THE QUIET DOGS

By the same author

JAMES BOND NOVELS
LICENCE RENEWED
FOR SPECIAL SERVICES

THE BOYSIE OAKES BOOKS
THE LIQUIDATOR
UNDERSTRIKE
AMBER NINE
MADRIGAL
FOUNDER MEMBER
TRAITOR'S EXIT
THE AIRLINE PIRATES
A KILLER FOR A SONG

DEREK TORRY NOVELS
A COMPLETE STATE OF DEATH
THE CORNER MEN

NOVELS
THE CENSOR
THE DIRECTOR
TO RUN A LITTLE FASTER
THE WEREWOLF TRACE
THE DANCING DODO
GOLGOTHA

THE MORIARTY JOURNALS
THE RETURN OF MORIARTY
THE REVENGE OF MORIARTY

THE KRUGER TRILOGY
THE NOSTRADAMUS TRAITOR
THE GARDEN OF WEAPONS

AUTOBIOGRAPHY
SPIN THE BOTTLE

COLLECTIONS OF SHORT STORIES
HIDEAWAY
THE ASSASSINATION FILE

THE
QUIET DOGS

John Gardner

BOOK CLUB ASSOCIATES LONDON

This edition published 1983 by
Book Club Associates
by arrangement with Hodder and Stoughton Ltd

© 1982 by John Gardner

Printed in Great Britain by
Richard Clay (The Chaucer Press) Ltd,
Bungay, Suffolk

For all my friends at
Hodder & Stoughton

Beyond the dark on a rock
Stands a tall house.
Birds are nesting on the rock,
But the house is empty.
But the house is empty.
The fire in the hearth has gone out long ago.
No voices are heard,
And only the wind, a wild guest,
Alarms the quiet dogs;
He has brought news from afar,
That the master has disappeared;
. . .

Shostakovich: *The King Lear
Ballad* (Source Untraced)

PART ONE

TRUST

1

MICHAEL GOLD HAD sported his oak, as the slang of centuries had it. In plain language Michael Gold had closed the outer door to his rooms in New Court, St. John's College, Cambridge, as a sign that he was engaged.

The young woman's name was Hilde, and Michael had met her casually the previous evening. Tonight, remembering the elderly undergraduate joke, 'Never make love on an empty stomach—always give her dinner first,' he had provided a meal at the Bath Hotel.

They would not be disturbed; for young Michael Gold, in his last post-graduate year, had a good understanding with his bedder, a Mrs. Florence, who knew all about the goings-on among undergraduates and graduates. She would turn a blind eye in the morning. But morning was a long way off. He leaned against the inner door, smiling at blonde and plump Hilde.

"So here we are." He briefly reflected on the inanity of his own remark.

"Yes." She had already indicated her willingness, over dinner, and came towards him—predatory, eager, arms encircling his neck, and lips closing on his as though she might devour him. An Amazon cannibal. A female spider hungry to consummate and then consume.

They reached first base on the old settee, and it crossed Michael Gold's mind that this particular piece of furniture, which must have served several generations of undergraduates, probably could have recounted a multitude of tales—love granted and received; troths plighted; lies believed; deceptions carried through; lust slaked. Tonight, Michael and Hilde would satisfy each other's lust. There could not be much about in Tunbridge Wells, he considered. Hilde was from Tunbridge Wells—an *au pair*.

He turned her slightly, lying almost across the settee, one hand reaching for a breast, the other falling, classically, into a casual caress of the right knee.

She moaned, and her tongue lashed at the inside of his mouth. Then came the pounding on the outer door, and the voice calling—"Mr. Gold? Mr. Gold, sir?"

Gold muttered a curse, motioning the girl into his small bedroom as the voice chanted its litany: "Mr. Gold, are you there, sir? It's urgent. Very urgent, the party says."

Still swearing softly, Michael Gold tucked his shirt into his trousers, smoothed his hair, opened the inner door, then unlocked the oak, to reveal one of the college porters.

"Very sorry to disturb you, sir." The man was out of breath, his face crimson. "The telephone, Mr. Gold. Said she was your mother. On the line in the Porters' Lodge. Unusual, sir, but the lady sounded, well . . . well, she has to speak with you, sir."

Heaven save me from possessive mothers, Gold thought, grabbing his jacket. Yes, he would come. He would be there in a minute.

The porter departed, giving Michael Gold time to slip into the bedroom. Hilde was lying, half naked, on the bed. "Sorry. Back in a minute." He smiled, loath to tear his eyes from her: the body good as he expected. Better maybe.

Down the stone stairs, and out into the chilly damp March air; running, just to get it over with. Along the cloister of New Court—the Wedding Cake as they called it, this great Victorian Gothic addition to the college. Over the Bridge of Sighs, footsteps echoing. On through the Courts to the Porters' Lodge at the main gate.

The Head Porter was on duty. " 'Evening, Mr. Gold. That telephone there," indicating the instrument with some distaste. It was not usual for members of college to receive calls at the Porters' Lodge.

Michael shrugged his apologies and picked up the phone. "Mother? Yes?"

His mother's voice was distinct in his ear. Michael Gold listened, incredulous. "What?"

10

The tone of his query made the Head Porter look up. He saw a look of stricken grief cross the young man's face—grief and shock and disbelief, all rolled into one. The Head Porter, a man of great experience, had seen that look many times, and knew exactly what it meant.

*   *   *

"I really came to see your gaffer. To see Old Soap."

"Soap?" Tony Worboys scowled his incomprehension.

Superintendent Vernon-Smith, of the Branch, gave a small, superior, smirk. "Cloak and dagger name with us. Kruger's cloak, and Kruger's dagger. Soap. Joke we had. Jest with your DG actually. It was him who gave us the name—Soap. Comes from a bit of doggerel: Boer War, I understand:

> Poor old Kruger's dead;
> He died last night in bed;
> Cut his throat on a bar of soap;
> Poor old Kruger's dead.

Soap, you see. Good, what? Haven't we met before?"

"Once." Young Worboys' mind ticked off the options. As far as he knew, the security blanket on Big Herbie's Berlin debacle (or cover-up as the Press would undoubtedly call it), had worked amazingly well. Now he had a senior officer of Special Branch—their sister service, MI5's, executive arm—asking questions. "Oh." He sounded genuinely surprised. "Oh, Herbie Kruger. My gaffer. Yes." Bland as unseasoned white sauce, allowing the light to dawn slowly on the youthful face, which was the main reason for everyone calling him *young* Worboys. "Gaffer. That's what threw me a bit. Yes, I'm sorry. Fact is he's been off sick for quite a time."

"Sick?" Vernon-Smith looked peeved. "Soap sick? Never heard of such a thing. Nobody bothered to tell me . . ."

"Well, with respect, sir, you do work with Five most of the time."

Vernon-Smith made a harrumphing noise. "Sure he's off sick? Not on some murky jaunt? Or in disgrace? You people

11

wouldn't tell me though, would you? Wouldn't tell each other, let alone me."

"Ah, er. He's fine again now. Back soon in fact." Worboys sounded, and looked, brighter.

Vernon-Smith was staring at him, a V crease between the eyebrows. "Yes, we did meet, didn't we? Few years ago. Some East German woman. Shooting, wasn't it? Herbie's crowd tried to get their noses in. Got 'em in as well. Quite a party at the end. Remember you now."

"Yes." Worboys was non-committal; even though he remembered it all with perfect clarity: the Nostradamus business. After all Worboys had been holding the fort since the night they had taken Big Herbie off to Warminster. The DG had dragged him over the coals. All things to be reported to those on high.

"Give Herbie a message if you like, sir. Unless it's very urgent of course."

"Well," Vernon-Smith looked down his nose. "It's a small matter." From the tip of his nose he could see his wristwatch, and thought he might just as well have saved himself the trouble and gone straight home. "Now I'm here. Only a small matter. Information might be useful to Herbie: need-to-know and all that." Lord, it was past six-thirty already. He'd be lucky to make the seven-five from Waterloo. "Street accident this afternoon." He spoke briskly, barking out the information as though giving orders. "One poor devil dead. Run down by a taxi. No Georgi Markov stuff. Nothing funny. Straight-forward. Fellow's own fault. Wasn't looking, and stepped out right in front of the cab. Worked for the BBC's Russian Department. Bush House. Know the firm? Live above the Inland Revenue Mafia, eh?"

Worboys knew all about BBC Overseas, and Bush House.

Vernon-Smith took out a neatly-typed five-by-three card, holding it halfway towards Worboys. "Victim, name of Gold," he said. "Alexander Gold. Lived out Catford way. Address on this." With a certain reluctance he parted with the card; like someone giving up his season rail ticket for the last time.

"And Big Herb . . . Mr. Kruger, should know?"

"Does already; or so it would seem. Not the death, of course, but the corpse. Fellow had Herbie Kruger's name in his address book—open and clear for the whole world to see. Name. Address; and *both* telephone numbers." He gave a small, petulant, sigh. "This number—here—is written backwards. A shade clumsy I thought. So . . . er . . ."

"Worboys, sir. Tony Worboys."

"Yes. So, Worboys, we ran him through the magic machines for luck. That's how we came up with the BBC's Russian Department. Already had Bush House, and BBC Overseas, of course. Thought he might be one of old Herbie's contacts. Seems he was lucky. Until today. Slipped the Yalta halter; got here with his young wife in '47. We took him in. Reason not clear yet. Anglicised his name. Model British citizen. Alexei Zolotoy. Zolotoy's Russian for Gold. Thought Herbie should know—his involvement does not show on the machines, by the way. Wife's in a state, naturally. Thought Herbie might be a friend in need. We've got nothing on Gold, by the by. Clean and sanitised. Not a whisper on him, nor the wife and son for that matter. Wife's name, Nataly; son called Michael—post-graduate work at Cambridge. Modern languages."

Worboys slipped the card into his pocket, saying he would give it all to Mr. Kruger. "When he gets in." The Special Branch man nodded; anxious to be away.

Alone, Tony Worboys sat, silent, for a moment. Then reached for the telephone. Ten minutes later he left the Annexe, walking fast towards Westminster Bridge. The Director General was expecting him; and other people besides.

13

2

THE CHAIRMAN OF the KGB, the Committee for State Security, arrived in Dzerzhinsky Square, Moscow, at a little before eight o'clock in the morning. This is his usual practice.

The sleek black Zil limousine—custom-built, with darkened windows and luxury interior—avoided the crammed pedestrian entrances to the large greystone building, known as Number Two Dzerzhinsky Square, and quickly negotiated the main vehicle entrance. The uniformed guards took little time in checking the Chairman's credentials, together with those of his driver and two bodyguards, before waving the Zil into the inner square and parking area.

The car was driven to the place reserved for the Chairman: close by the nearest entrance to his office. Then, flanked by the burly personal guards, the head of Russia's Intelligence Service and secret police, walked briskly into the building: across uncarpeted parquet floors, along the main corridors—with their décor of unremitting light green—and so into the elevator, which quickly carried them to the third floor.

Outside, snow still lay on the roofs, in parks, gardens, and by roadsides, though the sun shone, for the first time this year, with a startling brilliance, but little warmth. Perhaps the winter was at last ending, a few weeks early. There was a definite taste of spring in the air—even in the building that houses the executive and secretarial staffs of the KGB's Directorates.

There is some irony in the fact that the large structure of Number Two Dzerzhinsky Square was once the All-Russian Insurance Company's head office. It has gone through a number of changes in the years since the Revolution; and, like all bureaucratic offices, has long since become too small for the growing staff, let alone the needs of the Russian Intelligence Service.

Towards the end of the Great Patriotic War, the place was extended and enlarged: by German prisoners-of-war. But even with this new building, Moscow Centre—as it is known, both popularly and officially, within Intelligence communities the world over—is now the Centre in name only.

The Chairman's office, with its ante-room and secretariat, is situated in the bridge joining the original building to the extension: the suites of offices there being huge and well furnished.

Here, the parquet floor gives way to rich oriental carpeting, large armchairs and sofas. At one end of the Chairman's spacious inner sanctum stands a huge desk ("Big enough," he always joked with his children, "to land a Yak-36." The Yakovlev 36 being the Russian VTOL jump-jet, similar to the Harrier).

On the wall, directly opposite the desk, hangs the only picture in the room—the grim photograph of Felix Edmundovich Dzerzhinsky: his face set and hard; eyes narrowed; tufts of dark hair showing on the inner sides of his thin eyebrows, and an irregular crop of hair forming beard and moustache around almost invisible thin lips. 'Iron Felix', founder of the Cheka which was now, after many transformations, the Komitet Gosudarstvennoy Bezopasnosti— The Committee for State Security, known the world over as the KGB, though still spoken of by most Russians as the Cheka.

The Chairman, left alone by the bodyguards, crossed to his desk, scanned the day's engagements, and the brief intelligence résumé. On his way to the Centre he had thought about the first appointment: the meeting with General Vascovsky; remembering also that the day was particularly important, being the last Wednesday of the month. The last Wednesday of each month was the day set aside for the meeting of the First Directorate's Standing Committee for Forward Planning. Today the Standing Committee would

15

have an extra member, and it was important that he—as head of the KGB—should give Vascovsky the final briefing.

The Chairman took two paces towards the window, standing to look down into the square on Marx Prospekt. Yes, he thought, it was right that Jacob Vascovsky should do the job. For a man of Vascovsky's rank and experience, it had been a terrible failure—to lure one of the British Service's most senior officers into East Berlin; trap him, and then, after only a few days, let the man slip through the net. In the bad old days, in the times of terror—and under a chief like Beria—Jacob Vascovsky would have been recalled, and shot out of hand. The Chairman hoped they were more sensible now. If they had not brought Vascovsky back to a lengthy, friendly, interrogation, the truth might never have emerged. Now they had trawled his mind and gleaned facts. The few days which the General had spent with the man Kruger, proved to have brought forth a vital, and disturbing, piece of information. Instead of a bullet, or even a reprimand, the carrot of promotion had been offered. From Colonel-General to full General in one move.

Who better than Vascovsky to go in, now, to find the original source of Kruger's knowledge. The General was unlikely to talk, as it would only spread his own failure to a wider audience. Before Vascovsky left to start his crucial work, then, the Chairman had a duty to place the officer under a discipline of silence. Just to make certain. He turned again, glancing around the room, with its high ceiling, and walls, changed from the familiar green—which abounds through the rest of the building—to fine, sturdy, mahogany panelling.

For a second, the burden of power, and its attendant responsibilities, tripped across his mind—for the Chairman of the KGB, Member of the Politburo, and Central Committee of the Communist Party, is, arguably, the most important and powerful man in Russia—next, of course, to the Premier of the USSR and First Secretary of the Party.

The Premier was aware of the facts concerning Vascovsky. The case had, naturally, been discussed with the Chairman's

16

deputies, and the Politburo; though the files remained heavily restricted. The final, and worrying, facts—together with the decision—had been withheld from the deputies; but the seventeen members of the Politburo, who were conversant with everything, had unanimously agreed to the KGB Chairman's recommendation.

Now, seated at his desk, with its battery of telephones—including the famous Kremlevka and Vertushka phones, linking him directly with the Kremlin and Politburo members respectively—the Chairman pressed the small button to summon his adjutant. General Vascovsky was already waiting, he was informed. Also two senior First Directorate officers were standing by, to take Vascovsky to the First Chief Directorate headquarters: the true Moscow Centre.

The Chairman nodded, signifying he would interview the General immediately.

Vascovsky had not seen his chief for almost two years. Now, as he entered the office, he quickly reflected on the manner in which the Chairman had aged. He had always thought the man looked more like an academic than an Intelligence officer; but, in two years, this mien was even more apparent—the large head and broad shoulders further stooped; hair greyer; and demeanour increasingly reflective.

"Jacob, my old friend." The Chairman rose to greet Vascovsky—telling him to sit down, that it was good to see him again, asking after his wife.

"There was a moment," Vascovsky said, once the two men were settled, "when I thought your greeting might be more harsh than this."

The Chairman laughed: dry, without real mirth. Every man was entitled to one mistake. As long as he was not discovered in the million others he might make. "For your error you got promotion, anyway."

Vascovsky spread his hands, palms upwards. "I am a lucky man." The gesture had a French, rather than Russian flavour. Many remarked on the fact that Jacob Vascovsky always seemed more Gallic than Russian—a happy accident of birth which had been well used during his career. "I have

17

no doubt as to the pure chance which led Kruger to give me a couple of interesting exhibits during the few days I had him.''

The two nuggets Vascovsky had procured from the agent known as Big Herbie Kruger concerned secret facts about proposed operations coded Hallet and Birdseed, respectively. Kruger had known about them when there was no way in which he could have known—or, at least, *should* have known.

The Chairman asked if Vascovsky had been fully briefed on the importance of those pieces of information.

"Thoroughly. But would you expect anything else, Comrade Chairman? The briefing officer must have got it direct from yourself.''

The Chairman said it was not quite like that. The two aborted operations—concerning the American officer, Hallet, and the one with the Birdseed cryptonym—were known to three other people as well as himself. "But they are completely clean,'' he added. "Even in this world of ours, in which trust is not an easy commodity to come by, these, my personal staff, are an exception. Anyway, each one works in a vacuum. Not one alone would ever have known the full significance of either Hallet or Birdseed. No, my friend, the matter boils down to a betrayal, leading directly to the First Directorate's Standing Committee on Forward Planning; and that is very worrying. Let me check you out. Tell me what you know of the Standing Committee.''

Vascovsky was well-informed. Lucidly, and with that economy of words associated with a military background, he specified that the First Directorate's Standing Committee met regularly on the last Wednesday of each month; that their duties concerned the discussion of possible operations; changes in field structure; procedure; new activities; techniques. An average of three possible ideas were put forward each month—many of them concerning detailed proposals for operations. These ideas were formulated directly to the Chairman. No second or third party was admitted. The Chairman, alone, sifted the possibilities. Those which he

18

thought positive, or productive, were passed on to the Politburo for discussion.

"It is just before that stage when I would, perhaps, consult one of my staff. As it happens, the proposals for Hallet, and the operation called Birdseed, were discussed—with two different people. So, only myself, and the members of the Standing Committee, ever knew the full story regarding both of these cases." The Chairman put his hands flat on the desk, as though this was a gesture of some significance. "It's me who you have to thank for getting you off the hook, Jacob. Nobody else analysing your interrogations with Kruger, in East Berlin, could make head or tail out of Hallet or Birdseed. Those particular transcripts were sent to me as a last possibility. You can most surely rule out the two officers of my staff, as I have said. So, it's either me, or a member of the Standing Committee."

"Which is the reason for concern." Vascovsky's mouth tightened.

"The Standing Committee consists of . . . ?" The Chairman waited for the answer. Vascovsky reeled off the members quickly. They were four senior officers of the First Chief Directorate. The Departmental Heads of Directorate S; Directorate T; Special Service I, and Department V.

Four of the most dependable people in the Service. Each one a long-time Party member, with an unblemished record. All were over sixty years of age—two had passed their seventieth birthdays. Four men with spectacular personal histories, and incredible experience.

"You can see why I'm relying on you, Jacob." The Chairman's worry showed in the way he looked, spoke and moved. "At best, one of these men has merely been garrulous; talked out of turn, not obeyed the rule of silence demanded of him. This is distinctly probable. They are getting on in years. Yet . . . Yet . . ."

"Yet they are all lively and active officers: alert, trained in the hard school." Vascovsky put the Chairman's thoughts into words.

"Yes." Flat. A long pause. Then—"Jacob, I pray this is

only a small slip of the tongue, by one of them—to a wife, or trusted friend. If not, you realise what it means?"

Vascovsky said he recognised the most sinister implications all too clearly. If it was not a piece of loose talk, then it had to be professional. Given the ages, and length of service, of the people involved, this meant a distinct likelihood of one of them being nothing less than a long-term penetration agent. How long neither man would wish to guess.

"You're to be taken to the Standing Committee's meeting this morning." The Chairman spread himself in his chair, lifting his chin, pushing back his head, as though to exercise the muscles in the rear of his neck. Vascovsky recognised it as a tension-relief exercise. "I've given written authority, and made out the order. You are to be my representative on the Standing Committee: a new procedure, which goes into operation as from today. It's good enough cover, and will give you the opportunity to keep in touch with all four of them. I've also made sure their personal dossiers are at your disposal. Detective work, Jacob. A crossword puzzle with one clue: otherwise just the black and white squares. You will supply the other clues, and their answers."

"I can think of one answer to the first clue. Nightmare." The General was not being facetious.

The Chairman made a slight affirmative gesture. The twirl of a hand. If it was that bad, the essential move was to hunt down the offender; then clean him out. Another point had to be taken into consideration. If proof was brought against a member of the Standing Committee, it would be necessary to shroud the scandal. "I don't mean to sweep under the carpet. Maybe the British Service—if it is them—will wish to make some capital out of it. On the other hand, all parties could well desire a cloak of silence. No scandals. Nothing against people like ourselves, Comrade General." He gave Vascovsky a look: blatant and undisguised. Let us make sure we save our own faces, and our own skins, the Chairman was saying.

Aloud he continued—"To this end I must put you, Jacob, under the strictest discipline of silence. Do you accept this?"

"Naturally. As an officer of the Committee for State Security, I accept this discipline."

"Good. Before you leave, one more question. I understand you are still assigned to the Kruger business. Have you any information? Taken any action?"

Vascovsky chuckled. "A small campaign of mental terror. I'm fairly certain his people have put him under most rigid control. Maybe they'll dismiss him altogether. I'll know in a day or so. Whichever way it goes, I do not give up. He was a broken man; even though he got away. It is possible that I might yet reclaim him. Whatever happens, he will be forced to live a restricted life. If I know that man, this can only compound his frustrations. There are still levers we can use."

"You have a most personal vendetta with Kruger." A statement of fact.

Vascovsky did not hesitate. "Naturally. It would be strange if this were not so. I fought him in the dark during the coldest days of the Cold War. I lost him. Then I found him again and caught him, only to let him slip away. Yes, some of it is personal."

The Chairman rose. "Don't allow it to become too personal, Jacob. In our business we are like whores; we should not get personally involved with our clients. Keep your desires to nail him under some restraint." He leaned forward, pressing the bell to summon his adjutant. "Now, go and solve this other riddle for me. If we have a cancer in the Standing Committee, gouge him out. But use a pain-killer. Before we take him to the terminal ward we need him whole and well for a time. His memory is important to us."

Jacob Vascovsky smiled. "Don't worry. I'll cut him out and he won't feel a thing."

*   *   *

At about the same time as this conversation took place, Stentor was being fussed over by his wife, in their relatively luxurious apartment, on the third floor of a building reserved for high-ranking Party officials, in Kutuzovsky Prospekt. The sun may well be shining, Stentor's wife was telling him,

21

but this did not mean he could go without his best winter coat—the one with the lynx collar.

Stentor would have preferred to wear the other—the one cut in a military style. But he did not argue. Long ago, Stentor had learned the futility of arguing with women—be they wives, mistresses, friends, or colleagues. Besides, the doorbell had rung: two long rings and a short, which meant the bodyguard was waiting, and the car stood ready downstairs.

He allowed himself to be helped into the coat with the fur collar, put on his hat, glanced in the mirror, picked up his copies of the morning papers, and gave his wife a resounding kiss on both cheeks.

The bodyguard was the new, young man. Tall, bronzed and alert, he greeted the Comrade General good morning. Stentor smiled, and walked down the passage to the elevator. He did not, of course, think of himself as Stentor. He lived under the name by which all had known him since he was fourteen years old. Stentor was the cryptonym with which the British Secret Intelligence Service had invested him, many many years ago.

In the foyer, the usual two dark-haired day guards were on duty. Stentor smiled at them also. They did not smile back, but came to attention—showing respect for a hero of the Soviet Union. It was a cross one had to bear, Stentor thought: this business of being guarded twenty-four hours a day. The building had plainclothes guards, who undoubtedly timed your exits and entrances, passing them on to some unknown scrutineer, who kept account against the day of judgment, if it ever came. Days of wrath and doom were more likely to strike a high-ranking political, or military, figure, than the ordinary citizen. But then, the ordinary citizen came in for his fair share of judgments at all levels, Stentor reflected, so that might even the odds a shade.

But, whenever he went out on official business there was at least one bodyguard and the driver. In his other little secret world, Stentor found the lack of privacy restricting; yet he managed by accepting it as a challenge.

22

The bodyguard opened the rear door of the black Volga, allowed Stentor to make himself comfortable, then joined the driver in front.

The Volga pulled away, and Stentor settled back, opening the daily document case which had been picked up earlier from the Centre. More papers than usual this morning. The monthly Standing Committee meeting day often produced a load of documents. Stentor began to go through the daily Intelligence digest.

So, they had taken Svobodny, the poet, at last. Old M. I. Svobodny, well-known poet and pederast. It would have been around four-thirty in the morning—that was the traditional time for swoops like this: had been for centuries. In ancient Rome, Caligula probably sent his Praetorian Guard out at dawn to collect victims for the treason trials. The Gestapo certainly took people in the early hours, as did most modern secret police.

The cars, either noisy with slamming doors, or creeping, silent, around the block. Then the sudden rush of feet; the pounding on the door; all exits blocked. Bleary eyes, crying children—frightened from their sleep—the white-faced woman, waiting a few paces behind the man who opened the door.

At one time, when police came calling in the early hours, mothers would calm their babes by saying they were only the men who had come to catch mice—because mice appeared from their holes at night. The Mice Men Cometh.

Even Stentor had taken part in those kind of arrests; just as he had known many people who lived in terror of them. Stalin's orders were often obeyed like that. Stentor had obeyed them himself.

Well, this morning, at around four-thirty, they had come for Maxim Ivanovitch Svobodny, in his little apartment, lined with books from floor to ceiling, near Sokolniki Park. Maxim Ivanovitch was probably waiting for them, his suit-case packed. He must have been expecting arrest for days.

As Stentor read the short report, he smiled. Then his smile changed to a chuckle. Svobodny, in English, meant Free. For a moment the chuckle turned into a full-blown laugh, so loud that Stentor's bodyguard turned to ask if the Comrade General was all right. Yes, the Comrade General was fine. He simply had a strange and twisted sense of humour. The kind of humour that comes only with age, and a full life—a life lived near to the knife-edge of disaster.

Outside, the sun shone, so bright that the driver had to wear glasses. Traffic was normal and they drove fast, out on to the Moscow Circumferential Highway—out to the KGB's First Directorate Headquarters. The First Chief Directorate's Headquarters does not lie, as so many imagine, within the charming and enlarged greystone building on Dzerzhinsky Square. The true heart of Moscow Centre, in fact, beats some twenty kilometres from the city.

Stentor's black Volga covered the distance in half-an-hour, leaving the highway at the Yasenevo exit. There, a sign reads, SCIENTIFIC RESEARCH CENTRE. FORBIDDEN.

As far as members of the First Chief Directorate are concerned, the real Centre is only a few metres further on: hidden behind a thick green hedge of trees. Stentor's car was not forbidden.

The site itself stands in around three hundred acres, completely surrounded by a high wire cyclone fence. The car stopped at the main entrance. Passes and documents were examined, by uniformed KGB men, and exchanged for laminated plastic badges, each bearing a photograph of the wearer, together with rank and essential descriptive details. These badges were hung around the neck by thin chains. Stentor, his driver, and the bodyguard, donned them with an almost religious gravity. The General had once remarked that they should kiss them first—as the priest kisses the stole before draping it around his neck. The flippancy was greeted with much hilarity by his driver and bodyguard. Priests were out of season at the time.

The car then moved on to the second checkpoint—a ten-foot-high concrete wall. Here Stentor and the bodyguard left the car, walking past the metal barriers, while the driver turned in the direction of the parking lot. The area between the cyclone fence and concrete wall holds facilities for 1500 vehicles, together with maintenance garages, and, on the outside, a running track. The wall—cornered by observation towers, and topped by electrified wire—leads to the heart of the complex. Contained within this inner area is a gymnasium, swimming pool, and the big, five-storey Y-shaped building in which the major part of the First Chief Directorate's business is carried out.

Building A is the downward stroke of the Y; B and C being, respectively, the left and right angles. Stentor's office, as one of the senior departmental chiefs, was in building B. But, this morning, his first appointment—in fact the only appointment of the day—was in building A: Conference Room 110, a secure, 'silent', office; one of the many strong rooms, as they called them in the Yasenevo Complex. In the strong rooms it was impossible to filch conversations. Here, in Room 110, the First Chief Directorate's Standing Committee for Forward Planning held its monthly meeting.

*   *   *

By ten-thirty they were all gathered: the four men whose duties included advising the Chairman of possible operations, ploys, techniques, the realignment of agents on the ground, even changes in the programmes of those great electronic beasts which circled the globe providing the Centre with photographs and a mass of other data—the *Cosmos*, and other advanced satellites; plus the seaborne 'trawlers', electronically garnering intelligence.

Stentor smiled inwardly as he looked around the room at his fellow members of the committee. He had a personal name for the four of them, a cryptonym which he always used when sending information to his British masters. The whole quartet had seen vast changes in their lifetimes. Their combined span in years came to around two hundred and eighty, he supposed. By rights they were all nearing the time of dotage, and retirement, when the fangs of their power would be drawn. The Quiet Dogs, he thought. It was as good a name as any for this little group.

One of his colleagues joined him, greeting Stentor as an old, wise, and valued, colleague; asking advice regarding a proposal he was putting to the committee.

At that moment the guard who stood—a kind of jailor—in the corridor outside, rapped on the door and opened up. All four men turned towards him. Three newcomers, in civilian clothes, stood in the doorway—one carrying an official-looking pouch.

"Who is the Standing Committee chairman this month?" The man carrying the pouch, spoke with the arrogant snap of authority that comes from working as an aide to someone holding great power.

Oleg Zapad, once a junior professor of Physics at Moscow University—when it was still off Manezhnaya Square, straddling the two sides of Herzen Street—stepped forward. "Comrade?" he queried. "Who are you? And what is this intrusion?" Zapad had plenty of power himself, and could recognise the bullyboy approach of one whose rank was probably well down the scale, but carried orders, making him one of the *nachalstvo* for a day, or a few hours.

"You are the chairman, comrade?" The man with the pouch still retained some of the military bearing, once probably second nature to him. But he was a man now running to fat, living off his job in Dzerzhinsky Square no doubt, thought Zapad.

"Comrade General," Zapad corrected the leader of the three intruders. "Comrade General Zapad, Head of Directorate T."

"Good. I am Colonel Mironov, attached to the Chairman's staff. I come as the Comrade Chairman's representative." His hand reached inside the pouch, his head turning to introduce Major Striganov, also of the Chairman's staff. He then produced an impressive document, typed on a thick, almost parchment-like paper.

Stentor could see the signatures and seal. It could be an arrest warrant for all he knew. But his interest lay in the third member of the trio. He knew the face, but could not put a name to the slim, healthy-looking man with iron grey hair.

Mironov thrust the document into Oleg Zapad's hands. "You will see that this is a directive, signed by the Chairman himself; authorised by the Politburo. It calls for an alteration in the number of members to this Standing Committee. For some time the Chairman has felt he should be formally represented. You will note that the document calls for the addition of one officer to the Standing Committee. It is my pleasant duty to introduce him to you. The Chairman's personal representative, General Jacob Vascovsky."

The face and name both fell into place in Stentor's head. With the recognition came a twinge of worry; a tiny cloud on his sunny horizon. Could this possibly be the cloud he recalled reading about, years ago, in the Bible? The cloud no bigger than a man's hand, which would grow into a tempest? The fear that, one day, they would pick up a hint, and come to seek him out, had always been kept in the very furthest refuge of Stentor's mind. It peeped out now, just for a second, like some scaly poisonous lizard flicking its head from behind a rock.

Jacob Vascovsky stepped forward, holding out his hand to Oleg Zapad. "I'm sorry, Comrade General." He smiled: the charm of a practised diplomat, combined with that more sinister, bewitching, disarming, manner which Stentor had seen many times in his long career. Some claimed that he himself possessed this same kind of magic: the ability to gain confidence, to attract, as a Venus Flytrap entices. Stentor's well-maintained antennae now picked up the vibrations of danger from this new arrival.

Vascovsky lifted his head, looking at each member of the committee in turn, "I must apologise to all of you, comrades. I expect to be the unwelcome guest at your monthly feasts, but I ask you to bear with me. The Chairman has personally appointed me, and one does not argue with our Chairman." He turned to Mironov and Striganov, "I think you have done your duty, comrades. You have been good nursemaids, but I can manage on my own now. Thank you."

The unexpected arrival, accompanied by the unanticipated appointment of an extra, new, member of the Standing

Committee, took the small group a short time to assimilate. The first hour of the session was now concerned with introductions, and the business of Vascovsky getting to know his new colleagues.

Two of the four he already knew by reputation within the Service, and the dossiers of all four men were—as the Chairman had told him—at his disposal. In the car, the General had just managed to riffle through them. Starting at the back of each thick folder, Vascovsky memorised the latest photographs of the subjects, so he would have no trouble putting names to faces, to jobs, at this first meeting. The dossiers had gone back to Dzerzhinsky Square with Mironov.

As a man who had spent the bulk of his career in the field—mainly working the clandestine labyrinths of Europe—Jacob Vascovsky could only be impressed by these now elderly men, whose backgrounds provided an encyclopaedic picture of the Russian Service; its operations over at least the last three—in some cases, four—decades; and the current techniques of political, economic, military, and strategic intelligence-gathering, analysis, and manipulation.

As he sat with them, Vascovsky found himself amazed at the lucid agility of their minds, and the more prosaic fact that any single one of the men could be taken for fifty-five years of age, not the late sixties, or even seventy. All looked to be in their prime, displaying exemplary physical condition.

The man who was the current month's chairman, Oleg Zapad, for instance, though only of medium build, had the look of someone who could hold his own against trained men half his age. Though basically a physicist, his general demeanour was that of a jester, with the ability to both laugh at himself, and score amusing points off others. His wit ranged from the pithy one-line joke, to that kind of humour which scourged the recipient. Zapad would—Jacob Vascovsky considered—have made an excellent field agent. Maybe he had done a spell out there in the winter—as KGB argot had it. In spite of the humour, Zapad's face was like a blank wall. Anything that showed could be seen only in the eyes.

This, then, was the head of Directorate T—responsible for the theft of all data concerning nuclear weapons, missiles, the strategic sciences, space research, industrial processing, and cybernetics, in the West. The department worked in close conjunction, and was heavily represented, with the GNKT—The State Scientific and Technical Committee.

The tall, and fine-looking, Nikolai Aleksandrovich Severov was overlord of Directorate S, which dealt with the selection, training, and tactical disposal, of KGB operatives living in foreign countries under false papers, and, often, fictitious identities. Even at his age he sported a mane of white hair, smooth as an ermine's pelt; while his looks were enhanced by a very straight, classic, nose.

Vascovsky knew Severov by sight. What concerned him was the obvious conclusion that Severov—because of the position he held—almost certainly knew Vascovsky *very* well indeed. At least, he would be conversant with Vascovsky's record. If any man in the room was aware of the recent blunder with the British spymaster, Kruger, in East Berlin it would be Severov.

Vladimir Glubodkin: bronzed, as though he spent an hour a day under a sun lamp, was another who had kept his hair—though it was cut short in the military manner—and, from what Vascovsky could see, his teeth were also intact. Glubodkin was fond of flashing pleasant smiles at his colleagues, and seemed to be a bit of a dandy. A ladies' man in his day, the General assessed; or, by the look of him, probably still a ladies' man.

Glubodkin, Head of Special Service I—responsible for the distribution of all intelligence gathered by the First Chief Directorate (his department would issue the daily digests, for instance). Special Service I also undertook specially instigated studies for on-going projects, operating right from the heart of things. A very important man for this particular committee.

Vascovsky casually remarked to Special Service I's chief that he had noticed, in the day's digest, a paragraph concerning the arrest of the poet, Svobodny.

Glubodkin looked surprised. "Really?" he answered in a somewhat effete and disinterested tone. "I rarely read the thing myself. Anyway, that's Second Directorate stuff— Russian subject, Svobodny."

"It's true, though, Volodya," Oleg Zapad interposed from the end of the table. "I hear they've incarcerated him in the Bolshoi Ballet School. He'll be out in a year as an Honoured Artist of the Soviet Union."

The dry, almost coughing laugh, came from Andrei Tserkov whose pleasant, almost avuncular, manner; friendly, weather-beaten face, and chain-smoking habit, made him— to Vascovsky—the most chilling member of the group. For Andrei Tserkov fronted Department V—as in Viktor— thereby elevating him to the status of one of the more dangerous men in the Service: head of the black and sinister heart of the KGB.

Department V is probably the most secret of all sections, developed from the original organisation popularly known as *Smyert Shpionam* (*Smersh*), in the 1940s; and briefed to deal with political—or intelligence—murders, kidnappings, dirty tricks, and the covertly violent aspects of the trade they all plied.

As Zapad brought the meeting to order—welcoming their new member as the Chairman's direct representative— Vascovsky clearly saw, seeing these men in the flesh, what a truly bizarre situation faced him. Just to be in the presence of these four men was to touch the KGB's history, and be aware of their combined intellect and knowledge. Together this group was a powerhouse within the world of secrets.

Vascovsky, though brought up in a tradition of atheism, was vividly aware of that intense, and shining, example engendered by men and women who are believers in some form of faith. In the murky world of secrets, men of faith were needed. These four men were like people called to the religious life, but within the arcane society. You could feel the strength, just by being with them. Now, if one—only one—led a double-sided life; if one had, in another context, sold his soul to the devil, and dedicated it to God, at one and the same time, then the damage, over the years, could be impossible to assess. The General was a firm believer in his own faith and work. The Chairman had given him the job of unmasking the truth. Detective work, he called it. Vascovsky thought of it differently, almost fanatically. Looking around the table, he hoped, with all sincerity, that the tiny pieces of information—certainly leaked from one of these men—had arrived in Herbie Kruger's ear by accident, or through unguarded talk, and not by design. Whatever the truth, though, he would hunt it down, and tear it out, as a wolf would tear the throat from its prey.

Stentor guardedly watched Vascovsky throughout the long day's meeting. He even talked with him, during their usual break for lunch. The agenda was not of a high standard this month. Only three possibilities, about which they talked, bringing the collective mind to bear on values and viability. There was a suggestion regarding the already well-infiltrated Trade Unions of the West; another concerning a senior NATO officer (they were always popping out of the woodwork); and a final possibility—a follow-up over the question of an American senator who had placed himself in a situation which might well be exploited to advantage.

At the end of the meeting, only this last point was voted as a viable proposition, to be forwarded to the Chairman.

Through the day, Stentor watched, listened and spoke. Mostly, he watched. Stentor knew his own powers of intuition, just as he knew of his own secret involvement with the operation which this man, Vascovsky, had pulled off, and then bungled, in East Berlin. Stentor's own warnings had been too late to be of help to the British; but the final result of the business was a stalemate, with a slight advantage to the General.

Stentor therefore did not require second sight to know there was a special reason for Vascovsky being appointed to the committee. The knowledge was strengthened when, as they were concluding for the day, he heard Vascovsky invite one of the committee members to dine with him. "I must come to know you all a little better," the Chairman's nominee

31

said casually. "In due course I trust you'll all visit my home."

When the meeting broke up, Stentor went over to his own office and worked for a couple of hours. It was only when he was in the car on his way back to Kutuzovsky Prospekt that he started to feel deep concern. Throughout his lengthy double life, almost from the first moment—long ago—when he met the man called Trofimov, Stentor had rarely allowed himself the indulgence of worrying about his personal safety. He had a rare confidence in both his own facility for survival and the precautions taken by his masters. There had been tricky situations before. But this time? He was only too conscious of Vascovsky's reputation. If anything had leaked in East Berlin, then the whole weight of authority, together with its technology, surveillance, double-checks, and searches into the past, would come into play. Vascovsky was but the tip of the iceberg—a nasty and dangerous tip, below which lay unpleasant horrors.

Once back in the apartment, Stentor behaved normally. Not that this was difficult. A wife who is left to her own devices all day wishes to talk when her partner returns. Stentor's wife had, over the years, developed the idea that conversation meant monologue for a couple of hours. True, later in the evening, they would talk; but, by the time the evening meal was eaten, Stentor had not been required to contribute a great deal.

There was a television programme his wife wished to see, so Stentor excused himself, retiring to his study. Once there, he made a telephone call. Certainly it was tapped, but it was a call he made often—to his 'niece' who lived, with her husband and two children, in Leningrad. The conversation was pleasant—How was Ivan? How were the children?—of no consequence to any of the listeners, or to Vascovsky who, if Stentor was correct, would most certainly be listening to the tapes.

He could only risk one call through his 'niece'. If Vascovsky decided everything had to be covered, she would be under surveillance very quickly. Doing it now, and in this way,

Stentor would be assured of a drop and pick-up within the next few hours. The 'niece' would be out of her apartment, and making the contact he needed within seconds of the call ending. After that, Stentor would turn to his remaining four methods. Then silence. It was not worth the risk of using one of the methods twice.

The call finished with a particular phrase—"Take care of the little ones." On some occasions, it was "Look after the children," or "Give the children a kiss from me." Each had its own special meaning; innocuous enough not to raise suspicion. "Look after the children" meant that the 'niece' had to make contact with a third party, in Moscow, and end her conversation with yet another cipher phrase. "Look after the children," for instance, meant her conversation would end with, "Everyone sends greetings." All this ensured that the right person would be in the right place, at the right time.

Stentor now sat down to begin work on his message. Short, to the point, and operated by a book code. The book changed every three days, and the cipher was not easy—even if you knew which book was in use.

When Stentor had completed the cipher he copied the groups of numbers on to a two-by-four piece of flimsy, which he folded neatly, and locked in the metal filing cabinet that stood in the corner. Years ago, in the late 1920s, when his friends in England had taken him out—to a secluded house in France—in order to give him elementary training, and some idea of what he could do for them, one of the prime rules they dinned into him was, "Trust nobody. If you want to be absolutely certain, always do the job yourself."

So it was that when the car arrived on the following morning to take Stentor to the Yasenevo Complex, the small flimsy paper had been inserted into a packet of Lucky Strike cigarettes—his favourite brand, obtainable easily enough, at duty free prices, by the privileged classes. There was one cigarette in the packet.

Just before the black Volga pulled away from the kerb,

Stentor told the driver to take them to Granovskaya Street—a couple of blocks from the Kremlin. The driver nodded, smiling to himself. At this time in the morning, Number Two Granovskaya Street would be open for people like his boss. In the afternoon, wives and families of Central Committee staff, senior KGB officers, and the like, would have the run of the place. A visit to Granovskaya Street always meant a small luxury for the driver and bodyguard.

Number Two Granovskaya Street has one claim to historical fame. A plaque near the door commemorates the fact that *In this building on April 19, 1919, Vladimir Ilyich Lenin spoke before the commanders of the Red Army headed for the front.* The front was, of course, that of the Civil War. Even at his advanced age, Stentor still remembered the Civil War with the clarity of yesterday's events. As a child he had been ripped apart from the safety of his parents, and was still living in a state of terror six years later when the Englishman, they called Trofimov, discovered him.

Apart from the plaque, the building is nondescript: drab, with the windows painted over, and a sign which denotes it as The Bureau of Passes.

Stentor told his men he would only be a few minutes. One other car was parked in front of them. Apart from that, the street remained almost deserted.

Passing through the doors, Stentor felt in his inside pocket for the clear, plastic-covered, identification which allowed him entry to this small Aladdin's cave. Here, and in many other hidden places like it, those with the necessary rank, appointment, or position, could buy items ranging from vegetables to Japanese stereo equipment—all unobtainable in ordinary stores.

Stentor bought four 200 packs of Lucky Strikes, and a flask of Chanel for his wife. He took time over the small transaction, lingering, as though trying to make up his mind. Finally, as the purchases were being loaded into a thick paper sack, he glanced at his gold digital watch—another status symbol. The timing was right, and the only other customer had left. By this afternoon the place would be crowded with women

34

and children, and you might have to wait for up to an hour for service.

Outside again, he paused, taking the Lucky Strike packet from his pocket, removing the last cigarette, and lighting it as the bodyguard came over to help with the paper sack.

Crumpling the empty packet in his hand, Stentor set off towards the car. The few people on the street studiously took no notice—particularly those who had spotted the Volga's number plates, which identified it as an official vehicle.

As he climbed into the car, Stentor dropped the crumpled packet into the gutter, among the remnants of hard snow which still lingered there. Inside, he delved into the paper sack, tossing two of the packages of cigarettes to the bodyguard and driver. They thanked him almost casually. He was a good boss, but, over the past few years, the driver, at least, had come to know he disliked any effusive gratitude for small gifts such as these.

Nobody noticed the young man, approaching the building on foot, from the Kremlin end of Granovskaya Street. Almost opposite The Bureau of Passes, the young man hesitated, bending to adjust the zip on his short leather boots.

When he straightened up, the Lucky Strike packet was safely inside the pocket of his greatcoat. Fifteen minutes later, Stentor's flimsy ciphered message lay on the desk of a room deep within the British Embassy. The Ambassador, and his main staff, would know nothing about it; but, within the hour, the series of numbers were flashed to a clandestine receiving point in Finland. From there they continued their journey to GCHQ—the Government Communications Headquarters—near Cheltenham. Finally they reached the building near Westminster Bridge. All these journeys through the airwaves were made at high speed, and intermingled with other messages.

Allowing for the time difference, Stentor's message was on the Director's desk, in London, ready for deciphering, at nine o'clock in the morning—Thursday morning.

Deciphered, Stentor's message read:

WARNING POINTER TOWARDS QUIET DOGS/ OLD FRIEND JACOB FROM BERLIN GIVEN MEMBERSHIP/SUSPECT OFFICIAL INVESTI- GATION/POSSIBLE LINK WITH THE BIG MAN/ STENTOR

This message, combined with information concerning the death of a man called Gold in a street accident, tipped the scales. For some time, men in secret places of power had prevaricated over making a decision. Now there had to be action, and so it was that Tubby Fincher—ADC to the Director General of the British Secret Intelligence Service— received orders to bring Big Herbie Kruger, the Big Man, back from Warminster.

3

IN THE FIRM, they always spoke of the house as Warminster; though, to be accurate, it stands—a Georgian pile with some ugly Victorian additions—well back from the road, between the army camp at Knook and the village of Chitterne, some seven miles from the Wiltshire garrison town of Warminster.

The main house is centred in ten acres of open country, dotted with a seemingly haphazard series of prefabricated huts, and an acre of woodland: the whole surrounded by high walls, studded with invisible electronic sniffers.

Depending on their sense of nostalgia, or guilt, members of the Firm regard Warminster with either a feeling of warmth, or a shiver of fear. Dreadful things had happened there; as well as good.

Tubby Fincher stood in the Commandant's office, his emaciated frame silhouetted against the tall sash window, as he looked out across a stretch of lawn, towards the line of evergreens which hide the brick wall on the road side of the estate.

From the open door, Tubby appeared—to Herbie Kruger—as a Giacometti figure.

Fincher turned, smiled and put out a hand to the huge ungainly man as he entered. Searching for the right words, and not finding them, Tubby resorted to some banality about Herbie looking fit and well.

"The weight comes back easy enough," Big Herbie growled. "Life may not be as simple."

They stood facing each other; both ill at ease, until Herbie took the initiative, carefully lowering himself into a chair.

"You come to give me the bullet, Tubby?" he asked; the lumpy porridge face set in a deceptively stupid expression, as though he did not care one way or another. It had been almost a year since they last met—in cold and grim circumstances.

A little over a year before, Big Herbie—one of the Service's most experienced men—had been granted permission to carry out an operation, codenamed Trepan, to save an old, and valued, network in East Berlin. His brief had been clear—he was not to go over the Wall himself: that was too dangerous to contemplate.

But Herbie, whose field work had been mainly within the Eastern Bloc, had blatantly disobeyed orders—slipping into East Berlin, settling the problem, and getting himself neatly trapped into the bargain.

For a good week, Eberhard Lukas Kruger was the prisoner of Jacob Vascovsky. His escape was ingenious and lucky, but left a nasty taste in the mouths of his colleagues. From the day of his return, Herbie had been kept at Warminster. The Firm's trust in him was sadly uncertain.

"The bullet?" Herbie repeated. "The sack, and a bag to put it in? That's what young Tony Worboys told me—it's an expression, he says; his mother uses it. You get the sack, and a bag to put it in. The bullet. Fired."

Tony Worboys had been Big Herbie's assistant. Five years out of training but still known as *young* Worboys.

Tubby held up a hand through which the bones appeared to show clearly like an X-Ray. They were as alike as chalk and cheese—Fincher and Kruger. Young Worboys' mother would have said that also, Herbie thought. Alike as his last pair of confessors—the ones with the names like a firm of specialist leather workers: Fidge and Morray. Fidge with the warts, big hands and policeman's feet; Morray like his name, slippery, with a sting in his voice. Neither had been as good as Crawford, the Firm's old hand, brought out of retirement especially to deal with Herbie Kruger's case. At the time, Big Herbie had thought he should feel honoured. Crawford was exceptional. Never had there been a confessor to touch him; except, possibly, Skardon. Yet even Skardon had failed to break Philby.

Tubby Fincher found it difficult to look his former friend in the eyes. They had been close once, but that was over, and the thin senior officer had even fought hard to avoid this final scenario. Trust was a thing of the past.

"You're going home, Herbie," he said quietly.

"So where's home?" A shrug of the massive shoulders.

"The flat's still waiting for you. St. John's Wood. Just as you left it. I've a car to take you back. Tonight. You'll have a weekend to settle in, then the DG wants to see you first thing on Monday. Giving you a job."

"Cleaning latrines, yes?" Herbie looked at him with vacant, peasant-ignorant eyes.

What was going on behind the eyes, deep within that agile brain, Tubby wondered. He still felt a little guilty, not trusting the man, once such a close confidant. "Something like that." He tried to sound cheerful. "Cleaning up a mess anyhow. Mopping up your own vomit, if you want to think of it like that."

Herbie remained silent, staring at a patch of carpet between Fincher's shoes; an act which made the macilent Tubby even more uncomfortable. It was so simple to forget Herbie's ability. The big man was using technique even now, just by staring at the carpet in silence: the technique of secrecy, intrigue, and misdirection. Herbie was from the old school; from the days when men on the ground, and agents in place, were of greater importance than the evaluation of data, or infra-red pictures taken from intelligence satellites. Nobody should ever underestimate Kruger's mastery of technique, or his intellect.

It was because of these things, and the climate within the intelligence community, Tubby presumed, that the Director General had obtained personal clearance from the Prime Minister to bring Kruger back and use him in an active capacity.

"Tubby . . . ?" Herbie began, but Fincher did not want to be drawn. He forced his voice to stay neutral, and not betray hostility as he told Kruger to go and pack the few things they allowed him in this place. "We must leave within the hour."

Big Herbie gave a small smile, indicating that he realised the boot was on the other foot now—after all the years, the fighting, operations, planning, and arcane action. His hands came up, palms flat, lifting six inches from the knees, then dropping again, with alarming gentleness, as the great head gave one quick nod. "I get ready, Tubby." At the door he turned back. "You pay, my friend, believe me. In our business you pay in years, or months, or days. You pay in our own coinage—Trust. I'll mop up my vomit; then, possibly you'll trust again."

Tubby Fincher swung back towards the window, deeply disturbed.

*   *   *

Tubby sat in the back of the car with Herbie, and considered the change that had overtaken the huge man. Big Herbie was docile, staring out of the window, like a child being taken to an unfamiliar house. Fincher wanted to talk, but could not; just as he would like to banish all thoughts of betrayal from his mind. There was no evidence against the big man—Crawford had said it a dozen times: only that single inexplicable deviation from a lifetime's professional habit,

39

discipline and caution. Tubby Fincher wondered what went on in the mind of a man who knew he was suspected of treachery: what thoughts would plague him if the suspicions were founded in truth? What anxieties? Or what bewilderment if he was, as the Director General believed, clean and free of guilt?

Big Herbie had no wish to talk with Tubby Fincher. There was little desire to speak with any of them. He knew the suspicions, and he was conscious that they were unlikely to go away. Now he was simply puzzled by this new, and unexpected, move—taking him from the institutionalised life of Warminster, back to some kind of job which could only be another test, 'mopping up his own vomit': a jab at his loyalty.

As he had done in the field for all those years, Herbie started to use his strongest mental weapon. He watched the road, fields, villages and copses rolling past, allowing his mind to play the music he knew so well. It was an escape, a method of retreat, and of putting the mind either in neutral, or setting a task for the subconscious—a problem that would finally emerge solved.

The music in his mind was Mahler's Second Symphony— 'The Resurrection'—for he knew the works of Mahler by heart, and had no need of orchestra, recording, or tape, to listen when he needed to use the facility.

Crawford had understood his love for the composer. One of the other confessors—was it Morray?—had scoffed. An oaf, neither comprehending Herbie's devotion to the composer, nor the works themselves. Pretentious, the boor had called them, signalling by one word that he had no understanding of either Herbie's work, or Mahler's stature.

But Crawford was astute: a tweedy man who smelled of pipe tobacco, and some shaving lotion which Herbie could not identify. There was nothing of the bully, or inquisitor, about Crawford, who had put even Big Herbie—no stranger to the methods of interrogation—off guard.

Crawford had gone, first, not for the horrors—the recent happenings and folly which had brought Herbie Kruger to

Warminster—but back to the beginning: to childhood, and the trail of secret life which the large German had followed since his teens. It was as though Crawford realised Herbie Kruger was still in shock, drowned in night sweats and dreams of what had happened—the fact of love, the anxiety and sense of responsibility—those driving forces that had led him to the sin of disobedience, murder, deceit. No, he would never be free again; but in this profession you were not free, from the moment it embraced you. Freedom was another land, a different time. Possibly you could touch it for a moment in this life—but freedom was not the easy word of politicians.

Having just come back from behind the Berlin Wall—when facing Crawford—it had been simple for Herbie to talk about the past: of life in Berlin in the late 1930s; his father and mother; his father's death as a fighter pilot; and the young Herbie's growing distaste for the régime, for the Party, and the Führer. Then the hell of Berlin as the Russians drew near; the death of his mother; his own flight into the arms of the Americans, and the strange life that was to become his profession.

The work, as a lad of fourteen, undercover in the DP Camps of Europe, winkling out Nazis posing as refugees; then the change of pace when, in spite of pleas from his case officer, the American service refused him, rejecting all thoughts of taking Herbie into the fold of what was eventually to become the CIA. Yet, when one door closed, another opened—to the British, who saw his potential, and the great use to which they could put this mountain of a young man, who had an ideal deceptive air of stupidity. So, through those years when Big Herbie Kruger had become a legend in the British Service as an agent runner in the Eastern Zone, where his networks built him a reputation which had lasted until the previous year.

Openly, he had spoken to Crawford of the secret battle, during those Cold War years: the feud with the then rising KGB officer called Vascovsky; and the river of gossip, hard fact, and superlative intelligence provided by his people in

41

the East. Then the forming of that small and secret network, after the building of the Berlin Wall; and the final crash, when Herbie had seen his agents blown, killed, turned, and made suddenly invisible by Russian magic.

It became a passionate, vital, even emotionally gripping, story. Crawford had listened as one captivated by what seemed, in retrospect, and in the telling, an adventure; yet was, at the time, a terrifying period, interspersed with long dull interludes: and a final capitulation, when Herbie Kruger got out by the skin of his teeth, leaving only a handful of watchers still untouched by Vascovsky.

He told Crawford of the following years; of his work in Bonn: another blown cover, and the instructions that he was never to work in the field again. Then of the new cover—as a burnt-out case in London, with an office and facilities in the Whitehall Annexe, away from the tall, concrete, steel and glass building near Westminster Bridge which is the Firm's headquarters.

There Herbie spent his days, ostensibly involved in paper-work and vetting. In reality he had become one of the most knowledgeable Intelligence mandarins, with a special under-standing of—and responsibility for—East Germany.

From the quiet, neat office in the Annexe, Big Herbie enhanced his already brimming reputation—dealing with daily problems affecting the East, and slowly building a new servicing machinery for the few men and women on the ground in East Berlin. Because of this network; because of his old alliances; because of his reputation, and past success, the Director General had given permission for Operation Trepan—the job that was to cause Big Herbie's fall from grace.

So it was that Crawford finally led Herbie through his life, to those few days of horror, when the adroit Vascovsky had him close mew'd up on the wrong side of the Wall. Nightmare time.

Sitting next to Tubby, now, in the back of the car speeding towards London, Herbie felt the same old swell of depression, aware of the one constant—that his life's work, his reputation

42

and loyalty, had been shattered into fragments through one act of folly.

Slowly Herbie turned his head, conscious of Tubby Fincher's eyes moving away from him. Not only his old enemies were hiding in the dark, but his old friends also.

Tubby Fincher still wondered how it was for Herbie; though not a particle of his own senses felt compassion. The Director General could possibly allow the benefit of the doubt, but Fincher was unable to give way as easily. What had once shown the smallest chink remained unsafe for all time. He heard Big Herbie give a small sigh, and thought that it was all very well for Kruger to feel strain. Tubby Fincher still had a long session ahead, once Herbie was safely installed, back in the St. John's Wood flat. The long session would, in the end, have a final effect on Kruger.

They turned into the road Herbie knew so well. Yet now, he could hardly recognise it. Like a man returning to a childhood haunt, the street and buildings seemed smaller and more cramped. The year at Warminster had accustomed him to space.

4

ALONE ONCE MORE in the St. John's Wood flat, Big Herbie again experienced that sense of isolation, known only to those who have lived the strange double life of deceit, under cover in a foreign land.

It was as though he did not even know this place, with its large picture windows looking out across London; even the once-familiar, and comfortable, furnishings now seemed alien. The leather buttoned suite, metal and glass tables, expensive stereo equipment; the four oils of Berlin—executed by some

43

unknown artist in the days before the Third Reich. All were at odds with the experiences of the past year.

He wandered through the rooms, conscious that all appeared to be as he had left it—except that it was clean; spotless, and polished; as it would be, for Herbie was under no illusion that they had prepared carefully for his return. The cleaning would have been done after the electronics were installed, and he might just as well spit at the moon as try to locate whatever had gone in. Maybe, he thought, after a day or so he would try to do a small visual sweep. Both the telephones would be handled from outside, while the interior devices could range from high frequency sophisticated micro-ears, to those minute fibre-optic lenses leading either to cameras or VTR snoops.

Even the book he had been reading still lay on the bedside table—Jordan's *Edward VI: The Threshold of Power*. Herbie Kruger's other passions, outside his work, were music and English history. Seeing the book triggered an even deeper trough in his depression. Since Herbie had last put down that book, his world had shifted on its axis; in spite of the care, and professional skill, with which he had planned his own private trip over the Berlin Wall—to do what he truly believed could be accomplished by himself alone.

In honesty he now knew the folly, and its consequences: his own selfishness and indulgence. He also knew the cost of that action, and could even count the lives—trapped or ruined. All because he, Eberhard Lukas Kruger, had taken the law into his own hands, and come face to face with his enemy of the past, Jacob Vascovsky.

Nightly in the tormented dreams, he saw the faces of those he had failed; and sometimes, like now, in broad daylight. Girren; Schnabeln; Anna Blatte; Mortiz Winter; the sensual Martha Adler; Otto Luntmann, the eternal scholar; poor little Peter Sensel; Monch; and Ursula. Christ, Ursula, his Achilles heel.

Herbie shook his head, as though to clear the images from his mind, or blot out the echo of his own cry when Vascovsky had finally laid the news on him. Kruger gave a bitter smile.

What madness. He had even thought that the few days' inquisition—face to face with Vascovsky—had been simple. Those first questions had appeared to need no agile ducking or weaving. How wrong he had been.

At the time, the interrogation in East Berlin was not intended to last. The real thing would have been set up in another part of the forest—probably in some *dacha* near the Black Sea, with young tough KGB watchers sealing off the outside world.

Herbie had no doubts that it was pure chance which saved him from the whole, drawn out, business of confession by every possible means. Chance, and his own recklessness again: though, by this time, it was not courage that spurred him, but a need to get clear—even if it cost him his life. Even life did not matter, after Vascovsky had shown him the full picture: Herbie Kruger's professional career and reputation was founded on a series of betrayals and treachery.

Standing in his old bedroom, part of his mind computing where the musicians had their machines—in another flat? in this building? elsewhere?—Herbie wondered, with hindsight, which, in the end, would have been worse: the Black Sea or Warminster? Of one thing he was sure. Somehow, during those few days with Vascovsky, he had compounded the errors.

When Crawford really got down to it, back at Warminster, and began to draw the teeth of fact—without the benefit of anaesthetic—something had touched a nerve in the heart of the Firm. Either Crawford recognised a tiny flaw, or it came to light when the patient men were sifting through the daily transcripts of those long conversations, between Herbie and his wise and experienced confessor.

For all his personal guile, Big Herbie had let slip some diamond—which meant little to himself—placing it before Vascovsky, right there in East Berlin. Whatever it was, that small piece of information meant a great deal more to the senior men of Herbie's Service than it did to Herbie. Therefore its value was probably even higher to the Russian Service.

He had some idea that it was about Hallet and Birdseed;

for Crawford kept going back to that one point, and those two names. Later, when the other confessors took over, they also retraced the same ground. Hallet and Birdseed? Why should such a piece of chaff mean anything?

Slowly, Big Herbie began to unpack his case: hanging up the two suits; folding shirts; dumping dirty linen into the laundry basket, then carrying the beloved taped works of Gustav Mahler back into the main room: replacing them in the polished racks above the stereo machines. He traced the fingers of one hand along the ranks of taped music: Mahler, Bruckner, Shostakovitch, Britten, a little Mozart, some Bach, Richard Strauss, but no Rachmaninov.

They had even gone to the trouble of filling his fridge-freezer—probably to discourage him from going out—while the bottles on the drinks' trolley, in the main room, were all full: unopened. Herbie gave another of his heaving shrugs and started to build himself a mammoth vodka-soda.

With a large hand cupped around the glass, he turned, walking towards the window, glancing at his bookshelves as he went. Everything seemed in place, the classics of English history, mingled with studies of British statesmen, world leaders, and occasional rare books sought out during those more prosaic periods of peace in Herbie's burrowing active life.

At the window, the view suddenly became its old familiar self, the flat taking on its former perspective. It was as if he had wakened from a dream to find nothing had changed; that he was safe. Only the active sensors, in the back of Herbie Kruger's brain, told him nothing could ever be the same again.

Looking down on to the road below, his professional mind sought for the obvious: a closed van, an estate with blacked out windows—anything that might conceal the watchers he knew were there, adjusting their tuners to get better sound or picture as they rifled his present privacy.

Then he remembered the mail. At Warminster they had brought up his mail each evening, with the Commandant's daily box of papers. The mail had been impeccably opened and resealed. To the normal eye there would have been no trace. When Tubby brought him back into the flat, Herbie had been vaguely conscious of a small pile of post on the glass table. He crossed to it now—four letters. Two of the letters had window envelopes, and were not sealed. Circulars. The remaining pair had none of the usual marks. The same team—probably a day and a night man—had done all Herbie's letters while he was at Warminster, and it had not taken long to spot individual trademarks. One man always left a minute tear—a brushing of the fingernail almost—on the right side of the envelope flap, high up: as if he was impatient, and never quite allowed the glue-softener to complete its work, before he started on the flap.

The other searcher had a habit of leaving a small fragment slightly loose, at the point of the flap. Again minute, but Herbie had spent most of his life watching for trademarks.

Neither of the two envelopes before him now bore the traces. Either a new team had taken over, or they had pulled off the dogs. Taking a long draught of the vodka, Herbie opened the first envelope with deliberate care.

The letter was on government paper: typewritten with a neat signature.

Dear Herbie,

They have just told me you are coming back on Monday, and asked if I still wish to work with you. Why they should ask must remain one of life's mysteries. Of course I want to work with you, if you will have me. No hint of what the job is to be, but I expect they have briefed you. Need I say how thrilled and relieved I am to know you are coming back. Welcome home. It will be so good to see you again, and nobody could be more pleased than I that all has turned out so well. See you soon.

As Ever,

Yours,

Tony Worboys

Big Herbie smiled. At least there was young Worboys. Green perhaps, but untainted, as yet, by the deeds of treachery that went on within the world he had chosen. Herbie closed his eyes, remembering that it was young Worboys who had been there on his return over the Berlin Wall: bouncing around him like a puppy.

"You made it, Herbie." With his eyes tightly closed, Herbie could still hear Worboys' greeting. "Thank God. You made it . . . they had you, and you got away . . . At least you've come back a sort of hero."

Aloud, he laughed. A sort of hero? That's what Worboys imagined. Tubby Fincher, and heaven knew who else in the Firm, thought of him as the villain of the piece. Crawford knew more than was good for him. The Director General probably knew it all. Hallet and Birdseed? Why Hallet and Birdseed? Would they ever tell him? Was it right he should know?

The second letter was handwritten in violet ink. A woman's hand which, oddly, made Herbie's heart give a sudden lurch. This time his fingers fumbled with the flap, and he ripped at the envelope. Inside, a few lines of neat, Germanic script:

Herbie dear,

I am probably breaking all the rules, but they have not told me that I am forbidden to write. At least I am not including an address. Maybe they have told you they traded me for some wretched little KGB man. I am pensioned off and playing the lonely German widow without much success. They tell me you have been cleared of all responsibility. It would be nice to see you, and I am usually at this number (0590) 73637.

Fondest love and many memories!
Martha

The sun crossed the pitted, lumpy face as it gashed into a beaming smile. So? So one more at least was saved. He had condemned her by his folly, but she had been reprieved. Martha. Martha Adler, who had been arrested just after

48

Herbie had seen her in East Berlin. Martha, who he had recruited so long ago, in the agile days of his youth.

When he had seen her in Berlin, before the axe fell, she was still lithe, with a wonderful figure and hair the same shade of ash blonde it had been when they first met. Then she had screwed Russian officers, diplomats, and politicians of the DDR, just for the tidbits of information. She had even had an affair with Herbie before he recruited her. So long ago now. Martha Adler, from whom sex bubbled like a hot spring. Good. He would call her; see her. At least she would make him laugh, as he was nearly laughing now. Not from here though. He would go out. Make the watchers work for a living. Phone from a call box. Maybe they would even . . . Herbie started to laugh aloud. The thought, after all these years. At least he was absolved from one crime if Martha was back. Perhaps her testimony had helped the Director General make up his mind.

At that moment, as though on cue, the direct line telephone began its urgent bleeping. Herbie lumbered across to pick up the instrument. His hand shook, but his voice was strong as he answered. The Director General was on the line.

"Welcome home, Herbie," the Director's voice flat and without emotion, but not unfriendly.

Herbie muttered his thanks, Vascovsky's voice still an echo in his head.

"I'm afraid I have some news for you. Possibly bad news." The Director paused as Herbie grunted. The past year had been all bad news so what could be worse?

"A friend of yours has been killed, I fear. An accident. A real accident. Nothing sinister. You know a man called Gold?"

"Alexander Gold?" Herbie did not react immediately.

"The same. He was killed crossing the Strand. Walked in front of a taxi."

"Walked?"

"Definitely. There are witnesses. He stepped off the pavement without looking. I'm sorry."

Herbie remained silent for a second. He could see Alex clearly: at their last meeting, in the little house in Catford;

full of life, a little drunk. Shit, he said silently. Getting careless in his old age. Dropping Alex's name like that had been a test. Nobody . . .

"I thought you should know. Exiled Russian, wasn't he, Herbie? We've nothing on file." A mild hint of admonition? A query?

"It was private," Herbie did not say it too quickly. "A friend outside. There's nothing that connects. No return ticket to us."

When he answered, a more definite shade of accusation had crept into the Director's voice. "Herbie, he carried your name and address, openly . . ."

"So?"

"Together with your Firm address—the Annexe—and its private number, reversed, in his book."

Herbie counted to ten. "You want to talk about this now? On the phone?"

"Bare essentials, I think, yes."

"Okay. It was private. Goes a long way back. Back to the camps—you know my life story . . ."

"Most of us know a lot of it, Herbie."

"Well, it was in the camps. I've known Alex since I was fourteen, fifteen. He is—was—about four years older than me. I knew his wife also. Yes, I gave him numbers. Not so very long ago, the private number. That was because of his son."

"Michael?"

Herbie grunted an affirmative. "Recruits, Director. You always say we should keep our eyes peeled. I watch like anyone. Michael has a first class honours degree in modern languages: speaks Russian, lives Russian—old Russian, but Russian. A good, possible, bet. Not yet, though. In time a possible. Too young yet. That enough? We talk properly when I see you?" There was no percentage in revealing the shameless way he had used Alex—without making any written reports, except to call him 'a source'. Nobody was going to ask; it was the same way they worked in the Branch; the CID; journalists.

"Right, Herbie, we'll talk on Monday. Nine sharp."

"On the third stroke," Herbie chuckled. "I look forward to it."

"It'll be good to have you back." The Director closed the line.

Herbie realised the glass was still in his hand so he drained it, felt the bite of the liquor on the back of his throat, and saw, in the bookshelf, a copy of Halliday's *Shakespeare Companion*. A line, stunningly apt, came into his head. *Henry IV*—off hand he could not remember which Part. The tottering Mr. Justice Shallow, the trembling Mr. Justice Swallow, reminiscing about their youth: feeling their own mortality through the death of contemporaries, "And is old Double dead?" A hollow irony now. Double dead. Poor Alex; and is old Alex dead?

"And is old Double dead?" Herbie said aloud, smashing his glass towards the imitation fireplace, so that the splinters flew back in a sunburst shower.

So they thought him a fool, a traitor, a Judas. Okay, God help them now. The Director's voice on the telephone, and the news of Alex Gold's death, had been like a drench of icy water.

Too long, living with self-pity. No, he would not see Martha Adler this weekend. That could wait. He would plan a new campaign. Then, on Monday morning, he would place himself, like some kind of monk, under the Director's obedience. Whatever the job, though, Herbie Kruger would play a second game. An end game. Pride in his sordid profession was all he had left; the swamped lands of his career now needed draining, and the crops sewn anew.

With Shakespeare still in his mind, and no thought for the men who listened through their electronic ears, he raised his arms and voice, shouting, his bull-like head tilted back. "Herbie's himself again."

5

THE DIRECTOR GENERAL put down the telephone, turning to the men assembled in his office. Crawford, like a pleasant farmer; Tubby Fincher; Tony Worboys; and, sprawled in a leather armchair, his manner so casual as to make him almost invisible, Curry Shepherd.

"Private friendship, he says." The Director looked at each of them, like a good actor sweeping the house with his eyes, letting each member of the audience think he was aware of them as separate individuals. "Private friendship, from way back in the camps. No connection, except that he had an eye on the son. Possible material."

Fincher gave a short, brassy laugh. "Haven't we all? Spotted by our tame Cambridge Don. Michael Gold's been on our private probable list for two years."

"It's plausible, Tubby. On the cards," the Director spoke gently. "I know you aren't convinced, but . . ."

"I've been with him." Sharp, efficient Tubby. "I've *seen* the man. He's come through the best part of a year's interrogation, and I still consider a few more months would have broken him."

"Oh come on . . ." From young Worboys.

Fincher gave the junior a cold stare. "You're really going through with it, Director?"

The Director, behind his desk again, asked why he should not go through with it? Because the shadow of doubt still remained. Tubby snapped back. "The man's a walking land mine . . ."

The fact that no case had been proved against Kruger, made it more likely that last year's Berlin disaster was simply an act of passionate frustration, the Director parried Fincher. "Out of character with the rest of his known professional life,

I admit. But you will recall that he pressed constantly for permission to put matters right in East Berlin, on his own. We all had warning about that. I'm personally ninety-nine per cent sure that Big Herbie's one of ours and always has been."

With his eyes, the Director tested his audience. "Crawford?"

"Like you. Ninety-nine per cent certain, Director. Yet I've a sneaking suspicion that it matters little whether it's my one per cent or yours. The rule of thumb is that when there's a jot of doubt you suspend. Neither Milmo nor Bill Skardon could break Philby . . ."

"And look what happened there . . ." Tubby began.

The Director nodded. "Exactly the argument the PM put. But permission was granted: mainly because of the way I intend to use him. If Herbie is ours, then he's given them those two small pieces of silver in error. That is quite possible, as we all know. One of the few evils of the need-to-know principle."

Curry Shepherd stirred. "Sound as a bell, old Herb," he murmured. "Don't forget, I saw him in action. You heard what Martha Adler had to say. He went over to save, not to kill. Five-to-four-on favourite, Herbie Kruger."

Fincher remained unmoved, asking if they would get twice-daily reports on Kruger's behaviour and movements.

Since his own cover was blown, as the Firm's Berlin troubleshooter, Curry Shepherd had been appointed head of what was known, in trade circles, as the Watch Committee— training and operational surveillance: the leeches, who worked on foot, or in cars; and the privacy-thieves with their electronics, mikes and cameras. All were under Curry's control.

"So what's he been up to since I got him back?"

Curry uncurled himself and wandered towards the door. "Get you a news flash," he muttered.

The Director, anxious to convince his trusted adviser, began the argument again; directing it solely at Tubby Fincher. "You see, whichever way this goes we'll know. Also there's no harm done. After all, Stentor is expendable. We're trying to keep a promise, that's all. If it fails . . . well," he raised his hands in a signal that, in a priest, would mean God's will be done. "Truth is, Tubby, we're in error. Planning should be finished by now; and someone without a face ought to have completed training. We're buck-passing, whichever way you look at it."

Fincher remarked that young Worboys should not really be with them. Patiently the Director agreed, nodding at Tony Worboys: signalling he should leave.

But Worboys wanted a say. "Sir, the first time I worked with Herbie was on the Nostradamus business. I surely don't have to remind anybody that it was Herbie Kruger who unearthed what, we hope, was the last of the long-term penetration agents in the Firm. If it hadn't been for Herbie, that man might still be working here."

Tubby Fincher gave a frustrated chuckle, "And may I remind you, young Worboys, that when push came to shove, it was Herbie Kruger's gun that jammed; and it was Mr. Kruger who failed to put a tap on the wife's house phone, so allowing the gentleman in question to get away; and so causing us the trouble of arranging a search party, followed by an unpleasant accident. Techniques we try to avoid." He went on to say that this was the line he'd pursued from the start. He expanded. Herbie Kruger had come to them as a mere lad; refused by the Americans. There was some evidence he had already worked, as a boy, in the German anti-Nazi resistance. "And you know what they were—Communist Party members to a man, woman, and child. With the information we have now—since Berlin—Herbie's entire career with us is revealed as a sham: the great reputation built on sand. You only have to go down the list—agents blown, networks folded, and, finally, Herbie taken back after throwing all his people on to a dungheap. One got out, right. One man; then we did a deal for the Adler woman . . ."

"And she stakes her life on him," the Director murmured.

"Par for the course. He's a natural. I take my hat off to him. I still cannot trust him."

The Director told Worboys he had better be going, and Worboys had the distinct feeling that the Director General had to control himself from saying "Cut along, old chap." He cut along anyway, unhappy in the knowledge that he would have to play the subversive with Herbie Kruger. He passed Curry Shepherd in the passage, Curry looking, as usual, like a slightly seedy, cashiered officer. Worboys presumed it was the fading looks, the slightly worn blazer, and the suede brothel-creepers that did it.

Back in the Director's office, Curry launched into a quick résumé of Herbie's words, and actions, following Tubby's departure from the St. John's Wood flat. In silence, they heard him through to the end.

"Out of his tree," sneered Fincher. "Breaking glasses. 'Herbie's himself again' . . ."

"Parody of *Richard III*, Tubby." The Director coughed, "Refurbished by a Mr. Cibber, I believe. 'Conscience avaunt, Richard's himself again.' Curry?"

"The letters? What did they contain?"

Curry's tired, almost dissipated, good looks underwent a small convulsion, as one hand raked through the thinning blond hair. "Oh Christ."

The Director showed no anger. It was too late for fury. He baldly stated that Curry had called off the mail surveillance. Shepherd nodded.

"Then get it on again fast. If he does go out, put a man in to go through those letters." His head snapped towards Tubby Fincher. "You see, Tubby, even if I am ninety-nine per cent certain of Herbie, I'm damned if I'm going to get caught out. In the meantime, avaunt, gentlemen, I wish to examine the Stentor File in order to talk with Mr. Kruger on Monday—and, Curry, don't lose him over the weekend, will you?"

Curry managed a smile. "Not even if he defects to Bognor Regis, sir."

Quoting the supposed deathbed words of King George V, the Director grinned sourly. "Bugger Bognor," he said.

6

Big Herbie towered over the Director General, hands awkward at his sides. "Just remember it was not my idea to come back here." He gave no hint of a smile. "That is first. Second, you should know that I am aware Martha Adler is in England on part of the Firm's wonderful exchange programme. She wrote to me: telephone number but no address. I am not a mind reader so did not know how you felt about things, so I refrained from calling her over the weekend." The old grin appeared for a second time. "It would be nice to have your okay to visit her, yes?"

Herbie had an idea that, in his adopted country, his attitude would be called 'opening the batting'. He had given the Director General—who had kept him waiting, under Tubby's surly eye, for fifteen minutes—no chance to even greet him.

The DG raised his eyebrows, motioning Herbie to sit down. When he spoke it was with the calm quiet voice of authority: the velvet larynx covering a will of steel.

"Herbie, it's nice to see you. Good to have you back. But there's no need for you to come in with guns blazing. If anyone should blaze, it's me."

Herbie took a chair, lowering his bulk into it with some care. "I am under your authority, Director. I spend the best part of a year being questioned at Warminster; there is a Board of Enquiry; nobody tells me the result; Tubby Fincher comes down, out of the blue, on Friday to say you give me a new job—though he behaves like I am untouchable. Then I get a letter from one of my former agents, telling me something I should already know. You expect me to be calm and meek? I'll do my job—whatever it is—but I am uncomfortable. You don't have to be blessed with the huge IQ to realise that good old Herbie Kruger is still under suspicion: that some people think I'm a mouse . . ."

"A mouse?"

"Whatever they call them in the spy books. A mouse. A long-term penetration agent."

"Mole, Herbie. Yes, of course you've been under suspicion. What d'you expect? You spent a time in the Soviet nick, with one of their best men breathing down your neck."

"I . . ."

"Yes, you solved a problem. You can have credit for that. You put one matter to rights. But you then proceeded to have long-term agents blown, arrested, killed."

Herbie gave a passable imitation of a nodding Buddha. "Okay. I know. I'm sorry."

"Sorry? You're sorry, Herbie? What good's that to me? One of my most experienced field officers, invaluable to me here in London, now that we have to rely on fewer and fewer people in the field. That's what you *were*. Invaluable. Now what're you good for?"

"Stamping passports? Vetting visas?"

The DG sat looking at the big man, his eyes glossed with genuine anger.

"Sweeping floors?" Herbie tried again.

"You say the Board of Enquiry result has not been passed on to you? Right." He shuffled among some papers. "I'm not going to read the whole thing. Take too long. The result is that you are to receive a severe reprimand; that you are to be used only at my discretion; that you will never again be allowed to operate outside the confines of the United Kingdom; and that you will only be given limited access to priority classified documents and information."

"Then I cannot vet visas."

"Strictly speaking, no, Herbie. No, you haven't even the power to do that. Without my especial say-so. However," the DG leaned back in his chair, "I'm willing to interpret the Board's findings in a liberal fashion: only because you are good at your job, and we're short of manpower. Also I believe you went your own way—over the Berlin Wall—out of the best possible motives."

Big Herbie bowed his head, clearly thanking the Director, who gave a curt smile of acceptance.

"Okay, I'm vulnerable, that's obvious. Vulnerable to the Soviets, and to many here in this building."

The Director thought for a few moments, fingers drumming on the glass covering of his desk top, as the traffic rumble rose from the street below, a faint hum in the high office. "For what I had in mind, it is perhaps a good thing."

The Director gave a half smile, "And I see no harm in your being in touch with Martha Adler."

"And the work?"

"Ah. Would you relish an impossible task, Herbie? It's like the old fairytale. Candidates for the princess's hand in marriage're required to perform outlandish feats. That is what's required of you. Pull it off, and you get the princess. At least you regain trust. Will you slay a dragon or two in exchange for trust?"

"Tell me."

The Director laced his fingers, saying that Herbie should know, first, that the Prime Minister had been consulted. There was agreement to waive some of the Board of Enquiry's findings—"You are to be allowed access to certain highly classified documents and information; and make no mistake, the Prime Minister can't even take a squint at them. But it is necessary to the work in hand."

"And the work in hand?"

The Director asked what Big Herbie knew of Stentor. The workname of their most important source within the Soviet Bloc, Herbie replied. The name was chosen, presumably, because of its mythical connotations: Stentor being the herald before the city of Troy, known for the great power of his voice.

"You've handled, and had knowledge of, information directly emanating from Stentor?" The question was put hard, like part of an interrogation.

"You know I have."

"Did you ever handle information you only suspected came through Stentor? Intelligence, or possible hints, which you considered could have only come from one logical source?"

"You mean without official confirmation that it was Stentor?"

The Director inclined his head.

Herbie's brow creased; eyes flicking about the room, going back in memory through the vast amount of information that had passed over his desk, or been given to him in verbal confidence. He maintained there was nothing he could put his finger on.

"As it happens, you *have* been given such information—without being told the source."

Herbie sat quiet for a moment. Then his eyes slowly widened. "Oh Christ," he whispered. "Hallet and Birdseed?"

"You worked it out?"

Herbie acidly said it had not taken much working out. "First Crawford; then the others. They came back to it again and again. I gave Vascovsky Hallet and Birdseed for good measure. A bit of extra grain. Millet. They were just tips—came to nothing." His voice began an upward, angry, rise. "I fed them chickenfeed. Hallet and Birdseed were chicken-feed."

The Director chuckled, "I liked some of your chickenfeed, Herbie—even though the Hallet and Birdseed stuff *was* sensitive."

"Birdseed, yes. Chickenfeed. Good name. Glad you approved."

The Director nodded. He had liked the trivia, the details Herbie had thrown away about safe houses that were no longer in use; the two small watching operations—in Lisbon and Dublin—that were of no value. "It was Hallet and Birdseed I did *not* like."

Hallet was a NATO General. Eighteen months before, while stationed in Germany, with BAOR, the Firm had got wind of a discredit operation being run by the Soviets. Steps were taken; Herbie had been involved on the periphery, and the discredit came to nothing. Hallet was quickly moved back to England and retired on full pay.

Birdseed was also a tip. A Soviet disinformation ploy regarding the possible siting of American nuclear weapons on British bases. The ploy seemed to have been called off, because the whole thing went dead.

"I taunted him a little with Hallet and Birdseed. They were nothing," Big Herbie paused. "But they were something, yes?"

The Director shook his head. They were something and nothing, he claimed. The difficulty was that they came directly from Stentor. The larger problem was they could be traced *back* to Stentor.

"And Stentor is vulnerable?"

The Director did not answer. Instead, he asked when Big Herbie had first been made aware of Stentor?

"Two . . . No . . . Three years ago. You had him operating three years ago."

Wrong. Herbie could tell by the DG's face. "Three years ago, Herbie." The Director looked straight into his face. "Three years ago, the magic circle was widened. The circle with knowledge of Stentor's existence. True, there are others who know the workname: but that means nothing. Only six people in the entire Service know that Stentor is our one major Soviet source. Only three of those six are briefed on all the facts. Herbie, you are one of the six. Now you have to be the fourth to join the inner ring of knowledge. Would it surprise you to know that Stentor has been in the field—and in place—longer than yourself? Much longer."

Big Herbie cocked an eyebrow: waiting.

"Like you, Stentor began in the trade when he was aged only fourteen years. Which means he's a good deal older than you. He first came in as a fourteen-year-old boy. That was in 1925 . . ."

" 'Twenty-five?" Herbie again raised his voice.

The Director nodded, asking if he knew of the work done just after the First World War by Sir Robert Bruce Lockhart.

"He operated under diplomatic cover in Russia, during, and after, the 1917 revolution, yes?"

"Lockhart went out in 1918—you'll have to go through

the file—as British Consul-General in Moscow, and head of a special mission. He worked mainly to us—or, I should say, to the Head of Service. In fact, he ruined a rising diplomatic career because of his work for us. Stayed in Moscow until the collapse of Germany. You should read him, some time. A real expert on Russia, and the politics of the period. Became a writer of distinction.

"One of the many things Lockhart did was lay down a stock of agents. In those days we had a very good network inside Russia. In 1925 one of Lockhart's original people recruited a boy, briefed him—even brought him out for training in France at one time—and set him up as a long-term source.

"The boy was from an old family—aristocrats close to the Tsar, and the court. As the revolution took hold, and things got worse, his family tried to get out. They were caught and shot. The boy was hidden by a servant—it's all good penny novel adventure stuff; but it happened to a lot of people. He was hidden; survived the Revolution, and the Civil War. By the time Lockhart's man got to him, the lad was living in fear of being denounced; the very people who saved him had become frightened that his true identity, and background, would be revealed. Lockhart's man took care of it. He was an exceptional recruiting officer, with a long view—like Lockhart himself. Gave the boy a new identity, coached him in cover, until the lad almost came to believe it himself.

"Lockhart's stay-behind man had the cryptonym Trofimov and one of the things he did was play the boy straight to the Head of Service. Nobody else—not even people close to Trofimov—knew about the young recruit. In those days we weren't so sophisticated: certainly not about sleepers, and long-term penetration people. Trofimov, I suspect, knew the foresight of the Russian hierarchy. You must remember they were starting to sow their seeds over here. That's how advanced *their* thinking was. Only a few years later they had recruiting officers crawling everywhere—pulling the Cambridge set into their net. They looked to the future. So did Trofimov.

"His young recruit was briefed to take the Party line; get into the military; then squirm his way into their Intelligence Service if he could. His status as an agent; his work; and his potential, has, from that time, been played only to the Head of Service—or Director General when the new title came in. It's been like the Apostolic succession: passed on from Chief to Chief. Stentor would take instruction from no one else; and give nothing, except to the man at the top—a very good thing as well. He would've been rumbled years ago if it hadn't been for that golden rule. Then, three years ago, it became necessary to widen the circle of knowledge."

Big Herbie looked bemused. "If he was fourteen in 'twenty-five . . ." he began.

"Yes," the Director made a short, nervous, chopping motion with his right arm. "Stentor's over seventy years old now. Three score years and ten—and for around fifty-six of 'em he's worked, alone and silent, for us. He slogged away on farms, because they wouldn't let him near the army; then they took him, and he wormed his way into the Cheka. He survived the show trials, and Stalin's purges. He was even part of the Military Intelligence arm. Served under cover with the German Army. After the Second World War he still survived, and rose in power. There was a time when he seemed to be in direct line for the top job. You'll have to read the whole file, Herbie. For the last seven years, Stentor's been head of a department in the First Chief Directorate—a position of great responsibility; therefore of exceptional value to us. I suppose it could be said that, if Kim Philby was their mole, Stentor is our moth: laying his eggs and eating away at their fabric. The only difference is that Stentor hasn't been caught."

"Not yet." Herbie's voice unusually hoarse, as his agile mind leaped over possible ravines. "But I've put him at risk."

"Yes." A terse statement of fact, unflavoured by anger or concern. "Yes, Herbie, you've put Stentor at risk. But I accept—like Crawford—there was no way you could have known that the Hallet and Birdseed information came directly from Stentor. Neither could you possibly know that, in giving

Hallet and Birdseed to Vascovsky, you were handing them a direct link back to Stentor. We've been lucky; very lucky. When Trofimov recruited Stentor, his strategy was that of a long-term operation; but even he could not have guessed how long we would get away with it—or to what heights that fourteen-year-old boy would rise in the Soviet hierarchy.

"The point is that Stentor's now an elderly man: full of years; but with all his faculties, and a mountain of experience. Otherwise they'd have put him out to grass years ago. Already we've faced the fact that they might retire him at any time. The powerful Russians—politicians, diplomats and military—cling to their authority: sometimes even on their deathbeds. But now they'll either catch our man pretty soon, or put him in a *dacha*, among pleasant surroundings, for his last years—and then catch him. He's almost through: and there's the rub. Successive men in my place have, over the years, promised Stentor that, when the time comes, he'll be brought out. We've given him our word that the autumn of his life will be spent here—in the country he's served so long, yet never seen. Your actions have forced the situation. It's now a matter of great urgency. Stentor is not only drawing to the close of a distinguished career in the Soviet Service, and our own Service, but also he stands at the point of exposure. For the first time he is in danger of being well and truly blown."

Kruger opened his mouth to speak, but the Director raised a hand. "This is the real crunch. We have evidence that a ferret has now been put in to finger Stentor. So your job—the impossible—will be to get him out, as soon as it can be arranged. And this you will have to do without leaving London. You see, I told you, it is an awesome task."

Herbie Kruger looked as though he was thinking of something else, his eyes glazed in a faraway look. He blinked, coming back to the present. "A ferret, you said? They're putting a ferret in to drive him into the open?"

"Yes."

"How do we know?"

"From Stentor himself."

"Do we know this ferret?"

The Director General nodded.

With a slight trace of apprehension, Big Herbie Kruger asked, "Who?"

"General Jacob Vascovsky."

The two men locked eyes. You could hear the silence, as though it was tangible, lying there on the desk with the transcripts of Herbie's interrogation, and the thick flagged folder that was a record of Stentor's life and deeds.

7

HERBIE KRUGER SAT looking from the train window, as they pulled out of Lewisham. The rain plied its way down the grimed glass, and Herbie decided that Lewisham was not really the centre of the universe: particularly on a soaking wet afternoon.

"Stentor has five methods of communication with us," the Director General had told him. "They're nearly all old-fashioned—the tried and true Boy Scout dodges everybody knows."

When Stentor had taken up his last appointment, some seven years ago, he had acquired his 'niece' in Leningrad. The 'niece' had direct covert contact with the British Embassy's 'outside' man in Moscow. A simple telephone code would lay on a drop and pick-up. "Just like you read in the books." The Director was obviously unhappy about such simple tactics. He supposed that, if things got really bad, Stentor could make a run for it; but the Embassy would certainly send him packing. The other four methods of relaying information to London, ranged from similar drop and pick-up techniques, to a more sophisticated fast-sending radio link which the Russian used sparingly. "He'll keep that one until last," the Director prophesied.

"If Vascovsky's been put on to the scent, their surveillance lads'll be smelling around Stentor, and his three brothers in the Standing Committee, like wasps around the jam. We know the situation, so he'll probably remain silent—unless full-scale drama breaks out—until *we* make contact." The Director wanted his, Big Herbie's, comments within three days. How long had they got? A month, if lucky. Six weeks if luckier still. Realistically? A month—give or take a few days.

"And nobody on the spot?" Herbie asked.

All Stentor's contacts were cut-outs, Big Herbie was told: which meant there was no interrelation, and not one of them knew Stentor's true identity. That had always been essential: like it was essential they did not have a known 'face' making a pass at Stentor. Boiling it down, Herbie considered, it left only one chance. Send in a mystery, as they said in the Firm's jargon—a man or woman who could in no way be connected with the Service. Send him in. Give him cover. Show him a way to meet Stentor face to face. Provide a workable plan and bring them both out. After a suitable time lapse, they could then embarrass the Soviet Service by spilling the beans to the Press.

The Director General would be all in favour of spreading it over the front pages. Too often, of late, the Press had dug up old scandals; and raised hell over fictional new ones. Even wild guesses were being taken as gospel truth.

Tales of treachery—however stupid—were meat and drink to Press and public alike. The two Firms had come in for a lot of stick: particularly MI5, with the so-called Blunt scandal—about which the real truth just could not be told— together with various insinuations concerning officers, and politicians, now dead. A coup like this was politically desirable.

Herbie glanced out of the streaming window again, as the train rocked and twisted its way back to Charing Cross. It had been a melancholy afternoon, even without the rain. Alex Gold's funeral had been almost as quick as his death.

"He wanted no religious ceremony," the widow, Nataly, told Herbie. So there had been no prayers, no cleric—not even an Orthodox priest. Just the rain, the undertaker, and Alex, in a box, at the crematorium. The BBC was represented by a young man in a grubby raincoat, who refused Nataly's invitation to come back to the house. Apart from him, there was only the widow; Michael, the son—with a plain girl friend who cried—and Big Herbie.

Herbie returned to the house with Nataly, while young Michael took his girl home. Her name was Cynthia Perkins, and Michael promised to be back before Herbie left.

As the young man walked away, Herbie thought of the possibilities: and the irony. Alex had always sworn that neither Nataly nor the son knew about his other work. Big Herbie was inclined to believe him. Herbie would not have trusted Nataly with a minor confidence, let alone the important discipline of secrecy. As for Michael? No, Alex was dedicated to giving the boy a first class education—seeing him grow into a successful professional man. Neither would know of Alex Gold's dirty secret; and Michael now spoke German, French and Russian. Russian with his parents' Ukrainian accent. Perhaps. Herbie tucked the thought away, as he guided Nataly back to the little house. Perhaps, but certainly not yet. Yes, he had started at the age of fourteen, but that was a different world. Young Michael Gold really was too young, callow and inexperienced in life. Maybe, one day.

Desperately, he tried to see Nataly as she had been when they first met: but the picture was gone—changed to a phantom, like the ghost image you get on a faulty TV. He knew she had been a natural blonde and very thin. Now the blonde streaks in her hair remained only with the aid of chemicals; and the most charitable would call her buxom at least.

He also wondered at the fact that he had never known her maiden name. But why should he? They were all little more than children on that first meeting; and he thought of her, even then, as Alex's wife.

66

In the house, she expressed her grief to Kruger in great gouts of effusive thanks. "If it hadn't been for you, Herbie, we would both have perished years ago. Instead, you've given us a happy life together. Alex would want me to thank you in whatever way was best. You are welcome here at any time. You know that; you *do* know and understand what I mean?"

Big Herbie tried not to believe what he heard. There was only one construction he could put on her words, for they were accompanied by coy movements of her body and eyelids.

He sighed with silent relief when Michael came back, seating himself in the old horsehair easy chair that had been his father's favourite. It was as though Michael had consciously taken over the throne in this overfurnished room which, Herbie thought, had altered little since he had first seen it in the late 1960s.

Nataly constantly referred to the room as 'the lunge', which Herbie translated into 'lounge'—a word he detested. The only decent thing in the place was a little icon of the Virgin of Vladimir—a reproduction of the much larger work; but a good one: old and crafted. Herbie had not seen it in the DP camp, but Alex would almost certainly have had it there.

They took weak Russian tea, and very English cake—which Nataly called gateaux. There was sentiment, and many tears, before Herbie left. Michael drove him to the station, so there was opportunity for a short talk with the boy. Boy? You're getting old, Herbie: the boy was now in his early twenties. Yes, but young, romantic and immature for his age.

On the train, Herbie concluded that Nataly had never known her husband. From the very start of it all, she had not known him. For Nataly, Alex was simply a passport from hell. Now he was gone she probably felt relief: there had been much talk of how well Alex had done; how high he had risen in his field. Fantasy. The little house, and the old cheap furniture had become a mansion crammed with taste and wealth. Nataly lived in a world of fantasy, just as her late husband had lived in a world of double fantasy, and Herbie had come to despise it all, because Alex did what he did for money; not out of conscience. Had Alex ever been blessed with a conscience?

Strange, whenever Herbie had made contact and met Alex in recent years he was always able to see the original man— the boy—he knew for the first time all those years before.

Young Big Herbie was sorting the wheat from the chaff— for the Americans—in the DP camps, when Alexei and Nataly came into his life. Now he could not immediately recall which of the many camps they were in; but the memory, that it was Alexei who had made the first move, remained strong. He introduced himself as Alexei Zolotoy, and just hung around, with the girl; staying close to Herbie, for a few days, before making the real pitch.

It was the usual horror story. They had originally come from the same Ukrainian village, near Kiev. The village had been slap in the path of the Nazi advance, with its attendant scorched earth policy.

Some of the older men tried to put up a fight. In the end they had been stripped, led out naked on to the common ground, and burned alive, with a flame-thrower, in front of the other villagers.

There followed the usual mass slaughter, except for some of the younger men and women—including Alex and Nataly, who claimed they would never forget the sight of the village in flames as they were driven away.

Young Herbie had heard many such stories. "All over now," he told them. "This is a pleasant camp. Your cases will be sorted out. You will go home, and rebuild the village."

Nataly began to cry, and Alexei shook his head. "We were children, but they brought us to Germany. We were worked like little horses. Slave labour. Others came from Russia also, and we know what will happen if they send us back."

"What will happen?"

"You know." Alex, three years his senior, looked ready to spit at Herbie. "You're well in with them. I've watched you. You know the State has decreed that any Russian who worked for the Nazis has been declared a traitor to the Party. There are no excuses. We should have given our lives, rather than

68

work for them. If we are sent back we will surely die; or serve long prison sentences. Mostly we shall die."

"Then you ask not to be sent back." It appeared to be reasonable logic.

"This is what worries us. We hear, in the camp, that the Americans have been ordered to hand us over to the British. The British have agreed, with Stalin, that all Russian-born DPs will be returned to their homeland. We know what this means."

It so happened that Big Herbie had done well in that camp: flushing out several former SS officers and NCOs. His American case officer was pleased with him, so Herbie felt he could ask a favour. He made a plea for Alexei and Nataly, after asking the American if the story was true—about the deportation of Russians, and what would happen to them.

It was all too true, the American said. In fact the British detachment was already in the camp. The Russians would be sent back within a few days. "The British officer doesn't care for it at all," he told Herbie. "None of us do. But that's the order."

Big Herbie put in a further plea and, because of his good work, the American promised to see what he could do. In the end they were all lucky. The British officer had agreed to get Alexei and Nataly out, and into England, before the main party left. Herbie's case officer reckoned it was the Britisher's way of salving his conscience, and the couple were taken out a couple of nights later. Herbie recalled having to ask the American what 'salving his conscience' meant.

Six months passed, and Herbie had almost forgotten the couple, when he received a letter, which had gone halfway around France and Germany to get to him. Alexei and Nataly were safe in London. They were married, and there was a good chance of them being given British citizenship. Their name was now changed to Gold. They both had good jobs.

The next time Herbie Kruger saw Alex was in Berlin, in the late 1950s: when Herbie was working in the West, and agent-running in the East. The work in the West was, of course, concerned with debriefings, and operational orders. It was relatively easy then; before the building of the Wall.

All Alex wanted was to talk and drink. He invited Herbie to London. He could stay with them. Nataly would love to see him, for Alex Gold was now a responsible journalist: doing well, being sent on assignments all over Europe. Within an hour of their meeting, Herbie knew. Perhaps it was Alex's manner, or a hint in something he said. Maybe it was simply intuition, but Big Herbie knew he must keep his guard up, for Alex was working for the Soviets.

Once Big Herbie was back in London—between engagements, so to speak—before going out to Bonn, there was a full reunion. Since then the meetings had been mainly with Alex, with an occasional visit to Catford, just to keep up appearances. So, it was not long before Herbie realised the full state of play. Alex had been either coerced into working for the Soviets, or was doing small jobs for them—not for any ideology, just for the extra money. By this time his great success story had been exploded. Certainly Alex went on business trips, but his assignments all over Europe were mainly as a translator. It was the same with his work for the Soviets. Alex was no master spy; only an occasional courier.

But Alex liked to boast and hint, so Herbie eventually called his bluff, put an arm lock on, and turned him—all nice and private: nothing on paper, and no reports. All it meant was occasional claims for payments—*information from a special source*. In turn, that meant Herbie got first look at whatever Alex was couriering into some part of Europe. Over a few years Alex just about earned his keep; though Herbie was never able to get any headline material. Nobody in their right mind would have trusted scoop information to Alex. Not that he would have talked. It was more likely that, in fear or panic, the man would simply destroy the stuff to save his own skin.

He had been useful though, and, in spite of the terms of their trade, Herbie had a tiny soft spot for the man, hidden away in some far corner of his contempt.

As the train pulled into Charing Cross, Herbie Kruger spotted Curry Shepherd loitering with intent. He was to escort Herbie back to Headquarters. The Director General wished to see him immediately.

*   *   *

The two men sat, alone, in the Director's office, high above Westminster Bridge. Quietly, the DG went through the situation again for Herbie's sake—very conscious that he was setting the big man an invidious task.

"It's obvious that our go-between with Stentor has to be a mystery." The Director paused, waiting for the affirmative which came as a grunt.

"Sure, so we use a clean journalist, or some new sales rep, yes?"

"No." The DG leaned back in his chair. "Herbie, you remember when I broke the news about Alex Gold's death?"

A very wary affirmative this time.

"Well, you told me that you had an eye on the boy—Michael—for future use."

"The accent is on *future* use, yes."

"No." Fast, like a gunslinger in a Western movie, from the hip. "No, Herbie. Michael Gold's time has come . . ."

"That's . . ."

The Director raised a hand. "Just listen, Herbie. We need somebody really clean and with the right qualifications. Michael Gold has the qualifications. What is it? Speaks, thinks, lives Russian . . ."

"Has never been there," snapped Herbie. "Never been there, and he's still only a kid . . ."

"And you were only a kid when you . . ."

"Different. War makes people grow."

"It's no different. We've talked here. Sorry, Herbie, you were his father's friend, but the decision is that we use Michael Gold, if he's clean—and I don't see that being a problem."

Herbie's stomach turned over. Deep within him, gathered in the centre of his vast experience, he knew the choice was

71

wrong. Aloud, he said it was insane; stupid; even criminal. "The boy lacks guile. Yes, with a few years' training, the fact of his Russian background, and command of language, could be of help. But something like this—madness."

"Nevertheless, Herbie. He's to be your mystery."

"That an order?"

The Director General said it was very definitely an order.

"Then I resign."

The longest silence ever between the men. "No way on this one, Herbie. Win back trust and you can do as you like. But resign now and we'll have you locked up for ever and a day. I've set you the impossible, but you're under my orders. Michael Gold gets vetted, and then you net him—and I will not have spanners thrown in the works. You'll do it properly."

Big Herbie reflected for a moment. There were no doors or windows through which he could escape: only an impossible operation to be run from a distance; and now they wanted him to recruit Michael Gold who would hash it up.

"You understand? No spanners; no refusals from Gold because you tip him the wink?"

No options either, thought Big Herbie. He gave a deep sigh. "Okay. Okay so we try for him. We go for Gold, yes?"

The Director gave a tiny smirk of approval before Herbie continued, "But I make two things clear. One, I personally do not like it, am not happy with it . . ."

"But you'll give of your all?"

"Naturally." It was a weary, beaten voice. "Two, the vetting. I want Curry. Curry personally, because he's good, and just in case there's buried horror among the gold. I run it, okay. I give of my all, but only if Curry turns him inside out. Curry's very good, yes?"

"The best," the Director acknowledged.

"You tell Curry, then; and I'll brief him. That way we all know who's rowing the boat. I also want it on record that I do not approve."

The DG gave a sombre nod. He would get Curry Shepherd over to the Annexe as quickly as possible.

"He'll find me in Registry." Herbie gave one of his daft grins. "The dossier—Stentor's dossier—is very thick. Takes a lot of reading, and you won't let me do it at home."

"I should bloody well think not," the Director snapped.

8

THE DIRECTOR WAS correct. The Stentor File should not be allowed out of Registry. Eventually, Herbie presumed, when it was all over, with the loose ends neatly tied, the File would be put into cold storage for the requisite number of years. After that, the Press and historians would have field days galore.

To an amateur historian, the three great folders which made up the Stentor File were fascinating: living history; complete with the original written reports; letters under seal; and decoded information.

Big Herbie had already spent a number of hours hunched over the books, his ham hands touching the older papers— repaired and covered in clear plastic—with caution. Few would have believed those great hands and stubby fingers could be so gentle.

Whenever he signed the file out, Herbie Kruger found himself under the eagle eye of Ambrose Hill, the aging Head of Registry. Hill also knew the value of original documents. Stentor's file was both history and dynamite.

Since his return from Warminster, and assignment to the impossible task, Herbie had—almost overnight—truly become himself again. He did not even notice the snubs from people like Tubby Fincher—who flatly refused to deal with him. He just got on with the job, oblivious of time, food or the requirements of others. All his old expertise returned, like a man who has not swum for many years, taking to the water again.

More—apart from this new concern over using Michael Gold—Herbie found himself laughing; the legendary good humour bubbling, as a driving power began to force him into the logistics—the nuts and bolts—of getting Stentor out of Moscow, and into England. He even found himself forming an affinity with the man, as he plunged on through the pages of the dossier.

His first worry had been about the identity, and nature, of Lockhart's agent, Trofimov. During the period of the Revolution, and through the Civil War—well into the twenties—Herbie knew the Service had employed some odd people. This was always necessary—he was an odd person himself, as were the 'psychos' they brought in on occasions.

Herbie's long secret career had seen him working with thieves, forgers, and professional criminals, as well as rogues of all kinds. Nowadays, there were techniques of control. But in the twenties—as during what used to be called the Great War—the Firm took on both casual labour, and full-time people, who would turn coat at the twitch of a five pound note. There were no devious methods of restraint in the old days—particularly in Russia.

He need not have worried about Trofimov. The cross-refs were all there, and it took only an initial hour to establish the man's bona fides. His real name meant little—the product of a Russian father and English mother, having been born in the heartland of British respectability, Surrey.

Like many before—and since—Trofimov was a university graduate who failed entrance to the Diplomatic Service. In 1918, Lockhart took him to Moscow on his staff. The staff was constantly changing; soon coming under suspicion as a nest of spies: to the extent that, after the attempt on Lenin's life in the summer of 1919, Lockhart himself, and some of the staff, were placed under arrest. A diplomatic incident followed—the British Government responding by arresting the Soviet representative in London and not releasing him until Lockhart was freed.

The continual changes of staff, however, were exceptionally useful. Men and women, suspected by the new régime—because of their former position, or for more sinister reasons—could be got out by substitution. Papers and passports were doctored; the real original member of the special mission staff dropping out of sight, still in Russia, once his duplicate was safely in England.

Papers were readily available, and Trofimov was soon living as a genuine Russian, under the cover of being a former clerk. He quickly found himself lodgings, and reported to his local Bolshevist Commissar. For the next three years, Trofimov was in the thick of the bloody confrontation—the Civil War— which was to end in victory for the Communists, and the birth pangs of the new Soviet nation. By 1923, he had a job with the growing bureaucracy: Inspector of Rural Areas; a title which sounded very grand, but meant that he was required to tramp around an area of some hundred square miles, in order to register the peasant workers, and report on numbers of men and women who could be shifted from traditional farming to the more urgent work in newly-planned factories. It was a job he did not relish. Inspectors of Rural Areas had a habit of being found drowned, or in ditches with their brains distributed in some nearby field.

The peasants wanted only to live as they had always done—let the women slog in the fields, while the men got drunk, or occasionally assisted with the harvest. The idea that a governing body could move them from their homes and villages, setting them down to do factory work, did not immediately appeal. To them, an Inspector of Rural Areas was equated with the hated *zemsky*—the government official under the old régime, who usually lined his pockets at the peasants' expense.

Trofimov, however, must have had charm, and an appeal to the peasants, for he lived, worked, and sent in reports—duplicates of which arrived on the Whitehall desk of the Secret Intelligence Service's Head, together with long, personal, intelligence notes. The area was small, and he used great care and subtlety in choosing those who would

75

eventually be moved into industry. Trofimov was a long way from Moscow, his particular patch being on the edge of the Ukraine itself. Herbie concluded that the man must have been dedicated and trustworthy to a high degree. Life would be far from easy in his shoes.

It was in the Ukraine, after the magnificent harvest of 1925—when those who worked on the schemes for making the country self-sufficient were of good heart—that he came across the boy. News arrived, in the form of a long report, marked *Personal. For Head of Service Eyes Only*. Big Herbie went over the relevant passages again and again;

I have been to this village before; but they were always surly and difficult. A week ago, however, the mood changed. Nearly everybody had been drinking heavily in celebration: for the barns are full. The Agricultural Commissars will be around soon to proportion the grain. Then they will have a beano for a year.

If next year's harvest proves to be as catastrophic as 1921 they will be up in arms. These people never seem to learn from nature. Or God. Or both. Two bad harvests, and the whole country is in grave trouble.

One of the older men approached me during the evening, addressing me very much in line with the old, pre-revolutionary, style. He appeared to be greatly troubled, and sought my advice. There was a boy in the village— brought there as a young child, in 1917 or 1918: he could not say which. The couple who brought the child made no secret that they were hiding him, and that, formerly, they worked for some prince and princess. The boy has no documents, and is the offspring of aristocracy.

I felt sick at the fear this small fact produced. The whole community feels threatened by the presence of a teenage boy. They have probably heard about the scandal at Mozyr: a whole family shot in the public square, for trying to pass off the Tsar's niece—one of a hundred claimants—as a daughter. I have seen the boy tonight, and that is why I am marking this *urgent*.

He's a stout lad with plenty of spunk. Certainly frightened, but with an arrogance that would see him face a firing squad without a tear. He had no hesitation in condemning the régime to me; and that takes guts.

I think, with some elementary training, we could use him on a long-term basis. The Communists, as the Bolsheviks now call themselves, are here to stay. Believe me, this constitutes considerable danger to the Western way of life. Certainly to the Empire. If we could catch boys like this, and get them working for us, I am certain the time will come when they could be of great use. I await your instructions, and, in the meantime, will take the lad with me. I shall get him papers, and coach him in a cover.

Only a little under forty years ago; yet they talked, wrote, and thought, like that. Herbie shook his head over the letter, knowing that the words came from a man more advanced in the techniques, and tactics, of long-term intelligence than most of his day.

He turned the pages, skipping though to the point he had reached during his last session. The, then, Head of Service had agreed to try and make the boy into a 'deep cover agent' (they actually used those words); and Trofimov had managed to get him to Moscow, provide papers, and coach him in his cover.

I shall get him to a farm—Trofimov wrote to his Chief—and see that he is settled and established there. It has to be far away from the last place; but somewhere I can keep my eye on him—so I can visit about once a month. I did say his French is excellent, did I not? He is also picking up English from me at a remarkable speed. This will be a great asset. You will agree that time must be allowed to pass before we set him into play. About a year on a farm—they are full of the collective farms business at the moment, so there is much to do in order to keep my own cover. Also much work on the Five Year Plan, though it will take more than five years to get industry and agriculture running properly. Can you start making arrangements for me to come out—with our little Stentor—for training? A couple of months in France, I think. Somewhere remote, with a pair of really trustworthy chaps to help. You will have to visit him of course.

Two months' training. Good God, I am suggesting a couple of weeks for our man, Herbie breathed silently.

He was conscious of Ambrose Hill at his elbow, bending to whisper that Mr. Shepherd was waiting for him.

They walked over to the Annexe: Curry with his lope, head down, and scuffed suede shoes brushing the pavement with a swishing noise. Curry had a tendency to lope, and not put his feet down squarely.

"Job for me, the Old Man says, Herb old fruit." He spoke rather loudly, considering they were in the street.

"I want it secure, Curry." A drop of steel in Herbie's voice.

"Ah." Curry managed to place a forefinger alongside his nose, and continue walking steadily at the same time. Something, Herbie considered, a lot of world leaders might find difficult.

Worboys leaped to his feet when they entered the outer office. "No messages, Herbie." It was almost pathetic, Kruger reflected. Young Worboys had been reduced to a mere message-taker. "Inside." He jerked his head towards the inner office door. To hell with manning the phones, he'd let young Worboys learn a little from Curry. Break a few rules of his own—why not?

It took around half-an-hour for Herbie to give them the guidelines, and he was most careful to disguise his personal reticence regarding young Gold. "I stress that the subject must not know; and it has to be done last week, you understand?" There was no stupid smile. When he wanted, Herbie could be terrifyingly hard. "Not your ordinary, common or garden, positive vetting. Something special, yes?" Curry was to do everything, and Worboys would watch, learn, and give active support. "There's a possibility—a minor possibility— that you'll turn up some connection with friends of his late

78

lamented father," Herbie counselled. "I doubt it, but if that happens just pack up and come home."

"What you mean is that if he's even brushed shoulders with anything dodgy, it's no go," smiled Curry.

"Right." Herbie stressed the need for thoroughness, combined with speed. "No mistakes, Curry. If we're out by a millimetre, it'll blow up in our faces."

He then gave the bare essentials—rough date of birth; family address; schools; and the fact that Michael Gold was in his last post-graduate year at St. John's College, Cambridge.

"Just right, old fruit." Curry grinned. "Nice trip to Cambridge. Could do with the odd stunt in a punt. Right time of year; coming up April."

Worboys took the cue, "Ah, the Backs a blaze of colour; sun kissing ancient brick . . . ."

"Clowns I don't need." Herbie still did not smile. "Work and speed. Get to it. Day and night if you don't mind."

"Worry not, Herb. I'll put a girdle round Gold's earth in"—a wry look— "in a couple of days."

Thank Christ he could trust Curry. Behind the scuffing gait, at the back of the couldn't-care-less facade, lurked a ruthless professional, who could not be squeamish if he tried.

Big Herbie watched them leave; put a message through to say that he would be at Registry until about eight, then at the St. John's Wood number. Slowly he walked back along Whitehall, conscious that the surveillance teams—dogging him under the supervision of Curry Shepherd—were there, unseen, around him. This way of life took the strangest turns. People watching him, for a false move—or hint that he had gone sour—taking their orders from a man who had just been sent to do a job at Herbie's own bidding. But the world had gone mad anyway.

*　　　*　　　*

Secret inks; disguises; shadowing; photography; lines of communication; what to look for, and how to use what they called a one-time pad. These were only a few of the things they had taught Stentor all that time ago in France. There were pamphlets and books as well. He remembered a book by the Boy Scout man—what was his name? Baden-Powell. A brave man, but his espionage was in a different country—a strange terrain—and of a time past. How naive they were then: those earnest men in the chateau, preparing him for a job they could not really do, because the techniques had already passed them by—or they had missed the Indian signs, and taken the wrong trail. The war to come would be fought very differently. Two wars really—the war with Germany, and, starting even before that, the new secret war, played out in darkness, or on the air waves; even on the wind, in newspapers, among the gossips. War by photograph and manipulation. The war of whispers, distorting mirrors and silent death.

When you really boiled it all down, Stentor knew he had learned the professional side of his life by trial, error and cunning. You could not be taught the weird and black arts, they were soaked up over years of deception.

He chuckled to himself, glancing out of the window of his office. A group of neophytes, just out of training school, were being herded around on the usual conducted tour. Stentor could see their faces. They looked so young. Did he look as innocent when he first joined the army?

On the way back from the training in France, they advised him to go via Moscow, and volunteer for the army—even though he was well under age. He expected they would tell him to disguise his education, but that was the last thing Trofimov wanted. Together they concocted a story that was a kind of truth in reverse. He had been son to the Head Butler of the Prince and Princess Anashkov. Their son was about his own age, and their Highnesses had arranged for Stentor to take lessons with the young princeling. His own mother and father had a butler whose son took lessons with him. The butler, his wife, and the boy, had been killed in one of the first riots. Looking back on it, Stentor felt he must have been quite a bright lad—even though he had been bilingual from the moment he could talk, like most children of his class.

By the time he was ripped from his parents and the old

life—at just over seven years of age—Stentor could read well; knew his way around maps of the world; had some notion of the nature of history, and simple mathematics. In the seven years that went by before Trofimov found him, Stentor learned more practical things, but had still not forgotten the original lessons. "When they realise you're above average, they'll want you for their new Officer Corps," Trofimov maintained. "As long as you're a good Party member. Learn what you can from your local Commissars. It might seem dull, but it'll be your salvation."

The trip back by way of Moscow was really only to cover his absence from the farm. In Moscow, Stentor reported to the Recruiting Office, at the Znamensky Barracks at the end of Karetnaya Road—the old 'Coachmakers' Row'—where they welcomed him, asked many questions, gave him a raw cognac to drink—laughing when he spluttered on it—wrote, and filed, details of name, age, work, parents, and then told him to come back next year. "In the spring, little one," the sergeant called after him. "Come in the spring, and we'll make a soldier out of you."

So, in the spring, he returned, and they made a soldier out of him: not just a soldier, but an officer. By 1928 the young man was an officer cadet; by the end of '29 a junior lieutenant—what nowadays they would call an ensign.

The telephone hauled Stentor from his reverie. Vascovsky, oily and a shade too friendly, was on the line. A social call, he said. Would the General like to have dinner with him and his wife? The General—Stentor assumed Vascovsky's own unctuousness—would be more than delighted; he presumed it would be informal, and that his wife was also invited? But of course. So the date and time were arranged.

Stentor supposed all four of the Quiet Dogs were going through this small mill; Vascovsky's mill. From what he knew of General Vascovsky, his mill ground exceeding small.

*   *   *

Curry Shepherd, with young Worboys in his wake, took exactly three days to vet Michael Gold. Even by Big Herbie's

81

exacting standards it was a fast, and meticulously-detailed job. "Old Chinese adage, cocker." Curry switched on his brightest grin. "From womb to tomb, we leave no room."

"So what you come up with, Curry?"

"Michael Gold is what." Shepherd laid a plain folder on Herbie's desk. "All there. Even talked to the midwife. Educationally abnormal; brighter than St. Peter's halo; modern languages a speciality; very fast on the uptake. Politically clean as a new-born babe. Sexually normal, but *not* as pure as a new arrival. Lots of girls—and he's been leading one little darling up the garden path . . ."

"Cynthia Perkins," murmured Herbie.

"Why ask if you know it all, cocker?"

"Because I don't know it all."

"He's shrewd with cash; hasn't smoked dope, or taken magic pills; steers clear of contemporaries who do. Drinks little. Smokes ten a day. Health okay. Plays squash. Too good to be true; but you were right about the Papa." Curry winked broadly. "Then you would be, Mr. Kruger, you knew him pretty well. I tripped over *you* a couple of times, checking out the father-son bit."

Herbie shrugged. The father had been a source; that was all. "I'll read the file, of course; but you say he's okay?"

"Michael Gold? Wouldn't let him go on a nature ramble with my daughter; but I'd use him, if that's what you're after."

"Okay, Curry. Better get your boys on their toes." He gave an innocent, idiotic smile. "I threw them this afternoon. Had fun in Marks & Spencer. They didn't have all the exits covered, and couldn't get cars around fast enough. They presume too much, your boys, Curry. You should watch that."

"Mostly trainees on today, Herb. Don't blame 'em too much. You do anything naughty when they lost you? Like make phone calls to friends in the Kremlin, or that beautiful and ornate building in Dzerzhinsky Square?"

"I do it all the time, Curry. You watch me. *We*'ll be doing it all the time soon." Herbie switched off the stupid grin. "Just so you can brief the lads, I go to Cambridge tomorrow, okay?"

"If you have to. Changed since I was last there," Curry said mournfully. "Not what it was, Herb. Not what it was."

*　　*　　*

The Backs at Cambridge were, indeed, a riot of colour—a carpet of daffodils—but there were few people on the river, and even Big Herbie was forced to turn up the collar of his greatcoat against the fiercely cold wind. Herbie had vowed to be scrupulous over the recruitment of Gold. Act on your orders, he told himself. Do what must be done, though you disapprove. "Comes straight in from Russia, they say." Michael Gold laughed. "Nothing to stop it this side of the Urals."

The young man seemed to have inherited no traces of either father or mother; though Herbie occasionally thought he could glimpse a glitter in the eyes, which brought back memories of the young Alex.

"I'm sorry to thrust myself on you like this." It had been Herbie's idea to walk in the biting and blustery wind. Out of habit he had no desire to talk in Gold's rooms, in New Court. "Thrust myself? That's right, yes? The idiom?"

"Thrust? Yes. It's good to see you, Uncle Herbie." The 'Uncle' had always been Alex's idea.

Herbie grinned his stupid oaf-like gape, telling Michael to forget about the uncle. "Just plain Herbie'll do."

They went from John's to Trinity, then took the Hostel Bridge, walked up as far as King's, then turned back. "I had nothing much on, today." Michael's hands dug deeper into his pockets. "And you must know I'm always glad to see you. Though I was puzzled by the telegram. Mother's not ill or anything, is she?"

"You think your mother wouldn't let you know if she was ill?"

Michael laughed. Herbie was right; Nataly Gold would have telephoned, *and* sent a telegram, had she been unwell. "And got six neighbours to let you know also, Michael," Herbie added.

"You said it was urgent." Michael Gold did not even phrase it as a question.

Herbie stopped walking, turning towards the young man. "Have you ever been to Russia?" The question was put lightly; though, behind it, anyone with perception would detect a hint of suspicion.

Herbie watched Michael Gold's hands—there was no hint of movement. Then he switched to the eyes. A twinkle, spreading downwards: the slow smile crossing his face. "My motherland?" The smile turned to a one-syllable laugh. "No, Herbie. Neither of them would go back. They had a good reason, I gathered. As for me? Haven't had the time. One day, possibly. I really should see it all, I suppose."

Herbie's gaze switched. Over Michael's shoulder, a pair of young lovers were entwined, trying to keep in step; moving very slowly towards them. They appeared to be engrossed in one another. Herbie really would have to tell Curry not to pair off his people in the same way twice on one surveillance. Those lovers had been out and about in London the day before. Ahead, towards St. John's and the Bridge of Sighs, an elderly man loitered, as if waiting for Godot. Eberhard Lukas Kruger equals Godot, the massive SIS man considered.

It also struck Big Herbie that they probably had the listeners on him today—the team working very close, because there would not have been time to set up any directional microphones, or similar electronic legerdemain.

He started to walk again, urging Michael to keep at his pace. "Yes, you should see it all. I gather you could easily pass for a Russian; that your accent is Ukrainian."

"So?" Young Gold frowned. "What's this about, Herbie?"

"A favour, Michael. Something you could do."

"For whom?"

"Think of it as repayment for your father and mother. If they'd gone back . . ."

"Yes"—slightly irritated—"yes, I've heard the story till I'm sick of it. You got them to England. If they'd been sent back, the buggers would've killed them."

"You have no sympathy with the régime, I know that."

"Here," Michael lifted an arm in a gesture which took in the whole university, "it's not an altogether fashionable view. The Socialists flourish; the Communist ideal is just around the corner. A load of crap."

"I wouldn't be too sure." Herbie stopped walking again. "So-called Western democracy is the best, and easiest, target for Soviet propaganda—especially at times of political crisis: when there's a recession—or unemployment; or constant trouble with the Unions. In the West it's always propaganda time; and nearly always infiltration time. Wherever there's freedom—and the Left can call the police fascist pigs, just for keeping law and order—the Communist seed flourishes, because it's so easy to plant."

"I'll go along with that." They were pacing comfortably towards St. John's now, the huge Gothic 'Wedding Cake', that was New Court, ahead of them. "You didn't answer my question. The favour? Who's it for?"

"The people who pay my wages." Herbie gave him an on-and-off grin. Not so stupid this time.

"Dad said you worked for the Foreign Office."

"I'm playing at being a recruiting officer, today. Not for keeps, Michael. One job. In my trade they call it a quick in-and-out. Maybe two quick in-and-outs."

"You're . . . ?"

Big Herbie nodded. Yes, he told Michael. He was with the big bad wolves. "MI6. SIS. Call it what you will. We say that we work for the Firm."

"Like the Americans call it the Company?"

"So I'm told." Herbie backed off, becoming business-like. "This isn't our usual way of doing business, I promise you. But we have a small problem."

Michael still frowned. "And you want me to go to Russia for you? To do what? Act as a courier? Then get caught, and slung into the Lubianka where they'll probably unearth my parents' records, and bury me for good. I'm told they've got very long memories."

Herbie's large head moved up and down. "Very long. This

85

is more complicated than just acting as a courier. We need someone who'll pass as Russian, born and bred . . ."

"I thought you had people—or have they all come under the defence cuts?"

"Michael." Soft, but sharp as a scythe. "Listen to me. Of course we have people. But, in the current circumstances, it would not be safe to use them: so we use a 'mystery'. A 'mystery' is someone brought in for one job—one operation, if you prefer it. You see, if we used somebody already in circulation, there's no way of knowing if they have the finger on him. This way we do it clean. We have control of our man; we trust him. You would be trusted."

Michael took two paces forward, stopped, and turned. "It's all a bit dramatic, isn't it? Would the job be dangerous?"

Herbie laughed, "Only if you're caught. It isn't likely; and if you did run into trouble . . ."

"You'd disown me. That's what I've always read."

"A cargo of old rabbits," Herbie muttered, almost to himself. "In this case we'd own up, and get you out. No question. Wouldn't you like to see Russia, Michael?"

"When?"

"About a couple of weeks time."

"And do what?"

"See a man. Talk to him. Maybe come back and tell us what he says. Possibly go in again, and bring him out."

Michael shook his head. "You're joking."

Herbie did not joke about the important things of life. This was important, and, he was very sorry, but if Michael said no, they would take him away—now, this very afternoon— and keep him until the job had been done by someone else. "In the lap of luxury, of course. Not an incarceration in some damp cell."

"But don't you have to go through special training; codes and all . . . ?"

"Just a very little. Already you have most of the training— you look Russian, speak Russian so nobody could detect . . ."

"But why me, Herbie?"

"Why not?"

86

Slowly, they walked back into New Court, and Michael's rooms. Herbie still did not relish talking within the confines of four walls. He urged Michael to stroll around the court with him—arguing; persuading; cajoling; trying to make sense out of the nonsense he was putting to this, very normal, young man.

"It's like something out of Buchan." Gold was amused. "Like 1930s' spy fiction, Herbie. You come to John's, and invite me to take on a clandestine job, for Queen and country presumably . . ."

"No." Herbie restrained him with one large hand. "No. Not for Queen and country, Michael. For what we call democracy—not that it means all that much any more. For all the oppressed; the people you know about—those in Siberia; in the labour camps; in the mental hospitals. For the people who want to say what they feel about life, but can only whisper it. If you're religious, for Christ, or Mohammed or Krishna. For the sun even. No, it's not like Buchan, either. I've been given a job, and I cannot safely use the tools of my trade. So, like any other workman, I've got to go out and buy a new tool . . ."

"You offer me money . . . ?"

"If I did, I hope you'd spit in my face."

"You've almost convinced me."

It took nearly another hour. Herbie was at his persuasive best. Still Michael Gold could not take it seriously. After all, it *was* preposterous. Then, just as Herbie prepared himself for a really long siege, Michael capitulated.

"When do we leave?"

"I leave now." Herbie did not even stop to savour what little relief was afforded by victory. "You go back to your rooms. You tell nobody. We will arrange for you to send letters to your tutor, or Dean, or whoever. In a short time someone will come for you. Do what he says: whatever he says. His name's Curry, by the way. Curry Shepherd." For a moment Herbie did pause. Yes, it was ludicrous. Curry kept *him* under surveillance—because there were still people in the Firm who could not trust E. L. Kruger. At the same time, Curry had set up an elaborate series of moves, to take Michael Gold to Warminster that night. It was all mad. Especially using Gold.

At Warminster, the pair of ringmasters, laid on by the Director, could take over for a couple of days. It was time for Herbie to visit his old colleague Martha Adler—now in retirement, playing the German widow. Martha, with the ash blonde hair, long legs, and ways which coaxed information out of people, as a pickpocket will coax a man's wallet.

At the door of Michael's rooms, the young man asked, "Who is it I have to see in Russia anyway?"

"Oh nobody in particular." Herbie grinned: daft, peasant leering. "Only a senior officer in the KGB."

"Jesus Christ. You're crazy."

As he lumbered away from the court, Herbie glimpsed a loping figure scuffing its way towards Gold's stairway.

PART TWO

MOSCOW TOURIST

9

"TALK ABOUT FOOD, the weather, the usual grumbles you women share: but, I beg you, do not discuss my work." So Stentor to his wife, before they left for the arranged dinner with the Vascovskys.

"I know nothing of your work," his wife snapped. "You tell me nothing; you come in at all hours; you cancel arrangements at the last moment; you change holiday dates; but I know nothing of your work. Except you are KGB. For all I know, you keep a mistress."

"At my age, I keep a mistress? My mistress is my work. Well you know it."

"Then I shall say that if I wish."

"If you wish." Stentor nodded, with a great sigh. He should not have cautioned her.

"You say this man, Vascovsky, is powerful?" Stentor's wife asked, in the car as they headed towards Kalinin Prospekt, where the General had a luxury penthouse.

"Exceptionally powerful."

"Then, perhaps, he can arrange for your retirement. Some nice place in the country where I can see more of you."

"You'd be bored. You'd want to move back to Moscow within a year."

"Never."

"Well, *I* would." Stentor, with a sickening realisation, knew this was true: not just of Moscow, but Russia as a whole. He closed his eyes, and a blur of coloured lights formed, then re-formed, in the darkness. The art of living a double life was to believe it, down to the smallest detail. It was the first time he had even given his nationality a thought; which showed how deep his cover ran. For a few seconds, these reflections mixed together with the knowledge that

91

Vascovsky was a wolf, and Stentor the prey. He was tiring, and had few doubts who would be the loser. To lose meant leaving Moscow, and Russia.

A trough of depression swallowed him for a moment. Then he broke through the surface again, as though gulping air: pulling himself into the present, wrapping the shroud of his cover around him, so that he could face the General head on. It mattered little that Stentor was the ranking senior by several years. Power, not dates of promotion, was what counted.

Vascovsky's penthouse apartment made Stentor's own comfortable place look like a slum—and he lived in the same area as the KGB Chairman himself. The furnishings were Swedish; the décor like the pictures you saw in American or English magazines. Almost everything you looked at, or touched, was imported.

Vascovsky must travel a great deal, thought Stentor. He must also have access to the very best élite stores, a high *nomenklatura* rating. Vascovsky probably got the *kremlevsky payok* as well—enough food to feed himself, in luxury, each month: free food—the Kremlin Ration. If he travelled abroad on service business, he would also have access to the *Beryozka* shops, where you paid with certificate rubles, obtained in exchange for hard currency earned or collected abroad.

The main room of the penthouse contained a huge picture window, through which you could look out on the great spread of lights that was Moscow. The penthouse faced away from Kalinin Prospekt, thereby giving a magnificent view across to the golden domes of illuminated Cathedral Square, within the Kremlin Walls, in the distance. You could even just see the red star glowing bright on its tower above the Spasskaya—Saviours Gate, the main Kremlin entrance.

Vascovsky—like Stentor—was not in uniform. Also like Stentor, he wore immaculate clothes, tailored to exaggerate his slim build. He could easily have been a Western diplomat, as he came forward to greet them; paying a great deal of attention to Stentor's wife; playing host in an easy, relaxed style.

92

Stentor examined the rows of books which lined one wall: many superbly bound, and some in English. "You read a great deal?" he asked.

"When I have time. It improves one's knowledge of other languages. I read English, French and German—but you are also an expert in languages, Comrade General. Or so they tell me."

Stentor allowed his fingertips to touch the tooled binding of a book, by Graham Greene, and realised it was one of a whole set, similarly bound.

Vascovsky smiled. "You like the work of Mr. Greene? That is the Bodley Head collected edition. When a new one is added, I have it bound by a man I know in Berlin. But is it true, Comrade General, that you are also an expert in languages?"

"A little." Stentor gave a modest grimace.

"He's always reading." Stentor's wife: her voice far more good humoured than usual. "Always has his nose in a book."

"Yes. From what I hear, he is fluent in French, German and English. Ah." Vascovsky looked up as his wife entered— a woman much younger than the General: tall, dark-haired, with fine features, high cheekbones; and a mouth, which just stopped short of being too large, but, with a thick bottom lip, that gave her whole attractive face the look of uninhibited sensuality.

She wore a heavy brocade evening gown which had never seen the inside of any Russian shop, or tailor's workroom. Her manner was friendly, calm, warm, and very confident. Vascovsky introduced her as Yekaterina, adding that she had taken a new name when she became a citizen of the USSR.

"And before that?" Stentor asked.

It seemed a cliché to define her laugh as tinkling; yet there was no other description—high, melodious, like a little cluster of bells: a Christmas decoration. "Oh, I have a most secret history." She turned to her husband and spoke in French, "*Can I tell all my secrets, chéri?*"

93

"The Comrade General is in our line of business, darling."
Vascovsky moved towards the glass-topped table, picking up
a bottle, eyebrows raised towards Stentor, inviting him to
name his drink. Both Stentor and his wife took vodka; as did
the Vascovskys.

"So what is your secret, Madame Vascovsky?" Stentor
asked in perfect French.

"Ah." She laughed again. "Caught. Well, Comrade
General, I am a traitor. I came over—a long time ago now.
Fifteen years?" A query to her husband who made a give-a-
little-take-a-little gesture, saying it was almost sixteen years.
"I defected." The calm smile stayed in place. "From France."

"Yekaterina held a very high post with the SDECE. Codes
and ciphers. Her name in that life was Catherine. Her saving
grace is she worked for us—how long? Almost two years,
before things got warm, and she came out. Happily for me,
she arrived via Berlin, where I worked. I even had the luck to
carry out the first debriefing."

Yekaterina laughed again, still speaking French,
"Translate into English, chéri. That gives a most dubious
meaning."

They all laughed, except Stentor's wife, who spoke neither
French nor English. Stentor had to explain the joke in
Russian—not easy, and not really appreciated when she
finally understood.

"You speak excellent French, General." Yekaterina took
Stentor's arm, leading him from the large salon into an
equally elegant dining room. General Vascovsky took
Stentor's wife, as the young military servant, complete with
white jacket and gloves, announced that dinner was served.

"I've had a lot of practice with French." Stentor thought
the ploy was really quite subtle. Each of the Quiet Dogs
would be subjected to an evening with the Vascovskys.
He wondered if they always played it this way—Madame
Vascovsky probing the subject, while her husband chatted to
the wife.

Indeed, Stentor had fleeting doubts about Yekaterina's
authenticity. Possibly there was a different partner for each

94

dinner. While dismissing the idea, almost immediately, Stentor could not but admire Vascovsky's methods. Pairing his French defector wife with the subject was machiavellian mischief.

Yekaterina explained that the servant—provided because of her husband's rank—only waited at table. *She* was the one who slaved in the kitchen. "Just like any other good Party wife."

Stentor admitted she had slaved to perfection. Aloud he did not voice the opinion that she probably had the best possible food with which to work. The meal, he later told her, was—"a hymn in praise of the French culinary arts," adding hastily that this did not mean the USSR was without its particular flair for menus, and dishes.

They ate a rough pâté, bringing back many memories for Stentor; followed by trout in a pepper sauce; and, for the main dish, thin slices of veal, marinated in crushed juniper berries and thyme, then fried in onion and carrot. To complete the meal, Yekaterina announced her favourite pudding— *Tarte des Demoiselles Tatin*: an apple tart, in which the apples, sugar and butter were thoroughly caramelised.

At the outset of dinner, she continued to tax Stentor's French. He told her about being bilingual; and having been brought up as the butler's son in the Anashkov household. "But how fascinating, yet you cannot have mastered that perfect Parisian accent as a young boy?"

"No," Stentor admitted. That was part of the training.

"And the English, and German also?"

"I had a very small amount of English. But after they made me into an officer, and discovered I had a flair for languages, the Cheka claimed me, and trained me. That was in 1930. They called it the OGPU then. Later I was transferred to the GRU,"—the Chief Intelligence Directorate, concerned with military intelligence. There had always been a rivalry between the Cheka and the GRU. "It was with the GRU that I had field experience." He gave a chuckle, knowing it would be all too easy to make mistakes with this lady; perhaps drop some tiny morsel, out of character: a morsel upon which Vascovsky would no doubt chew until he had extracted all the juice.

It was also difficult not to be distracted, and try to hear what was going on between Vascovsky and his own wife; but he simply had to blot out their conversation from his head. The General was constantly filling her glass, and they both laughed a great deal. Stentor's wife—who knew nothing of his other life—was a liability. There were so many small things she could mention: tiny pieces of wool, at which Vascovsky might grab, pull, and so unravel his life.

"Why do you laugh?" Stentor caught the faint hint of an expensive scent, as Yekaterina bent close to him. Should a man, seventy years of age, still lust after young flesh, and feel the need? He had heard that the senses of lust, and desire, diminished with age. It had never seemed to change for Stentor.

"I laugh because you are French; and my first field work was done in France. For several years I ran French agents in, and around, Paris. I even had a job with the SNCF. Working on the railways, eh?"

She laughed also; and to get it over and done with Stentor went on, as though rambling about his life. "While I was away there were the purges. Stalin—as you very well know—became periodically paranoid about his senior officers. Before the Great Patriotic War the best of his General Staff were purged. He had a go at the GRU also. I suppose it was luck. They recalled me from France—there was word that someone had sold me out anyway. I came back expecting a reception committee with a machine gun. Instead, they brushed up my German. I spent some of the war with the German Army."

The last words came out in silence, for Vascovsky and Stentor's wife had suddenly stopped talking. "You must tell us about Stalingrad, General. I understand you are one of the few people left who was there with the wrong side."

Stentor heard the guns in his head, from a long way off down the years. For a few seconds the memory of intense heat and cold seized him: there for a second; then gone. "That is an exaggeration. Just not true." He explained how they

96

had infiltrated him—back through France—into Germany. "I suppose it was precarious, but the papers and cover were very sound. I was given contacts with people who later became known as the Red Orchestra. Brave and loyal people . . ."

"Most of whom perished at the hands of the Gestapo." Vascovsky paused, as if reflecting, before he finished his sentence. "Or returned to Russia, to be accused as traitors by Stalin."

A tragedy of enormous proportions; Stentor still experienced pain when he thought of the risks and courage of those convinced men, full of political ideals, who had fought for their faith; provided the Centre with exceptional information, yet perished—one way or another—for their beliefs.

"I knew many of them." It was the only epitaph he could give; for it had been a strange time, that alliance with traditional enemies, who were—for him—both friends and masters. In those years he was forced to split himself many ways—providing necessary intelligence for the Centre, duplicating it for London, and, outwardly, playing the role of a good German.

Sitting at Vascovsky's dinner table, Stentor realised the thinness of the line he trod, when talking of the Second World War—the Great Patriotic War. One of the lessons, learned in a long life of deception, was never to turn and run from the subject. As the English say—you had to keep the ball in your court. "My life, from around the winter of '39, until the winter of 1942, was that of a loner. Back to France, as a German national. My papers claimed me as an official of the Reichsbank." He laughed, a loud and jolly chuckle. "Odd, those papers did not let me down. On the contrary, the Centre had them so well prepared they became my undoing."

Stentor explained his instructions were to use existing networks only when absolutely necessary. "My briefing concerned the Nazi economy—though I learned little about economics. The Reichsbank knew me as a name. I was on their files. It is still difficult to know how that trick was done. But I had official clearance, even to go into restricted areas.

For the Reichsbank I was supposed to be submitting a report, on the manner in which the military occupation forces were conducting monetary matters—that was after 1940, of course. Before the great *blitzkrieg*, my reports were of a general nature. I merely travelled and observed the situation in key cities: mixing with bankers and money men. I can tell you, I was truly out of my depth.

"Then, after the occupation of the European continental countries, the role changed. Report to the Reichsbank on the military handling of the economy; report to the Centre on the Nazi methods of handling the resources of the occupied countries. Easy? No, I made a terrible error. Reports to the Centre were, apparently, good. The same did not apply to the Reichsbank."

In his pause for breath, the real fact whirled through his mind: memories half forgotten; journeys on crowded trains; fatigue; writing pages of notes in hotels that were unwelcoming, and gloomy. A girl, in Amiens, who gave herself to him out of mutual attraction, not for the usual mercenary reasons of the time.

He went on to tell of the sudden summons to one of the Berlin offices of the Reichsbank—leaving out the urgent messages, flashed between himself and the Centre (they used a radio provided by the British, which a Communist cell had taken over near Nantes) and the final instructions. He was to go; keep his cover, and implant himself within the Reichsbank staff in Berlin.

"It was a farce—you understand, Madame. I was accepted as their man without question. They had no suspicions. Yet, I had been recalled to Berlin because my reports were so bad. I was incompetent." He spread his hands. "So I was dismissed. Three days later—they had provided a room in a guest house for one week—my call-up papers arrived: brought by a corporal, who stood over me while I packed my belongings. I became a soldier. As simple as that."

"On the wrong side at Stalingrad," beamed Vascovsky.

Stentor beamed back. "You listen to gossip, Comrade. *That* is the legend. The truth is a matter of official record.

98

I could not let myself serve the Supreme Soviet as a private in the German Army. It was not possible to get advancement, or be posted to a General Staff. Nor was there any hope of becoming an officer, where I might just have been able to pass on a little useful stuff. No, I had been trained, and trained, and trained. Trained for attack, and for cannon fodder. I did indeed end up, still a private soldier, heading for the Eastern Front. Summer 1942. About to have to fight my fellow Russians, and what I saw in those first days sickened me beyond belief. So, the first chance that came my way, I surrendered to a Red Army patrol. Early winter 1942, and many kilometres from Stalingrad."

It sounded nice and easy, seated around the Vascovskys' sumptuous table. Leave it like that, Stentor's intuition told him. Leave it easy and simple; the bare bones. Keep away from the horrors; only hint, and don't even mention that your life hung in the balance, for an hour or so, after you surrendered. If Vascovsky wanted all the facts, he could get them, easily enough, from the files. Unless they had completely changed history, by altering his own file, the full story was there, with all its harrowing description. Had he not sat for almost six weeks, in a little green room, with two experienced debriefing officers, giving it to them? He still did not know what saved him from any further enquiry, or trial—even accusation. People who returned from so many missions, ended up in Siberia; or against a wall in the Lubianka. Stentor just went on—transferred from the military arm into the Ministry of Internal Affairs—and began to rise in responsibility, and power; finally leading to his present position within the KGB.

They all sat looking at him. Even his wife's eyes glistened. Strange, he realised that he had never given her a hint of his wartime experiences.

"You are an interesting man, General." Yekaterina appeared to have dropped the prefix 'Comrade', on purpose. "A book should be written."

"You, my dear, ought to know better than that." Vascovsky studied him closely: eyes unsmiling, fixed as though boring into Stentor's mind. "But tell me, Comrade General, how did you come to be in the army before the transfer into GRU?"

"I volunteered, like many. I began as a farm worker."

Vascovsky lit a cigarette. "Ah yes. From prince's palace to peasant."

"The times, Comrade, were out of joint. I was a child. People protect children when the world goes mad: or at least they try to guard them. Today's children are tomorrow's people."

"When the world goes mad?" A thin stream of smoke rose towards the high ceiling. "You think the Revolution was mad?"

"Neither the reasons nor the cause, Comrade. But the doing has to contain some madness. Do you believe the Revolution to be completed?"

"No. It has changed course, but it can never be completed. Not now."

Stentor gave a coughing laugh, "That could be treasonable talk, General . . ."

"Oh yes; treason, I'm sure. But truth. You know it, and I know it, dear friend. The Revolution will never be completed on this planet; running out of living space, fuels, grain. The Revolution is doomed, together with mankind."

"So we shall all go, dying with a knowing ignorance."

Vascovsky's brow creased. "Who said that?"

"With a knowing ignorance? A Christian—St. John of the Cross."

"So, the butler's son turned peasant-farmer, knows his Christian books. I suppose you learned those in the prince's house; or was it in the Ukraine?"

Stentor always kept himself on a tight rein. In any case, he could not tell if Vascovsky was teasing or really baiting him. Very quietly, he answered, "Both, General; and don't forget I returned to the Ukraine—with the German Army. I saw the houses burned; and men, women, and children—who could have been the children I worked and played with— and *their* children, hanging from trees, and poles, like rotting

100

fruit. Or with their bellies prised open. Yes, I remember my Christian books."

Vascovsky made a gesture, as though to say, "Enough. No quarrel." Aloud he changed the subject, "And you have no children?"

"No . . ." Stentor's wife began; but before she could finish, Vascovsky spoke again—

"Your good wife tells me you have relations, though. A niece, she says, in Leningrad."

Stentor looked him straight in the eyes. "I hear from her sometimes; but she never comes to see us. I have a nephew, also, who I have not seen."

His wife opened her mouth to say more, but Stentor went on speaking. "He will come some day, I'm sure. He writes regularly, though."

"And where does this nephew live?"

"He appears to travel a lot. He works for the Supreme Soviet—like us. Though not in the same line of business."

Vascovsky motioned Yekaterina to refill the glasses. The servant had disappeared after the last plates were cleared. "For a butler's orphan you've done well. And very well to trace relations, Comrade. I shall have to use my influence. See if we can arrange a family meeting."

"Would you? Would you do that?" Stentor sounded almost pleading. Inside, the pulse quickened, and his guts turned over.

Vascovsky twirled a finger in the air. "Oh, some time; when you're feeling like it, give me the names and addresses, and I'll see what can be done. Shall we go into the other room?" His diffidence was masterly. But Stentor had no doubt the moment would come. Not now in his home; not tomorrow; but soon, Vascovsky would ask. A telephone call, perhaps, when he was going through his files on the four Quiet Dogs. He would pull the niece and nephew out of his hat, playing his king, and at that moment, Stentor would have to drop an ace from his sleeve.

Another of his four remaining, precious, lines of communication would have to be used. Tomorrow.

They were drinking cognac now—an excellent bottle, not the raw liquor one could buy in any of the stores, but the real 'liquid fire'. Stentor was careful. At his age there was a tendency to overdo it, and he certainly could not take as much drink these days. Even five years ago, a bottle of vodka and a few brandies, of an evening, would still see him lucid, and on his feet. Age had taken its toll regarding alcohol, and he did not dare risk loosening his own tongue.

His wife was not so cautious. But why should she be on her guard? There was nothing for her to hide: no thread of life to follow. With Stentor, taking the wrong exit meant ending up in the marshland of deception. He refused another drink, but Vascovsky was insistent.

"A little music, I think." Going to the shining Japanese stereo unit, looking through the line of recordings, in their long mahogany rack. "Shostakovich?" he suggested.

"Why not?"

Vascovsky selected a record. "Now that he is dead, why not? You've read the so-called *Testimony*—the edited memoirs, published in the West? The usual propaganda?"

"I've read them," Stentor was not so sure that Dmitri Shostakovich's memoirs, of disenchantment, and torment, with the Party, were actually the work of disinformation experts. The Party and Supreme Soviet had to take the propaganda line. He heard the stylus come down on the record; then his heart lurched. The sombre pianos, following the clear bass of Nesterenko—

> Beyond the dark on a rock
> Stands a tall house.

The King Lear Ballad, from which Stentor had taken his own cryptonym for the four members of the Standing Committee.

> But the house is empty.
> But the house is empty.

What did Vascovsky really know? Was he playing cat and mouse, by choosing this music? This song? Was it a signal, to Stentor, that he knew, and would pounce when ready?

> And only the wind, a wild guest,
> Alarms the quiet dogs;

Stentor cocked his head—an old man whose hearing was slightly impaired—listening to the voice; straining for the words.

The ballad ended; the music changed.

On the way home in the car, Stentor's wife prattled on about how pleasant the Vascovskys were, and how they should be cultivated. Stentor hardly heard, his mind reaching for the logistics—racing ahead.

There was no way in which the Shostakovich record could have been a warning. The danger lay in Vascovsky's seeming indifference to Stentor's 'niece' and 'nephew'. That side of things had to be quickly blocked up.

In his study, Stentor worked far into the early hours. Phrasing the message; putting it into cipher; then copying it on to the thin paper. Around six in the morning, before the dawn, he made a telephone call, listening to the distant signal ring three times. Replacing the receiver, he made as though to try again, allowing the number ten rings on the second occasion. The number of rings changed with the day of the month. For the benefit of those who might listen to the tape of an unsuccessful telephone call, he made an exasperated grunt; grumbling loudly as he replaced the receiver.

Stentor then burned everything, except the final, small, piece of paper with the numbers written neatly in groups of tiny figures. He folded the paper inside a ten-ruble note, offering a prayer that the second of his five methods of communication would go without any hitches.

Back in the apartment on Kalinin Prospekt, Jacob Vascovsky sat alone, with a glass of cognac, his mind concentrated on General Vladimir Glubodkin, Head of Special Service I, who—with Madame Glubodkin—had been his guest that night.

Cunning, he thought: cunning and full of guile. Also highly placed in an appointment of exceptional importance, with access to mountains of sensitive material.

Vascovsky could not rely wholly on suspicion, but that strange extra sense, developed over years of hunting in the dark, jangled like a chorus of bells. General Vladimir Glubodkin, the bells said.

10

IT WAS FOR their own security—Herbie imagined—that the daily trip, between St. John's Wood and Whitehall, was usually made by car. The driver, Paul, was long known to Herbie as an old hand, who had worked with the lion tamers—as they called the élite bodyguards—and the Watch Committee. There was little doubt that Paul, the driver, was, at the moment, employed by the Watch Committee.

As yet, Big Herbie still needed to ring Martha Adler. He had gone as far as to check the dialling code from her letter. Martha was out to grass in Lymington—a small southern town, complete with marina, and an exit to the sea—almost opposite the Isle of Wight. The marina was a favourite haunt of people who messed about in boats, including famous yachtsmen, and women, of the day. It was also a quiet place of retirement, only a few minutes by car from the New Forest. Big Herbie would ring Martha, and—with luck—get himself invited down for the weekend, before facing the rigours of working with Michael Gold.

Of Gold he need not worry; the ringmasters would be hard at it, putting him through the hoops of cover; dinning

Moscow into him, so that it would seem like a second home by the time Michael arrived in Russia.

It was Friday; complete with the usual traffic chaos. Only a week ago, Tubby Fincher had appeared, like the genie of the lamp, at Warminster. So much had happened in that short time, that Big Herbie could hardly believe it was only one week.

Paul saw him right to the door. Curry's other watchers, around the service flats, still eluded Herbie. They had certainly been camouflaged with all Curry Shepherd's devious and expert knowledge. In any case there was little point in trying to flush them out.

During that Friday evening's drive, Big Herbie hardly spoke to Paul; his mind besieged by the demons conjured from the pages of Stentor's dossier. During that afternoon, Herbie had read the complete text of the man's original report, concerning his experiences in France, Germany, and, finally, with the German Army, in his native Russia.

Herbie Kruger, who knew all too well the weight of living a double life in the field, was deeply affected. The cold, translated, text, needed experience to read between the lines. Herbie's own familiarity with the loneliness, fear, and isolation of the field trade made the document even more moving.

The grand inquisitors of Dzerzhinsky Square were a demanding crew. Stentor's record of his work, undercover, as a Reichsbank official in the occupied countries—and the times which followed—became, at their probing, almost a daily trek through actual incidents: travels, meetings, and even fragments of Stentor's conscious stream of thought. Indeed, the pages were littered with footnotes giving minute alterations—*The subject realised, after thought, and at a later date, that he travelled from Paris to Nimes in July, and not June as stated.*

To the everyday human being, the work would be suspect; for how can a man recall all his actions—even his thoughts—three years, or so, after the events? Yet, to Big Herbie, there was nothing odd about this. To live under a deep cover was to be ever watchful. In time, the cover takes over the personality; but the trained memory becomes almost automatic: sifting and filing away what can be retrieved if needed. Herbie Kruger could, if necessary, sit down with trained confessors and—over a lengthy period—pull, from the depths of memory, actions, thoughts, dates, words, and even conversations from that time spent living the life of an agent-runner in East Berlin, during the late fifties and early sixties.

The sections which Kruger found most moving took place in Russia, with Stentor in the guise of a German soldier, during the late summer of 1942.

I was back in the Ukraine, where I grew up. Memories of my own childhood played tricks that, time and again, led me to greater caution. It was on a Friday in early June that we reached the village of Sumki, which I had known as a young boy. It is impossible to describe the carnage. The barns still smouldered, while over thirty bodies, including those of children—who could have been no more than ten or eleven years of age—swung from a makeshift gallows, their eyes already pecked out by birds, clothes starting to rot with the flesh. The stench made some of the men retch. I retched also, but not at the smell. The thoughts were enough: who were these people? Had I known the older ones in life, as children? What had they done?

The answer was soon forthcoming. At the edge of the village, our sergeant called for us to stop. I had noticed nothing—my mind too disturbed by what we had just witnessed. Suddenly a group of men rose from the ground ahead, where they had lain hidden. They turned out to be from the 5th Division: a patrol sent on an anti-partisan mission. Their sergeant approached us, saying they had 'made an example of the village'. There was no evidence—as far as I could see—that the victims had anything to do with partisans; but the sergeant was one of the most brutal men I have ever met. He laughed with our sergeant, describing how the villagers had 'squealed like stuck pigs', and had to be beaten to the gallows. He seemed to take a particular delight in the terror of the little ones, whom he had made stand and watch, as their parents were dispatched.

His men were lying in wait for the partisans. We moved forward, only to find the same scenes of desolate violence in the next village; and at a farm, some three kilometres down the road. There, the farmer, his wife, and some others had been killed—but not before terrible torture. One young woman lay on the wooden steps of the house, her throat slit. Her body, which was naked, showed the marks and wounds of burning, and whipping, not to mention the obvious, obscene, signs of rape. She looked as though a whole section of soldiers had been through her. The final knife cut must have arrived as a merciful release.

A squealing noise came from behind the barn, and I thought it was probably an injured animal. Our sergeant went to investigate, and a few seconds later the squeaking rose to a shriek. Then silence. Apparently, it was a child of about five years. A girl, with both legs broken. All Sergeant Zipperman said was that he had put an end to her with a bayonet—'there was no point in wasting precious ammunition on a sub-human like that'. I was certain I would kill the man before we were through.

Big Herbie understood the last line, for he had also seen revolting scenes of injustice. The statement caught Herbie Kruger in the throat and heart. Stentor was merely recounting what he saw, in the barest terms.

At the St. John's Wood building, Herbie said good night to Paul, and took the lift to his flat. There had been an afternoon mail delivery. On the floor lay a small brown package.

Gently, Herbie picked it up, placing it on the table, then removing his coat. With scissors, he clipped away the sellotape, alert to any possible device hidden inside.

There were no sinister traces: no wires or leads. Big Herbie tipped the package on to its side, and a pre-recorded cassette fell, with a clatter, on to the glass table top. Wrapped around the plastic box was a printed slip bearing the heading of a well-known mail order record and tape firm, and the legend—*Please find your order enclosed.*

He had ordered nothing. Certainly not this, though it was

on his list of recordings to purchase. The music magazines had reviewed it well: *Mahler. Symphony No. 4. Israel Philharmonic Orchestra ZUBIN MEHTA*.

Odd. Big Herbie prided himself on having a collection of the finest recordings of Gustav Mahler's works. For the Fourth you would have to go a long way to beat Szell with the Cleveland Orchestra, and Raskin singing the final little poem.

Well, never close your mind. He would drink some vodka and listen. Sliding the cassette from its box, Herbie lumbered towards the tape deck. A few feet from his goal he stopped—standing statue-still and alert. Holding the cassette by one corner, his finger and thumb had encountered a small sticky patch.

He held the tape up to the light. There, on either side, at the top, were faint traces on the plastic. Maybe the tape still held some of Mahler's Fourth, but a pound to a Deutschmark not all of it.

Pre-recorded tapes have small oblong indentations in the plastic, at each end of the top narrow section—to prevent accidental recordings being made over the original, for no tape machine will operate on *Record* with those small holes in place.

There are many ways of overcoming this—matchsticks, for instance; though the easiest is to cover the holes with small pieces of sellotape. Someone had undoubtedly already done this to the Mahler tape in Herbie's hand. So, instead of the Israel Philharmonic there would be a voice, or voices. The thought was both intriguing and worrying.

Slowly, Herbie Kruger opened the drawer near the tape deck and removed a pair of lightweight headphones. Adjusting the headphones, he slipped the tape into place and pressed the *Play* button.

Three opening bars, then the steady beat of basses, with the violins taking up the first, deceptively jaunty, main theme. Ascending basses and answering horns. Then a sudden cutting of the music, and a voice whispering in his right ear—sending a shiver up the back of Herbie's neck.

It was a most ingenious recording, done with first class

equipment: using a stereo microphone so that the voice began in the right ear and then moved away, behind Herbie. There was even a creak—the sound of a loose board?—which made him turn, expecting to see Jacob Vascovsky standing directly behind him, the face looking, as always, oddly more French than Russian.

Herbie could almost smell the room in the old Magdalenen-strasse jail, to which Vascovsky had him taken after the final entrapment. To have once been in the hands of men like Vascovsky—knowing that you hold precious secrets deep within your head—is to know true fear. That same sense of terror returned, momentarily, now, at the sound of the General's voice on the tape: whispering, lulling, soothing, like some beckoning siren.

"So, Herbie, my friend, you think you have escaped. You really believe it's the end between us? Well, I have things to tell you. I understand they've finished cleaning you out. Are you a husk, now, Big Herbie Kruger? A shell of a man? You should be, for it was I who fractured the legend of your great career." At that point, the voice seemed to move behind him, clear in both ears. "I gather they've been foolish enough to give you a little work. It will be very little, I assure you." He paused for a single hard laugh. "They've given me more work also, Herbie. Quite important, because you gave me so much—though I doubt if you knew it.

"Now listen carefully, my friend of darkness, my secret adversary, my enemy. At this moment I have only one way of keeping in touch. Later there will be another; but I think it is important for me to talk with you.

"Herbie Kruger, you are a worthy man in our line of business; but the world has changed. Our own kind of work alters with it; practically every day. You know the truth as well as I—and please don't close your eyes and ears to it. This message is not a lure: our time for traps and lures is gone. This is a genuine offer, believe it or not. Listen, I will meet you; I wish to meet you; I will meet you anywhere"—again the laugh, but more of a chuckle this time—"without any hired guns or hoodlums. Please, I beg you, think about this. I do not know what they have given you to do; but I *do* know the mentality of your Service. In your deepest heart you know also.

"Herbie, have you had time to really feel it yet? That they don't trust you? That they will trust you no longer? You will be like a man who is grounded, tied to a desk job after years of flying experience; or an active soldier pensioned off, rooting in a garden, and living on memories. What is worse they will be memories with a bitter taste—the gall of not being trusted at the end. The past is no good for either of us; it is the *now* that matters. Now, and the future—what is left of it: for there cannot be too many years left to this troubled planet.

"I belong to what they call a superpower; while your adopted country is reduced to being a missile site, launching pad, and giant aircraft carrier, for another superpower.

"When it comes, the new holocaust will concern the survival of the few; and their survival will be in the most primitive of conditions. The days of our great technology are numbered. Do you, like myself, think that mankind is basically psychopathic by nature? We bring our own destruction into the world as snails carry their houses; and the further mankind has travelled along the slow road of discovery, the more dangerous it becomes.

"This time, the wheel cannot be stopped. The food will run out; the harvests will not feed our countless millions; and the battle will come—over grain, and oil, and what we think of as the bare necessities. When it is over, and the destroyers have done their job—with neutron, atom, plague and blight—some must remain to build a path through a barren planet. Men of different races and political beliefs, but similar knowledge of specialised techniques will be required. We are such men, and need a freedom to act and use our qualities.

"Your people will never give you that freedom now they've lost trust. *We* can give it, and we *will* give it. Soon, I shall let you know how to reply. Consider it, Herbie Kruger. Consider meeting me alone. Consider hard and long, because you have been a worthy adversary."

Big Herbie—shaken at the fact of Vascovsky's ability, even now, to reach out to him—listened to the tape again. He then poured himself a very large vodka, sat down and tried to out-think Jacob Vascovsky. There was a strong, and logical emotional appeal, together with a moral argument which sounded sincere enough—if you happened to be one who really believed in the inevitability of a world laid waste by the superweapons and greed of man.

Desperately, Herbie wished he could figure Jacob Vascovsky's angle. There had to be a reason for this. More— the reason must be one of some urgency.

Slowly, Herbie Kruger got out of the chair and walked to the direct line telephone, hoping the DG would still be in his office.

He was there, snappy and gruff, but silent while Herbie told him about the tape.

"Yes." The Director General appeared to have relaxed. "So glad you told me about it, Herbie. I listened to it this morning. Interesting, isn't it? Posted in the West End yesterday morning. Curry's checking on the mail order firm now. No luck as yet. I wonder how we can use it to our own advantage? You might like to think about that, what?"

Herbie muttered an obscenity in German and replaced the receiver. He felt depressed and jittery that Vascovsky could come so close, and be so accurate. Perhaps Martha would help sweep away the gloom.

*   *   *

Herbie had last seen Martha Adler during the final phases of his ill-starred, unofficial visit to East Berlin. For a while, then, he had not trusted her.

She seemed to have lost a little weight. Apart from that, Martha looked incredibly healthy: her skin bronzed and the ash blonde hair silk smooth. To Herbie's eye, she had changed little since the first time he set eyes on her.

In the split second of their meeting—at the door of a small mock-Georgian bungalow, attached to a row of similar buildings—Herbie re-lived their past.

East Berlin, 1959. Herbie was recruiting. Saturday night at the Rialto, a hotbed of pro-Communists. She had come into the bar—a striking girl, with a tipsy Russian officer. A scuffle. Herbie to the rescue.

She worked for the ruling hierarchy, whom she hated, but held to a philosophy of the nearer you were to the centre of power, the more damage you could accomplish when the time came. She lived for that time; meanwhile, Martha got all she could. In sexual matters she was honest. She usually had a lover; but, between lovers, it was open season. That is how it was when they met; and, for a short time, Herbie had been her temporary lover—for she needed men with power, to supply her personal economic needs. She did not take much recruiting. One of the best who ever worked for him.

Now, all those years from that first, smoky, Saturday night meeting, Herbie put down his suitcase, opened his arms, and gave her a great bear hug.

"They've done you well." He looked around as she closed the door. A neat room with carefully selected furniture—mostly nice old pieces, late eighteenth century. On one wall, a painting of cliffs and sea; a large gilt mirror on the other.

"It's comfortable, Herbie. But lonely. More lonely than the East, I can tell you."

"In a place like this?" Herbie showed genuine surprise. "You'll capture yourself a nice, retired, well-off widower, and live happily ever after."

"God help you, Herbie. That's what I don't need: and you know it. I've never needed it. A drink before lunch?"

Herbie grinned enthusiastically. He had quietly put his small suitcase just inside the door. Martha looked at it; and then at Herbie. "Schnapps?"

"Perfect."

"You've known me for a long time, you great oaf." Her hands moving expertly over the glasses and bottle. "You know what I need. Life. Nights on the town. The comfort of knowing that you're cared for, even if it's only transitory. I've never believed in love being for ever. For ever if you only want comfort. Not for ever if you get your highs from passion,

112

and life lived at full stretch." She handed him a glass. "Prosit."

"Cheers." They seemed to be alternating between German and English.

"Herbie, you *know* me. Being cared for—just for a while; knowing there's someone around; a little companionable fucking."

Herbie laughed, "From what I remember it's a lot of companionable fucking."

She smiled—an imitation sweetness. "Well, you'll be reminded, tonight. There's only one bedroom and one bed."

Herbie glanced at the sofa. Martha Adler smiled her false, sweet, smile again. "No," she said. "You don't come down here to keep me company over a weekend and then do that to me, my teddy bear Big Herbie—*Schnitzer*." The last word—*Blunder*, in English—had been a cryptonym for both Herbie and his first East Berlin network.

They lunched on a consommé—"It came from a tin, darling. Can you see me sweating to make this?"—and a delicious *Sauerbraten*, complete with potato dumplings. "Yes, darling, I did sweat over this. I have a long memory."

It came back to Herbie. She had cooked *Sauerbraten* for him when they were lovers—and Martha between semi-permanent lovers.

Children almost. Puppies playing games. No, Herbie should not think like that: for, in those days, you were full-grown, emotionally advanced, streetwise, and full of the world's darkest knowledge, by the time you reached your teens. Martha was barely out of *her* teens when they first met.

Over the meal, she made him laugh. "I shall go mad, here. The available men are too frightened—they paw and pet and make noises: 'I say, old girl, better be careful, what?' " Her parody English accent made Herbie smile to himself.

"As for the retired married ones. Well, horny as hell, but scared stiff of their wives." She threw back her head to laugh at the little play on words.

"That's good for someone who does not speak really excellent English." Big Herbie grinned.

"Oh I learn, here. I learn, Oxo. Not until the sun crosses the yard-arm. Coffee Morning. You must come to dinner. Drop in any old time. Jumble sale. Sale of work. I learn. No wonder we have Communists. The bourgeoisie still triumph in these enclaves, Herbie."

Big Herbie nodded. "You get used to it, my dear. Like we got used to cover. By the way, who did they exchange you for?"

"Didn't you know? Oh, some little turnaround defector. KGB. Name of Mistochenkov." Herbie said he thought as much. Pavel Mistochenkov had been Vascovsky's ADC at one time. Then he asked what had gone on, when the KGB had her in Berlin.

"The usual things"—a bitter, one-note, high-pitched laugh. "Irony, Herbie. I'd been screwing the little bastard who arrested me. He tried coaxing. Promised the earth. Then it got unpleasant for a while—sensory deprivation. You know."

Herbie knew. A cell in which you could neither stand fully, nor sit in comfort. Darkness and solitude. Occasional noises off. Unless you'd had training—or practised meditation—it took around two days to become disorientated; four to six days before you thought you would go mad.

They walked in the afternoon. Down by the yacht club, and out along the coast. She still had that long, leggy, stride he remembered so well. The wind whipped in from the sea, blowing her hair into an untidy mop, and she hung tightly to Herbie's arm, as he rolled and lumbered over the grass.

Herbie did not speak of the immediate past. Instead, they talked of the times two decades ago: the early 'sixties. Over tea, in a snug café, Herbie felt the old trust; that special intimacy—between control and agent—returning. It crossed his mind that his future could be worse. She was intelligent. They both knew the job. He supposed the DG could provide a reasonable pension for him. Life might be very comfortable with Martha Adler.

The telephone was ringing when they got back to her little bungalow.

114

"It's for you." She frowned, holding out the receiver.

Herbie covered the mouthpiece, looking at her eyes. "I have to tell them where I'm going. They know anyway. Surveillance, because of what happened last year."

She gave a little nod of understanding, as he heard Curry Shepherd's voice in his ear. "Awfully sorry. Fun and games over. Urgent, from the boss man. Needs you in London pronto. Car in ten minutes be okay?"

"Yes"—putting the phone down; turning to Martha. "I'm so sorry, my dear."

She raised her arms, straight, from her sides; then let them fall back into place. "There goes my fucking weekend."

"There can be others. A lot of others."

Martha nestled in his arms, holding him very close. "You mean that, Herbie. Not just saying . . . ?"

"Not just saying. I'm on duty, my dear."

She clung even harder. "I'm so bloody frightened, *Schnitzer*. It must be age catching up. I'm more frightened of the loneliness here, than I ever was out there. Please come and see me—properly see me—soon."

"Very soon. I'll call you from London, tonight. Don't be afraid. Please."

All the way back up to London, Herbie worried about Martha Adler. Never had he seen her like this. Always he thought of her as one who could exist alone in the Sahara, if necessary: the Sahara; or the cold wastes of Siberia. She had changed, and he had seen people like this before. At that point they usually went private, because it meant the nerve had gone. Or they had been turned, and could not live with the turning.

115

11

Tubby Fincher still viewed Herbie with guarded hostility. The Director General, seated behind his desk, signalled fatigue in the dark pockets under his eyes. Big Herbie sensed an atmosphere of uncertain concern in the pleasant office, with its buttoned leather chairs and paintings of military victory from other times.

"I'm sorry, Herbie. Gather you were preparing for a quiet weekend with Miss Adler." The Director moved his chair forward, settling himself more comfortably. It crossed Herbie's mind that as Martha Adler's pretty little mock-Georgian bungalow was probably wired for sound there would be some titters among the younger members of the Watch Committee as they listened to the tapes.

"You'd better sit down, Herbie." Tubby's voice was flat; but a step in the right direction. At least he looked Kruger in the eyes; and called him by his Christian name. "This may take some time."

Herbie sat, and the DG passed a typewritten flimsy across the desk. At the top was a cipher number; time received at GCHQ, Cheltenham; followed by the words *For Director General SIS. Or G Staff Eyes Only*.

The transcribed message read:

POSSIBLE NIECE AND NEPHEW WILL GET FULL CHECK TREATMENT SOONEST/ADVISE YOU COVER ME/MOST URGENT/STENTOR

"It came by a route he hasn't used for over a year." The DG gave the impression of speaking to himself: as though summarising events in his own mind; for his own benefit. "We have a courier, who occasionally works in the newspaper

116

kiosk at the Moskva Hotel. It's a hit and miss business, with a telephone ring code. If he gets the call, the courier has to try and alter his shift, to suit Stentor's requirements. There's a fall-back system, but that's not easy for someone in Stentor's situation. To get something to our postman, Stentor has to have some excuse to visit the Moskva. This time it's worked; though it was probably delivered early this morning. A late arrival for us. The problem is his reference to the nephew."

Herbie asked if the niece was the contact in Leningrad, and was surprised when Tubby answered, his manner slightly more friendly and less formal. Perhaps Tubby was getting the message. "Yes, she's Leningrad. Successive DG's have had problems with Stentor's communications. Until he reached his present, exalted, appointment it wasn't too bad. Now there are constant difficulties. A man with his responsibilities, in the Russian Service, is given adequate guard practically around the clock. Even his apartment block has watchers. The 'niece' was found for him some five years ago."

The Director took up the brief. Herbie, he knew, was conversant with most methods of communication; and the way they worked the couriers, within the Eastern Bloc and the Soviet Union. "There are a handful—and only a handful—of trustworthy nationals for message-carrying. We needed one with cover, just in case Stentor ever came under suspicion—as has now happened—and there had to be verification.

"Ambrose Hill provided us with a 'mystery', who didn't know what it was all about: an academic; a historian, with special interest in the period just before the Revolution."

They had sent the mystery in, with all co-operation from the Soviet authorities. He was given access to the pre-revolutionary archives. It was virtually impossible to be completely accurate and establish certain, and lasting, family connections—because so many people went missing during the cataclysmic events of the abortive 1905 uprising; the great October Revolution and the Civil War.

Against all the odds, the mystery professor discovered that Prince Georgi Nikanorovich Anashkov had employed a Head Butler—a major-domo—by the name of Gregory Orlov. Most of the Orlov family was on record as having gone missing, during the riots and lootings early in 1917; but there were some details of surviving kinship. Stentor, it was found, had a brother and sister—the brother a year younger; the sister also his junior. Further, the brother, Mikhail, was last recorded as living in Leningrad. It was established that he had married, and there was a daughter. As for the sister, she disappeared completely.

"We already had a good postman in Leningrad." The Director smiled. "Married with two children: husband's name Ivan Morozov. We set her up as a Stentor contact, and got a professional in, so that the local records showed her maiden name as Orlov. Then by a series of false passes, brought the two together—letters, and then telephone calls: the letters from Stentor, after he was seen to spend much time examining public records. He had found a niece; difficult in the circumstances, for he continued to live under the assumed name, taken when he was moved from Moscow as a child."

Herbie quickly interrupted, asking how their 'expert' had tampered with local records.

"That one was lucky, and simple. The only paperwork we needed to worry about was the marriage certificate. The clerk at the Morozovs' local House of Marriages was old, infirm, and just about ready for retirement. We got the Morozovs to apply for a new apartment. For that they needed all the documents, including the certificate of marriage. Our girl went to collect and saw the old clerk alone. She threw a scene. Said the maiden name was wrong; that there'd been an error. The clerk didn't want trouble; didn't want to blot his copybook just before retirement; didn't want to get his pension docked. Made out new certificates with the Orlov name inserted. Even destroyed the original and had it re-run."

Big Herbie did his nodding Buddha impression. "So, Stentor has a niece. Okay, what's that got to do with the price of eggs?"

"For some time now we've been considering preparations for lifting Stentor, mainly because of his age. This is where we're slightly off course. Stentor has an assumed kinship with a nephew. 'Nephew', in fact, has always been our crypto for his personal Messiah—the man who'll be sent to get him out. Michael Gold is to be that nephew: a great-nephew, in fact. The genealogy would put him as Stentor's sister's grandson. Knowing Stentor, he will direct Vascovsky towards the niece. That should be safe. He knows his nephew has a government job and travels a lot. The problem is one of time. First, to get more information to Stentor concerning the nephew. Second, to get the nephew to him very quickly. How quickly can it be done, Herbie? I mean we need him there last week."

Big Herbie sat, unmoving: still, as an animal is still when waiting to pounce on prey. When he spoke, it was with slow deliberation. "I wish to get this straight. You are telling me that if Vascovsky begins to question about kinsmen, Stentor will talk of a niece and nephew?"

The Director inclined his head in an affirmative.

"The niece he can produce."

Again an affirmative.

"He knows who the nephew should be—the relationship, I mean. A great-nephew?"

"Yes."

"But he has no proof? Nothing else?"

Tubby Fincher replied, "That's what the DG's just told you, Herbie. We've been working on a plan to get him out, using a cover nephew . . ."

Herbie raised his voice, "And the plan's gone wrong, yes? Events have overtaken you. With this"—he raised the copy of Stentor's message—"with this, you've been blown to pieces. They're catching up on him, before you've even reached the first planning stage of an operation to get him out."

"I'm afraid that's about the strength of it, Herbie. Well, I mean there is an operational plan; but no trained nephew. Only Michael Gold."

Even the Director General jumped, as Big Herbie's fist came smashing down on to his desk, and the voice barked out. "So you fit me up. Something goes very wrong, and Herbie is in charge, yes? And you give Herbie a baby, an infant with romantic ideas to work with—Michael bloody Gold; babe in arms not know his ass from a hole in the ground. You give me a peashooter to destroy a tank."

"No. We're putting you completely in the picture, Herbie. Giving you a crisis report."

"You've screwed it." Herbie looked at each of them in turn, the bitterness etched minutely on his pudding face. "You've argued, no doubt. You've had little lunches, and tête-à-têtes, trying to fix on who's to be the nephew; what cover you're giving him? All the nuts, bolts and nails. But you've—what's the word you use?—waffled? Yes. You've waffled on, and not come to any decision; not started any training. Until now. Until Stentor is suddenly caught with his ass bare. The nephew needs a minimum of six months' detailed training. A year would have been better—a year, with information being fed to Stentor as you went along. Now the poor bugger's right in it. Read the message." Herbie flourished the paper under the DG's nose, "Read it—ADVISE *YOU* COVER *ME*/ MOST URGENT. I should think so. *Most* urgent."

"You landed him in the shit, Herbie." Tubby Fincher, quiet and full of malice. "Hallet and Birdseed . . ."

"I didn't know, you . . . you rasher of wind. Nobody had the sense to brief me, when I got that information. No. All you need have said was, 'Herbie, this Hallet, and this Birdseed. They come from the most sensitive source. You stay silent, yes?' Instead it looks like chickenshit . . ."

"Feed," the DG corrected. "Chickenfeed."

"Feed? Shit? What's the difference? Stentor's life, yes? Or don't you care that he's already given all those years for the Service. Over fifty, living cover; worming his way in. God knows what good stuff he's passed your way." Herbie took a deep breath. "I tell you something. You ask how long for Michael Gold—the nephew—to be prepared? We want him

120

now. All that rubbish. You either give me a full hand, or take me off this. Now. Am I still on?"

"You're in sole charge, Herbie." The Director docile.

"In writing," Herbie snapped. "I want in writing, that I am in full charge; but, if anything goes wrong—if they get Stentor and, or, Gold—it is *your* responsibility. You spell it out. The planning, for lifting that old man, should have been further advanced. The fact you ordered me to use Gold. Not my choice. You do that?"

The Director General nodded, his face an open book on which you could almost read the word shame. There were no doubts between any of them. Herbie had control. If it went wrong, the resultant Enquiry would be told the facts: too little planning, and too late. It would be the end of the DG's career; and almost certainly Tubby Fincher's as well.

"Before I leave this office, then." Herbie did not smile. "If Tubby could draft it, get it typed, and you sign it, sir. Copy for me; copy for Registry; and one for the Stentor File. Okay?"

The Director exchanged a few words with Fincher about the form of words.

"I need a car also. To Warminster. I also need young Worboys. You do that for me, Tubby?" He turned to the DG, "And you authorise Worboys? I need a moment alone with you in any case, sir."

The Director nodded to Fincher. "Everything as he says." Brisk; leaving no room for wasting time.

"I'm sorry, Herbie," he said as the door closed. "Yes, I suppose we were treating you shabbily. I do have to say, however, that I was in no way trying to shift blame on to you, should there be errors—if you didn't get Stentor out. There was no plot there—no night of the long knives."

Herbie smiled, "I take no chances. Now, sir, another matter. I spent some of today with Martha Adler. Already you know. I have known her for many years. She is changed and it worries me."

"She had a bad time after her arrest—and that *was* partly your responsibility, Herbie."

"Yes. Yes, I know about that; and about the bad time. It's more. It could be connected. After all, somebody's popped a love letter from Vascovsky into the mail to me. Have you been seriously concerned?"

"Can you be specific?"

Big Herbie sighed. "Is her place wired?"

The Director frowned. "That's classified, but I'll tell you. The phone's wired."

"Anything interesting?"

"No. Why?"

"Because I really *do* know her. Something's very wrong. Either her nerve has gone; or she's been turned, and cannot live long with it. If it's nerve, then she could still be turned—particularly if she's close to me: and she wants to get very close."

"I'll put the musicians in. Thank you, Herbie."

"I care, sir. I care that we get her off any hook she might already have swallowed. Just like I care about Stentor. He must be brought out; and a great deal will depend on how bright, and what sort of idiot we have in Michael Gold. There is also a question of your own decisions—arrangements yet to be revealed to me: Gold's cover; how we get him in; how he can come out—if that's necessary—and how he can bring the old man out with him." Big Herbie was not, normally, a sarcastic man, but you could sense the acid as he added: "Providing your planning has got that far."

"The paperwork only needs Michael Gold's photograph. The arrangements are a matter of a couple of messages." The Director looked wearily at his watch, leaned back and continued, "There is a mining engineer from Rostov—by coincidence only, within five years of Gold's age . . ."

"You mean he's five years older?"

"Older, yes. He'd only just come out of university when we chose him. Not married; but father and mother still live in Rostov. He's under the impression—as a good member of the Party—that the Russian Service has asked him to undertake something different; something out of the ordinary. A sort of test. Name, Piotr Kashvar. Works mainly in the

Central Ural chain, and has saved up some of his leave. Kashvar, on a word from us, will obtain the leave and travel permits. In his position that takes exactly two days. He thinks of it as a great game; something very secret, and to do with mining prospects. Job prospects. If his parents receive a cable from him, saying he has arrived in Moscow to see his uncle, that is the story they'll tell—no matter who asks. It's amazing what a loyal Communist, and his family, will do when they think we're the KGB.

"Kashvar will fly to Moscow, on our word, and then go up to the Baltic. Stentor has his summer *dacha* there—on the Latvian coast. Our man Kashvar," he allowed a tiny smile, "has a letter of permit, and the key to the *dacha*. He's to stay there; as though on holiday. Whoever we send in, simply flies from Heathrow to Moscow, and stays in one of the tourist hotels. During the day—or one evening—he moves in on Stentor: a telephone call from one of the railway stations, anything like that. His secondary passport and papers will be under the name Piotr Kashvar. Once with the old man, he prepares him for the lift."

"And if there's a problem?"

"We send him a telegram. Needed at home urgently, love Amy—you know."

"He comes back, and you sort it out."

"That was the general idea. He could always fly out again in a few days, as long as nobody's on to him."

"And, if Stentor can be ready?"

"They go to the Baltic, and we lay on a cloak and dagger jaunt. Spirit them over the sea to Stockholm and away."

"Leaving the mining engineer in charge of the *dacha*."

"His instructions are to stay for two weeks. Then leave. If nothing happens, he will return, refreshed, to his labours in the Urals; and receive the grateful thanks of the Supreme Soviet. If Stentor is ready."

"So, this Kashvar will be out of the way while his substitute operates. You have all this organised without Stentor's approval?"

"He knows we have spare keys to the *dacha*."

123

"But nothing else. Not even the name of his long lost nephew?"

The Director shook his head. "We wanted . . ."

"You wanted to find the right man to play the mining engineer, Kashvar. Michael Gold probably knows as much about mining engineering in the Soviet Union as I know about . . . about . . ." he stumbled, "about micro-surgery. Why, sir? Why did you arrange it this way? Surely, the first priority for something as important, and vital, as this, is the agent; the nephew. You need a man trained in all the black arts; someone who knows the Soviets; who knows Russia like his hand. You need a high-priest, not just a Russian-speaking acolyte. What's the use?"

"I am aware," the Director said smoothly. "I accept responsibility, Herbie. You've already said it all: we had lunches and meetings. We went to a great deal of trouble with method; getting at the man Kashvar—setting him up; conning him. It's no excuse, but we're all under pressure. The Stentor business lagged; and you're right, Herbie, we should have had an old hand in training; standing by. Gold is a last chance. Risky. Yes. But we're committed."

Big Herbie sat there, biting his lower lip, hands crossed on his lap, out of long and disciplined habit (because, they said, it is the hands that give you away by sudden movement). "I do what I can with the Gold boy. It'll really have to be a quick in-and-out. Anything goes wrong, I have to think of him, and not our precious jewel—Stentor. You understand?"

The Director General barely moved his head, but it was acknowledgment enough. Above him, Nelson's *Victory* battled with the French fleet—sea, smoke, flame and sail: man grappling with man.

"One other thing." Herbie rose, towering over the DG's desk. "I know the strict rules; but if I'm to be with Gold—cramming him? Is that what you say? You cram people for examinations, yes? If I am to be mainly at Warminster with him, then you'll have to put the Stentor File in a steel box, chained to a lion tamer's wrist, and with one key in my pocket.

124

To get Michael Gold ready, I have to know all there is to know about Stentor."

"Done." The Director spoke as though making a deal, just as Tubby Fincher returned with the typed documents, absolving Big Herbie from the sins of failure.

They all read the agreement, and the Director signed all copies. Ambrose Hill, waiting in the outer office, was summoned, and given instructions about keeping the documents safe—Herbie folded his own copy and placed it in his breast pocket. The Director then gave further orders about the Stentor File. It was to be brought up, in one of the fire-proof and thief-proof cases; then placed in Mr. Kruger's keeping.

The Head of Registry tried to remonstrate, but the Director merely repeated the order: saying he would take full responsibility.

When all things were done, they went to the outer office, where young Worboys waited, his face carrying a perplexed and baffled look. When he saw Herbie, he made a questioning grimace. Herbie winked at him.

Seated in the back of the car, the boxed Stentor File at his feet, Big Herbie Kruger started to initiate Worboys into the explosive secret which lay at the kernel of their Firm.

*   *   *

The pair of ringmasters were putting Michael Gold through his paces, inside one of the small complexes of prefabricated buildings which stud the estate, surrounding the house at Warminster.

Not even the Commandant knew who was there, as the team had arrived in darkness, and in cars with dark glass windows. There were worknames, and they kept within the group of buildings, which were laid out in the form of a cross. One bar of the cross contained work sections and equipment; the rest made up reasonably comfortable living quarters, to which food was brought—placed in an outside trap, with a bell, so that, like lepers, the staff did not see them.

This was just as well, Big Herbie imagined. The Commandant would be unhappy to see him there, after the hostile reception of the last year.

When Herbie and Tony Worboys arrived, Michael Gold was being taken through the streets of Moscow, aided by film, photograph and map. The two instructors spoke nothing but Russian, firing questions, and expecting immediate answers.

"You are standing at the corner of Frunze Street. Walk towards Arbat Square. Describe. Now."

"I am on the left side of the road. The right-hand side is the Lenin Library. Number Eleven—Basic Library of Social Sciences of the Academy of Social Sciences. Number Twelve—Empire-style house with a statue of Marshal Frunze in front. Large building at the end of the street—Military School."

"What's the significance of the Military School?"

"It was one of the main strategic defence points of the Tsarist army, during the October Revolution. Its former title was the Alexander Military School."

"Good." The instructor saw Herbie beckon. In English he said, "Okay. Let's take five."

"Well?" Herbie raised his eyebrows.

"Quite incredible, Chief. Two days and he knows the lot. Mind like a camera. You'd think he'd lived in Moscow for years."

Herbie nodded. At least Michael was smart in the brain. That was something: a small plus. "That's useful. He might be there this time next week."

"Bloody hell," muttered the instructor. "You want to talk?"

"Alone; and to the subject. Everyone else out of the way."

Big Herbie sat, with Michael Gold, in one of the small offices. For an hour he went through the situation, step-by-step—plotting the moves; pointing out the pitfalls; playing the Devil's Advocate, and genuinely attempting to present the gravest dangers to the young man.

"It is still not too late, Michael. Nobody's going to think

126

the worse of you if you decide to back out now. But this is truly the last chance."

Michael Gold did not smile. Herbie could plainly see the worry buried deep in the young man's eyes. Yet, when he spoke, the voice was calm. Herbie looked at the hands. Not a twitch or nervous movement. "Herbie, now you've given me the full picture, I'm more determined than ever. In Cambridge, I thought it madness; then decided it could be a bit of a lark. Now I want to help. You've said that your people can't use what these boys here call 'a face'. I'm around; and there's an old man waiting in Moscow. He's spent over fifty years working for England—doing what my father would probably have liked to do. No, Herbie. I'm going. Just show me the best way."

God help us all. Big Herbie felt the stab of irony, as Michael mentioned his father; then, smiling his most stupid of smiles, he reached out, resting one great paw on the young man's shoulder. "Okay, Michael. I'm told you have to be ready very quickly. We're going to cut things down. The two instructors'll give you a couple of days, running through the establishment behaviour; so you won't give yourself away in the first ten minutes. Then I'll have you for two days: forty-eight hours without sleep. I have to lead you through the black arts, and teach some simple tricks. After that, one day's rest. One day's briefing. Six days from now, and you'll be ready and running."

Later, Herbie spoke to the Director, on a secure phone. "One week. I'll have him ready in one week. Told him six days, but we give him an extra for the insurance. You'll have to map-read him through the way out with Stentor; and give him specific instructions about an abort. You do that directly before he leaves: the day before. Start booking the tickets, sir. He'll be as ready as I can make him."

12

In MOSCOW THE days were still bright and clear; the sun dazzling, reflecting from buildings and the remaining packed snow. The thaw had not started in earnest. There was no warmth in the sun, and the time was not yet ripe for true spring, with the thrusting of the grass, budding of trees and flowers.

Jacob Vascovsky thought of the spring. True, he loved Moscow at that time of the year, when the blood surged, and new life appeared in the city—even showing on the faces and in the walks of Muscovites, as they put another bitter winter into the bed of their memories. Yet Vascovsky hoped that, by this spring, he could get the present matter over and done with. They might even give him leave. In any case, there was the chance that Kruger would fall for his quiet pressures, and that would mean one trip out of the country. Business combined with pleasure.

The reverie came to an abrupt conclusion as Vascovsky's driver parked the car in the space reserved in the Dzerzhinsky Square inner lot. The bodyguard opened the rear door, taking up the standard position—a little to the left, and slightly behind—as Vascovsky walked quickly to the entrance which would take him to the 'Bridge', and the Chairman's office suite.

The adjutant was expecting him. No, he was not late, but the Comrade Chairman said he was to go straight in.

The Chairman rose from the huge desk, opening both arms in a symbolic gesture of welcome and greeting. The arms dropped, and the Chairman gestured to a chair drawn up close to the desk.

Vascovsky walked the considerable distance to the desk and sat down. There, in front of him, as he had expected, lay four matt photographs. The faces of his colleagues from the First Directorate's Standing Committee for Forward Planning stared unseeing from the prints.

"Well, there they are." The Chairman allowed himself a chuckle. "You've guessed why I called you in. There's been time for evaluation. I need an unofficial verbal report. What progress you've made? What ideas? A suspect even?"

Vascovsky smiled. Always smile when things are not straightforward. For him it was a rule of life. Remaining silent, he looked at the photographs:

Tserkov, the avuncular, chain-smoking, weatherbeaten head of Department V. The sinister one, whose very friendliness sent a chill to Vascovsky's bones.

Severov. A fine head of hair—remembered thinking it was like an ermine pelt—straight, tall, and fine-looking, with good features. A man who could be taken for a sixty-year-old instead of his seventy years plus. The Head of Directorate S. The one who probably knew more about Vascovsky's career than anyone else.

Zapad, Head of Directorate T. The blank face with biting humour. The former professor—scholastic, with a mind teeming, crammed full of secret knowledge.

Last in line, the dandy, Vladimir Glubodkin—bronzed, with a good head of hair in spite of his age. Very fit, with that disinterested air which was undoubtedly a studied pose. Head of Special Service I.

"You've had a chance to talk to each man : . ." the Chairman began.

Vascovsky made his habitual hand-twirling movement: the right arm raised, with the hand, loose-fingered, twisting from the wrist. He had seen each of them separately, over dinner with their wives. His own wife had been a great help. It was all most interesting.

"But, any conclusions, Comrade General?" The Chairman picked up one of the photographs—Zapad, by chance. "This one, for instance?"

"I don't think he's our man." Vascovsky shook his head. "I have to admit there are difficulties, Comrade Chairman."

129

"Failure? At this stage?" The Chairman raised his eyebrows.

Again, Vascovsky smiled, shaking his head. "Oh, far from failure . . ." The Chairman seemed about to speak once more, but Jacob Vascovsky held up a palm. "No, sir. I have had opportunity to examine each of the suspects at close quarters. I have also gone through their records, and dossiers, with a microscope. Their telephones are wired. Also their apartments. The first problem is that they are elderly men. The youngest is sixty-eight, the eldest, seventy-two. All of them have led similar lives. They come from peasant, or proletarian, stock. Each has had some kind of an education; some better than others. All four joined the Red Army in the years after the October Revolution. All came to the Cheka, and served in various departments. At least two did a spell with the GRU. All have some field service. These things are common to the whole membership." He continued; voicing his opinion regarding the subjects' possible faults: the chinks in, otherwise, unblemished careers. Zapad drank too much, though that was common enough—even among chekists; Glubodkin still liked women, and took some small risks there. Severov, a fine-looking man, tall and straight as a lath, also had tiny secrets—at home, his wife pampered him to excess, and he hated too much exercise.

As for Tserkov, the sinister one—well, what could you say about the Head of Department Viktor? He smoked too much?

The Head of Department Viktor had his own defensive system; his own private army. It was necessary, and always had been, for the chief of that organisation.

"You have to look for means and method, don't you agree, Comrade Chairman?"

"Explain." The Chairman's head cocked to one side, taking in everything Vascovsky said: weighing it; testing the ground.

"Well, at first sight I would look, among these four, for one who talks too much: in the hope that the Hallet and Birdseed information was dropped in a moment of indiscretion. There is only one candidate for that—Zapad . . ."

"You've already eliminated him. You said so just now."

130

"As a traitor, yes. If this business is indiscretion, it is a different matter. If you want a loose tongue, Zapad is your man. You'll see what I mean if you listen to the tapes. His wife also drinks to excess, and Comrade General Zapad talks to her. The woman knows as much as he does. Every night he talks. If she, in turn, mentioned Hallet and Birdseed, in a tipsy moment, to the wrong person . . ."

"And they know the wrong people?" The Chairman leaned forward, glowering, as though he was on to something.

Vascovsky laughed aloud. "That is where the indiscretion theory falls flat on its face. The Zapads are models. They share each other's company, and that of few others. This, incidentally, applies to all four; and that is why I rule out both Zapad, and indiscretion."

The Chairman relaxed his body, sagging back into his chair.

"Normally I would go for those who have regular access out of the country," Vascovsky continued. "If we do have a long-term penetration agent, then he has to have ways of getting information out. This would mean that he *must* have the ability to travel. However, I do not count this as an absolute qualification. If we have a burrower on our hands, his lines of communication would have been well established years ago. All the candidates attend official functions; each of them know, and are known to, security officers in the Western Embassies—and people outside." He leaned forward and removed two of the photographs. "Zapad, I reject as a possibility. Also Tserkov. I doubt that even the most hardened operative could be as successful as Tserkov, and still act as a double."

"Which leaves . . ." The Chairman allowed a heavy forefinger to touch each of the other photographs.

"Nikolai Aleksandrovich Severov. He travels little, but his assistants fly hither and thither like pollen. He is also a mine of intelligence information. Ideal. As is Vladimir Glubodkin; and he hardly ever travels. Either of them fit.

"But this one." His hand lifted one of the photographs from the desk. Vladimir Glubodkin. "This one has a strange past.

131

He has no linear relatives, yet there is a niece in Leningrad whom he telephones but never sees; and a nephew he has sought out, but never met. I am having them checked most thoroughly. *He* is my prime suspect, and I'll play him—with your permission, Comrade Chairman—like a fish. My staff are making enquiries about the niece now. Soon I shall drop in on him, to ask more about both niece and nephew. When we talked of it last, I gave the impression of being un-interested." He gave a wolfish smile. "But I am very interested indeed. The man's background, after the October Revolution, is odd. Nothing you can put your finger on, but there are some anomalies. If, by chance, he is our man, the niece and nephew could be cut-outs: messengers, setups, fixers." It was Vascovsky's turn to lean across the desk in a close, con-spiratorial, manner. "What is more, it would seem the niece and nephew have appeared only since he was appointed Head of his Department. Before that time, things would have been easier for him. It is where my money lies, Comrade Chairman, with this one." Vascovsky's forefinger again tapped the photograph.

The Chairman's face drained of colour. "It is difficult to believe . . ." He paused, swallowing hard, pulling his senses together. "No, no, I suppose not difficult to believe, for we all know the ways of our world. But it is difficult to accept. For all our sakes, I think I should neutralise him in some way. Remove him without suspicion. He's near to retirement in any case." Again the pause, a hand passing over his forehead. Then the Chairman's face underwent a strange and terrifying change. He was in control once more: the hard and ruthless man; a man of steel; a Chairman in the mould of 'Iron Felix' himself. "Unless, Comrade General, you wish to try the old methods. Interrogation of the old style?"

Vascovsky gave a quick shake of his head—fast and very definite. "Comrade Chairman, no. No, I beg you. If I cannot discover the truth, with complete certainty, here in Moscow—with everything at my disposal—there is one last card."

"Your trump?" The icy sharpness did not diminish.

Vascovsky nodded, violently and quickly. "If I cannot build a dossier of evidence now, there is a chance that I can get the truth from another source . . ."

"Ah?"

"Kruger. I still work on that. It is a gamble, but there are possibilities with him. A chance. If I get near enough, and apply the correct pressure, we will know for sure." He paused for a second, taking a deep breath. "I have one more favour to ask."

The Chairman did not reply: looking Vascovsky in the eyes; waiting for the favour to be asked, like some monarch of old weighing up the boon to be granted by him.

"If my pressure on Kruger works, it may be necessary for me to leave Moscow at a moment's notice," Vascovsky began. "Naturally, I would let you know. But I need permission to act freely, and on my own initiative. If I disappear for a day or two, I trust it would be with your blessing: without question, or surveillance."

"Naturally. You have that power." The Chairman rose, turning towards the window and speaking without looking back. "I should warn you of one thing, Comrade General. It was through me that you received promotion, and this particular assignment. Others were not inclined to be so understanding. I fought hard on your behalf: mainly because of my belief in you and your ability. Let me down; play me false; and it will be the last time. I trust you understand. To err is human, and, in your case, it uncovered something potentially dangerous. A second error can have but one ending, and you are well aware that it cannot be escaped. If anything went wrong, which I am sure it will not, you will be in an unpleasant situation. If something does go wrong, and you are foolish enough to attempt running from it, I—your friend—would not hesitate to have you hunted; and you know how good Tserkov's people from Department V are at that sort of business."

He turned, to see that Vascovsky had risen to his feet. The slim, elegant General looked relaxed and unruffled. He even gave a small chuckle. "Comrade Chairman, I'm not a fool.

133

I'm a loyal servant." He tossed the photograph of his suspect on to the table. "I'll get him for you; and with enough evidence to squeeze him until his brains pop through his eye sockets."

*   *   *

General Vladimir Glubodkin stood at the window of his office, in Building B of the Yasenevo Complex. He felt a sense of relief, and had done so all day.

Like all Heads of Departments and Directorates, Stentor had access to the foreign newspapers. Indeed, it was part of the job. There was an entire staff who did news analysis from the foreign Press, and nobody thought twice about the senior officers who strolled in, daily, to take a quick look at the newspapers and magazines, brought each night and morning to Yasenevo.

Stentor only visited the Media Room on an average of once every three days; for his British masters made crash contact through the Personal Column of the London *Times*—the message repeated for three consecutive days.

The ciphering was complicated, and the Flash word changed each four days. But it was there; that morning; and Stentor took only nine seconds to memorise the tiny paragraph. After all, his life had been spent in committing things to memory. Far back, in the days just after the Great Patriotic War, when he had worked solely on evaluation, in a cluttered room at Two Dzerzhinsky Square, Stentor was quick at mastering the technique of speed reading, and memorising.

Today's Flash word was DOMINIC. The whole paragraph read:

> DOMINIC please phone Father. Mother now accepts your apology. We all want to see you and understand. Love Lucy.

In his own office, Stentor—the desk littered with papers— used a pocket calculator, transcribing the message into numbers, then breaking them down into the familiar groups. Less than an hour later he had a translation, locked away secretly in his head.

STENTOR: expect contact and visit from your nephew Piotr Kashvar mining engineer. Piotr should reach you within one week. At present preparing for leave from site in Urals. CODEX.

So, at last it had come. After fifty years and more, his masters were keeping their promise. It was an odd sensation, for he knew this had to be an end to the life of Glubodkin: the only way of life known to him.

A rap at the door broke Stentor's train of thought. His Assistant, Polnikov, stepped into the room. There was a General to see him. The one who had just been appointed as Chairman's representative to the Standing Committee. Vascovsky. He wished to see the Comrade General.

Stentor nodded and smiled as Jacob Vascovsky entered with an apologetic word—"I was just passing. Hope I am not disturbing you, Comrade General, but I suddenly remembered you asked for my help, the other night, concerning your niece and nephew. You would still like to see them? Arrange visits?"

Stentor sat down quietly. Of course. But he did not believe they should be frightened. He was getting on in years, he knew. But, in family affairs, it was not his way to pressurise relations. If they did not wish to come to Moscow, he certainly would not demand it of them.

"I've always believed in family responsibility," Vascovsky sounded treacle smooth. "If you have their names and addresses . . ."

Of course he had their names. An address for his niece; but, as for Piotr, the nephew—"He is a mining engineer. The last I heard, he was in the Urals. You know how they move around?"

Vascovsky agreed. Nowadays, people in professions such as mining engineers were moved around more than soldiers.

"They are soldiers. The spearhead of Mother Russia's economic survival."

The two men stayed silent for a few moments, as though making individual decisions on weighty matters.

"Piotr . . . ?" Vascovsky queried.

"Have a quiet, friendly word with my niece first . . ." Stentor began, giving the Leningrad name and address. "Kashvar. That is my nephew's name, Comrade . . ." As he spoke, there was a light tap at the door, Oleg Zapad of Directorate T came into the room.

"Oh, I'm so sorry. I did not know you had such illustrious company, Volodya. I shall leave at once. The General," he indicated Vascovsky, "has the ear of the Chairman himself. Did you know that? They tell me you're always nipping into Dzerzhinsky Square to run errands for him." He grinned broadly.

"Come in, Oleg. You're always welcome here." Stentor looked pointedly at Vascovsky. "The Comrade General was about to leave anyway."

13

Big Herbie had his own small room off the complex, in the Warminster grounds. As always, he carried a small case of tapes, together with his miniature portable stereo unit and a lightweight headset. At night, and when not sitting in on the work—while the ringmasters were putting Michael Gold through his paces—Herbie would lie for hours: his mind a rest—or reading the Stentor dossier—while the works of Gustav Mahler flowed into his head.

Herbie soaked up the music he knew so well, while his subconscious worked away, distilling the massive amount o technique he would have to crowd into Michael's mind, before taking the lad for his final briefing with the Director General. There was so much, the bulk of which could only really be learned by extensive experience in the field. Herbie's job was to give young Gold the essentials; sifting methods, choosing only the things he might have to use on this particular job.

During the days, Big Herbie sat in on some of the tough sessions with the ringmasters. They were well named, as he knew from his own past experience. These were men whose agile minds battled against their pupil—putting him over hurdles: going progressively higher; and whipping him through hoops, which eventually blazed with fire.

By the time it came for Herbie Kruger to take over, Michael Gold knew Moscow in the dark. He could see it; smell it; hear it. He was as familiar with the transport systems of taxis, 'collective taxis', buses, trams and the underground—named so aptly after Lenin himself—as he was in London.

Gold also knew Stentor: his looks, habits, likes, dislikes, communication systems, idiosyncracies. He could get to the apartment on Kutuzovsky Prospekt blindfold, and was completely familiar with the best exits from the well-guarded building.

The ringmasters also ran him through the short cuts of elementary small arms' training, and self-defence. "There's no point in trying to give him the works," one of them told Herbie. "As long as he knows the standard hand weapons in use—the Makarov and that bloody big Stechkin—it's enough."

Herbie had grinned. "Good idea if you tell him which end is which; and where the *safety* is."

Basic holds; easy throws; the quick arts of physical deception, made up the self-defence course. Herbie had to turn away, and gaze silently out of the window as he listened to the hardest of the instructors telling the old, old story. Things changed little—"Remember, Mikhail," the leathery little instructor advised, "there's always a weapon to hand: a box of matches converts into a hard object that will break a nose;

137

a book of matches, if handled with the right misdirection, can be flared in the face; a pen will take out an eye . . ." These were things taught years ago; things Herbie had learned, in this very place; and the Director, also, many decades ago, during the Second World War.

The boy had to be as ready as they could make him. Lying on his bed, the night before starting his own two-day marathon of technique training, Herbie listened to the magnificent Mahler Eighth—the Symphony of a Thousand—and made the divisions in his mind: Anti-Surveillance, watching your own back; Throw-offs and Back-doubles; Misdirection; Emergency exits—just in case there was no other way. The Director could do the rest—the Piotr Kashvar briefing, and the way out with Stentor: to the Latvian coast *dacha*, and that final dash to Sweden.

Big Herbie slept fitfully that last night, knowing there would be a forty-eight hour stint ahead. Yet, in the shallow vales of sleep, the dreams came back—as they so often did. Dreams that should have been peaceful, but to Herbie, were nightmares—dreams of a Dürer print and ruby wine glasses with fluted stems; of the woman he had loved in East Berlin; of Vascovsky smiling like a head waiter, bending over him. Then, far off, the KGB man beckoning to him from the end of a tunnel, while a girl led Herbie nearer to Vascovsky, scattering paper: a paperchase, right into Vascovsky's waiting arms. He even heard the Russian's voice. "Come, Big Herbie. It's the only thing to do now. Come to us, man. It makes sense: ideologies are things of the past now. It's us against them." It did not seem odd that Vascovsky spoke to him in German.

He woke, in a boiling sweat, with the quiet voice still in his head. Dawn was breaking; and, with the light, Herbie saw traces of hammerheaded clouds through the window. The thunder came; and lightning. For the entire two days with Michael Gold it teemed with a rain so dense that you could only see clearly for ten yards or so from the windows.

Alexei would have been proud of his son: if only because he was such an apt pupil. Herbie telescoped knowledge, garnered from a lifetime, and the young man had it fast in his head as quickly as Kruger could pass it on: blanking his own doubts and worries from his mind.

"All the tricks of the trade, Michael. Remember, the whole time, that they're following you. They probably won't be near, but think it: that's what matters. Now, give me the signs. What you look for?"

Young Gold reeled them off, and even Worboys—who had remained quiet—was impressed. "Watch for the same car numbers; then look for the faces. Always watch the shoes, and wristwatches—teams change clothes, but often forget the small things."

"Yes, watch faces, Mickey. Always the faces. One turns up twice: you take a dive, okay?"

"Okay, Herbie."

So, and so. Such and such. On and on. At the end of it all, Michael Gold still appeared fresh. Herbie felt himself to be a wreck. Age, he thought. Over the hill, Herbie. Maybe Jacob Vascovsky is right. Time for *me* to take the dive and vanish. Maybe. See if this one works first.

They allowed twelve hours for rest, then it was a pile into the cars, with the dark windows, and a fast drive to London. The rain had disappeared, and—with the inconsistency of English weather—the sun shone, cool, from skies of pale blue wash.

Curry's boys were to have a go at Michael Gold, so Herbie let him out in Swallow Street. Gold knew they would be working the area, just as he knew there was a time limit: two hours to throw them and get to the safe flat near Kensal Green.

The safe flat was off the far side of Harrow Road, the once opulent building flanked now by an Indian Restaurant and a launderette. You had to go up two flights of stairs, past peeling walls, and the noise of Reggae music, rattling the cockroaches from the woodwork on the first landing. Behind the doors on the second turn of stairs, West Indian voices screamed—a man and a woman: it could end in murder, and the police might not know for days.

139

Safe flat, Herbie thought ("Whata fuck you know, maan. *I* know. You believe that now . . . ?" "Yo shut your fuckin' mouth, woman. I say what goes on here. My house. Get it. GET IT . . ." Then the sound of a blow).

"Charming neighbours we have here." Curry smiled as Herbie opened up the Chubb dead-lock. Curry's hand slid into sight again from inside his jacket. "Bit niffy as well, old cocker. Scents of Arabia and all that."

Herbie leaned his great bulk against the door frame. "Good hard-working people, Curry. Very hard working in this area. I tell you. I know. Been using this place a long time."

"Well, it'll remove any glamorous ideas from friend Gold—or Troilus, as I understand our beloved Director wishes him to be called. He's bloody good anyway. You'll be pleased to hear, he lost my boys. Boots, the Chemists, in Regent Street. Straight through and out. Thought they'd pick him up in Great Marlborough or Carnaby, but he just vanished. Well done Warminster."

"You only had your probationers on, though, Curry. Yes?"

"Actually, no. Mixed team. Thirty of them . . ."

Two sharp rings on the bell, heralded Michael Gold's arrival. He was hardly inside when the telephone squeaked, and Curry answered. "Our lord and master's on his way. Everything clean as starch." He congratulated Michael Gold whose face showed nothing but wary concentration.

The Director General arrived, as arranged, with young Worboys riding shotgun. He took no notice of the others, looking straight at Curry, to ask if they were clear. Curry nodded, and the Director introduced himself to Michael Gold. "We've a lot to do. If Curry would arrange coffee or something . . ."

Curry Shepherd cocked an eye at Worboys, who disappeared into a small kitchen while everyone else arranged themselves on the shabby furniture.

In the trade they called it the moment of truth: when the full news was laid on the agent. The Director General had a long briefing ahead. Michael Gold's cover as Kashvar, passwords; drops; what to do if they went to pieces, and he had to take a dive. Most important, there was the operation itself, once Stentor had agreed to go. The stations, trains, methods. What was to be done at the *dacha*, then the complex business of getting them out, and away—across the Baltic to Stockholm.

Big Herbie had heard it all. He knew that, at this moment, there was a merchant ship, under a flag of convenience, departing from Harwich, ostensibly to pick up aircraft parts from Stockholm. The *Artemis*. What the manifest did not show was the four Gemini inflatables, plus several crates of arms, brought on board under cover of darkness. Herbie thought also of the Island class patrol-craft, *Jersey*; now lying in the safety of Rosyth, under sealed orders which would eventually reveal a dash across the North Sea—not the most pleasant trip at speed, in this 195 foot, 925 tons vessel—through the Kattegat, and into the Baltic on a 'good-will-show-off' mission.

The Director began to speak, addressing Michael Gold personally, going through each stage with care; emphasising every point. On the small table, maps were spread out—street plans, drawings, timetables; while, put to one side, was a pile of documents: Gold's own passport with the necessary visas and papers; the Russian passport, and travel permits, in the name of Piotr Kashvar.

Herbie felt himself drifting from the briefing, the Director's voice becoming blurred, as words on paper will go out of focus when fatigue overcomes the reader. He was not nodding into sleep, however; merely letting his mind roam over Stentor's dossier, which he had spent much time studying when waiting for the two-day stint with Michael.

Reflecting now, Big Herbie was amazed at the amount of solid information they had taken from Stentor. In the early 1950s, with the war over, and his field work done, Stentor spent time with the cipher department at Moscow Centre, graduating quickly to other, more important, and useful, posts. Then, for two years, he contributed little. The First Chief Directorate had shipped him off to the training school, near Minsk, to do the full interrogation and debriefing course.

This turned into a blessing in disguise during the following decade, for Stentor became one of those who interrogated possible defectors; and many things Herbie had suspected, regarding the handling of certain doubles, now fell into place like pieces in a jigsaw.

Stentor's value, at the heart of the Soviet intelligence community, was not so much that of a provider of hard secret facts; more often he gave a stream of comment and warning from the very core of Moscow Centre. Page after page of the material from the 1960s appeared to be direct transcripts from interrogations, and briefings; together with the arterial thinking behind Soviet subversive and clandestine action.

The details are not known to me—Stentor reported in one lengthy statement—but I have little doubt the recent Cuban missile crisis (this was in 1963, before President Kennedy's assassination) was manufactured. Penkovsky is still alive, and not executed, as announced after the trial. It would seem that the US Government, the CIA, and the President went for what is called in vulgar language, 'a sucker ploy'. More on this when I have it.

Many times in his list of different lives, Herbie had been through case files. Nine out of ten were terse; even unimaginative, and dull: the signals kept short by necessity. But, with Stentor, while there were many Flash messages, in which a wealth of information was packed into a few words, the major reports were long and finely-honed. Sometimes, these reports read like lengthy letters to a friend, in which gossip mingled with hard, sometimes devastating, facts.

Big Herbie's mind swam away from the realities going on around him, in this dingy and uncomfortable room smelling of Indian food, and stale, musty, disuse. When he had been *in extremis*—last year in East Berlin—it was Stentor who had tried to warn the Director. Now, almost out of respect, he dragged himself back to the all-important briefing, knowing he was gambling with Stentor's life, as well as that of Michael Gold, and, perhaps, his own.

The Director continued his cold, weighty, monologue; punctuated, from time to time, with sharp, telling, questions, fired like darts at Michael. Herbie Kruger concentrated also. Tomorrow, this young man would be on his way to Moscow. Face to face with Stentor. Ready to bring him out: Troilus, not the betrayed son of King Priam, but Troilus the guide and protector of an old man who, while betraying his own country, had served another with great loyalty.

It was late and dark by the time all the questions were done, and the long briefing over. The Director left after Curry Shepherd, who went ahead to check on a clear coast for everyone. Herbie nudged Worboys on his way, and turned to Michael Gold.

"Do it well, Mickey. Break an arm and a leg, yes?"

Michael took the huge hand. "I'm scared shitless, Herbie." His palm was clammy.

Big Herbie shrugged. "So are we all. So we all know. Just do it well. If it goes wrong, dive out very fast. Take your Uncle Herbie's advice. Hell is full of heroes—old movie title: yes? Don't be a hero."

When Michael had gone, Herbie Kruger went to the window, watching from a chink in the curtain as the young man walked down the street. A girl came out of the shadows to offer herself, but Michael Gold kept on walking. Good boy, Kruger thought. That would be what he needed now: a bed and a woman; some small comfort before it all started. Insecure, with all the papers he carried; yet he would have wanted it.

With a start, Herbie realised it was what *he* wanted. Crossing to the telephone, which was completely sterile, he called the office, asking if he could be out of London for that night. The Director had just returned and they put him through. He did not see why the request should not be granted. "Nothing any of us can do until he's made contact. As they say in those dreadful old war films, 'It's hell—the waiting.'"

Herbie thanked him, asking if he could use the car and driver. He then made another call—to Lymington. Martha Adler was more than happy. "I'll cook us a late supper," she told him.

Herbie did not stop off at St. John's Wood, but had the driver take him straight down to Hampshire—pausing at a still-open chemist's shop to get a toothbrush and spare razor. If he had gone back to the flat, the whole thing might have been different.

14

THE ADVENT OF General Oleg Zapad, into Stentor's office at the Yasenevo Complex, had no immediate effect. In spite of Stentor's comments, and Zapad's wry sarcasm, Vascovsky did not leave. He merely lit a cigarette, sat on the corner of Stentor's desk and chatted amiably for ten minutes or so. Smooth he certainly was, but the smoothness was that of glue.

"Gives me the creeps; makes me expect a knife in my back, that one," Zapad said after Vascovsky finally left the office.

Stentor—General Vladimir Glubodkin—smiled with no hint of concern. "Oh, they come and go. The Chairman's ferrets. This one's already blotted his copybook, Oleg. Don't lose sight of that. When you screw something as badly as he did, there are three possibilities: they retire you to a pleasant spot where you can do no harm, you disappear to an unpleasant spot where you can do no harm; or they promote you and, possibly, set you the most difficult job going: you fail, and then it's curtains. Humour him."

They talked together for a time. Zapad had come with a small problem which needed sorting. He also required the advice of Special Section I's Chief regarding suspect documents on the US Space Programme.

When the Head of Department T finally left, Stentor got back to his own work, heavy in the 'In' tray—there were two reports to write, and three dossiers to examine. Within the next few days, General Glubodkin would be briefing three officers posted out of Russia—one to London and two to Washington. It was a part of his routine duties to personally brief officers leaving the country, and, in his role as Stentor, this became a work of major importance.

When the jobs were completed, Stentor's fingers strayed along the row of buttons on his desk console. Finally, as though making a great decision, he pressed firmly on the end button. A few moments later, a tap on the door heralded the arrival of a short dark-haired girl of around twenty-five. She was just starting to get a little plump around the waist, but Stentor rather liked that.

"Is there something I can do for you, Comrade General?" The girl was dressed in uniform shirt and skirt; a notebook and pencil were carried in her right hand, and she wore no jewellery.

Stentor smiled—a grin of great charm, which made him look more of a forty year old than his seventy-odd years. "I'm sure we'll think of something."

She smiled back and walked across the office, towards the door at the rear which led to his night quarters. As she passed through the door, the girl was already unbuttoning her shirt. Stentor followed, almost lazily, closing and locking the door behind them.

It was almost nine in the evening by the time the black Volga got him back to the apartment block. As soon as he opened the door, Stentor knew there was a visitor. His wife called out, as he went down the short hallway into the main room.

Vascovsky sat there, a glass of vodka in his hand, a self-confident smile of greeting on his lips.

"See who's come to visit," Stentor's wife gushed. "The General took me quite by surprise. If I'd known he was coming . . ."

"You would have baked a cake." Stentor grinned mischievously.

"*Chto?*"

"An old American song." Stentor slipped out of his coat. "Comrade General, you mind if I join you in a vodka? You seem to be haunting me these days."

"Just passing by."

"Like at my office this afternoon?"

"He brought me chocolates, see." Stentor's wife held up a massive box of Lindt. "Swiss. They make the best chocolates in the world."

"They once made the best wristwatches." Stentor poured himself four fingers and a thumb of vodka, and tossed it back, relishing the fire bursting in his throat. "Until the Japanese digitalised them almost overnight. It was like Hiroshima for the Swiss watchmakers."

"But, my dear General"—Vascovsky raised his glass—"you know, my friend, that *we* have always made the best watches—just as everything we do is best. It's what the proletariat believes." His chest heaved with a silent laugh.

Stentor grunted, walking over to take Vascovsky's glass. "So, twice in one day, General. You are seeking us out . . ."

"And why not?" snapped Stentor's wife. "Jacob is a good friend. They are both good friends, Jacob and Yekaterina."

"Ah, so we are to be comrades and friends . . ." Stentor first filled Vascovsky's glass, and then topped up his own, despite his wife's outstretched arm and tapping foot.

"When you hear what he's done for you, you'll dance another kind of jig."

Stentor was pleased to notice his hand did not even tremble. Passing Vascovsky his vodka, he finally took his wife's glass, and asked what the General—Jacob—had done for them?"

"You're to have a visitor. He's asked what *you*'d never ask, because *you*'ll ask no favour of anyone."

Stentor raised an eyebrow, in query at Vascovsky, who smoothed his already sleek grey hair and nodded. "Your niece is coming to visit," he announced.

"There." From Stentor's wife. "Your little Glasha from Leningrad."

Stentor tried to put on an air of surprise. "Is this true?"

146

Vascovsky gave a tiny nod. "Aglaya Mikhailovna Morozova."

Even down to the patronymic, Stentor thought. Aloud he asked if Ivan and the children were also coming?

Vascovsky made a helpless gesture. Alas, Ivan could not take time from his work; and the children should not come out of school. But his niece would arrive—probably in a couple of days, maybe three. She would stay for a week.

"Then I'll know for sure." Stentor's wife pouted.

"Know what, woman?"

"If she's a niece, or a mistress."

Stentor was truly angry. "You stupid woman. You old idiot. My niece. God knows it took me long enough to find her."

"Ah."

Vascovsky stirred. "There's something else. I should visit the shops. Get plenty of food and drink in store."

"Something else? Oh?" From both Stentor and his wife.

"Your nephew. You know, General: the one who works in the Urals. The mining engineer: Piotr Kashvar?"

Stentor put on an inquisitive face. Inside his body, he could feel the heart pounding; blood sweeping to his head. God, he thought. Heaven save me. For a moment he was convinced a heart attack was imminent.

Vascovsky continued to talk, and Stentor heard him as though through some kind of barrier: like a fog of the ears— red fog. "I told you I'd do what I could. You should see your relatives. Happily, your nephew seems to have had the same idea. I traced him, and telephoned his superior. Piotr applied for leave a couple of days ago. Apparently I just missed him. He left the camp early this evening. He had leave due in any case. Rejoice, my friend; he told his colleagues that he was going to visit his uncle in Moscow. So, your nephew, Piotr, should be here tomorrow night."

"Why . . . ?" Stentor began. In his head the thoughts whirled, fragmented, and came together in a tangible pattern, like a kaleidoscope. So, they had done it. Tomorrow night, the nephew would come; and Vascovsky was waiting. He

147

would dangle them; then haul on the line. It was a matter of agility now. Speed, when the nephew arrived. Great speed.

"Is this really true?" Surprising how training would out. Not a trace of the agitation he felt inside. "I'm going to see them?"

"I'm glad you're pleased." Vascovsky sounded genuinely happy—and why should he not be? "Yes, you should see your nephew by tomorrow night; and your little Glasha within a couple of days." He tossed back his vodka. "Now, having broken the good news, I had better go to my Katya. She does not like to be kept waiting."

At the door he said, "I'd also like to have the chance of meeting your relatives while they're here. Please invite me, my friend."

Stentor told him that he was welcome any time. "Invite yourself, General; and, thank you. As my wife says, I would never have pressed either of them to come."

"I didn't have to push the nephew," Vascovsky snapped, and was gone, striding down the passage towards the elevator.

*   *   *

At about the same time as Big Herbie Kruger was driving through the New Forest, Scandinavian Airlines Flight SK528 made its final turn, lining up with the main runway of Stockholm's Arlanda Airport. The giant A300 Airbus wheeled its way over the flat, thick, forests and lakes; touching down gently, then turning from the runway to taxi down the ramp into the disembarkation bay.

Among the 190 passengers who walked through the quiet, and orderly, modern airport building, nobody queried the four British businessmen—travelling in separate pairs. Certainly, for men who carried passports stating they were sales managers, or executives, of two British-based concerns, these men looked exceptionally fit and well built.

Within the hour, all four were registered, and booked into rooms at the Grand Hotel, overlooking the harbour. Only one of these visitors made a telephone call. It was to a London number, and the line was open for less than two minutes.

148

In the Secret Intelligence Service Headquarters at Century House, near Westminster Bridge, the Duty Officer took a call, on the secure line, from the Special Air Service HQ in Herefordshire.

When the Director General arrived at his office on the following morning there would be a flimsy lying among the other signals in his tray. One word—TIVOLI—would tell him that the two pairs of men, from the Special Air Service, were in place; ready, when needed, to make their dash, to cover the lifting of Stentor.

*   *   *

It was like slaking a thirst that had built up over a long period. Martha gave Herbie a light supper—melon, which she remembered he liked; followed by a dish of scrambled eggs, liberally laced with chopped smoked salmon and onion. They drank champagne—"A treat," she said. "After all, I suppose it's some kind of celebration: a visit in the night from the great Big Herbie."

Herbie forked a mouthful of the eggs, took a sip of the champagne, and gave her a tired grin. Throughout the meal he remained oddly silent, to the extent that Martha Adler twice asked him if anything was wrong.

"Just the usual, Matti. Long day. Hard decisions. Tension and stress. Like the old days, remember?"

She remembered all too well. The odd paradox was that she had banished Herbie from her bed then. It was best that way. He often admitted it later; for she was more use to him, in the old days, when her lovers were either ranking Russians, or government officials close to the heart of the Communist Democratic Republic of East Berlin. It had only been when Herbie began to get serious with the other woman that Martha Adler had recognised the symptoms of jealousy within herself.

She stretched an arm across the table, and took his hand. "It's funny, Herbie. There I was, screwing around, working for you; yet I always resented her."

Again, Herbie said nothing. He merely smiled. The ways of women were far too complex for him. All he knew was that he needed comfort now.

As though sensing it, Martha's hand tightened on his. "Is it bad? A really difficult one?"

He nodded.

"You want to talk?"

Yes, of course he wanted to talk, though he could never say it aloud; or give her the facts. In honesty, Big Herbie longed to tell her everything—Stentor, the old man; and the young, inexperienced one, he was sending off, in the morning, to do the impossible. Michael Gold—Troilus—had become *his* agent. The rules, and all the years of field experience, told him never to become emotionally involved with those you controlled. Experience had also taught Big Herbie that, for him at least, this was asking the impossible.

The Director General could go on all night to Gold—telling him they would not let him down; that he was different; if anything went wrong they would not deny him. But Herbie knew, again from the deep well of experience, that, if it went wrong, they would abandon Michael like a sinking ship. He had always found this particular hypocrisy difficult to live with.

But now, Martha made him feel young again. He was the old Herbie of the late 1950s and early '60s—and, heaven knew, she had the ability to work the magic. Martha Adler's memory had always been a strong point. However many lovers she had taken, since that short period with Herbie, she could still recall his tastes.

They took to each other's bodies as though nothing had ever separated them—time, other lovers, age, or circumstance. Perhaps it was a trick of memory—or of the light, as the Firm would have had it—but Herbie sensed that Martha Adler was the very best physical experience of his life.

On her part, Martha appeared to feel, and react, in the same way Their loving was tender, caring, and then wildly passionate; subsiding, at length, into the caress of a satisfied aftermath.

They lay close, and naked, afterwards; smoking and not looking at one another. They talked, but not about what had just happened. They spoke of the long past, and of the even longer future. Then silence. It was comfort; a feeling of stability for Herbie; sleep for Martha, cuddled close to his warm and fleshy chest.

But sleep would not come for Big Herbie. Martha moaned, dreaming, then started to cry out, to mutter—"No . . . no . . . no . . . I can't do it to him . . ." Silence again. This time Herbie floated into dreams. He was on board an aircraft, with Michael Gold; yet not with him, for he could see the pattern of the skies, and their aircraft persisting on its course towards another plane—silver and bright in the sun. Behind them a swarm of black snarling fighters. Their aircraft, the silver plane, and the fighters all on a collision course, and no way in which the ultimate horror could be avoided.

Herbie woke with a start, aware of what was going on in his subconscious; and of other noise: Martha weeping, clawing at his shoulder.

"Matti, what is it? What's wrong?" For a few moments he thought she was crying in her sleep; but now Herbie saw she was awake, looking at him, her face a mixture of concern and pain. Herbie repeated the question, but she simply bit her lip, shaking her head wildly. He had the same sensation as before. There was something very wrong with Martha Adler. He should prise it from her now. Force out the truth. So many times, Herbie had seen that look—the moment before a subject let go; into the darkness of disclosing everything.

He propped himself on one elbow. "Martha, tell me." Their need had been mutual: for him an escape, burying himself in a woman who happened to be an old and trusted colleague. For Martha, another kind of escape. Both of them wanting to be lost in the act of loving sexual relief.

"Tell me. God in heaven, Martha, it's me. *Schnitzer*. Blunder. Herbie. What is it?"

And again, as if on cue, the telephone started to ring—it seemed to be shouting with great urgency.

151

"Sorry, Herbie." He knew it was Curry Shepherd before even hearing the voice. "I've asked the car to come for you now. Monitoring your mail. You'd have picked it up last night, at the flat if you'd gone in. My boys collected it this morning."

"You got the keys as well, Curry?" Herbie heard his own voice become very harsh.

"Sorry Herbie. Rules of the game. Whoever your postman was he came personally. You've got another tape, and it seems the DG feels this one's very important."

Rage boiled up; then reduced to a simmer. They still could not trust him. The mail, telephones, personal surveillance, even stealing the private moments here. "Go to hell, Curry. I'll be ready. Ten minutes." He slammed the receiver down with a violence that made even Martha Adler jump, as she stood in the bedroom door, naked, the tears still damp on her cheeks, and her eyes an angry red.

"I got to go, Matti. Stay in. Stay here, please. I get back quick. You don't have to tell anyone else. I come back and talk. It'll be okay, I promise. Whatever, it'll be okay. You promise me, yes?"

"I'm not going anywhere, Herbie."

He dressed, cursing; shaved, cursing even more; keeping up a flow of talk, as though Martha could store it and hold on while she was left alone.

The car was outside, waiting. At the door, Martha finally spoke, "Herbie, thank you. Thanks for everything—for the whole thing. Berlin. Everything."

"You okay?"

"I've told you—I'm not going anywhere."

It left a sour sense in Herbie's mind. Now he was certain. There was something there, in Martha, with which she could not cope alone.

To his surprise, the driver pulled up at the Crown Hotel, in Lyndhurst, on the London edge of the New Forest.

"Came down specially, cocker. Brief you before you see the DG."

Herbie waved him aside as he settled into the car.

Curry leaned forward, pulling the soundproof partition closed.

"You keeping a twenty-four hour watch on that woman?" Herbie looked at Curry, his face vacant; dull.

"Again, sorry, Herbie; but yes. You did ask . . ."

"I'm asking again. You trust your people there?"

Yes, Curry had good people on the spot.

"Then tell them to be extra careful. Tell them to watch her. She mustn't leave until I've seen her again."

"No sweat. I'll get a message off now." He re-opened the partition, telling the driver to stop at the first public phone booth he saw. When it was done, Curry came back into the car. "Tight as the proverbial drum. You expecting trouble?"

"I'm cautious, Curry. You know that. Well—cautious most of the time."

Curry gave a sage nod, producing a headset, and Sony miniature stereo from his briefcase. "The tape's in. All ready for you. As I said, you were meant to get this last night. The boys picked it up this morning. DG says 'Listen, mark and inwardly digest.' Then he wants to do a King Arthur—old round table conference."

It was the 'Resurrection'—Mahler's Second Symphony. Four bars only, before Vascovsky's voice purred through the headphones.

"Herbie, my friend. It is time for me to put all the cards on the table—as the English say. My superiors know I am in touch with you. They do not know how; nor do they know what I am really proposing. As far as they're concerned, I'm trying to lure you—which, in a way, is true. I know your own situation must be precarious—I've already spoken about that: the lack of trust, which will dog you for all your days now.

"In some ways I am in a similar situation. Yes, they've promoted me, and given me a job to do. That work is almost completed. In fact I should have it tied up before the week's out. After that? Who knows? They may decide I've served my purpose. My feeling is that I shall be posted to some

153

backwater; and that does not suit my style, any more than the lack of trust, from your own superiors, can suit you.

"I have some ideas about this. Enemies can become closer than old friends. You remember Ursula, Herbie?" There was a small, humourless laugh on the tape. "Of course. How could you ever forget her? She could be with us. You, Ursula, myself, and my own love—Yekaterina—who you've yet to meet.

"Now, I can't—dare not—put my proposals on tape. It must be a personal meeting. Face to face. I will show trust. I will meet you anywhere reasonable, in Europe, at twenty-four hours' notice. There. That's trust. I'll show myself; risk myself; for I'll come alone, with no hired guns—if you'll do the same.

"Name the place. Give me the day. Old telephone double-talk—the day you give me will be the day before the real one. Time? Give me two hours in advance of the real time. Okay? I'll come alone. I do not expect you to believe me as you listen to this; but we both have to trust someone. How do you pass the message? That's easier than you think, old friend. Easy and untraceable. Just tell our mutual friend Martha Adler. She'll know exactly what to do."

Big Herbie snatched the headset from his ears. "Stop. Turn the car round. We must go back."

Curry rested a hand on his knee. "It's okay, Herbie. No panic. We've really got her sewn up. She's not going to run away. I've heard the tape."

"Bloody fool," Herbie bellowed. "That's exactly what she's going to do. Get back there, or you'll have one dead source on your hands. Turn round, I'm going in there. Just turn around, and don't let your goons within a mile of her door."

Curry sighed. "Okay, cocker, but you take responsibility."

"I take your throat out if we don't get back fast. Responsibility? Of course. She *is* my bloody responsibility."

As the car swung violently through the Cadnam round-about, heading back towards Lymington, Big Herbie glanced at his watch, praying they had time. It was exactly 11.45. At

Heathrow, Michael Gold's flight would just be leaving for Moscow. Silently, Herbie wished him good luck. Break an arm and a leg.

15

THE ILYUSHIN 62, of Aeroflot's Flight SU242—London–Moscow—was cleared for take-off on Heathrow's 28R runway. The four Soloviev turbofans wound up to full power, and the brakes came off.

Michael Gold, sitting in the mid-section of the Russian aircraft, felt his stomach tighten as the ground began to slide away below him. They passed over Staines' Reservoir, and Michael tipped the seat back, reaching for his cigarettes.

His mind was clear, and the Director General's briefing remained in his head like a tape he could switch on at will. He was visiting Moscow purely as a tourist. Around him, the other members of the group chatted excitedly. The woman sitting next to him fiddled in her handbag, checking travel documents for the eighth time since they had boarded the aircraft. In due course she would engage him in conversation, and he would have to respond. "Try not to be too aloof with the rest of the tour. But don't get close," the DG had cautioned. "I know it's difficult, but it's possible, and you mustn't be conspicuous, either by your friendliness, or by being too stand-offish."

They had assured him that going in a group tour would mean less chance of thorough, and inquisitive, checks at the airport. That was the last thing anyone wanted; for, while it was unlikely the Russian documents would be discovered by a normal examination, the clothes would certainly be spotted very quickly.

Everything in Michael Gold's case was available in Russia, including the clothes on his back, and the case itself. His clothing was modest—either Eastern-Bloc-produced, or from normal Russian import stock. He carried nothing that could link him with either *Beryozka*, or other privileged stores.

They would be at Sheremetievo Airport by six-thirty, local time. If lucky, Michael thought, he would be settled into the Intourist National Hotel by seven-thirty. After that, the night would start in earnest.

*   *   *

Big Herbie broke the door down with his own shoulder, which stayed bruised for several days.

She was stretched across the bed; still breathing, but obviously near to a coma. The small bottle of tablets lay empty on the night table, and there was no note. Only the empty tumbler smelling of whisky. Herbie turned her, face down, over the side of the bed, and walked quickly to the tiny kitchen, in search of salt and warm water. Curry was already telephoning for an ambulance; but when it arrived, Herbie still held her—head back—trying to force a saline mixture down her throat. It took Curry, and the two ambulance men, to get her body from him.

Herbie insisted on being in the ambulance. Curry, after another fast call to London, followed in the car. The Director had simply told him to 'nobble the quack'; so nobble the quack he would.

Herbie Kruger's usual calm had disappeared, when Curry saw him at the Infirmary, which was the nearest place for them to take her. Later, they said, she would be moved to the local hospital; for the Infirmary was kept for the aged, and those whose condition was considered terminal.

"They say she'll be okay, Herb. But why the fuss? She doubled on us. I mean, I know you were fond, and all that, but . . ."

"I warned him . . . I told the DG." Herbie was very quiet now, his hands moving a great deal, fingers locking and interlocking. "That's why you had to step up the watchers, Curry. I knew it—knew she'd doubled; knew she couldn't live with it. Christ, you know the games they play: the long arm; death in the night; no escape; and there must have been something else as well. A relative, perhaps. The bastards had some hold, or she would have told me. She came very near to it this morning; and I can guess why. If I was supposed to get the tape last night, she must have been expecting a message from me. She wept this morning. No message, so she had failed. If she had failed, they would do whatever they promised. Someone. They have someone?"

It was almost two hours before a doctor appeared. Martha had taken enough Nembutal to kill an elephant, but they'd got most of it out of her. She would sleep for twenty-four hours, and wake with a nasty hangover, and a worse depression. What about the police? Curry took the doctor to one side and, to use the Director's phrase, nobbled him. Then they arranged for three of Curry's ladies to stay on—he revealed they had a team of four men and five women in Lymington. One would be constantly at Martha's bedside.

Herbie could return tomorrow. In his mind, this meant the small hours. In the car, Curry confided that they would probably bring Martha back to the clinic in London, as soon as she was fit to move.

*　　　*　　　*

The Moscow Flight landed ten minutes late—just after six-thirty in the evening—and the group with which Michael Gold was travelling passed through the usual formalities without a hitch: except for an interminable wait at the passport clearance desk.

Their passports had been taken from them on the aircraft. It was the Russian way, they were told. Now, as he stood in the queue, waiting for the document to be returned, for the first time Michael felt a true hint of vulnerability. A post-graduate student of foreign languages, yet he was really an innocent abroad. More than that—an innocent caught up in the clandestine trade of diplomacy.

"Gold?" The passport officer did not smile as he looked at Michael, comparing the face with the photograph. It reminded Michael of first days at school, when one went in fear of everyone in authority.

"Yes."

"Michael Gold. He speak foreign language?" The officer's English was not exceptional. "No. You *study* foreign language." Still no smile.

In his passport, under 'Occupation', it simply said *Student*. Michael's throat went dry. "How . . . ?" he began; then thought better of it.

The officer flourished the tourist office form. "Here it says you study foreign language. What language?"

"German. French . . ." Michael paused; then, in bad Russian, with a distinct English accent, "Also a very little Russian."

The officer still did not smile. "Like me a very little English, eh?" He held his forefinger and thumb a fraction apart. "You must practise Russian while here." He wagged a finger, "But not too much with our girls, ah?" For the first time, there was the hint of a smile, then he waved Michael on, handing back the passport. "Have good time in Russia."

"*Spaceeba*—Thank you." Still with the accent in all the wrong places.

There were some twenty people in Michael Gold's group, shepherded by a pair of Intourist guides—a thin man in his late forties, with the air of a harassed schoolmaster; and the most stunning blonde Michael Gold had ever seen. But, then, most blondes were, to Gold, stunning on first sight. Though this one was truly exceptional—more Scandinavian than Russian: tall, slender, with a tilted nose, lips that issued a thousand invitations, and large eyes, deep blue and twinkling with what could very well be mischief of the most pleasant kind. She wore Western style make-up, and the blonde hair hung, heavy, to her shoulders and bounced—like other attractive parts of her anatomy—as she moved.

The guides spoke excellent, if not correct, English. The group would be taken to change money now; then there was a bus ready to carry them to the hotel.

"It is very good. One of the best hotels in Moscow," the girl told them, her voice pitched low, and a shade husky. Michael Gold was lost, almost immediately, in dreams of conquest.

The National Hotel, though extensively modernised, still gives one the impression of entering a Victorian railway terminus—with its marble arches; high, ornate ceiling, and huge chandeliers.

Michael was pleased to find that he automatically registered a sense of familiarity once they entered the city. The workouts at Warminster had provided him with such detailed knowledge that he could now feel Moscow embracing him like an old friend.

The Director, and his advisers, had chosen the tour well— particularly by placing him at the National; for the hotel stands on Marx Prospekt, behind the far end of Red Square. A very central base of operations.

Once again they had to stand in line. This was another chore which called for the surrender of passports. "They will be returned to you later, or in the morning." The Intourist girl seemed to smile directly at him, and Michael imagined there was some special significance when she repeated, to each tourist, "Tonight you are free. Dinner is served until eleven-thirty, and tomorrow we all meet here, in the lobby, at nine-thirty sharp, for the first day's tour."

Michael smiled back—that glazed and set grin of the sexually smitten—then picked up his own case, in spite of the porter who was about to reach for it, took the token for his key, and walked across the polished hallway to the elevator. He was on the sixth floor, which he considered convenient, exchanging the token for his key at the little desk, manned by a severe looking Floor Lady dressed in black.

The room was functional, bright, and reasonably pleasant. From the windows you could see out over Red Square—GUM, the Lenin Mausoleum; with St. Basil's clearly visible in the cold city lights.

They had told him to move as quickly as possible. "You have to spend as long as you can with him on the first night," they said. "It's essential he understands there's a time limit to the operation; just as it's most urgent for him to know the exact chess moves." Some of the moves would obviously have to be invented by Stentor himself. "He has to set up his own *modus operandi*, for leaving the city without attracting too much attention." The Director General had said Stentor would almost certainly choose the weekend, and advise Michael regarding the method of travel—whether by rail, car, or air. It would probably be air. There were plenty of regular internal flights.

Michael worked fast, unpacking, and going through the routine they had dinned into him. Putting on his overcoat, and the fur hat he had brought against the cold nights, he quietly left the room. His personal first phase had taken only seven minutes.

Out on the street it was as cold as an English mid-winter. It was not yet spring for Moscow. In a month or so it would be warm and pleasant—the so-called urban heat island effect keeping the city temperature above average.

Michael walked steadily, though not fast enough to cause suspicion; knowing exactly where to go, and pleased that he had not been asked to do this in the middle of winter—when unacclimatised lungs can become so affected by the cold, that long walks outside are impossible.

He reached the Marx Prospekt underground station, and followed the great arched underpass to the Sverdlov Square platform. When changing his money, Michael had made certain he had a few five-kopeck pieces, one of which he fed into the access machine. Three minutes later he was riding the train out to Airport Station.

Nobody appeared to take much notice of him, and he had followed all the initial precautions—doing two double-backs, and three pauses. Inexperienced he may be, but Michael considered that, so far, he was clean.

160

There was one nasty moment, on disembarking from the train at the Airport stop, when a uniformed policeman asked for identity papers. Michael had not wanted this to happen before doing the quick change act, but handed over the Russian passport and work documents, only to be ordered brusquely to produce a *spravka*—the authorisation permit, to prove that he was allowed to be away from his work in the Urals. As the officer glanced at the papers, so Michael committed the man's face to memory. He did not wish to bump into this officer twice that night. A taxi took him to the airport.

He did the quick change in one of the public toilets of the departure area: unbuttoning his coat, pulling the neatly folded soft plastic holdall from inside his shirt, and filling it with the overcoat and fur hat. He would feel the cold through the light raincoat he had worn under the greatcoat, but that would only be a minor discomfort. Clear-glass spectacles, and a denim cap completed the effect. He walked from the convenience feeling, oddly, the complete Russian.

Michael used a public telephone booth, dialling the number he knew by heart. Stentor answered on the fourth ring.

*   *   *

"The situation with the Adler woman changes matters, of course." The Director was working exceptionally late, seated, with arms folded, behind his desk. "But I still need your views, Herbie."

Big Herbie sat directly opposite the DG; while Tubby Fincher, young Worboys, and Curry Shepherd were ranged around the room—all fairly close to the desk. The curtains were drawn, and the room illuminated from the striplight above the desk, and a couple of large table lamps. In one corner a blank TV screen glowed, linked directly to the Communications & Cryptanalysis—'C & C'—offices, on the top floor of the building. Any Flash information would show on the screen: including an early warning of an 'Eyes Only' for the Director.

Big Herbie shrugged. "You know what I know. They've obviously got something very heavy on Martha. We go back a long way. Normally she would have told me straight out. She's not a natural double, I'd stake anything on that. The suicide attempt. Unnatural. Something very heavy. She couldn't live with the Judas thing."

"I'll buy that." The Director was like a statue: not even a muscle moving in his face. "What really interests me is Vascovsky. You think it's genuine? A dangle? What? You think he really believes you'd go for what he's peddling, Herbie?"

Herbie allowed a mocking smile. "Do you?"

"Not now," the Director volleyed back. "A few months ago . . . Well . . . maybe. But not now."

"I tell you the truth,"—Herbie looked around at the others, as though he was hoping someone might offer him a drink—"If I thought General Vascovsky was on the level, I would have considered it."

There was a sharp intake of breath from Tubby Fincher. Herbie's head whipped around. "Yes, Tubby. I'd have considered it. For the very reasons he's given. I spend my life in the business, okay. Good. One mistake and everyone thinks I pull the pin on loyalty. Like a fucking leper, I feel—if you excuse me, sir. This job's the end anyway. I do this and go private, right? Better tell you all now. But I'll do the job first, and do it properly."

"Herbie?" A note of warning from the Director.

"Who's to stop me? Maybe I open a little shop somewhere. Sell music—records, tapes, listen to Mahler all day, and read. If Jacob Vascovsky could be trusted he's right. Maybe he thinks I'm ripe for plucking; that I get so pissed off with the cold shoulder here, I go and listen to his bright ideas for a quiet future—what's left of it."

"But you don't think he's got those kind of plans, do you?" Curry Shepherd lit a cigarette.

"You think he believes he could entice you again, Herbie?" Tubby Fincher sounded almost friendly after the outburst. "You know he's not safe. What's he really after?"

162

"You tell me." Herbie laughed. "Plain as the nose—your nose, Tubby. Bastard wants to lift me. Like always. Playing it long; Vascovsky's a gambler."

The Director looked around the room. "We use the situation in any way?"

"You would let me go? If it suited a purpose you'd allow it?" Herbie sounded incredulous. Then he smiled his dopey, stupid, grin. "Of course. You let anyone do anything if there's gain: if the scenario works, you let me go."

"It might just be wise to set it up." The Director kept the enigmatic and frigid expression. "Not alone, of course, Herbie—you're not allowed to operate out of this country in any case. A dozen of Curry's goons; maybe more, so they can't snatch you . . ."

"Snatch *him*?" Curry queried. "We snatch Vascovsky?"

Slowly, the Director shook his head. "No. Snatching would bring down the wrath of diplomatic incident. Draw him. Draw Vascovsky off Stentor and young Michael Gold for a few days. Where'd you suggest, Herbie?"

"I have to talk with Martha first. In the morning."

"It's morning already, dear heart." Curry stretched like an animal.

"Yes." The Director still calm. "But, all things being equal, where'd you suggest?"

Herbie did an impression with his hands—a couple of scales. "Paris. I could work him in Paris."

"And you?" The DG turned to Curry. "Could you handle Paris?"

"Always could in the old days." Curry gave a pleasant grimace, running a hand lightly over his hair. "Used to enjoy Paris in the old days. Yes, that would be okay, as long as Herbie doesn't try to be clever. You try that, cocker, and they'll snatch you quick as a cat."

"I talk with Martha first."

"Yes, but if you're happy, then perhaps . . ." The TV screen flickered into life. They all turned to see the computer read out come up.

MOST URGENT DIRECTOR OR G STAFF EYES
ONLY. TROILUS.

"It'll be down in a moment." The urgency undisguised in the
Director's voice. Tubby Fincher was already halfway across
the room to intercept the cipher clerk outside.

It took fifteen minutes for the decipher—Tubby and the
DG closeted in the office, while the other three waited outside.

Fincher called them back, and nobody needed telling that
the news was not good. The closed faces of the Director, and
his ADC, spoke of disaster; though the DG, as usual, put it to
them as an understatement. "We seem to have a problem
with Stentor, gentlemen," he announced.

*   *   *

The thinking behind Michael's journey out to the airport—
to do the quick change, and make his first call to Stentor as
the nephew, Piotr Kashvar—was an elementary precaution.
Stentor's telephone was certainly wired. They also probably
had an intercept system, to trace the origin of call. Kashvar
had just arrived in Moscow, and the airport was a better bet
than a railway station.

There had been only the slightest pause, a tiny break, in
Stentor's reply when Michael introduced himself: then the
effusive full flood. Piotr must come straight over. Did he
know how to get to them? Where would he stay? He was
welcome at Stentor's apartment. Come as quickly as possible.

So, Michael again rode the Moscow subway, passing
through its great stations with their marble and ornate
designs; their statues, chandeliers and paintings. He changed
platforms, once more, at Sverdlov Square, and sat back,
adjusting to the new smells, noises, and background of the
city and its people ("Feel yourself to be one of them," the
ringmasters had cautioned. "Be Russian; think it; act it.").
So, at last, Piotr Kashvar arrived at Koutouzovskaya Station,
and walked the few hundred metres to Stentor's apartment
block, where the guards asked for his papers, and telephoned
up to Stentor who urged them to let his nephew in.

All the way there, Michael had double-checked. He did not seem to have any tail, or team, on his back.

*   *   *

A few miles away, high in the Kalinin Prospekt block, Vascovsky's telephone rang. They were halfway through dinner—alone tonight, and eating, with the rest of the evening planned by unspoken, mutual consent: sucking the juice from prime artichokes; savouring tender lamb cutlets, cooked in herbs; spooning in the sensual, delicate flavour and texture of zabaglione; drinking a dry pleasant White Burgundy from Sauvignon de St. Bris. Both Jacob and Yekaterina Vascovsky had creaking bedsprings in mind.

Vascovsky answered the persistent ring. It was his own monitoring room.

"The nephew's arrived. Just phoned from the airport." The news came from Vitali Badim, a small, bald-headed major—one of Vascovsky's most trusted aides.

Vascovsky spoke low and quickly. "Set the teams up near the apartment. Mark him. Report anything unusual. Right?"

Badim acknowledged, smiling to himself. This whole business had occupied his superior's mind and concentration to a high degree, verging on obsession. Now, at the moment of breaking, the Comrade General obviously had other things on his mind.

Major Badim picked up another telephone and spoke to the officer in charge of surveillance. Once the nephew was inside the apartment block, on Kutuzovsky Prospekt, they had him bottled. When he left, they could follow his every move. Neither Badim, nor the surveillance officer, chose to question why the nephew of such an exalted officer of the KGB should be of interest. They simply did as they were trained. As far as the surveillance teams were concerned they would do the job very well indeed.

*   *   *

Stentor's wife wanted to fill the boy with food and drink— "Stuff him like a goose," she said. But Stentor would have

165

none of it. Piotr was tired, and had said he would not impose on them. ("Though how a nephew who has never met his uncle until today can impose, I have no idea.") Some salt beef, beetroot salad, and vodka would do fine. That's what Piotr wanted, and that's what he would get—particularly the vodka: as much vodka as he could hold.

In the meantime, Stentor told his wife, he wanted the boy to himself. There was family business to discuss. Family business from the past, and nothing to do with women. The wife went away muttering and cursing like a trooper, though she smiled to herself as she cut the salt beef. Her husband's happiness showed on his face. It was good.

In his private room, however, things were not good. Stentor told Michael they were safe. "I personally sweep this room; and there's no way they can get directional microphones on us."

"We have a lot to do," Michael began, but Stentor held up a hand. "No," he said.

"But . . ."

Stentor smiled. It really was like being with an uncle, Michael thought. "Look, sir." He began to argue. "They're close to you. Vascovsky's very close to you. We have to get you out . . ."

"Please listen." A hint of pleading in the old man's voice. You could tell he was not asking favours. It ill-suited him. "I know you are at great risk: that you want to get on; and that your superiors want to honour their promises to me—what are the plans, by the way?"

In four or five quick sentences, Michael Gold outlined the whole thing—the escape to the *dacha*; the British patrol-boat that would be in the Baltic; the SAS team ready in Stockholm—to be picked up by the merchant ship, then dropped with their Gemini inflatables. "One of our people will come alone in a Gemini," he finished. "If we're there on time, he'll take us off, land us on the patrol-boat, and we'll have you under cover; on the way to London in no time."

Stentor smiled patiently, nodding. "All clever. Not fool-proof, but clever. We would probably have got away with it."

166

"Have?"

"It's simple." Stentor gave him a look tinged with a weight of sadness. "I can't come." The words had a finality about them: the mind made up; no arguments.

"But, sir . . ."

"Just listen to me; then, perhaps, you'll understand. At least I have to see you safe, and back in your own country." The old man patted his knee gently.

There was a pause while Stentor's wife came in with a great tray of food and drink. It was obvious she wanted to stay, but Stentor shooed her out, saying there would be plenty of time, later, for her to talk with Piotr. She went grudgingly, still muttering to herself.

"That's one of the reasons I can't leave," Stentor told him when the door was closed. "Just one." He laughed. "Oh, there are days when I've thought—longed—for the moment to come: the call from your people, for me to leave Moscow and travel to London. Sometimes she drives me crazy; so it would be an initial relief. But only for a time. We're used to each other and I've always returned to her. Yet that is not the only thing. Ever since I realised the good General Vascovsky was breathing down my neck, I have thought of little else— getting out in one piece. The game is finished, I know that, my nephew. London's had its last messages from me, and I feel I've done good work for them, through the years. It's over. As I say, I've thought of little else. Meditated—that's the word—I've meditated for long, and come to certain conclusions. They are not easy—but nothing is in this life, nephew Piotr, or whatever your real name is." He poured vodka, raising a glass in toast, then passed food to Michael before he continued—"There was a Christian mystic—St. John of the Cross: you know of him?"

Michael said he had heard the name, but was not a Christian. Stentor doubted if he was a Christian either. "However, I do read a great deal. This St. John of the Cross, you should read; for his work can be applied to many ways of life. His greatest mystical poem cannot be unknown to you— *Noche Obscura del Alma: The Dark Night of the Soul.* The soul must pass through a darkness; a terrible period of non-belief, and the torment of questioning, until one reaches a state of union with God. In many ways I have, for the past days, been experiencing a dark night of my own soul . . ."

Michael concentrated, eating in silence as he listened. The salt beef and beetroot brought back waves of nostalgia. Home, in the old days, when his father had been away. The joy of his return, and the meals they had shared. He took a swig of vodka. The nostalgia deepened and with it a flavour of depression.

"It is not a question of belief in any political ideal, you understand." Stentor poured more vodka. "The dark night of my soul is connected with my faith in Russia, not in God. You see, I am Russian; born, bred, through and through. To leave Russia now would be a worse betrayal than that which, I am certain, the Supreme Soviet will believe I have already committed. It is a viewpoint. To the Party, and the country, my work over these long years has been for Britain. In my own mind, though, it has been for Mother Russia herself. I am of this country's soil, Piotr; and, unless you are a Russian you do not know what significance the soil of Russia holds for her children."

"I've never been here before," Michael cleared his throat. "But I'm Russian. My parents came from the Ukraine. I know about the soil. We have a little gold box in my home. It is filled with soil from my parents' village. They brought it with them. Carried it through the camps and horrors."

Stentor was silent for a second or two. "Then you understand. The Russian and the soil of Russia are intermingled. I cannot leave Russia, even if I do not hold with the way our masters run the country. Yes, I would like to feel safe in London. But the fact of leaving would, I believe, kill me as quickly as they will do it anyway. Do you see?"

"I think so."

"My dark night is over, Piotr. I have faith in my country; and this means I cannot leave it—no matter what the cost."

"You're committing suicide."

"Perhaps."

"And putting others at risk."

Stentor shook his head. "That is why I tell you now. There is time to lift others; to cover tracks. They'll get little from me—even with their drugs and hospital techniques. Save the others now."

"You're sure of this?" The heavy depression would swallow him, Michael thought. He could have wept at the placid, though firm, acceptance of this man he had come to save. "You're sure?" he repeated.

"You do not look a fool. I have told you. That should be enough."

"There's nothing we can do for you?"

"Not unless you can devise some way of discrediting Comrade General Vascovsky."

"I could ask. It may be possible. I just don't know. My real duty, now, is to talk with you: persuade you."

Stentor said that was an impossible duty; his nephew was only wasting time. "You know your Chekhov?"

Michael had studied all the great Russian writers and playwrights.

"Bring to mind *The Cherry Orchard*. When that play was written, it was a prophecy: a seer's view of the cataclysmic change about to take place. Mind you, if any man had brain, and wit enough, at the time, the whole pattern of history should have been obvious. Though, maybe not. Who knows?

"But it is all there, nephew. The social change; the Revolution. You remember the stage directions, during the scene at the picnic? And, later, at the very end of the play?"

"You mean the noise? The string snapping?" Michael had always felt that was an uncertain dramatic device.

Stentor made an affirmative gesture—"A distant sound is heard, coming as if out of the sky, like the sound of a string snapping, slowly and sadly dying away," he quoted.

"I remember."

"The imagery is wonderful. Change, as the snapping of a string, in the distance. I've often wondered how many men, in the history of mankind, have heard that sound: for it has often been heard—the herald of great change. Change snaps many strings. The past dies away—slowly and sadly.

169

"I like to think I've heard it again, in my fast-approaching old age. Only this time it is change for all mankind, not merely one nation, race, or people. The world has reached a point near to climax. There has to be a new way ahead, through the problems. The string has snapped once more, my young friend. That is why I have come through my dark night, and placed my soul with Russia, where these bones will be buried." He thumped himself on the chest. Michael found it difficult to believe the man's age, he looked so fit, and far from his seventy-odd years.

"But, this time," Stentor went on, "this time, the changes will be so vast that I believe all men will truly come together—maybe through darkness, war, famine, pestilence. However, the outcome will bring some final sense of purpose. For my Russia, not the hypocrisy of a great political ideal, but something more democratic; and for the West, a drawing together with the Third World, and this great country. It will mean a shift from the kind of democracy your statesmen preach; but the end will be as a new dawn."

"I wish that I could believe it."

"You will come to it. Now, were you followed here?"

"No." Michael told him exactly how things had been managed.

"That is good. However, we have to get you back—to the National Hotel, as Michael Gold. This will not be easy. Maybe you were not followed here, but they'll certainly be out in force when you leave. So—I think I have a plan . . ."

"If our people could compromise Vascovsky . . . ?" Michael began.

"I think it unlikely. If I were you, I should concentrate on getting out in one piece. You say there is a method by which you can go, and return in a few days?"

Michael repeated the ploy of the dying aunt, which would allow him to leave and rejoin the tour in three or four days.

"Well, Piotr. If they have some way to put the screws on the General, and, possibly clear me—so that I can retire and live to a nice ripe old age, watching the world change and

170

reform from the sidelines—that would be good. You could return and brief me."

"I have to make one last try . . ."

"For what?"

"To make you alter your mind." Michael knew the answer; so he quickly added, "There, I've made it. My one last try. You've done wonderful things, sir. Personally I think you've made a brave choice: one I respect. If they can do anything for you in London, I'm certain they'll try."

"You have a way for communicating?"

"Several. This calls for a Flash. A risk. I daren't dive for cover to the Embassy." He gave a quick smile. "Just in case they want me out and in again."

"So." Stentor started to talk; telling Michael exactly what he should do about avoiding the surveillance teams. "I shall tell my wife—your aunt—that you were so tired I insisted on you taking my car and returning to see us tomorrow. When you don't come I shall report you missing. It would be nice if we could meet again." He picked up the telephone, knowing it was wired. Before dialling, Stentor asked Michael—once more—if he understood exactly what he must do?

"Everything." Michael smiled at the old man's audacity.

"They will not keep your passport, because you're a Russian citizen." Stentor was enjoying his plot. "You have all the papers? Good, they'll examine those. Nothing else. Now." He dialled, making two telephone calls.

*   *   *

Yekaterina's clothes were scattered about the apartment. Her dress was crumpled on the dining-room floor, near her chair. Shoes and stockings made a trail through the main living room; slip, panties and bra led, in rotation, through the bedroom door—right up to the bed itself, where she now lay panting, with Jacob Vascovsky astride her, thrusting hard, as she groaned with the pain and joy of it.

Yekaterina adored her husband's sexual strength; just as he respected her own sensuality—for often it was Yekaterina who took the initiative, grabbing and seducing her husband.

171

But not tonight. Tonight had been a mutual melding of their bodies. Tonight they would ride each other; rest, and ride again into the small hours.

They were mounting to the greatest peak of pleasure when the phone rang, shrill by the bed.

Yekaterina's body went limp. "Shit," she said, as her husband groaned and picked up the instrument, answering with a sharp, breathless, "Yes?"

Major Badim stifled a laugh. Oh, what a story. You might almost be in the same room with them. He could hear Madame Vascovsky's heavy breathing, and muttered oaths, in the background.

Quickly Badim pulled himself together. "The subject, Comrade General."

"Yes." Vascovsky's breathing under control now.

"We've monitored two calls. He's booked a room for his nephew. At the Metropole."

"Then the job's easier. He book in the correct name?"

"Piotr Kashvar."

"Good. And the other call?"

"His driver. Said his nephew had flown in for a few days; that he was very tired and wanted to stay at an hotel: get some rest. He's told the driver to bring the car to the apartment block. Take his nephew to the Metropole."

"Then we've nothing to worry about. It's all sewn up. Just let the surveillance teams know."

"Comrade General."

"And tell them to make sure he doesn't slip away. That shouldn't tax them over much."

"No, Comrade General. Good night, Comrade General."

"Badim, we'll give them a couple of days. I want the niece to arrive. Then we can hold a family party. Just don't let the surveillance people lose anybody. Understand?"

"Yes, Comrade General."

*   *   *

At the Hotel Metropole they were most solicitous. After all, the man Kashvar was nephew to a most senior KGB officer.

172

It didn't matter that he looked as though he had come out of some back street, with the dirty raincoat, and his little cheap plastic zip bag. Any relative of General Vladimir Glubodkin had to be treated correctly.

They made a very quick examination of his documents, including the *spravka*, which proved, beyond any doubt, that Comrade Kashvar was on leave from his highly important job, as an experienced mining engineer, in the Urals. Then they gave him an exceptionally good room. In the Metropole that meant something. It was a first-rate hotel.

Michael wished he could stay. The room was certainly better than the one waiting for him, on the other side of Red Square, at the National. As Stentor had explained, they would almost certainly give him a 'clean' room, by which he meant one that was not wired. Also, the Metropole was only a short distance from the National.

Contrary to popular opinion, and the grossly exaggerated accounts in both Western popular Press, and television programmes, not every hotel room in the Soviet Union is either bugged, or has its telephone tapped. Stentor banked on this; as did Michael Gold.

He sat on the edge of the bed, re-thinking the final ten minutes he had spent with Stentor. During that time Michael had asked questions regarding Vascovsky's personal life: surprised when Stentor could tell him very little, as he had only visited the General at home on one occasion. There was, however, a bit of gossip, and a good description of the apartment above Kalinin Prospekt.

Michael made certain he had those facts straight, then took out his small notebook and began to work out a ciphered signal. It had to be kept brief; just as he had to make the telephone call as short as possible.

Finally, when he had copied the rows of numbers neatly onto a page of the notebook, he picked up the telephone and dialled out. The number was unlisted in any Moscow directory, belonging, as it did, to the clandestine SIS control in the Russian capital.

This man—a Russian born—had access to the British

173

Embassy, and the resident SIS officer there. It was the clandestine controller who did much of the message-taking, and even Stentor did not have the number just dialled by Michael Gold. An ingenious electronics expert had managed to tap this particular telephone into the system, without the knowledge of anyone connected with the Moscow telephone authorities. The clandestine SIS controller also had a normal number, and an exceptional cover: for he was by trade a journalist—the music critic for one of the leading Russian newspapers; a most unlikely candidate for the real post he had held over the past six years.

When his telephone rang, the music critic picked it up, but did not answer until he heard the word *cello* in Russian.

"Secure?" he asked.

"Yes," Michael lied. He could not be certain, but this was as secure as he would ever get.

"Okay."

Michael quickly read off the groups of numbers, adding the urgent word, "Flash".

"Serious?" asked the music critic.

"Most."

"Straight away then." The line closed.

The Floor Lady who looked after the keys, on the first storey of the Metropole, had been dozing when the porter brought Michael up. He could only hope she was still nodding off.

With the same speed he had used at the National, Michael Gold transformed himself back into the guise of an English tourist. The glasses and cap came off; the plastic zip bag folded into its small square, and went inside his shirt. Overcoat and fur cap on; and, last, the page from his notebook burned, then flushed, in tiny black specks, down the lavatory.

Vascovsky's surveillance team had the hotel surrounded. They even had a couple of men in the lobby. But they watched for one Piotr Kashvar. All of them had managed to glimpse him as he left the apartment block—a man in a short, thin raincoat, denim cap and glasses. They took scant notice of the foreigner, dressed in a heavy coat, and fur hat, who walked slowly through the lobby and out into the street.

It took Michael Gold five minutes to reach Sverdlov Square underground station, and a further three to walk through the underpass to the Marx Prospekt exit. In all, he was entering the National Hotel within fifteen minutes.

The first person he saw, on walking into the vast lobby, was the beautiful blonde Intourist girl, wrapped in a military style greatcoat, a leather shoulder bag swinging casually by her side. Her black boots made a martial click-clack as she headed towards the main exit.

Gold went into another of his smiling trances, and she looked up, seeing him, returning the smile and pausing. "You are one of my tour?" she asked.

"Yes. Yes, I'm one of your tour." Gold felt a sudden lack of confidence. Heaven knew why his stomach turned over, and his head reeled. Usually he was most efficient with young women. But this girl? Crikey, he thought, she *really* is something.

"You have had food? Your room is comfortable?" She still smiled, the large blue eyes swallowing him.

"The room's fine, but I haven't eaten yet. Went for a walk."

"Ah," she wagged a finger. "You must get something to eat. It is late, but there is a small cafeteria on the second floor. I would advise . . ."

"Will you join me?" Thank God; his voice had steadied.

The Intourist girl shrugged, making a sad face. "I am so sorry. I would like to do that. Really I would," her leather-gloved hand rested, for a second, on his arm, and she repeated that she would like to join him, but she still had work to do. "I have to go to my office." Moving a little closer, eyes scanning his face. "Tomorrow? After the tour. Tomorrow you would like . . . ?"

"That would be wonderful." Tomorrow he would not be there, but maybe they would let him return. He could feel the static between them. There was something—he had experienced enough of women, in his young life, to know that: sense it; and feel it. They stood looking at each other, neither knowing the other's name, yet both loath to leave. Finally she squeezed his arm. "Tomorrow." She gave a little

175

smile, dragging her eyes from his. "I must go. Sorry." And click-clack, her boots sounded on the marble as she walked quickly to the exit and disappeared.

Michael Gold stood, rooted, for a moment; then slowly headed for his room.

*   *   *

By the time he arrived, the music critic, who was clandestine SIS officer in Moscow, had danced a complicated, and fast, choreography to get the message to his resident at the British Embassy, with its magnificent view of the Kremlin walls across the Moskva River.

The high-speed transmission went out less than an hour later—slipped into the middle of some routine trade signals which would, normally, have been left until the morning.

The department at Moscow Centre responsible for monitoring all radio traffic from foreign embassies, made a note of both the signal and time. The tapes went immediately to the Centre cipher section who reported, the following morning, that an unfamiliar sequence had been transmitted among the normal trade ciphers.

That unfamiliar cipher travelled, by the usual route, to GCHQ at Cheltenham. It was the signal that reached the Director General while he was in late conference with Fincher, Curry Shepherd, young Worboys, and Big Herbie Kruger.

16

THE DIRECTOR GENERAL read the deciphered message aloud:

SUBJECT ADAMANT/REFUSES COME OUT/ASKS IF BUGBEAR SUITABLE FOR COMPROMISE/ TROILUS

Bugbear was the cryptonym given to General Jacob Vascovsky.

"It looks very much like Paris." The Director still wore his grave face. "You want to go down and see if the Adler woman'll talk now, Herbie?"

Big Herbie indicated an affirmative with his large head. "She'll talk once they have her conscious."

"Well, she's the message-carrier. Point is we don't know if she can simply lay it on by telephone, or whether she has to do it on her feet."

Herbie cut in, his voice sharp. "If it can only be done on her feet, she'll do it," he said with unusual conviction. "Will somebody call Lymington, and see what the situation is?"

Worboys took the hint, sliding from the room, unobtrusive as a chameleon.

"And Paris, Curry?" The DG slid his stocky body to one side, leaning towards Shepherd.

"Whenever you say. Take an hour or so to clear it with the SDECE." He spoke of the French Secret Service: *Service de Documentation Extérieure et de Contre-Espionnage*.

"Do it myself," the Director snapped, turning to Tubby Fincher. "Tub, activate the Aunty Amy death, for Michael Gold. Three days out of his holiday. I want that Paris meeting set for tomorrow. Lunchtime if possible. It's now, what . . . ?" Squinting at his watch.

"One o'clock," supplied Curry. "Little after. Three in the morning, Moscow. Have to put your skates on, Herbie. What's the sequence for date and time? The day before the day you really want. Time, two hours in advance of real time. Can't be done. You'd have to give today as the date. Today, Wednesday, for a Thursday meeting. Have to advance, sir. Thursday for a Friday meeting."

"Not if we make it an evening meeting." Herbie's voice had taken on a throaty urgency that worried the Director.

"Tonight for Thursday night. Right?" The DG regarded Big Herbie with suspicion. "Why the speed, Herbie?"

"Same reason as yourself. I wish for Vascovsky out of Moscow. Off their backs."

"No funny stuff, Herbie, or Curry'll have you. We're

breaking the strict rules anyway, as far as you're concerned. A night meet okay for you, Curry?"

"Prefer daylight, but we've got cameras that'll do it. Herbie, can you arrange a public place? But somewhere we can get good snaps."

"I give you everything, Curry. Don't worry." He turned to the Director. "While we're at it—the tapes . . ."

"What about the tapes?"

"Have you not got wizards who can do some doctoring? Splice them up, and give me a message: a message with some real meat in it."

The Director smiled for the first time. "We'll doctor the tapes, and a few other bits and pieces. You sort out Adler; liaise with Curry; and we should be able to send Gold back to Stentor on Saturday—at the latest—with a real bag of goodies."

Worboys returned with the news that Martha Adler had regained consciousness. "They've put her to sleep again, though. Should be ready to talk around eight this morning."

"You're going to have your work cut out, Herbie . . ." the Director started.

"Let me worry about that, sir. Can we formulate a plan of meeting; type of compromise, and forward action, before I leave for Lymington?" It was the professional speaking, and everyone in the room knew it.

Tubby was dispatched to get the Aunt Amy death message off to Michael Gold, while the rest of them drew in around the desk. Already, Tubby had unlocked one of the filing cabinets and removed the Paris plan. With care, the Director started to unfold a large-scale street map, while Herbie leafed through drawings of public buildings and parks.

There was the usual muttering and pointing; odd looks; shakes of the head; fingers tracing the paper streets; but Big Herbie remained aloof, quietly going through the file on his lap.

At last he looked up, speaking loudly across the general buzz of conversation. "I think, gentlemen," he said "the Gare de Lyon."

Curry's jaw dropped. "Christ, Herbie. Not a bloody railway station. You should know better than that. Railway stations're murder. You have to use teams of a hundred a time. No way."

The DG shrugged, scowling, throwing Herbie the kind of glance he usually reserved for the criminally insane.

Big Herbie took no notice. "Will you listen—please." This time, like the good actor he was, Kruger dropped his voice to gain attention. "I have reasons, and—Curry— I *don't* mean the main concourse. I am talking about the restaurant . . ."

"Oh God." Again from Curry.

The Director leaned back from his desk. "Tell us, Herbie. Then we'll have done with it."

Herbie thanked the Director, without a trace of sarcasm. "I do not speak of your British Rail sandwich bar." For once he did not give them the benefit of his stupid grin. "The main restaurant at the Gare de Lyon is, as our American buddies would say, a classy joint . . ."

"Only in old Howard Hawks films, Herbie." It was the first time young Worboys had talked back.

"Hawks, doves, who cares? But it's not British Rail, with the spilt tea, and the sausage and mash. The restaurant at the Gare de Lyon is what, here, you call a protected building. It is also very good. Not Maxims, or Fouquets, I grant you; but they call it *Le Train Bleu*, after that famous express. The décor is old railway—tables like in the Victorian trains, the metal signs, and plenty of room. There is space—take a look. I know it already." He passed the necessary section of the file over to the Director. Curry stood at his elbow.

After a few minutes they started to nod. "We can, presumably, book tables, and there seem to be only two entrances and exits." Curry sounded more enthusiastic.

"One from the station itself—up a stairway; the other is an elevator on the street side—the station forecourt."

They talked for about an hour, going through the available drawings and photographs. Curry agreed that, once he had the go-ahead, his people would make the trip over and set things up. Herbie was right, this place had perfect cover. In the meantime, the Vascovsky tapes would go to the Director's wizards; and another team would begin work on what the DG called "A few little surprises from the past".

The Aunt Amy death message had already gone off. "Telephoned the Embassy myself"—so Tubby Fincher. "Make it more personal that way. Sank a few ideas into their heads."

It was six in the morning when Big Herbie—now shaved and bathed, in the executive washroom near the Director General's suite of offices—left to talk with Martha Adler.

"Move it, old son, won't you," Curry called to him as he reached the door.

"I go as quick as possible. No quicker." Herbie sounded determined and tough. Herbie was more than just anxious and nervous about the meeting with Martha Adler. The Director General had ruled that he was not to see her, or interrogate her, alone. Fincher was to be with him on this trip. Still there was a lack of trust, which meant they remained suspicious of both Martha and himself.

At the door, Tubby Fincher turned back to the DG— "Better recall the SAS boys, and that part of the operation, okay?"

Herbie leaned back into the room. "At your peril, Tubby. Please change nothing. I may need them even yet. Life has taught me optimism. That alright, sir?" to the Director.

"We'll talk when you get back from Lymington, Herbie." The Director did not even look up. "In the meantime, everything stands."

*   *   *

She would not meet Big Herbie's eyes when he went into the small private room, off the larger ward. One of Curry's ladies, who had been sitting with her, gave him a nod and left quietly.

Tubby Fincher stood well away. "When we get down to the heavy stuff you sit next to me," Herbie had told him sharply on the way down. "Just don't crowd me, Tubby, eh?"

Surprisingly, Fincher was good about it. He had probably listened to the tapes of their pillow talk, Herbie considered.

Even so, there was still bitterness in his mind. It all boiled down to trust in the long run. Trust and lack of trust. Everything was hand-stitched with suspicion. When they reached the hospital, Herbie had decided, 'To hell with them. I go my own way with Martha. They would listen in any case.'

Martha Adler lay, propped up by pillows, looking like death itself—her face drawn, the cheeks hollow, and skin like a transparent parchment.

Herbie carefully took off his coat, drew a chair up to the bedside, and gently sat down, reaching out to take her hand. She turned her head away.

"Martha, my dear, why? You could have trusted me; you should know that." He glanced to where Tubby Fincher stood, and whispered, "Don't worry about him. Just minding me. Why Martha? Please why?"

Martha merely shook her head slightly. He knew she was crying. Through a sob came the words, "Why couldn't you have just let me die?"

"Because you're important. You are important to me, and to a lot of people." He spoke very quietly. "Martha, we haven't got much time, and I have to know—one way or another. You are weak, and please don't think I threaten you. But there are others who can be most unpleasant. If I do not come out of here with answers, pretty damned quick, they'll have you in an ambulance on the way to London."

He told her there was a clinic the Firm kept especially for the purpose, "Also for anyone who gets hurt in the line of duty. They have a doctor there who the boys call Mengele. It's a sick joke. His real name's Harvester, and he'll put you through hell and back. He will also do it at speed—like today. You're weak enough already, and I don't suppose any of that lot would care if you came out of the clinic in a box."

"Good." She snuffled.

"Martha." Big Herbie remained unruffled, speaking softly, choosing words as though his life depended on them: knowing the lives of others *did* hang on what happened in this hospital room. "*I* would care."

181

For the first time she turned to look at him. "Balls." She choked. "All men're the same. You get what you want— money, sex, piece of cake—then you care no more. Well, *they*'ve got what they want. I now wish to die, because there's nothing more for me."

"Do you remember the first time we made love, Martha? A long while ago. Before you came to work for me in East Berlin."

Sullenly she said she recalled they did it, but not the details. "You went off with the Zunder woman soon after."

"Soon after you told me you'd got yourself somebody permanent, from whom you could screw information," Herbie reminded her. "I tell you something, Martha. I remember all details about that first time with you. *All* details. That's in spite of what happened later. You wore a black dress—almost twenty years old you were. Almost. A black dress, and black underwear. Silk, I remember. We had a joke about it. When I made love to you, I remember what you said."

She looked at him, puzzled; then a tiny flicker of light showed behind the dullness of her eyes.

"In the middle of it all, you clung on to me. Dug your nails in my back. You said, 'Lie to me. Lie to me, please. Tell me you love me, and that there's never been anyone else. Please, Herbie, tell me!'"

"You remember that?" Her voice breaking. Oblivious to Tubby Fincher who now moved closer.

"Remember? I've always remembered. I also deduced. Martha, you need to be loved. You require to be needed..."

"And now I've been needed too often; loved too often."

There was a long pause, as Herbie braced himself for the Sunday punch he hesitated to deliver. Then—"If I tell you—on that particular night, all those years and months ago—*I* did not need to lie; would that make any difference? And the other night—would it make a difference if I told you I was going private, after this one job's finished? If I told you my mind was made up; I was going to ask you to come and live with me. Maybe even marry? Cheeky of me, yes:

182

Arrogant. Male chauvinist pig, yes? But I had made up my mind, Martha."

She did not believe him. He could tell by the face; then the quick look away. With her head turned from him, she said, "You wouldn't ask me now though. Not after this."

"Don't be sure, Matti. You should not be sure of this. I had a watch doubled on you—after the first time I came down. My chief will have the memos if you want to see them. I told him you'd been turned. I told him the bastards had turned you, and that you, of all people, could not live with it. I said you were on a knife edge, and existing in danger. When I got Vascovsky's last tape—I presume you were the postman—I had them bring me back here double quick. You see, I had not heard that tape when I came down. I didn't go near my flat. Came straight to you from my office."

Her head turned fast. Too fast for whatever pain was there. She winced, wrinkling her brow and screwing up her eyes.

"They must have had something very big to hold over you, Matti. But you have to tell me. Everything you must tell." Herbie leaned close. She smelled of antiseptic and doctors. Now Fincher was beside him for the last rites—the confession. Herbie felt a flare of fury at his presence.

"It'll make no difference." Her voice almost a whisper.

"You are wrong. Tell it all; tell it now, and I'll put Vascovsky out like a light. That, I promise. Then we'll talk about the future. Please, Martha, remember it's me. Did I ever let you down?"

She tried to raise herself up on the pillows. Big Herbie put an arm around her and lifted. As he did so, her arms circled his neck. He bent low and kissed her, then gently laid her back.

She said nothing for a minute, which seemed like an hour. Then, with a slow inclination of the head, Martha Adler began to talk.

*   *   *

Michael Gold was having breakfast, in the National's large dining room, when the Intourist girl came to his table, her face troubled.

"Mr. Gold?"

"Yes. We met last night. Tonight you said you'd have . . ."

"You mind if I sit down a moment?"

He rose, making a movement with his hand towards the spare chair, knowing what was to come; heart pounding, and manhood awakened even by the simple way she moved. He asked if she would like coffee, and the smile broadened. She ordered some for herself, then leaned over the table. "I'm afraid I have some bad news. I am sorry." The smile did not change. Michael thought it was rather like an oriental who will sometimes say 'yes' and shake his head; or 'no' and nod.

"You have a brother, 'Erbert Gold?"

"It's not Herbie?" He made it sound fast and anxious.

"No. Mr. 'Erbert Gold, your brother, telephoned our London people this morning—very early. You have an aunt. A Miss Amy Wilcocks, is that right?"

"Yes, Auntie Amy. She hasn't been well."

"Mr. Gold. I'm sorry. They felt a woman should tell you. Your brother said you were—how do you say it?—fond? Fond of your aunt."

"She's a bit like a second mother to me."

"I'm afraid she is died, Mr. Gold."

"Oh." He paused for effect, and then said "Oh," again. Then—"Poor Auntie Amy. She wasn't well . . . But . . . dead?"

"I'm afraid so. They bury her on Saturday morning. Your brother thought you should be there because you loved her; and because of the reading of the beneficiaries . . ."

"The will."

"Yes. You are to get something it seems. Perhaps you will be rich, Mr. Gold."

"I don't think so. Just a little extra. Poor Auntie Amy. Who'd have thought it. Yes. Yes, I suppose I should be there. Saturday you say?"

She tried to be consoling, reaching out, touching his hand with the tips of her fingers. Then she withdrew them, as though burned. "Our London people have worked it all out

184

with your brother 'Erbert. He says your aunt would not have wished you to miss your holiday. Not altogether."

"No. No, she was like that, Auntie Amy. Can't believe it. Went to see her; day before yesterday." A voice in his head told him to cool it. The voice told him he was not Lord Olivier. He was not even a member of the cast of *Dallas*. Certainly not playing opposite this girl. Michael still could not understand how the sight and touch of her could throw his mind into such turmoil. Playing the newly-bereaved required a great deal of concentration.

"We have arranged you go to London tonight. Ten-past-six there is British Airways flight. If you feel like it, we can take you on today's tour—the Kremlin. Your brother says you can return to your holiday on Saturday; after the burying, and the reading of beneficiaries. Intourist will pay your return fare because you would miss three days of holiday. You like to do this?"

Michael said, yes. Yes, he thought it a very good idea. The Intourist girl said again that she was so sorry about his aunt; but, when he returned to Moscow, on Saturday evening, she would be at Sheremetievo to meet him. "Personally," she said. "You will be rich. Perhaps you like to take me to dinner?"

Would he not? At the moment, his mind turning circles, all he really wanted to do was talk with her, get to know her, hold her, kiss her. He was like a schoolboy with his first crush. This was deeply disturbing to someone like Michael Gold, who always thought he could take 'em or leave 'em: the old adage, find 'em, fornicate with 'em and forget 'em. But this girl? Christ, he did not even know her name. A tiny thought crossed his mind. Should he speak with someone in London? You heard about people being compromised. Oh, how the hell could this wonderful lady . . . ?

Still like a blushing schoolboy he touched her hand, hesitantly. She put her palm in his and squeezed. "Thank you," he said, then clumsily rose and went upstairs to pack before they left for the day's tour.

It was a full, and exhausting, itinerary. They walked

around the Kremlin Walls and saw all the towers—the Borovitsky Gate; the Tower of the Annunciation; the Tower of Secrets; the Beklemishev Tower; Tocsin Tower; Tsars' Tower, and the others; they visited the three main cathedrals; saw the Queen of Bells—heaviest in the world—and the King of Cannons—"Which never has been shot," the smiling Intourist girl said.

They tramped into the Praesidium, with its huge theatre; and, wearing muffs on their feet, padded around that most dazzling of artistic museums, the Armoury—or Palace of Arms—which contains treasures of untold wealth.

And throughout the day, she seemed to single him out; keeping near to him, flashing him smiles as though to signal an unspoken pact. Once, alone and apart from the rest, she shyly spoke. "I have good feelings for you. Take care and come back soon." The pact, Michael Gold thought, was sealed. Oh hell, there was Stentor and all the cloak and dagger stuff, but he wanted to get back to see the girl. Could he, of all people, have been caught? Was this the stupid, foolish thing the sloppy books called love at first sight? Romantic piffle. Michael did not believe in love anyway. But this one? Well, she *was* different.

It took the full day, with a pause for lunch. By the time Michael had been driven out to the airport, and taken through the customs routine, he had mixed feelings about being on board the British Airways Trident: not a little surprised to find they had booked him executive class—"Courtesy of Intourist," the steward told him. "Sometimes they have heart. Understand there's been a death in the family."

*　　　*　　　*

They had started in the usual way, Martha told Herbie. Softening her up for the feast: the question and answer routine, right down to the nice cop, and nasty cop business.

"You know—better than I do. They told *me* what I'd been up to; and what you'd been up to as well; and they got it right. That's the disconcerting part."

Herbie agreed. For the subject, it was always worrying

when the interrogators appeared to know every item. They would start by telling you they knew; then asking questions. You did not believe them; but, out of the blue, they told you, and did not ask questions. Then the questions started to come from a different angle.

"They asked me about things I couldn't tell them: because I just didn't have the knowledge."

It was usual. The third phase: the fishing expedition.

"Then they began the turning; and I refused."

"So things got difficult." Herbie still held her hand, coaxing her through.

"Not to start with. They suggested things at first. Why didn't I do some work for them? They could get me out: exchange me. I'd be free, though they would keep a good eye on me. Once over here, the British would almost certainly employ me in sensitive work—it was around then they told me you had sold out, by the way. You'd left everyone, and saved your own skin." She gave a bleak, thin smile. "I didn't believe them. Truly I didn't."

"Thank you. When did it get nasty?"

"Once they had made certain definite proposals and I'd flatly refused. I told them they could go to hell, and that I'd finished. I wouldn't work for them. It was final."

Good girl, Herbie thought. Good girl; though foolish girl. They obviously wanted her badly and, though she had no way of knowing it, for them to push that hard could only mean one thing—they could produce some kind of a hold.

"Drugs?" he asked, and she shook her head. No, not drugs. With her they took the old-fashioned scenic route.

"You sure you want to hear?"

Herbie said he was positive.

Vascovsky had done it. Three nights in succession, with about six of the strong-arm boys watching. Rape. "They say when it's inevitable, just lie back and enjoy it."

"You enjoyed?"

"No woman can. Oh, have no fear, Jacob Vascovsky's a good lover. No doubt about that. But this was calculated rape. On the first two nights, anyway. He was violent, and

187

they laid everything on—the plush bedroom; kinky undies for me; the whole thing. It was so obscene, with them watching. Obscene and degrading. I was on display, like some porn exhibition." She looked pointedly at Tubby Fincher, who, to his credit, could not meet her eyes. "Then, on the third night, he came alone and tried to seduce me."

"And you let him?"

"Of course. What else do you do?"

Herbie felt an odd pang of jealousy; blinking on and off like a leering wink. "I understand."

"You have to act. I thought that might be the end of it."

But it was only the beginning. On the following morning, they had brought breakfast in bed. Then Vascovsky told her to stay where she was. He would be back.

Only it wasn't him. "They came, stripped me, and the sensory deprivation started." She could not, even now, say how long it lasted. After all, that is partly the object of the exercise. She was put in a tiny, cold, airless cell. "You couldn't stand up, or sit down, or lie down. I had no clothes; there was no light; no sanitary facilities. Only the noises. I managed to work out three days, after that it could have been a month, or a week. I've no idea. Couldn't even tell by my own phases. All that stopped once they had me."

She thought she was really going mad. It could happen quickly enough; Herbie knew, because he had done it to people. Not the nicest thing in the world, but it had a fearsome effect, and was always carefully monitored by a doctor—otherwise you ended up with a subject fit only for the booby hatch.

Martha was a gibbering wreck when they brought her out. "They asked me, again, if I would go over and do some work for them. Like a fool I said there was no chance. Anyway, I asked them how would they know if I doubled back on them. They just laughed and told me they had ways of dealing with that. Vascovsky himself said they had so penetrated the Firm, they would know within hours. Then they would finish me off."

She recalled him saying that not only the Bulgarian Service

188

had access to poisons like Ricin. She had not known what this meant until they explained it at Warminster. That was the kind of comment she was able to make during the short debriefing at Warminster. "I was surprised they didn't dig deeper. Vascovsky warned me to expect a thorough going over by the Firm. In fact it was positively routine."

Herbie must have been there at the same time as Martha Adler. Funny to think of that. "They kept their eyes on you. Thought you had gone through a lot and come out unscathed. So, Vascovsky threatened you with death—the long arm of Department V—if you tried to be clever."

"They went on about it the whole time. Even when I was refusing every offer."

She continued to refuse for a long time; and paid for it. "Odd days of sensory deprivation, alternated with the noise treatment." She meant the other method of disorientation: hooded and placed in an uncomfortable position, then bursts of white noise poured through headphones; and, if that did not do the trick, they shut you in a soundproof, pitch-dark cell, and fed the most disconcerting, and painful, noises through high frequency amps.

"You cracked after that?"

Martha told him that she was rather proud of having lasted so long. She knew it was only a matter of time before she would agree to something. "I was right on the edge. It was like being staked out close to a crumbling clifftop."

They must have been monitoring her very carefully, because the final hit came right on target.

Her face sagged, and the small light went out of her eyes. "We didn't talk much about my family—in the old days, I mean. When we were in the East." She stopped, asking for a glass of water. A nursing sister came in and made clucking noises. The patient has had enough. Mr. Kruger and Mr. Fincher should really go. Herbie's look would have terrified even the most militant of hospital matrons.

"During the last days of the Battle of Berlin, I was separated from my family. I never saw them again. We were right in the path of the Russian advance. Logic told me they were dead—father, mother, and my young sister, Eva. But, some-how, I always had this odd feeling that they were alive. They were."

Giving Martha up for dead, the Adlers had moved North, to Anklam, in Pomerania. Her father had been unfit for military service; a cabinet maker by trade. The authorities put him to work in a factory—making off-the-peg furniture. Eva married, and they all settled down together.

"Vascovsky had managed to find them." She was weakening, finding it difficult to concentrate. Herbie had to push her on to the limit. After that she could rest. They would take her to the clinic in London, and she would get protection, with medical help of the best possible kind.

"I was ready to crack when they said I had visitors. I couldn't believe it at first . . . I . . ." She faltered, then broke down, starting to weep. "My father had never been very fit; but you know what they say about creaking doors. He was thin, like a ghost; and my mother was frightened. Eva seemed fit enough, but they had just taken her from her husband and two young children. She pleaded with me to do whatever they asked. All she wanted was her husband and the kids."

So Martha said yes—naturally.

"It was one of Vascovsky's sidekicks—the Major, Kashov, the one I'd been screwing: the one who arrested me. He said I was to do as I was told. One job for them. They would know if I sold out—will they know, Herbie?"

Big Herbie shook his head. No, they would not find out. He was certain of that.

"They would know, Kashov said. If I doubled on them, I would die: suddenly and unexpectedly. But I would die in the knowledge that, after I had gone, my father, mother, and sister, would also die: slowly, and painfully, in one of their special hospitals in the Soviet Union. If I did as I was told, they would get me back. We would all be reunited and . . ."

"And you'd live happily ever after." Herbie grunted. "You believed all that? Yes, of course you did. And you thought you'd failed, when I did not give you any message."

Her head moved, wearily, on the pillow, and she raised an arm to brush the long ash blonde hair from her eyes, wet with tears.

"What," Herbie asked her, "were you to do for this paradise?"

"Be exchanged for one of their people. Go through the Firm's debriefing, and do as they told me. Eventually I was to make contact with you and send you, by mail—or personally by hand—two tapes. They said you would react. There was no doubt. They believed it completely. You would react very quickly after I delivered the second tape. You did." She managed a thin smile. "Only you hadn't received it, even though I took it in personally. Did you know they had the dogs on your place in St. John's Wood?"

Herbie said yes, he knew. She was very clever to get in and out without being spotted. "I would give you a message?" He pushed.

"Yes."

"And you were to pass it on. How?"

She gave a long, tired, sigh. "The easiest way imaginable. They showed me how to manufacture a fault in my telephone; in case it was wired. I was to ask any clean friend if I could use their phone. A straight, and direct, call to Moscow with your message."

"Cryptonyms?"

"I was Lara—as in *Zhivago*—which was somewhat ironic." She gave a small sob of laughter. "You were Kolya."

"Simple as that. What about Vascovsky?"

"Yuri. Vascovsky was Yuri. Yes, it was that simple. They said it would only be a matter of weeks, after I sent the message. A matter of weeks before they'd lift me."

"Okay, Matti. Will you send the message? If you do, I'll see to it that your parents are safe." He paused, and she saw his great lumpy peasant face harden in bitterness. "I shall also see that Vascovsky's balls are removed. One at a time, and without anaesthetic."

He thought she would never answer him. The silence stretched on to a moment when Herbie, himself, could almost stand it no longer. Then she gave a small indication with hand and head. Herbie spoke quickly. "You need sleep; and I shall see you're moved to safety, in London, while you sleep. But this has to be done quickly. Now. Just stay awake for a short time, my dear. Do it, and we'll almost be there."

Fincher, himself, volunteered to fix a telephone, leaving them alone, moving fast to speak with Curry's people. When he had gone, Martha asked what the message would be.

"You tell them who you are—Lara. Then you say that Kolya will be alone, to meet Yuri, tonight at six o'clock, at *Le Train Bleu* Restaurant, Gare de Lyon, Paris."

"You're going to be there?"

"Oh yes. Nothing'll stop that pleasure."

"He'll try to snatch you, Herbie. Vascovsky's never forgiven you. He'll lift you."

"Eventually he'll try. But not on this run. On this run I'll snatch him; and the beauty is that he won't even know."

Curry's people—together with Tubby Fincher—had a word with the infirmary's Powers, and arranged a telephone for Martha's room. They also saw the doctor, and Herbie made a fast call to London. After she had made one telephone call from the bed, they would see that she slept. While she slept, a plain ambulance would take her to London.

He sat beside the bed as she made the call—taping it with a pocket recorder and suction mike.

Tubby took the telephone away himself, before the doctor arrived. Herbie told her that he would see her in London. "By then it will be all over and we can talk." He bent to kiss her, and she clung to him, but with no power in her arms.

"Herbie," she whispered, the tears starting again. "Lie to me. Lie to me, please. Tell me you love me, and that there's never been anyone else. Please, Herbie, tell me."

He kissed her once more. "I cannot say there's never been anyone else. But I don't need to lie to you, my dear girl. I love you." For what she had given him that day, he was not lying. Further than that, Big Herbie Kruger could not say what was truth, or what were lies. He had lived too many lives; existed too many lies; warped too many truths. The only thing of which he was certain at the moment, was that, tomorrow night, he would be at *Le Train Bleu* in Paris.

There, he would set up General Jacob Vascovsky once and for all. The rest could be silence, as far as he was concerned.

*   *   *

"It's all fixed," Herbie told the Director. He had gone straight to the Firm's headquarters on getting back to London. "Tomorrow at eight."

Curry Shepherd was there—"Just passing through, cocker. Off to gay Paree as soon as I can get out. Ten chaps there already. I'll dine at the wretched station place myself tonight."

"Before you go, Curry." The Director indicated the portable tape machine on his desk. "Like you both to hear the first piece the wizards've put together, from the Vascovsky tapes. Just listen." He switched on the machine. Vascovsky's voice filled the room. The tape and recording experts had done a brilliant job: extracting words, matching them, and rearranging sentences. Their prototype was short and ingenious.

"Herbie, my old friend. It's finished, and they're on to me, I'm certain. We have had a good run. Now I have to get out. Can you please do something quickly. I'll wait for your message as usual."

There would be others like it—"and the documentation, of course. I'm not even starting them on that until Michael Gold's back. Young Worboys is going out to pick him up at Heathrow."

Curry cheerfully said his farewells, quickly going through the routines they had arranged previously—in the small hours—for tomorrow night's meeting.

"Vascovsky has the signal by now. He'll also be casing the place for sure," Herbie cautioned.

"Don't worry; none of his lads are going to see mine—and, for Christ's sake, Herbie, be early tomorrow. I want you seated well ahead of schedule. My photo boys're like prima donnas when it comes to candid camera. Lad called Pat will

193

mike you up, and nobody'll suss you. The stuff's well shielded. All the latest equipment at bargain prices."

When he had gone, the Director started to talk. There were things he had to say before Michael Gold—their Troilus—arrived.

* * *

At around noon, Moscow time, Stentor telephoned his wife from the Yasenevo Complex, to ask if Piotr Kashvar had been in touch. When she said he had not, Stentor made some remark about the boy probably sleeping late. He then put down the telephone and dialled the Metropole Hotel, giving his name and rank, before asking for his nephew, Piotr Kashvar.

The girl at the switchboard was respectful, requesting him to hold on for a moment. There was no reply from Comrade Kashvar's room. Would the Comrade General like someone to try and locate his nephew?

Stentor hung on for nearly ten minutes. Then he was put through to the hotel manager's office. The man to whom he now spoke was plainly distressed: Stentor could detect, not only anxiety in the voice, but also a touch of fear. He felt it best to speak personally with the Comrade General. Comrade General Glubodkin's nephew, Comrade Kashvar, had not spent the night in his room. There was no sign of him; no clothes; the bed still made up, and unused.

Stentor murmured thanks, asked his name, and said he would be in touch. He then dialled the Moscow Militia Headquarters, on Petrovka Street, asking to speak with Chief Investigator Genik.

Misha Genik of the People's Militia—the MVD—was an old friend. He would know the best man to deal with a possible missing person case.

Stentor smiled to himself. It was natural for him to telephone the MVD. Of course. How could he possibly know that anyone from the Committee for State Security had an interest in his nephew Piotr?—particularly anyone like his colleague and friend Jacob Vascovsky.

194

Stentor did not, of course, know that only a few moments before his call to the Metropole Hotel, Vascovsky had also received a message of great urgency. So urgent that he immediately instructed Major Badim to hold a watching brief on the matter of Stentor's nephew; and the niece who would be arriving from Leningrad.

At this very moment, Vascovsky was on his way to the apartment on Kalinin Prospekt. From there he would, eventually, go to the airport, leaving no instructions regarding his whereabouts—apart from a curt message to the Chairman, saying that he would be out of Moscow for about two to three days, as he had predicted during an earlier conversation.

Even Yekaterina Vascovsky would not know the General was on his way to Paris—via East Berlin.

17

IT HAD BECOME most apparent that the Director was not taking any chances with Herbie Kruger. The outburst, when Kruger had spoken of leaving the Service—going private— once this job was done, had not furthered his cause. The admission that, under certain circumstances—and if Vascovsky could be trusted—Herbie might seriously consider dropping out of sight, with the KGB man, had not endeared him to his chief.

Alone now, in the office high above Westminster Bridge, the Director General read the riot act: probing into the action Herbie eventually proposed to take against Vascovsky.

To discredit the KGB General, on his home ground, was one thing. Herbie's part in it, however, which would mean him being on the loose in Paris, and, perhaps, elsewhere, was contrary to the initial findings of the enquiry into Big Herbie's outrageous actions during the East Berlin affair of the previous year.

"I've had you pull strokes on me before, Herbie." There was no give, or glitter, about the Director. "It's *not* going to happen again."

"It may be the only way of saving Stentor." Big Herbie opened his hands, after the manner of a magician showing he had nothing up his sleeve.

"Maybe. But, in the end, Stentor is expendable. If the whole thing gets tricky, I'm not risking diplomatic incidents."

Big Herbie went through the several possibilities: presenting at least three different scenarios of what could happen. "You'd have me covered all the time," he said, the ingenuous, open and stupid look blank on his face.

"We'll see." Big Herbie Kruger did not, for a moment, convince the DG.

So they talked: going over the fine brush strokes of the operation to discredit Vascovsky, again and again—modifying here, pruning there, adjusting timings to possible events. They were still at it when Worboys arrived, from Heathrow, with a tired Michael Gold.

Then the talking began in earnest—the Director General himself probing Michael, firing question after question, while Tubby Fincher made notes. Eventually Fincher left them, to type up the fine print of what Michael had learned from Stentor—particularly what he had discovered about Vascovsky: the General's habits, lifestyle, and, above all, Stentor's description of the apartment on Kalinin Prospekt.

For a quickly-trained tyro in the trade, Michael Gold had done a good job. Particularly returning with such a clear picture from Stentor. "We knew about Vascovsky's wife, of course," the Director acknowledged. "Done very well for himself there." Nobody missed the smile playing, for a second, over his lips.

Then Worboys—prompted by the mention of Yekaterina—asked if their present situation had been cleared with the SDECE. He was worried about the current political climate in France; and, from the outset, feared they would get a rejection—disallowing them an operation on French soil.

It was all taken care of, the DG said. "You should know I don't leave things like that to chance, young fellow-me-lad." There were still some secret and subtle pressures the Firm could bring to bear on the French Service, though they were never the most co-operative when it came to exchanging information.

During this highly tense council of war, the Director also took calls from Curry's second-in-command, regarding the run-through they were to have at *Le Train Bleu* that night. ("Curry thinks of everything," he nodded approvingly. "They're even using Russian film and tape.")

While Big Herbie was still present, word came through that Martha Adler had been moved to the safety of the clinic in London. "She's comfortable, a shade fretful, and asking for you," the Director General gave Big Herbie a quizzing look.

When he finally left, complete with tickets and other travel documents, Herbie became even more conscious of Curry's teams working around him. It had ceased to worry him by now; in many ways there was comfort from the fact. With Jacob Vascovsky on the rampage, who knew what devious methods were being used to watch his progress? If any mystery teams showed up, they would almost certainly abort the operation, switch plans, or drop Herbie out of sight. He reflected on the Director's ruthlessness—'Stentor is expendable'—shocked at himself agreeing; but still firm in his resolution towards Vascovsky.

Big Herbie took a taxi to the clinic, which looks like a normal, unmarked, block of flats in New Cavendish Street—off Marylebone High Street. There he spent half-an-hour with Martha, who was tearful, but obviously pleased to see him. She had thought he would be in Paris: particularly after the message she passed on to Moscow from Lymington. "Double-talk." Herbie grinned. "But I'll be away for a couple of days."

She asked him—pleading—to come and see her the minute he returned.

"Try and stop me." He winked, kissed her, and left—his mind humming a snatch from the Mahler Ninth. Why the Ninth? he asked himself, in the taxi on his return to St. John's Wood.

So, they continued their lengthy discussion with Michael Gold, who was now in an advanced state of fatigue. At the moment, if everything went to plan, Gold would be called upon to return to Moscow on Saturday and make one highly important drop to Stentor. It was possible that the headiness of one very fast clandestine job would quickly wear off. Gold now knew the dangers. Both the Director and Fincher had to make certain the young man was in a fit psychological state, while still retaining the confidence, and momentum, to bring off a second go.

"I'm sorry." Michael felt a little stupid, fuzzy-headed, and jet-lagged. "A night's sleep and I'll be okay. But, yes, I'm quite determined. It may sound foolish, but the short time I spent with the old man was an eye-opener. He's incredible. If I can do anything to help . . ." In the back of his mind, the blonde and blue-eyed Intourist girl twirled in his arms.

They told him to take a rest. A day off. They would talk again—on Friday. So, with Worboys as nurse-maid, Gold was removed to a quiet hotel in Knightsbridge.

*   *   *

In Moscow it was not until quite late in the evening that Major Badim's surveillance teams became anxious. All exits to the Hotel Metropole were covered; watching teams had been changed, and Badim saw to it that only the best personnel were on the job. Everyone was familiar with the likeness of Piotr Kashvar; yet, as far as they could discover, the man had not left the hotel.

Even Badim began to feel uneasy by the early evening; but, when darkness fell, and there was still no sign, he knew it was time to make some gentle enquiries. The last thing he wanted was to stir up the waters, and produce mud—the

198

Comrade General played things very close to his chest; even the Chairman himself might not know what was going on.

Badim suffered from that most pernicious of Russian diseases—passing the buck. He would hang on for as long as possible. If anything went wrong, on his account, while the General was away, it would be him—Vitali Gregorovich Badim—who would carry the blame, by way of a drop in the promotion scale, or the removal of some coveted privilege.

However, it would do no harm to check the day's reports. He went through the two pages of typed messages with more than usual care. There it was: standing out like the blush on a bride's wedding night. Time: 14.23. Arrival at main entrance. One plain Volga with MVD plates. Four plainclothes officers, including the driver. Senior officer identified as Chief Investigator Fedyanin.

Then, a little further down the page: Time: 15.45. MVD party, headed by Fedyanin, left hotel. One officer remaining in place.

Great Lenin's balls, Badim thought, hastily picking up his telephone to dial the People's Militia Headquarters. Two minutes later he was in possession of the knowledge that Chief Investigator Fedyanin was an expert on missing persons—not just an expert, but head of the Moscow area department for missing persons. A minute or so after this, Vitali Badim had Fedyanin on the line.

It is no secret that love is not lost between the Committee for Security, and the People's Militia; but, on this occasion, Badim knew he trod on particularly thin ice. He went out of his way to be precise, cordial, and co-operative.

Fedyanin was prickly, and, obviously, very busy. Badim respectfully suggested that he had been carrying out an investigation at the Metropole Hotel that afternoon.

"There is no new thing under the sun," the Chief Investigator growled unpleasantly.

"No." Badim was stuck.

"So, I was carrying out an investigation at the Metropole? What has that to do with the KGB, Comrade Major?"

"We are also carrying out an investigation at the Metropole. I wished to make certain no toes were being crushed."

"I doubt it. My instructions came from the Senior Chief Investigator—M. A. Genik. I understand he was tipped by your people."

"*My* people?" At heart, Vitali Badim was a simple, home-loving man.

"Not yours in particular, but a very senior KGB General. *Very* senior."

"Ah. Just to make certain, Comrade Investigator, is it a missing person?"

"Why? Did your Yetis bundle him into a car? Is he at this moment, e'en now, undergoing a quiz at that nice hotel you run behind Two Dzerzhinsky Square? The Lubianka?"

"No . . . No . . . NO. It may not be the same person. I just enquire, that's all. The missing man would not be a Piotr Kashvar by any chance?"

"Who said it was a man? and who's your superior?" Fedyanin asked sharply. From Badim's end of the line it sounded as though the investigator had been jabbed with a sharp instrument.

"General Jacob Vascovsky . . . But he's out of touch; out of Moscow."

"And he's interested in Kashvar?"

"There is a surveillance on him."

"You know he is the nephew of a most senior KGB officer?" The Chief Investigator was loath to name the General concerned.

"It is probably a security matter," Badim said sadly, wishing he had not opened this particular can of worms. Heaven knew what would be at the end of the road.

"Well, he's missing, and that's all there is to it. His uncle thinks as I do. Kashvar's been working hard in the Urals—a mining engineer of some talent. He visited his uncle last night, but insisted on staying at an hotel. Like his uncle, I believe he's gone off on a vodka binge, with some local talent thrown in. He's probably sleeping it off in a Komsomol

Square whore's rabbit hutch. Don't worry. The MVD'll do your work for you. Give me your number."

Against his better judgment, Badim gave the number, his extension number, and name.

"I'll get back to you." Fedyanin put down his telephone in Petrovka Street then immediately picked it up again, asking the switchboard if Investigator Genik was still in the building. He was, and they spoke for a few moments.

Within the hour, Genik had telephoned Stentor with the news that one of Stentor's colleagues—Vascovsky—had eyes out for the General's nephew. Stentor thanked him. After all, what were friends for?

*   *   *

In his deep sleep, Michael Gold dreamed. It was not usual for him to dream of women. Even his closest friends said he had no real feelings as far as girls were concerned, and he knew that was near to the truth.

Yet now he dreamed, most vividly, of the Intourist girl. Her name was Irena: he had discovered that much, and in the dream they were together, blissfully happy in some warm climate and it was roses all the way. Gold's subconscious appeared to have collected every detail concerning Irena for he saw her face with the clarity of an accurate photograph— every pore; the bright blue eyes; the way one eyebrow was a fraction higher than the other; the tiny creases—laughter lines—on each side of her lips and around the eyes; even the minute scar below her right ear.

The dream changed, and Gold saw her as he imagined, unclothed—and he had thought about that enough times as he watched her move through the tourist group during that one day in Moscow.

He woke with a start and a great physical longing. Yet it was not only physical. He lay there in the early morning gloom, feeling the immense distance between them: wanting her close and longing to talk to her, to get into her mind as well as her body.

In a word, for the first time in his life, Michael Gold was besotted. He sighed, like some lovesick boy in a cheap romance, then dropped gently into sleep again.

*　　　*　　　*

Curry Shepherd's man, called Pat, turned up very late at the St. John's Wood flat, giving a prearranged telephone signal.

The wiring was easy enough—quite standard in fact: gold cufflinks with highly sensitive inlaid microphones, but tuned only to pick up the human voice. They were very sophisticated, Pat said. They were also real gold, and needed no wires trailing to back pockets. Curry would give him the receiver in Paris, if he thought it necessary. Otherwise they would pick up his signal from some nearby source. Pat did not know any details, but his orders also included fitting a homer in one of Big Herbie's shoes.

Kruger smiled—he'd had trouble with homers before. This time he was forced to play it clean. For Paris, he would wear his business suit, which was hell, for Herbie did not like to be restricted by collars, ties, or heavy smart suits; you could never give Kruger a best-dressed man award.

He waited until the expert neatly fitted the homer, and replaced the heel of the black shoe, using tools from a small briefcase. The job done, Pat wished him good luck and left.

Somewhere, out in the dark, Big Herbie was certain that Curry's watchmen would have noted the times of entrance and exit. Unless he was superlatively ingenious there was no way in which Big Herbie could slip the leash unofficially. Well, he considered, if it has to be done, then it must be with official, or semi-official backing. There were ways. Already his mind leaped ahead.

Pouring himself a king-sized vodka, Big Herbie Kruger stretched himself out in his favourite chair and listened to Mahler's Ninth Symphony, with all its obsessions of farewell, death and transfiguration. He did not feel morbid: the notes

202

of death and last goodbyes were not for himself; this time it would be Jacob Vascovsky. Already the moves were in an advanced stage. Paris first, with a face-to-face meeting, then a further arrangement at which Big Herbie would be present.

If anyone was going to say their final farewell it would be Vascovsky and not Herbie Kruger. But not yet; not just yet.

PART THREE

THE MAIN EVENT

18

THE FIRM STILL kept two safe houses in Paris, as well as an external resident—who worked the covert side, directly to their man in the Embassy. They took Big Herbie to the house near the Place Voltaire, as it was the most convenient for the Gare de Lyon: all very discreet. Curry had always done a nice line in locals. The driver was French, and the taxi real. The house was, in fact, a four-room apartment on the second storey. There Curry waited for him.

"Nice trip, Herbie? Good. We've had a run-through. No problems. Got you fixed up with the right table, and I defy the good Comrade General to mark our people—mixed bag: some local labour, and a few of my own boys."

As far as Curry could tell, Vascovsky had not yet arrived in Paris. "But you never can be sure. I'm not exactly blanketing the place. Calls for about two hundred bodies this one. I'm using fifty. That way I keep control—I mean, we don't need to know where he's off to after the meet, do we? As long as they don't try to snatch you: and there's no evidence of the dreaded red menace on the ground as yet."

Curry had a sidekick at the safe house—a lion tamer, as the trade has it—called Perce: as tall as Herbie, but less flabby. "Where I have fat, this one has muscles, yes?" Herbie laughed, and Perce gave a quiet, good-natured smirk. He would be at Big Herbie's back once they were on the street, or at the Gare de Lyon.

Now, he brought drinks and a light snack on a tray for Herbie, while Curry went over the scheme. He wanted Kruger in the restaurant by six that evening, "You can sip the odd glass; tell them you think your friends might be delayed; anything like that."

"And we just pray Vascovsky hasn't decided on the same."

Curry gave a sly smile, running a hand over the thin blond hair. "They're taking no bookings for tonight—except ours of course. Our friends here saw to that. They're also watching the airports, stations, and ports for us. I think we'll at least know when the General arrives. In operational matters our Gallic brothers are unpredictable—won't play ball often as not. This time they've really come up trumps. Gives me the feeling they've got a hidden interest: card up their sleeves and all that."

Spreading out a plan of the restaurant, Curry explained the seating. With his usual eye to both detail and the unexpected, Shepherd really had managed to get them boxed in. He went on to explain the equipment. Later they would tune Herbie's cufflinks to the correct frequency. His conversation would be picked up by three separate receiver/recorders—one at the table behind where he would sit; another in a suitcase deposited in the cloakroom, and a third carried in a watcher's shopping basket below *Le Train Bleu*, on the station's main concourse.

That took care of the sound. Photographs and film would come from the table immediately adjacent. "We're going to get the initial meeting, when he arrives, from across the room. I don't want the main team there when the Comrade General walks in," Curry explained. "He'll be edgy enough as it is. Better they should get there just afterwards."

The previous night's test had proved, "Ninety per cent perfect," Curry claimed. One small case held a miniaturised video camera with self-adjusting focus; while a briefcase was fitted with a more conventional camera; again with self-adjusting focus for light variations. Both were equipped with fibre-optic lens attachments, so no aperture showed in either of the cases—the fibre-optic end being no thicker than a pencil.

"They've got their marks on the floor, and the cameras will run for three hours—that's three hours of constant video that can be reprocessed on to film; and four stills a minute, for three hours, on the other one—bloody great magazine fitted on the side. All you do is sit back and lead him into whatever little trap you're planning."

Herbie nodded with the ghost of a smile which made Curry slightly uneasy.

The one thing they did not discuss was how the evening would end. Herbie had his own ideas about what Vascovsky would propose. His plans would, undoubtedly, be dictated to him by the heavy and muscular Perce; and nothing, at this moment, would tempt Big Herbie Kruger to even dream of tangling with Perce.

*   *   *

Big Herbie had an abiding memory of the main restaurant at the Gare de Lyon. In 1937, when he was only six years old, his father and mother had taken him on a holiday from Berlin. It was the only holiday Herbie spent out of Germany with his, now long dead, parents. Doubtless, his old mental pictures were warped by the erosion of time; but there was no doubt that it had been a golden and exciting three weeks.

They had stayed in Paris for a few days, and then took the famous express—The Blue Train—to the Côte d' Azur: to Nice. When Herbie thought of childhood, he held on to those days of endless sun, splashing in the water, eating ice creams; feeling free and happy, with the big, tanned, energetic man whom he loved so much—playing with little Herbie; carrying him on his shoulders; laughing and teaching the child to swim.

There were other retained pictures. The railway station in Paris, at what seemed an unearthly time of night to the little boy; a great metal staircase—two staircases, like a pyramid—rising to a huge restaurant, with zinc tables, and paintings covering the ornate wall. Most of all, he remembered the Spanish omelette and fried potatoes, and those murals, in vivid colours, executed within plaster ovals, and depicting, his father told him, scenes of Southern France and Italy.

Then there was the exciting train ride through the night; waking, at dawn, to see the sun rise along the coast.

There must be many people who carried similar memories from both before, and after, the Second World War. Though it still runs, the Blue Train is not what it used to be. Air travel has decapitated the glamour from that great thundering beast, just as it has reduced so many other famous European expresses. Yet the memories were always there: the old Blue Train which raced across France, down to Marseilles, following the coastline as the early sun rose to reveal the deep blue Mediterranean—Toulon; St. Tropez; Frejus; St. Raphael; Cannes; Antibes; Nice; Villefranche; Monaco; Monte Carlo—that small station bright with bougainvillaea—Menton; then over the border, at Ventimiglia, and up the Italian Riviera dei Fiori—Bordighera; San Remo and so on, to Genoa where it turned north to plough towards Milan.

As Big Herbie came out on to the main concourse of the Gare de Lyon, he could almost smell the station as it had been in those old days—the mixture of heavy smoke, from the steam engines, mixing with wine, garlic, French cigarettes and people.

There it was, the twin staircase of wrought iron, just as it had been all those years ago; smarter now, and the restaurant marked with a new sign—*Le Train Bleu*.

Big Herbie stood, among the bustle and chatter, the soft loudspeaker voices giving platform locations, and the shouts of travellers, as though he was completely alone in the huge throng, building up at this time of the evening—just before six o'clock. The commuters; passengers for long distance trains; and those just disembarking—jostling their way through, to find the vast taxi queues outside—eddied around Big Herbie, in a surging sea. Lovers entwined, and made their way past this hulk of a man; men in vociferous argument sounding as though they would come to blows at any moment; quiet debaters; and people just going about their own business of getting home, or on holiday, or to friends, or lovers. For a few seconds, Big Herbie Kruger was an island in the middle of all this.

From his perch in one of the SNCF offices—thoughtfully

provided by the *Service de Documentation Extérieure et de Contre-Espionnage*—Curry Shepherd whispered to himself: "Come on, Herbie. You stand out like the proverbial spare organ at a wedding. Don't doze out on me now."

With relief, he saw Herbie hunch his shoulders against the crowd, and start to move towards one of the exits, which would take him to the large station frontage.

"He is good, your man?" The French liaison officer, who was known to Curry only as Marcel ("As in wave, old cocker," to Herbie before they left the safe house) raised his eyebrows.

"Best there is," Curry spoke fluent French. "Made a gaffe last year that's put him off his stride, but when he's good he's very good—old English nursery rhyme." The Frenchman nodded. He didn't understand the English, and made no bones about it. "Except *that* rhyme's about a girl," Curry added, confusing Marcel even more.

"He'd better be. We don't want any foul up." Marcel used the French colloquial expression.

The French officer had arrived at the Place Voltaire apartment ten minutes before Herbie Kruger was due to leave. He brought news that the Russian General had arrived, just after four, on a flight from West Berlin. "A roving commission," Herbie murmured.

There was nobody with him. "Not even his wife," Marcel added.

"Doubt she'd risk a trip here, eh?" Curry laughed, referring to Vascovsky's wife.

In Marcel's car, discreetly driven on a different route from the taxi Big Herbie had taken, the Frenchman opened up to Curry, this time in English. "We have money resting on this operation also," he began.

"Oh?" Feigning surprise, as his suspicions seemed to carry weight.

"There is the faint possibility that I might be able to give you some useful hints before you leave. We also have sources; and when the cat's away the mouse . . ."

"Yes?" Curry gave him a sidelong glance.

211

"Just wait. In the meantime, I said nothing in front of your friend, but the Russian, Vascovsky, appears to have come into the country clean. None of my people have spotted known faces for the last twenty-four hours; and none since his arrival. On the last count, there was no activity in the Gare de Lyon area. Nobody is watching his behind, as you say."

"Back," Curry prompted, and they switched the conversation to French.

In the little office, that afforded a good view of the main concourse, Curry checked his own teams. The watchers—thin on the ground—were strategically placed, both in front of the station, and on the concourse itself. The three man, one woman, team which made up the camera unit, was scattered around: the woman, with one man, drank inside the *Tour de Lyon*, on the corner of the Boulevard Diderot and Rue de Lyon; the two other men were separated—one sitting, reading *Paris Soir* on the concourse, the other loitering around the bookstalls.

The three sound teams—made up of two pairs and a singleton, all kitted out as passengers—had started their various journeys, timed to arrive at the station within minutes of each other.

Apart from the watchers, on and around the station, Curry had three cars, circling the area, on radio control; while the seven other assorted men and women, who would use *Le Train Bleu* restaurant to complete the boxing-in of Herbie's table, were also passing the time in various bars nearby; or around the concourse itself.

There remained Perce, who had three burly assistants—two watching Perce's back, the other doing an arse-end-Charlie for the team. Perce was alone, in a souped-up VW which he had parked illegally in the forecourt, after doing a watching tail on Big Herbie's journey to the railway station.

Perce was the most vulnerable, and he knew it. If anyone was to be spotted by Vascovsky as Herbie's back-watcher, it would be Perce—though they had taken elaborate precautions to avoid the contingency. Large and muscular as he was, Perce wore a conservatively striped suit. He could have been a businessman from any EEC country.

Now, as Big Herbie moved, Curry surreptitiously crossed his fingers. The hands on the clocks of Paris were all moving closer to six. Herbie plodded around the front of the Gare de Lyon, to enter the small hallway and elevator that was the outer entrance to *Le Train Bleu*.

Even though he was aware of the tremendous refurbishing of the restaurant, Big Herbie's mind had been so dominated by the memory of a six-year-old child—from a different world and life—that the impact of the new interior came as a distinct surprise when he stepped from the elevator.

He found himself in an entrance foyer, heavily panelled, and leading into the first of what were now two large dining areas. The ambience was distinctly 1930s. Already a few people were seated, and enjoying dinner. Herbie paused, unbuttoning his overcoat as a happily-grinning black page boy, in livery, and a pill-box hat, approached to greet him.

Herbie's French came complete with German accent. "Kruger. I have to meet a friend here; though he may be late."

The page boy was followed by the Maître d'hôtel who recognised the name. Monsieur Kruger, ah yes. There was a table. He called to another waiter, saying it was Mr. Kruger. The page boy took Herbie's coat, signifying that the cloakroom was at the far end of the first room: situated in a wide passageway which led to the second dining room.

Herbie was ushered to a table on the left-hand side of the first room—against the wall, and with a good view through to a section of the other dining room. The tables were well spaced, and, while not made into booths as such, each table was enclosed by a framework made up of hatstand, brass work, luggage rack, and wooden half-wall. The impression was of being in one of the old Wagon-Lits restaurant cars.

Herbie took a seat nearest the wall, so that he could see, through the wide passage, into the station side of the second room. At least that covered the station entrance. By shifting his body slightly, he had a good view of the path he had taken, from the outside, elevator end. He sat, glanced around, vaguely registering that a couple had followed him in, and were being placed in the far corner to his right; almost certainly the first camera crew, who would be shooting the initial stills, before the main crews arrived. He quickly took in the pattern which Curry had gone through, at the safe house, with the aid of a table plan. The main camera crews would, eventually, take their places at the adjacent table. This left four other tables: behind, and in front, of him; and behind, and in front, of the camera table.

He knew Perce would be around; but Herbie did not look for him. The waiter approached, asking if he wanted to order. Herbie explained he would simply take a carafe of house wine. "The friend I am meeting—I think he must be delayed. I shall have to be patient." He grinned.

Of couse. A carafe of wine. Wait as long as you like. You will enjoy your meal when your friend arrives. The waiter disappeared, his long white apron flapping against the black trousers.

In their eyrie over the concourse, Curry and Marcel watched, and listened out. One of the observers at the front of the station came through the powerful walkie-talkie: clipped and laconic. "He's going in. Gone." A few moments later— "First *lumière* team going in. Gone."

Curry, his eyes fixed on the double iron staircase, saw Perce emerge from the crowd and begin his climb. "Just to be on the safe side," he muttered; then, pressing the button on his set, spoke quietly—"First 'sound' in please."

They waited for a few moments, then saw a middle-aged couple, both carrying baggage, begin the ascent. In one of their smaller cases, padded in foam rubber, lay a receiver. This case would go into the cloakroom, on one side of the passageway between the dining rooms. Curry wanted at least one receiver there, just in case of early arrivals.

Perce was shown to a table in the second dining room, set near to the passageway, and facing the first dining room. This had been chosen as his vantage point because of a mirror, which ran the length of the wall between the two

214

doors leading to the washrooms—opposite the cloakroom. From his place, Perce had a clear mirror-view into the area of the first dining room in which Big Herbie was now seated. He picked up the menu, ordering a dry vermouth, and saw the elderly couple quietly arguing about whether to tip the cloakroom attendant before, or after, their meal. They argued with American accents, and Perce gave the waiter an amused look, raising an eyebrow. The waiter, being of the old French school, did not react. The couple decided, a little louder, that they would tip later. Curry had described them as one of his 'speciality acts'.

Big Herbie, keeping his eyes moving regularly towards both possible entrances, had now almost cast off the nostalgia, though traces remained. The oval wall frescoes were still there—depicting in a washy colour views of the Riviera that no longer existed: coming, as they did, from a time long before the package tour, and rise of the beehive hotels.

Vascovsky took his time. There were fast, checking, calls, between Curry and the watchers. Seven o'clock went by. Seven-fifteen. Seven-thirty. "Looks as if he's playing it long, and for real." As Curry said it, a voice came from one of the forecourt watchers. "He's here. Cab just pulled up."

They waited—Curry and Marcel—in silence, until: "That's it. Out of the cab; paid off, and going in . . . Now . . . Gone."

Curry pressed the transmit button. "We're running . . . Running to all units . . . Now," he said. In quick succession the responses came up. Without any undue hurry, the various people who would be involved in stealing conversation, and pictures, started to make their way towards the railway station.

Herbie caught Vascovsky's arrival in one of his swift, routine, glances towards the elevator entrance. He turned away. Best to let the General think he had been surprised.

"Herbie?" Vascovsky's voice came from behind him.

Big Herbie turned to see the tall, elegant, man standing close to his elbow. "Ah," Herbie said. "I was a little early. Good. So are you. How are you, Jacob?" The stupid smile did not leave his face, as he stretched out an arm, grasping the KGB General's hand, then motioning him to sit down.

"I didn't think you'd come, Herbie." Vascovsky removed a cigarette case, offered it to Herbie, and lit up. "You got rid of the dogs, I trust?"

Herbie allowed the smile to fade. "I am good at that; but my time is limited. The question is, have you slipped your leash?"

"Oh yes." Vascovsky looked tanned and fit—as elegant as ever, in a grey tailored suit. "I've slipped the leash alright. It's my turn to go out on a limb this time, Herbie. Things run in cycles. Last year, you stole secretly into my patch. This year, I'm doing the same thing. The only difference is that I come unarmed, and without a retinue."

"Good." Herbie did not allow himself to sound friendly: a thin barrier should be kept between them.

* * *

In London, Michael Gold slept late, and breakfasted in his room. They had told him to take it easy. Rest. Relax. He would not be required until Friday and Saturday. They even made sure he had money. At around eleven, Tony Worboys called him at the hotel—"Just to make sure you're okay."

Michael said he was fine, asking if there was any ban on him going out.

"Do the town as far as we're concerned," said Worboys happily. Once the phone was down, though, young Worboys made a fast call to Curry's deputy—just to make sure they had some quiet leeches on Gold. They would not want him getting into any scrapes, or meeting the wrong kind of person before going back to Moscow.

Michael thought of telephoning his mother, but quickly decided that was not on. A call to his mother would have led to a visit, and questions. Instead he went out and treated himself to lunch, as it was on the Firm. From the moment of waking he could not get the blonde Intourist girl out of his head. It was as if he had been bewitched, for her face floated in his brain, meddling with any other thoughts. There appeared to be no logic except for her voice, lips, and fantasies of her body. He was sure she would give him her body, once back in Moscow.

The spell she cast began to take effect on his own body: this was not unusual for Michael Gold, whose life was permeated with more than a fair share of lust. Yet this was not lust alone. He wanted to share with the Russian girl: tell her of his life, ideas, future plans, feelings; and, in return, he needed to hear about her. He wondered what the girl's background contained—her family? her life? friends? memories? This he had never wanted of a girl before.

Intermingled with these thoughts was the constant thread of sexual desire. The mere thought of her brought on all the pangs of physical desire, so that she floated in and out of his head naked; half clothed; always sensual, constantly desirable.

By the time he finished lunch, Michael Gold had decided he must return to Moscow bearing gifts; and, as the sexuality became more urgent, he decided on feminine presents.

There was one point when he thought he should mention the business to Worboys—for you heard things about people being compromised in the Eastern Bloc countries: compromised with women. What the hell, he considered, he really wouldn't mind being compromised with his blonde Intourist girl. Best to be on the safe side, though; even if it was only for old Uncle Herbie's sake.

So, Michael Gold left the restaurant, and took a cab to Knightsbridge. After all, with a wallet full of the Firm's cash, he could afford the best in the way of female fripperies, to delight his lady in Moscow.

*   *   *

Jacob Vascovsky had, of course, not come alone and unprepared. He was too old a hand in the trade—too wise a dog to take any of Moscow Centre's field heavies either into his confidence, or to Paris. His reason for coming to Paris via Berlin had method. In East Berlin, Vascovsky had picked up two men, unknown to the British and French security services.

Then he had crossed to the West, and contacted three other similar ghosts. In all, these chosen few had done odd jobs for him in past years: being experienced in surveillance, and playing nanny to field agents. Two members of his team, known only as Kurt and Klaus, carried West German papers; the remaining three were neatly split—an American-documented woman, known as Anna; and two men with full sets of British papers: Frank and Gordon.

Vascovsky's cunning, and contacts, went very deep, after the years he had spent in East Berlin. Nobody could blame either the French SDECE, or Curry's people for not spotting 'faces'. There were no known, or even suspect, faces to spot, and Vascovsky only wanted to be certain of two things. First, that Big Herbie was not doubling on him from the outset; and, second, that he—Jacob Vascovsky—was not going to be lifted. His quintet was carefully briefed. Their first duty would be to report, after the meeting was over, on any possible external surveillance; while, if an attempted snatch took place, at any time during the Paris interlude, they were to move in and pull Vascovsky clear—using whatever force was necessary.

Ten minutes before Vascovsky's arrival at *Le Train Bleu*, Kurt and Anna had entered the restaurant—one to each entrance—and were already ordering their separate meals, one in each of the dining areas, by the time the General arrived.

Klaus, Frank, and Gordon remained outside, in front of the station building, and on the main concourse: constantly changing their positions, acting like travellers with time to kill. They mingled, bought magazines, sat quietly at vantage points, loitered, took the occasional drink, and did what all good watchers were trained to do—listened and noted anything unusual, without drawing attention to themselves. At no time was any of them far from one of the entrances to the restaurant.

Inside, Kurt found himself in a far corner, with a good view of Herbie Kruger—instantly recognisable from the briefing. Without shifting, or appearing to take any interest he also noted other things: like the fact of an American couple who talked, and acted, a shade too noisily for his liking. Kurt had a good memory, that pair at least would be described, so that Vascovsky could run them through his personal files.

In the far room, Anna found nobody of definite interest: only, possibly—and she put a large mental question mark against it—one man sitting alone. As a woman expert in these things, she wondered first about his clothes, for the man was obviously in fine physical condition, and alert in that seemingly relaxed manner of a professional. Secondly, she instantly recorded that he sat at a table affording a good view, via the wall mirrors, into the other dining room— particularly the area occupied by Herbie Kruger. She could see all this because she sat only a table away from him.

Outside, it was virtually impossible to mark people as suspect. Anyone, or everyone, could be part of a team. The three men circling, and watching, discovered this in a few minutes, and each decided their best course would be to remain vigilant against any possible snatch.

At their table inside *Le Train Bleu*, Jacob Vascovsky and Herbie Kruger faced each other. Both, for a moment, reflected the same thoughts—conscious of time and its changes; that no man or woman remains the same person from year to year. Kruger, Vascovsky knew, was not now the same Big Herbie of the tense and nervy days of the Cold War, when he ran his all-important networks in the East. On his part, Kruger felt—more than saw—that his old enemy of the secret labyrinths, was changed by time, experience, and the altered circumstances of two decades.

A waiter appeared. The restaurant began to fill up around them, but each man centered his concentration on the other, squaring up like two world class chess champions. For Big Herbie there was a necessary dialogue to be followed—to draw the Russian, so that the electronic thieves could pick up words, and phrases, to be reshaped in their workshops. These would emerge as tapes which might, eventually, lead Vascovsky to perdition.

Vascovsky also had an end in sight—to play the big

219

German; seduce him; make him believe, and so bring him safely into the net, and within reach of the deadly barbed gaff.

They selected a simple dinner, neither man much bothered by the thought of eating—a seafood cocktail for Vascovsky; soup of the day for Herbie; steaks for both. Vascovsky insisted on choosing the wine—a sensible Château Grancey.

As the Russian ordered the wine he was conscious of the adjacent table being occupied by a boisterous party: three men and a woman, chattering away in French. Obviously business people from the same company. A small suitcase and a briefcase were set on the floor by the table—left there and not bothered about through the serious act of eating.

On the other side of the room, Vascovsky's man, Kurt, noted the group, wondered for a second or two, and then decided to remain watching: giving them the benefit of the doubt.

Herbie now knew the cameras were in place—at the adjacent table—and the meeting was being recorded for posterity. Vascovsky was nobody's fool; so Herbie hoped to God that Curry knew what he was about: that they would get away with it.

"I really wondered if you would come, you know." Vascovsky voiced the opinion for the second time.

"I'm here." Herbie's eyes held Vascovsky, who felt a tingle of unease. "So let's get on with it." Herbie appeared relaxed, perhaps too much at ease. "You have some kind of proposition?" he asked.

Jacob Vascovsky touched his knife, breaking the gaze for a moment, giving himself time to choose the correct words for his important opening gambit. Deep inside he knew he was now committed. He simply had to trust those who were watching out for him. This was the moment to get in close, twist the knife; pull in on the line. "The fact that you're here at all gives me hope," he began, glancing around. Kurt gave no warning sign, so he leaned forward and plunged. "You cannot be happy, Herbie. Life *has* to be grim for you. You wish to talk about it?"

His large opponent shrugged, the face open, readable. "You seem to know it all anyway. Me? I'm a leper. Your tapes said it. There is no more trust . . ."

Vascovsky made a mental lunge, and broke in, "Nor will there be. Never again."

"Unless . . .?"

The General thought he detected a plea in Big Herbie's voice and eyes. He did not allow the internal smile to break through to his own lips or eyes. "Unless you can pull off some great coup, eh?"

The plea vanished, and Herbie grinned. "If I snatched you, Jacob. That would be a coup. Or if I talked you into doubling."

Vascovsky willed himself not even to move his head in Kurt's direction. Relax, he told himself. Make yourself at ease. "Oh, I'd come to you. No hesitation. I'd do a walk-in, or leap over the border, at any time . . ."

Vascovsky watched Big Herbie do a clown's face, drooping his lips: a caricature of the mask of tragedy. "Then we could go now. It would by my pleasure," He hunched closer over the table, dropping his voice. "Just walk out of here, and drive to Charles de Gaulle. A couple of hours and I'd have you tucked up safe and sound."

Vascovsky laughed, knowing what would happen if they walked out together. For a second he played the scene over in his mind—his little team cutting off all the exits; Herbie manhandled; quietly put away even. "There's no percentage in it. Herbie"—he now followed Kruger, becoming conspiratorial in tone—"Herbie, I put it on the tape. This meeting is to iron out the fine points. You're a leper; you're not even British by birth. You've served them well; now they want you out." He raised a hand, sensing Kruger would interrupt. "You know it, Herbie. But the British have a way of doing things; they still pretend to play the game—as they say—even when they hold all the aces, and have the cards stacked against you. They send you to Coventry; give you the cold shoulder and a pile of useless work. What they wish is that you will, eventually, say

221

you've had enough. Then they'll send you private, on half pension."

If I don't do it in my own time, Big Herbie thought. Aloud, he said, 'Something like that," believing this was the way the Firm would handle matters if necessary. Inwardly he gave a mocking laugh, for he not only believed it, but also knew it. Had he not seen it happen enough times?

"With us it is different," Vascovsky saw the light at the end of the tunnel. "They promote me. Make me feel at ease. They've given me a job of high importance." An acid smile to denote distaste at the tactics of his service. "Oh, I shall do it: do what they require. But," wagging a finger, ". . . and it's a big but: once that job is done; once I've been lulled into thinking all is well, they'll cut off. My form of leprosy will be more permanent. A posting to some godforsaken place; maybe even a transfer to the GRU with a brand new set of orders. Not the pleasures of Berlin this time. For me it will be Commandant of one of those places—like the Gulags; Siberia; the Arctic. Wherever, it will be most unpleasant." Pause for the effect. Count to six. "We're in the same boat, if on different tracks, my friend."

He could tell nothing now, looking at Herbie's face. The large German just seemed simple. "Well, come with me," Kruger spread his hands wide, in a gesture of invitation.

Vascovsky had to will himself to remember Herbie Kruger's inbred cunning and ingenuity. He wondered what was going on in that agile brain, behind the bland look. "You think that would be the end?" he asked. "I might just as well say the same thing to you—Herbie, come to Russia. You think my problems would be over if I snatched you now?" He shook his head, pausing as the waiters arrived with the seafood cocktail, and Herbie's soup; letting them get well out of earshot before he continued. "Herbie, my destiny's already planned. With my masters it's like the whole thing's been written in the stars. You got away from me last year. So, that's over and done with. Even if I was able to take you back, by force, now, things would not change. Whatever happens, General Vascovsky is finished. My career stops when I complete my present assignment. Finish. Finis. The End. A wasteland." He had rehearsed that particular speech well. Now he waited to see if the big fish would bite.

"Then come to us." In the back of his mind, Herbie heard a voice from several years ago, reciting—'We are the hollow men . . . We are the stuffed men.'

It was Vascovsky's turn to spread his hands. "I've said it. Where's the percentage? There are better ways. Together we share many secrets. We are men of a particular technology— a dying technology. They're phasing us out, Herbie." Another careful pause. Hold back a fraction, Vascovsky told himself. Now—with confidence, "But, Herbie Kruger, if we go together, with a pooling of knowledge, we would have all the techniques, and all the ways. We could act as cartographers to the new secret world—when it comes." He raised an eyebrow, ready for the testing question, "You believe it *will* come, don't you?"

Herbie spooned soup into his mouth. Twice, giving him time to out-think the device Vascovsky was using. "What I believe has no bearing on the matter."

"But you believe we're near the end?" Pushing.

Herbie gave one of his gigantic shrugs. "Five; ten years. Yes."

"The computers have already taken over; the spies in the sky provide military data. No, I agree, they're not yet fully grown; and, before they're perfect, the new world will come. The population is already too large; the world's food supplies lie in a state of imbalance; the natural resources are running out at a terrifying pace; gasoline, oil, minerals—all are measurable. It is over these things that the final days of our civilisation will end and fail. The war will not be fought over ideologies or creeds. The next holocaust will come from greed, not politics. It will be short, sharp and devastating. Then, when it's finished, and youth dead as stone, the world will need to pick itself up. Technicians will be forced to pool their knowledge—the experts in industry, mining, agriculture, and the rest. All will be needed—even the military technicians; policing; and, my friend, people like ourselves who know the secret ways." He leaned back, looking around casually. Kurt was still flying the 'safe' signal—his cigarettes and lighter in view on the table.

Vascovsky was sure, by the look on Herbie's face, that he was halfway to winning. He knew how this kind of approach could outflank and psychologically persuade a man as bitter as Herbie.

For a full minute Kruger said nothing; allowing his face to show a mere gleam of interest. In fact he did not even acknowledge the thesis—attractive as it was. Did Vascovsky really believe Herbie could, or would, fall for this kind of approach? At last, as the waiters cleared away the plates, he asked—as straightforwardly as he could—the real question of the evening: what was Jacob Vascovsky's true intention?

The General waited until the steaks were served, and the wine poured. "I have a small place, unknown to anyone but my wife, until now," he began. "I do not intend to give you the exact location, but it is tucked away in Switzerland. Now, Herbie, if I complete my present assignment, I know ways of making a great deal of money. The job is crucial, and I can write my own ticket for the inside story of my life—to be published in various Western magazines and journals. What we can earn from that will keep us safe—and very, very secure—in Switzerland, for a long time."

Herbie saw the whole thing in a flash—the scales dropping from his eyes like some blinding revelation. In spite of the glimpse ahead, he held up a hand, palm towards the Russian, "I could not think of living on your earnings, Jacob. I have none of my own—well, no real capital, that is."

Time for the charm, Vascovsky thought, throwing out his most winning, friendly smile. "Oh, but you don't understand, Herbie. I have almost completed the job they have given me in Moscow. There are a few loose ends—and likely to be more. If we are to have a partnership of mutual trust, I would need your help—to clear up those loose ends as it were."

Herbie grunted. Oh yes, Jacob would need some help—and what help. "You honestly believe I would give you my trust?" He felt a tiny sliver of ice slide down his spine as he used the word *trust*.

"You've come to meet me, on neutral ground. You've listened to me. This is the start of trust. If you need further proofs, then I shall satisfy you."

Now it was coming. The sucker bait. Vascovsky saw it as the true lure.

Herbie, allowing the whole ploy to revolve in his mind, chomped on his steak. The meat was tender and oozing blood. "Melt in the mouth," Herbie said. Then, "So what is it you want of me?"

Vascovsky slid a hand into his breast pocket, bringing out two folded papers. His present assignment, he declared was to identify a long-term British penetration agent within the KGB. "If you're a leper, Herbie, there's a reason . . ."

Thrust. Now the parry. "Yes, they believe I was about to defect. They still have doubts; still wonder if I work for you."

This was not what Vascovsky had expected from Kruger. He knew there had been a tiny flicker of surprise in his eyes, and he hoped the German had not seen it. Slowly, regaining balance, he shook his head. "They do not trust you, my dear Herbie, because, unwittingly, you gave me information that narrowed down the field, as they say." He was pleased to see the look of shock spread, for a second, over Big Herbie's lump face. "The information has led me directly to the culprit—the long-term agent within our Service."

Soft; then hard, Herbie thought. He allowed a feigned gasp of surprise; smothered it; then let out a single ironic laugh. "If that *is* true, no wonder they're treating me as though I have the plague."

"Oh it's true." He had Herbie now: sure of it. "Certainly it's true; and I shall have their man—your man—within days now."

Herbie looked grave, even downcast, with small lines of worry between his eyes. When he spoke, the voice came out soft and unsteady. "If you're so certain . . . then what do you want of me?"

Vascovsky drummed his fingers lightly on the thick, starched tablecloth. He had his man. Herbie was inside the box. All he needed to do was drop the grille. "I need the details from your end." Smooth without a trace of oil, or greed. "I need the British dossier on your man, working within the KGB. For that dossier, I offer you a safe retreat; and a safe future—should the time and need arise."

He watched Kruger's face and hands, eyes flickering from one to the other, trying to fathom any body language. "You see, Herbie, I'm certain of my man. I know who he is; I am building evidence. However, your assistance will make things more simple. Your attitude, if I judge it correctly, is one of great bitterness towards your masters. And why not? You're German born—not even an Englishman. Your career, like mine, is washed up. Only I freely admit to you that I feel no bitterness. My motivation is one of pure fear. If I can present my masters with a full, and complete, picture of the past, it will set them off guard: help cover my tracks; give me breathing space. It is in both our interests for survival."

He still held the papers. Now he laid one sheet in front of Kruger. Big Herbie took it in both hands, allowing his fingers to tremble slightly.

The page carried a typed list of names, and the positions at present held by each person—

Oleg Zapad. Head of Directorate T. etc. etc.
Nikolai Aleksandrovich Severov. Head of Directorate S.
    etc. etc.
Vladimir Glubodkin. Head of Special Service I. etc. etc.
Andrei Tserkov. Head of Department V. etc. etc.

Vascovsky noted the trembling fingers, and knew the target was in his sights. "You've heard of these men, no doubt?"

Herbie said everyone in the trade knew of them. "They're all very big guns in your Service. So?" His tone played down, a shade too casual for Vascovsky.

"So?" the General repeated. "So, one of them has worked, for a long time—I believe—as an agent of your Firm. You know about this?" Vascovsky smiled to himself.

Herbie's hesitation was too long; he had no idea. "I would find it hard to believe. Very hard."

"My own masters found it difficult also." Vascovsky on safe ground now. He could almost feel the solid stone under his feet. "I also found it hard. But, Herbie, it is true."

Slowly he passed over the other sheet. On it was typed one name, together with a formal list of the man's appointments since he had first joined the Cheka. The name was that of General Vladimir Glubodkin—Stentor.

Herbie remained stone-faced. For good measure he allowed his fingers to stop shaking.

"As an old chekist, myself, I find belief hard," Vascovsky continued. "But there is little doubt. You see, Herbie, it would save us much time if you would secure this operative's dossier for us. A copy, of course."

Herbie's guffaw was perfectly genuine. He had been correct about Vascovsky's ploy. "You joke, yes?"

"I seldom joke about important things like this."

"I am a pariah." Big Herbie's face was a map of desolation. "If what you say is true, then the dossier will be in a steel box, wired with alarms, and guarded by the Royal Marines."

Oh, got him completely. Vascovsky gave an inward sigh of relief. "Maybe. But you are Herbie Kruger. You can do the impossible. That dossier will obviate much trouble. It will save my masters from long, and arduous, interrogation; and it will give them some idea of what damage this man has done over the years. A last, difficult, case for Herbie Kruger. Think of it as getting your own back."

Herbie said he could only think of it as quite impossible. He carefully folded the two sheets of paper together, holding them tightly by one end, passing the white oblong across the table to Vascovsky.

The General took the papers, not even noticing that Herbie held on to them for a few seconds, so that each man had his hand on the object.

227

A nice one for the cameras, Herbie considered. Who was passing the papers? Who was receiving? The big German still rumbled with laughter. "And if all this is true? If I could get what you want—and let me say now, I'd be glad to be rid of them all—*if* I could do this, what would I get in return, now, as a sign of good faith?"

Vascovsky believed Herbie could still do such a thing. "After all, you know your way around. If the dossier exists, I should imagine that, at this very moment, you know where to look."

Vascovsky did not take his eyes off Herbie, as the big man scowled, then gave a quick nod. "Maybe."

"You wish a sign of good faith. Okay, Herbie. You take this." Vascovsky drew out yet another sheet of folded paper, passing it across the table. "I give you two names. Both have worked for the KGB, within the British establishment, for the past ten years. All the details are there. You'd have no trouble proving it. That's my sign of good faith."

Big Herbie seemed to hesitate, his fingers hovering half an inch from the paper for a second before he took it. Vascovsky felt a twinge of warning—there and gone in a moment.

For Herbie it was more insurance for the cameras.

"If I'm to do it," the pause lasted for what seemed to be a full minute, as the men again locked eyes. "If I'm to do it, you want it quick, uh?"

"Fast as possible."

"I promise nothing. I know nothing." Herbie pushed his plate away. "All I say is that if it is true, I have a fair idea where the dossier can be found—*if it's true*." Again the eternal pause, leaving Vascovsky in doubt for a few seconds longer. Then—"Yes, Jacob. Yes, you're right. I want out. But I must warn you. You double on me; play me false, and I make sure you pay."

"We all pay. One way or another, we all pay—some time." As Vascovsky said it, Big Herbie remembered he had used almost the identical words to Tubby Fincher, on the day the Director General's ADC had come to bring him from Warminster.

He sat, very silent, as though reflecting on Vascovsky's offer. In reality he wondered at the arrogance of the General. Yet, Herbie could only but admire the professional risk the man was taking—putting his career out on a limb to catch him, Big Herbie Kruger. At last, he said, "If I can do it at all, it *will* be fast. You wish to meet here? Or shall I come closer, to show my own trust?"

Like taking candy from a baby, Vascovsky thought, glancing up in the act of lighting a cigarette. "If you wish to come closer . . . Well, of course. You have a suggestion?"

He watched Big Herbie scowl in thought, then nod. "I may know a way into the Baltic. Give me a code, and method. I'll let you know."

The General preened at the thought, asking where Herbie had in mind.

It was then that Big Herbie Kruger began to talk, and set up what he was all ready thinking of as 'The Main Event'. With many interruptions, and slight modifications, they had method, cipher, and place arranged after half-an-hour's discussion.

By the time they came to order the pudding, the people at the next table had left.

In the other room, Anna decided she had been quite wrong about the man in the business suit—the one with muscles. Perce was taking his cue from a body sign given by Big Herbie, a good twenty minutes before he and Vascovsky went their separate ways.

Across the room, Kurt was certain Herbie had come alone. Outside, the team had no ideas: only the instinct of professional watchers.

*   *   *

In Moscow it had been a busy day for Yekaterina Vascovsky. She rose late, took a light meal, then bathed and dressed.

Her toilet completed, Yekaterina went to the desk, which was commonly accepted by the couple as her property, and stood by the master bedroom window.

Without undue haste she unlocked the centre drawer, slid it out, removed the neatly packed contents of notepaper, envelopes, and other writing materials, before removing the false bottom, which was really only one thin, tightly-fitting, inner lining. Beneath this pliable piece of wood lay several sheets of flimsy paper, crammed with tiny, neat writing.

Yekaterina had waited for almost a month to deal with the matters gathered together on these sheets. The writing was in French. To the ordinary eye, they were merely copied pages, with annotations, from the works of Colette. To the cryptanalysts of the French SDECE, the information contained in these extracts from *The Last of Chéri*, *Gigi*, and the like, was of paramount importance. After a long wait, yet another covert operation was about to bear fruit.

At just after three o'clock in the afternoon, Yekaterina Vascovsky was driven—by her husband's chauffeur—to the main Moscow store, GUM, on Red Square.

She made her way through the vast building, along the wide catwalks, and across the bridges—which make the interior seem like some large open market—up to the third floor, where Section 100 is tucked away: Section 100 being the special privilege store for clothes.

After making a few simple purchases, she left Section 100. It was as she reached the stairway, leading down from the third floor, that she bumped into the wife of the French Embassy's Third Secretary (Trade). Both women politely apologised.

Before five o'clock that afternoon, the envelope containing Madame Vascovsky's sheets of closely-written French, had been carried—in the Third Secretary's wife's shopping basket—to the French Embassy on Dimitrov Street.

*   *   *

In London, Worboys checked again with Curry Shepherd's deputy. Their boy, Gold, had enjoyed a heavy lunch at the *Tibereo*, followed by a short walk. After that he took a cab to Knightsbridge.

"A small shopping spree," Curry's deputy said. "A couple of select shops specialising in top people's lingerie."

"Top people?" Worboys was puzzled. "Male top people?"

"No, dear boy, female. Friend Gold's either a pouf transvestite, or has good taste in ladies. Bought some very jolly knickers our fellow tells me. Very jolly, and bloody expensive."

Worboys decided he would talk to Curry as soon as he returned from Paris.

*   *   *

Curry Shepherd was delighted. "The sound's perfect. Already on its way to London." He paced the main room of the Place Voltaire safe flat. "And the camera people say they'll perform miracles. The film's also on its way back."

Marcel had come with them—both the Frenchman and Curry waiting, together, for Big Herbie's arrival. Herbie was followed, a few minutes later, by Perce.

"Can't be certain, but I think there was a woman watching his back from where I was sitting." Perce did not seem unduly concerned.

Herbie grunted. "Difficult. Could have been a man in our room. Caught him glancing a couple of times, but Vascovsky's too much of an old pro to come in without protection."

"You think the idiot's on the level?" Curry shook his head.

"Don't you believe it, Curry my old horse. He's playing a hunch. If it works, he'll have the crown jewels—the Stentor dossier, and me. Look, friend, I put myself on offer to speed things up. Now he probably thinks I'm easy meat. He's out to snatch me on his home ground. But I doubt if the old man, our beloved Director General's going to bend the rules that much. He's already looked the other way a couple of times. I'm officially not allowed to operate outside Britain. Can you see him letting me swoop about the Baltic, landing on Russian soil even?"

"Does it matter?"

"I suppose not, but I'd like to be there for the kill. Just to make sure."

231

They spoke in lowered voices, out of earshot from Marcel, who had been called to the telephone in the other room.

The Frenchman returned, looking pleased with himself. "I have a great favour to ask of you," he began. "In return for my people watching out for you. It is a favour that might pay handsomely."

"Ask away, my friend," Curry was in a state of high exuberance.

"The names the Russian gave to Mr. Kruger—their people working for you. Might I be allowed a small peep?"

Herbie and Curry looked at each other. It was Herbie who spoke. "I shall leave the paper on the table, here, while Curry and I take a look out of the window."

They stood, gazing down at the night traffic, Curry glancing at his watch. They had a flight to catch, at Charles de Gaulle, within the next ninety minutes, and Curry wanted the departure from the safe house to be as clean as possible. Both men knew the names Vascovsky had given them—two junior officers with Military Analysis, who had served for a year in Moscow, at the Embassy.

Behind them, they heard Marcel whistle. "He's pumped you chickenfeed, I fear."

"Running to form," Curry said cheerfully.

"If you would listen for a moment." Marcel sounded concerned. "We have our own operation in Moscow. I told you, Curry, I might have news for you before you left. I've cleared it with our people, and an official report will be going to your Director General, first thing tomorrow. Indeed, the two names here are suspect, but very small fry. Our operation has dug out five important French sources in Paris; and several in your own Service." Slowly he passed over a scribbled list to Curry.

Herbie leaned over Shepherd's shoulder to read. Certainly the two names, given to him by Vascovsky, were on the list. More important were three others—the second-in-command at Warminster; one senior officer in the Section dealing with liaison between the Firm and the Foreign Office. Last, and most important, was one of the three female secretaries who worked in the Director General's suite of offices, at headquarters.

19

ACTION WAS TAKEN first thing on Friday morning, in London. They kept the whole business in the family—no calls to the sister Service, MI5; certainly no application for arrest warrants from the Branch. At Warminster, the second-in-command was discreetly removed from his office, and walked quietly to one of the interrogation complexes.

At the London Headquarters, the Director General saw each of the other suspects without giving them any opportunity for collusion. One at a time they were taken away, by car, or plain van. By midday all were settled in new quarters at Warminster, where the confessors prepared for a high old time.

Other officers visited families, quietly whispering excuses; while local telephone exchanges received Home Office warrants for phones to be wired.

All this unpleasant activity failed to take the edge off the Director General's pleasure at the success of the Paris operation. He had tape and film men working around the clock; while some of the document experts were reported to be well ahead with their particularly devious machinations. These included copies of cipher messages, in an original word and number code, the key to which lay in the Bodley Head collected edition of Mr. Graham Greene's works. The fact that Stentor had reported Vascovsky's own specially bound series of this edition—to Michael Gold—naturally played a large part in its choice.

The recording engineers came up with three high-speed tapes, in clear language, taken from the Vascovsky-Kruger messages. Each of them created damning evidence that Vascovsky had been controlled, by Herbie Kruger, for a long time—maybe even in the days when Big Herbie ran the East Berlin networks, during the late 1950s and early '60s.

Now, the same engineers were putting together two recordings of meetings between Vascovsky and his British control—Eberhard Lukas Kruger—taken from the three sources which had stolen the previous night's conversation at *Le Train Bleu*.

"It's really quite shocking," The Director grinned, almost with glee. "Everything sounds, and looks, so genuine. I almost believe it myself."

They planned a council of war for the early evening. Michael Gold would be there, and the specialists—sound, documents and film—were instructed to have the whole package ready by then. In the meantime, Herbie waited, in the DG's ante-room, while young Worboys and Curry Shepherd went through last minute snags.

Worboys, a shade casually, mentioned Michael Gold's day of fun and purchases to Curry, who put it to the Director and Fincher.

"He hasn't had time to make any liaisons in Moscow." The DG was distracted by the mass of manufactured evidence, which he called, 'The dirty trick of all time'.

Curry screwed up his nose, pursing the lips in a sign of indifference. "Probably getting ready for a mild celebration when he's back. Nothing wrong in buying a few pairs of drawers for a lady. Done it meself before now."

"Horses for courses," mumbled the Director. "Look at the grain on that photograph. Wonderful."

"Do anything about it?" Curry asked.

"What?"

"Gold."

"Oh, get Worboys to have a word," as though Worboys was not even in the room. Then, realising he was—"Just put him in the picture; though there's not much call for sexual

234

blackmail these days. The lads from Dzerzhinsky Square've given up in disgust. Just a quiet word, Worboys. Right?"

Worboys said he would do just that. He did not write it down. He was not likely to forget a small chore such as this. On the way to the airport would be a good time.

Only in the end, it was Curry Shepherd himself who took Michael Gold out to Heathrow, which accounted for the warning not being given.

*   *   *

Herbie Kruger used all his varied talents on the Director General. He charmed, played the dumb oaf, cajoled and, finally, shouted. He did not lie down on the floor and drum his heels; nor did he weep. The Director General would not have been surprised if Big Herbie had resorted to these tactics.

"My dear Herbie, we've gone a long way already. You know that; I know that. When the Minister has the full report, I'll get a chewing out in any case. Your performance in Paris was admirable; but even I—blessed with an imagination which my wife considers bizarre—would not have thought you were serious about the Baltic coast meeting."

They were already a long way into the argument. Big Herbie sighed. "Someone has to do it, if not me. I can prophesy, here and now, exactly how Stentor's going to play this. We should direct him—yes. But he will not put in the dagger by himself; he'll leave it to someone more openly ruthless, and that someone will need to catch Vascovsky in the act. We stitch him up, okay? But we also have to set the snare—is that correct, setting a snare?"

"Snare? Yes. Snare or gin, whichever you like."

"Gin's a drink. My god, and I thought I knew the language," Herbie threw up his hands. "The English language could drive a man to suicide."

"So could a trip over the briny to . . . where was it you suggested?"

"There's a small, fairly deserted, cove between Ventspils

235

and Lyserort on the old Latvian coast. Fir trees to within a hundred yards of the beach. I thought we could use the same plan we had for getting Stentor off—only I would offer myself. I'd need cover, and let myself be seen early enough for them to make their snatch. But it *has* to be me, otherwise the fit-up will run aground."

"How about a lookalike, Herbie? I'm sure . . ."

Herbie grimaced, uttering an obscenity. "You find a lookalike for me? You search all the loony houses for miles. You might find, yes. But not easy."

The argument volleyed back and forth. Herbie's bulk was but the outward and visible sign of a stubborn toughness, and he fought all the way, knowing he had the Director in a very difficult situation.

"Who's really running this, anyway?" he asked, almost pushing himself over the desk.

"It's a joint thing. We're all playing our parts, Herbie. Interlocking."

"But it was *me*," Big Herbie thumped his chest like a gorilla, "*me* you asked to perform the miracle. So I do it, and your man will not come out. So I then set up another way. Remember, sir, Martha Adler will work to me. In fact she holds the aces, and we have to get a final message to Vascovsky."

After ninety minutes of this verbal battering, the Director partially gave in. "Tell you what I'll do, Herbie . . ."

The DG then outlined the concessions he was prepared to make. The result was almost total victory for Big Herbie. At least he gained enough to turn the business to his own advantage. The Director was prepared to seek ministerial permission for Kruger to travel as far as Stockholm, in company with Curry Shepherd.

The Director clearly saw the necessity for some kind of vessel to be standing off the Latvian coast, at an appointed time; he also realised that craft—probably a Gemini—would have to give the impression that it contained Big Herbie himself. As far as the Director was concerned, once he had the ministerial thumbs up, the finer points could be left to Curry and Herbie—in consultation with the SAS boys who were still quietly hiding out in Stockholm's Grand Hotel.

"All that remains, then, is for Vascovsky to know time and place for the rendezvous."

The Director shuffled his papers. "And with Vascovsky, also Stentor," he agreed. "When your protégé, Gold, takes in that package tomorrow, it also has to contain Stentor's final timings and instructions."

Herbie said that would be best. He could set Martha off like clockwork. It was really a question of timing. He suspected Vascovsky would be getting back to Moscow that night—a day ahead of Gold, who would have his work cut out in order to see the package in safely, and on schedule.

In the darker parts of his mind, Big Herbie worried, in case Vascovsky lost his nerve and plunged for Stentor's arrest, before receiving Herbie's confirmation that he held the key to the KGB man's suspicions—the dossier itself.

He left the Director's office, heading straight for the clinic, and Martha Adler. Now was the time for long-range manipulation. Tomorrow, as Gold left for Moscow, he decided, Martha Adler would have to make contact: a preliminary, telling Vascovsky the goal was in sight. The full moment could be left until either Sunday evening, or even Monday morning. At the council that night, Herbie would propose Tuesday as the final day. The early hours of Tuesday morning. The day when Jacob Vascovsky, General of the Committee for State Security, the KGB, would be lured to a dot along the Baltic coast, and there meet with that nameless spectre which haunts all men and women whose lives are spent deep within the trade of secrecy.

Martha appeared relieved to see Herbie. She was sitting in a chair, near to the window; her body covered in a towelling robe, which fell open as she rose to greet him, revealing the greater portion of those lovely long legs.

The pallor appeared to have gone, confidence returned and her eyes were clear. Herbie detected a slight trembling of the hands, and that same clinging need, which spoke volumes.

Martha was, he concluded, still terrified of the retribution promised by Vascovsky if she failed.

She held on to the big man, her lips reaching up to touch his ear, asking him, in a throaty whisper, if it was all over.

"Not yet. Nearly. Soon now. You have two more small jobs, my dear: another pair of messages—telephone calls to our mutual acquaintance. After that I shall be away for one night, maybe two. Then it will be over."

She shook her head, saying it would never be over; she would not believe it until there was real proof.

"You'll have your real proof, Martha. Very soon now. Have I ever let you down?" Echoing the argument he had used with her before.

She became more docile, after that, asking when it would be safe for her to go home, to the bungalow in Lymington? And would Herbie see her there? Had he meant what he said before? Was there a chance that she would not be alone any more? "It's been a relief here. People understand; just as you understand, Herbie."

Now was not the time for Herbie to think of future long-term plans; now was the present, and a time for the netting of Vascovsky.

He sidestepped the issues with Martha Adler: soothing her, kissing the smooth hair, and tiny ears, feeling her push against him, as though she wished for physical satisfaction here, in the clinic's private room. He made no specific promises, leaving the impression that all would come right for them, once this particular job was done. He would return tomorrow, when she was to make the first telephone call to Moscow.

She begged him to stay, but he pleaded duty; kissing her, embracing her with a bear hug, then disentangled himself from the clinging body.

On the way out he met the doctor, Harvester—a man with cropped hair and metal glasses whom Herbie disliked, but respected. He often thought Harvester was one of the most ruthless men he knew. Now, however, the doctor proved friendly; seeming to be genuinely concerned about Martha

238

Adler's welfare. "It'll take a few years. But, with help, and the knowledge that people love her, there should be complete stabilisation."

"I need her lucid and stable tomorrow evening, and on either Sunday night or first thing Monday morning." It was Herbie being ruthless now. As he left the clinic, he wondered if he could ever give up this life of professional secrets. Would there never be a real escape?

*   *   *

At the Yasenevo complex, Oleg Zapad—responsible for data on military sciences from the West: Head of Directorate T—brought the small meeting to order.

It had been called at a moment's notice, and not all the members of the First Directorate's Standing Committee for Forward Planning could be present. In fact, around the table in Conference Room 110, Block A, sat the original four officials—Zapad, with the blank face and wry sense of humour. The tall, fine-looking elderly Nikolai Severov, of Directorate S, who held, under that thick smooth white hair, the knowledge of all KGB foreign operatives. Vladimir Glubodkin—Stentor— the dandy, bronzed and fit, chief of Special Service I. Last, the sinister, chain-smoking, Tserkov of Department V.

Nobody had been able to locate the Chairman's special representative, General Vascovsky. He was out of town, according to the General's sidekick who posed as his adjutant: Major Vitali Badim.

The meeting had been called, on instructions from the Chairman's office, to formulate possible First Directorate reaction to a leak from the French Secret Service: the SDECE. News had arrived, in a flash signal that morning, signifying that five important agents, planted within the French establishment—and their SDECE—had been quietly lifted during the previous night. A sixth source—missed by the French—had remained to give the warning.

The Standing Committee for Forward Planning were not to know that the Chairman, aware of General Vascovsky's absence from Moscow, sat in on their meeting, via the miracles of electronics. The tapes and video would reach him later in the day. This was a quick concealment operation, for the Standing Committee were still under the impression that they used a 'silent' room.

Severov was anxious. After all, the five agents were known to him. He had seen to their infiltration, following a long wooing by his own selectors.

"We cannot deny there has been a very serious blow-out," he began. "These men and women have only held operational status for a matter of months. Certain small items have reached us, I believe, but there's no way of avoiding the fact that they've been nipped in the bud. It's a catastrophe." He shook his head. The mane of white hair moved, then settled back, perfectly in place.

"And the source from whom the information came?" Glubodkin's disinterested voice seemed to be tinged with concern for his colleague.

"Very long-term. Buried deep. Took over from . . ." Stopped himself from giving the name aloud. "From an impeccable operator. She got out several years ago, after giving us a long run."

"She?" Tserkov was known to mistrust female recruits from foreign powers. He was of the old school. Women in the field could be good, if they were Russian women: trained to perfection. Foreign women, in place, were always a danger, as far as the Head of the dreaded Department V was concerned.

"It was a woman who had to get out. A woman took her place. There was no interrelation." By this, Severov meant neither woman had known of the other's recruitment, or placing.

"You're absolutely certain, Nikolai?" Vladimir Glubodkin's effete manner, they all understood, cloaked a devious and professional mind.

Zapad tapped the table. "Nikki"—he looked at Severov with the usual bleak and inscrutable stare—"Volodya has a point. I think you should look carefully into the background of the woman who had to get out. The French have trawled

240

well, but left an obvious hole. They're devious bastards who'd fuck their sisters for advancement. First . . ." he began to tell off the items on his fingers, "we should advise the normal, and precautionary, measures in this kind of situation—plugging gaps; backtracking on those who made the original selections; reappraising every single officer who had anything to do with training; interrogating the controllers concerned . . ."

"I've already seen to it. They've been recalled. As soon as the Chairman's office informed me, I asked if this could be ordered." Nikolai Severov ticked off items on the pad in front of him.

"Good." Zapad knew this was not in their brief, yet was relieved to hear steps had already been taken. "At moments like this, it is always better to advise on standard procedures. Yet—as I say—General Glubodkin has a point. Note I called Volodya by his rank. That's for the record." It was the first, and only, hint of humour they had from Oleg Zapad that day. He continued—"Always we think our field agents are shielded from the truth. Nikolai Aleksandrovich, you had to pull a woman out, from SDECE Codes and Ciphers, some years ago. What if she doubled? You are the only one who has her bona fides, but it *has* been known, Nikki—an agent is blown; they let the agent know; they re-programme to their own specifications; then they allow a getaway."

Nikolai Severov laughed. "Oleg, my old comrade, you know not of what you speak. Our French lady, who got out by the straps of her bra—if you'll pardon the expression—is Caesar's wife. She *has* to be above suspicion."

"Why?" snapped Tserkov, all traces of the avuncular manner gone. Even these high-ranking Generals went in fear of this deceptively friendly man.

For a second, Severov looked cornered; shifty around the eyes: a man about to betray a confidence. "If I must say it aloud, then so be it. But this is highly restricted information." He swallowed, unable to retain his usual composure. "Our French agent, who worked so well in their codes and cipher department before she was blown, is now here in Moscow.

241

She married well. Her husband cannot be with us today, but he is the Chairman's representative. Our former agent is now married to General Vascovsky . . ."

"Who, it is well-known and documented, has French blood flowing through his veins." Glubodkin, half-yawning, straightened his immaculately knotted tie. His old heart sang. What if . . .? No, that would be too good; but the very fact of Yekaterina Vascovsky's involvement being revealed to the Committee now, was of great assistance.

"And Vascovsky cannot be with us today." Andrei Tserkov paused, putting a flame to yet another cigarette. "Yes, we should add this to our list of recommendations—that a complete documentation, a detailed Curriculum Vitae, of Comrade General Vascovsky's wife be made available. Also that her lifestyle, and work, should undergo a reappraisal. If the Comrade Chairman wishes, I can deal with this myself."

Zapad made a note, adding the suggestion to their list. "That is about all we can recommend, gentlemen . . ." He seemed to be on the point of adding something, when the telephone began to purr softly on the table. Zapad answered, listening intently. "Andrei," he called to General Tserkov. "One of your people is looking for you. He says it's urgent, so I've told him to come up, and wait outside."

The Head of Department V gave a dour nod, excused himself, and left the room.

"Can anyone think of a missing link? Something we could add as an extra guideline for the Comrade Chairman?"

There were some muttered, almost private, conversations; but nobody could suggest any further recommendation.

"Then I'll have this list made up, and sent directly to Dzerzhinsky Square." As Oleg Zapad spoke, so General Tserkov re-entered the room, his usually friendly face now turned to a thundercloud.

The remaining trio of the Standing Committee turned towards him, as he began to talk almost before the door closed behind him. "Gentlemen, an interesting point has just emerged. I may well have overstepped the boundaries of my responsibility; but General Vascovsky's appointment to this committee has given me cause for much thought, since it was first announced. In no way did I think the Chairman was deliberately making an error, but most of us are aware that Vascovsky's career hung in the balance last year." Tserkov stood, cigarette in hand, just behind Zapad's chair. "The General emerged with flying colours; though I've never been completely happy about him. To this end I ordered a light watch to be kept: not a permanent surveillance by my department—that would tie up too many men and women. I merely wished to follow his movements, in a loose kind of way." He paused, for effect. "It may strike you all as highly significant, but the Comrade General left Moscow yesterday and flew to Berlin. I have just had a report that he did not stay in the East. What he was doing there remains a mystery, but General Jacob Vascovsky spent the whole of last night in Paris . . ."

In the tense silence, the Head of Special Service I, Vladimir Glubodkin voiced the obvious. "And last night"—brushing imaginary specks of lint from the razor-sharp trouser creases—"five of our people in Paris were quietly removed for interrogation." What a bonus, thought Stentor.

"Quite," Tserkov did not even bother to hide his irritation.

Later, that particular information was also to shock the Chairman of the KGB as he watched, and listened to, the video tapes. It was the one thing for which he had not bargained; and, in some way, he felt responsible. Had he not allowed Vascovsky complete freedom of action?

At the time, Stentor—Vladimir Glubodkin—wondered: The Quiet Dogs? Is this the wild wind, come at last, to alarm the quiet dogs?'

*   *   *

Jacob Vascovsky arrived back at Sheremetievo Airport late on the Friday afternoon, surprised to find Major Badim waiting, with his chauffeur. He was not completely at ease, for his five watchers from the Paris trip had all muttered vague uncertainties regarding Herbie Kruger. Nothing definite, but the feeling, not willingly shared by the General, that Kruger was not alone in Paris.

"I thought you'd be manning the station." The car pulled away, taking the City Exit, and Vascovsky spoke sharply.

Badim smiled, "No need, Comrade General. Our kind friends of the Militia are doing the job for us." He saw Vascovsky start in concern, and quickly added, "It's under control. I have a direct link with the officer in charge. He knows what's expected of him. As soon as Kashvar emerges, he'll be picked up by the MVD, and we'll have him neatly hooked."

Vascovsky did not like either the smell, or sound, of what he heard. He liked it even less when listening to Badim's version of what had gone on during his absence.

Like most officers with responsibility to a hard taskmaster, Vitali Badim told the story from a slightly stronger, if warped, viewpoint. He did not lie, in the strict sense; but sinned by omission. Kashvar, as his version went, had decided to go out on a little expedition. "You know what these people are like, Comrade General. They get some leave, come to Moscow, and expect all the decadence."

"What you're telling me is that our teams lost him."

"Not exactly. He went on a vodka binge, and got mixed up with undesirables. The Militia want him. They have a good man on the job, who tells me Kashvar will surface tonight—they as good as know where he is: with some little Komsomol Square whore, the investigator said."

"And what about the niece, the Morozova woman? Has she arrived?" The General wanted to get straight back to Yekaterina. He had perfume, and other small delights for her. From Paris.

"Not yet, Comrade General. But we'll know as soon as she does. I've still got the Kutuzovsky Prospekt apartment under watch."

"I hope to heaven it's not swarming with people," Vascovsky sounded very irritated now.

"A very light, but efficient, team. Standing well back

They still have your orders—watch and report, but do not interfere."

"Well, thank the stars, something's been done properly." The General decided that Badim was probably correct. The Militia would let them know; and, as long as the suspect's apartment was still under light watch, he would be told, almost to the second, when movement occurred. He ordered the driver to take him straight home; yet, in the back of his mind, Jacob Vascovsky wondered what had become of the niece, Aglaya Mikhailovna Morozova. The General's 'Little Glasha'.

*   *   *

"We've had confirmation," Tubby Fincher announced. "The Morozovs are out and safe—tucked away in our Helsinki place."

"Leave 'em there till it's all died down. When it's all finished." The Director spread various items out on the desk, ready for the main meeting.

The council of war had been set for eight-thirty, and the 'Ladies of the Manor', as the Director liked to call his catering supervisors—for most were twin-set and pearls girls from military backgrounds—had laid on a cold buffet, with thermos flasks of coffee.

Tubby's people had moved in the projectors—for movie and stills—while extra chairs were set up in the main office. The final briefing was to be in two parts. First, the DG and Fincher were to be joined by Curry, Worboys, Herbie, and—later—the most essential, Michael Gold. This was the most important of the two conclaves: the briefing of Gold.

Herbie had constantly harassed the Director—plugging away, again and again, at the necessity for a fast delivery of the material. For Herbie Kruger, everything depended on the tapes and forgeries being in Stentor's hands by the following evening—Saturday—if the main event was to run smoothly.

By the time they reached part two, Troilus would have been excluded: spirited away by one of Curry's cohorts. For this meeting the council would grow, to include an SAS liaison officer; Curry's deputy; an officer from Naval Intelligence; and two other men, expert in their particular fields.

Part one began on time, with the Director going through the items Troilus would be required to take into Moscow. Gold, himself, was already in the building—kept safe, and apart, while the material was itemised. The less he knew of the contents, the safer the operation.

In all there were six tapes—all re-run on to standard Russian tape, and recorded from originals on Russian machines. As well as those put together from the Vascovsky-Kruger tapes, there were three conversations—all taken from *Le Train Bleu*—which could have been taped at long intervals, and different times. These left little to the imagination: the words and sentences arranged to give the damning impression that Vascovsky was speaking to his British control—Big Herbie Kruger.

On one tape, part of the dialogue ran—

Kruger: You think they're that close, Jacob?

Vascovsky: It's only a matter of time. My masters, I have to admit, Herbie fill me with nothing but fear.

Kruger: It has to be done quickly, then?

Vascovsky: I'd leap over the border, tomorrow.

Kruger: Why not tonight?

Vascovsky: I have to think of Yekaterina. There's no percentage in it—just leaving her.

Kruger: If I can do it, it will be very fast. Can you make the Baltic coast within twenty-four hours—a day's warning?

Vascovsky: Of course.

Kruger: The same rules as always, then. I'll get a message to you—there's an isolated cove, between Ventspils and Lyserort: our people've used it before. I'll send you map reference, day, time and fall-backs. If you're lucky I'll come for you myself. Don't worry, I'll have you safely tucked up in London in a matter of hours.

Vascovsky: I can get myself a little breathing time in Moscow. But come quickly. It has to be in a few days.

After hearing that particular tape, there was applause from the assembled team.

Other documents were examined. Again, these were executed with singular precision: cipher messages; notes; lists of names; drawings; plain language copies of agendas, and transcriptions of meetings. They all went back over many years.

Next, the photographs; all culled from the stills and video—some of the latter transcribed on to film, to blow up individual frames—taken on the previous evening. Once more, the forgers had produced startling results, indecipherable from the real thing. There were photographs of the two men meeting at *Le Train Bleu*, naturally; but, by the magic of the dark room, and some delving into files, the complete set included shots of Vascovsky and Herbie Kruger meeting, at different times and seasons, in places as far apart as West Berlin; Bonn; Paris, and even London.

Last, and most important, a small blue sheet contained a cipher of exact instructions for Stentor. If the old fox adhered to his orders, the main event on the Baltic coast would not go awry.

When all the items had been examined, Michael Gold was sent for. He sat, quiet and attentive, as the Director himself went through the ways they had camouflaged the material.

The tapes were easy: placed in commercial cassette boxes, each with a false, peel-off, label. The documents were inserted into two books—a popular novel, and a book on Russian history. Pages had been ingeniously made into thin pockets, designed to take both documents and photographs: the ends neatly sealed, so that they were virtually undetectable.

Gold was made to go through the number of items, and their importance, several times. As always, his agile and retentive memory did not let him down. Within minutes he could repeat the objects, and their hiding places, backwards, forwards and, as he said, "Sideways if you want it."

The kit included a jiffy-bag, into which he was to seal the whole consignment, once safe and at the National Hotel, ready for the drop. "It is most important"—the Director

247

repeated with some sternness—"most important, that you get on with things. Your drop has to be made at the earliest opportunity after arrival."

"Michael," Big Herbie towered over him, "this is most serious. If you've any doubts, now is the time to speak up. That drop *has* to be made some time tomorrow night. You think it can be done?"

Michael Gold nodded. "I'll do it, and then enjoy the rest of my stay."

The way he spoke gave Curry Shepherd a small jolt. For a second, he had the feeling that the boy was on to some jaunt of his own in Moscow. But only for a second. Curry dismissed the possibility almost before he admitted to the thought.

Herbie spoke about techniques. Then the Director took over, adding ideas of his own. The whole thing, while fraught with tension, and the kind of atmosphere which attends all briefings for dangerous missions, had about it a calm professionalism.

Michael Gold soaked in the instructions, like a sponge. Nobody else was to know that the larger part of his mind dwelt on his obsession with the girl from Intourist, and the fact that he would soon be seeing her again. He realised the importance of the assignment, but could not help himself. His mind and body tingled with anticipation. For him, the package, and its delivery to Stentor, was the simple thing—an act which could be performed quickly, and without a second thought. The overriding infection in his brain was the girl.

*　　　*　　　*

One of Curry Shepherd's men escorted Michael Gold from the building. The faces in the Director's office changed. Big Herbie Kruger was on stage, and planning for the Main Event began with a short word from the Director General, who then took his leave. It was up to Curry and Herbie to fight out the details between them. The DG had obtained the okay for Herbie's trip, as far as Stockholm. After that, they all

248

knew the rules. If someone broke those rules, and anything went wrong, there could be no mercy.

It was up to Curry and Herbie, between them, to see that nothing did go wrong.

Well into the night they talked, examined maps and charts, made contingency plans, and questioned alternative arrangements. When the meeting broke up, the final decisions had been made. The whole thing could now only fail if Stentor did not receive the goods from Gold; or if, for some reason, old Stentor was prevented from taking their suggested action.

As they left the building, Curry unknowingly made a step towards possible disaster. Since an essential message would have to go directly to Big Herbie—who would be with Martha Adler at the clinic—Curry took control. He always worked on the principle that, if there was danger to follow, the parachute should be packed by he who was to jump. Thus Curry dismissed Worboys, and gave the order that he would take Troilus to Heathrow, by himself. Once the aircraft had departed for Moscow, Curry would speak to Kruger. After that it was up to Big Herbie.

*   *   *

For the second time in the space of a week, Michael Gold sat in an Ilyushin 62, waiting for the heart-racing moment when the giant aeroplane would be propelled down the runway, lifting off to climb, and set course for Russia and Moscow.

Curry Shepherd, at his own private vantage point, waited and watched as the machine trembled at the threshold, then began its roll. Five minutes later he stood in a public telephone box, dialling the clinic's switchboard, and asking to be put through to the number given him by Herbie Kruger. After a pause, Big Herbie came on the line.

"Okay," Curry said. "He's running."

Big Herbie grunted, and put down the telephone. Turning to Martha Adler, who was now fully dressed and looking almost her old self, he pushed over the sheet of paper.

He had written out the message in block capitals. Martha smiled back, leaned over, gave Herbie a light kiss on the cheek, then started to direct dial the Moscow number.

On the paper were the words—

LARA HAS SPOKEN TO KOLYA WHO SAYS IT IS ONLY A MATTER OF DAYS. DO NOTHING UNTIL YOU HEAR AGAIN, PROBABLY TOMORROW OR MONDAY. KOLYA WILL BRING THE BOOK WITH HIM BUT IT IS ESSENTIAL FOR YURI TO RECEIVE IT.

It was just before noon in London; on the Saturday morning.

*   *   *

At three in the afternoon, on that same day, in Moscow, the telephone rang in General Jacob Vascovsky's office, at the Yasenevo Complex. Major Badim answered.

The woman at the other end of the line asked to whom she was speaking. Badim told her, and, as though by some intuition, said the General was at home. Did she have his number, if it was the General she wanted? She did not have the number, but it was very urgent.

Badim paused for a moment, knowing he should check with the General. "Can I call you back?" he asked.

The woman said it was difficult, but she would telephone again.

"Five minutes," Badim told her.

When he got through to General Vascovsky's number, it was Madame Vascovsky who answered. When he told the General, who came directly to the phone, Badim did not expect his ear to be deafened by the fast and angry shout. He gathered it was very much in order to give the General's private number to the caller.

After another call to Vascovsky's office, the telephone eventually rang in the Kalinin Prospekt apartment. Jacob Vascovsky smiled to himself. He recognised the voice, and the message delighted him. So, his personal analysis was correct. Big Herbie Kruger had swallowed the bait. He could afford to wait for a couple of days. His people were placed at a distance from the subject; Badim would give him word as soon as the nephew, Kashvar, was discovered by the Militia; and they would also know the moment the niece arrived in the city.

He went through to the main living room, aware of Yekaterina singing the latest popular song in the bathroom. Looking out over the rooftops, General Jacob Vascovsky was not to know that his apartment was under surveillance from Department V, who had installed a team in one of the nearby buildings. There was another team in a car across the Prospekt, on the main exit side of the building.

Already, the incoming telephone call had caused some raised eyebrows, and there was argument about whether General Tserkov should be alerted and disturbed over the weekend.

*   *   *

In her room at the National Hotel, the Intourist girl—who had the afternoon free—luxuriated in a warm bath. Her very best clothes lay on the bed, and she lathered herself with an expensive French soap, obtained through a friend who had access to cosmetics and perfumes.

The car was ordered. At six-thirty she would be out at the airport to meet the nice Mr. Gold—the Englishman. She hoped he was not too sad, for she was a genuinely kindly girl. Anyway, she would soon make him happy. In a funny way she had quite fallen for Mr. Gold. Now that he would be feeling rich, as a beneficiary of his aunt's will, he would probably buy her some gifts from the *Beryozka* shop at the National.

She really looked forward to this night, and had it planned, down to the last detail.

The girl was also very proud that her KGB adviser—as he liked to be called—had approved her choice. "I don't suppose he'll be of any use to us," the adviser, Pankov, told her. "But he's young, maybe an idealist. Who can tell? Give

251

him what he wants; woo him; see how pliable he is. Anything important, you always know where to get hold of me. We shall see."

She hoped, nonetheless, that there would be no need to make any recommendation to Adviser Pankov. She would not really like to feel that the Gold man was a subject for use by the KGB. She did not care for the KGB, but working with them was part of her duty as a good Party Member. It was also necessary if she wished to keep her job.

* * *

Looking out at the cloudscape, from the oval window of the Ilyushin, Michael Gold had no sense of flying, or speed, or even the urgency of his mission. He could not even see the clouds. Even with his eyes open, Michael Gold saw only the Intourist girl

20

IRINA LOBANOVA, FOR that was the Intourist girl's full name, waited inside the terminal building at Sheremetievo; watching, as the great Aeroflot Ilyushin taxied into its parking bay. They had confirmed Mr. Gold was on board, which pleased her, so she kept taking little sideways glances at her reflection in the window. The smile which she so carefully nurtured, flashed back at her. Irina considered that she looked good, in the green coat, with gold buttons and fur collar, below which her black knee-length winter boots gleamed with polish. Like glass itself, she thought.

Below the coat she wore her best winter suit—the smart, pepper-and-salt tweed one that her mother had made. Her mother was a skilful seamstress, and it had taken a long while to get the suit exactly as Irina wanted it—looking just like the drawing on the pattern purchased from GUM. The nice light brown blouse set it off perfectly. Irena knew Mr. Gold would approve.

Certainly Michael Gold approved of what he saw, as he emerged from the queues in the bleak customs and immigration hall. Nobody had queried his baggage, which was still marked up for the original tour. She was as gorgeous as he remembered—for it now seemed like weeks since he had seen her.

He had half expected Irina not to be there; but to see her now made his stomach turn over and heart pound. Was this really to be? Was he in that state of which he had always jeered—the thing romantics called love?

There was, of course, the whole question of delivering the package. "This time it's really dangerous," Big Herbie had said. "They'll be expecting the nephew, if they've got around to watching." Herbie also said it had to be done quickly. Come to that they all said it. Faster the better; and here he was, in Moscow, with this girl, and the possibilities she held for him.

"You see, I promise to be here, Mr. Gold," Irina greeted him. Michael burbled a kind of thanks, as she led him through to the car outside. He stood back to let her climb in first, before settling beside her.

"Your aunt? The burying was well?"

"Oh." Aunt Amy had almost gone from Michael's mind. "Yes. Well. Well, you know how these things are. Relatives; tears. It was all sad."

She touched his arm with a gloved hand. It was like fire: a fuse lighting his blood. "But now it will be better. You are a beneficiary and will be rich, I think."

"Not rich; no. She left a little money."

"You will take me to dinner, though. You promised dinner, Mr. Gold."

"I must go to the hotel first." It was his last chance. Perhaps she would wait for him. It should not take long—a short trip out to the Kutuzovsky Prospekt. An hour at the

253

most. That was it. Slip her at the hotel, and meet her later. That package had to be delivered: had to take precedence.

"We will have dinner?" The smile reached up to the light in her eyes. In the gloom of the car she really looked stunning, with a wisp of hair peeping out from under her fur hat, which matched the fur on the collar of the green, rather military, coat.

"Of course you shall have dinner." Then, before he could stop himself—"And I have brought presents for you."

She gave a little squeal. "You should not. No. Oh, Mr. Gold, what have you brought for me? Can I see?"

"Later." Suddenly Michael was quite calm in the knowledge and truth about the pair of them. "You shall see later. Please. Please call me Michael."

"No. I call you Mikhail; and you must call me Irina."

"Yes." He nodded. "Yes, Irina."

"Good, then that is settled. You get washed at the hotel. Already I have ordered a table at a very good restaurant. You see, I knew you would take me to dinner. What have you brought, Mikhail?"

It was getting very hot in the car; the heat began to centre around his loins, and there was a new pounding of anticipation in his head. What was it Herbie Kruger had said? ". . . that drop has to be made some time tomorrow night." Tonight. Some time tonight. *Some time.* Even though it was important, all would be okay; just as long as it was done tonight. Really there was plenty of time. Once it was done with the girl, he would feel better: refreshed; more capable of taking on a dangerous mission.

Irina moved closer to him. "What did you bring me, Mikhail?"

"Oh." His throat felt constricted. Dry. Must be the flight. Flying always dried up the throat: something to do with the air conditioning. "Oh." He looked at her, smiling. "Female things. Pretty things."

"Mikhail!"

For a moment he thought it had gone wrong: that he'd overdone it. Then she giggled, "That's naughty of you. But

254

nice. I shall like that. Pretty things from the West . . ." She moved even closer.

It was no good. The drop had to wait, for, when they arrived at the National Hotel, Irina seemed all set to go straight out to dinner. After he checked in, leaving the Gold passport, she gave him no chance.

"I shall wait here for you. We must not keep the car for too long, otherwise I shall be in trouble. Get ready quickly, Mikhail, and it will save having a taxi."

Michael Gold allowed the porter to take his luggage. In the room he did not even unlock the case, simply sluicing his face with water, and tidying his hair, before going downstairs again to join the girl whose smile seemed to have broadened: catlike. Feline—that was the word. Feline; nubile.

It was almost half-past seven, Moscow time.

*   *   *

Stentor felt nothing but anxiety. His wife just would not be talked out of going to the reception. "You must be there. You must," she had said time and again during the day. "After all, the Chairman of the Supreme Soviet will be there; all the Politburo. It is important."

As if he did not know it. Of course it was important. The reception, to be held in honour of several Eastern Bloc leaders, meeting the Supreme Soviet for what, in the West, they called a summit. Yes, the reception was very important. Yet Stentor knew that, if there were to be messages, he should stay in the apartment. Indeed, he hoped for some kind of message earlier in the day. The only hope, at this moment, lay in the new anti-Vascovsky interest sparked off at the Standing Committee's meeting.

As he pinned the long line of medals on to the breast of his dress uniform jacket, General Glubodkin wondered who would watch who. There was irony in it; for they would all be at the reception—Vascovsky and his wife; Tserkov and the wizened little woman with bad teeth who was Madame Tserkov.

The thought made Stentor chuckle to himself. He put the

255

finishing touches to his tie and hair, then slipped into the jacket: standing back to admire himself in the mirror. Vascovsky would almost certainly have people watching him, Stentor. In turn would Vascovsky know that the Head of Department V had him, and his precious beautiful French wife, under surveillance?

The irony was very Russian, with a touch of French farce. Yet this did not make Stentor feel less uneasy. Tonight he had the senses of an animal. Possibly thunder in the air; even though it was still cold. A storm? No; more than that. In the dark world, the years teach you to tune intuition, as an experienced electronics man will tune a set.

It was in Moscow. Now. Tonight. Help and threat in equal portions.

As they left, the General told the night guards that he might have a visitor. If someone arrived for him, they were to telephone this number at the Kremlin and ask for him personally. He wrote the number on a card.

All the way in the car, his wife chattered. Why leave a number? You're getting too old for this kind of thing. Always you have to be on duty—twenty-four hours a day. Duty; duty; duty. That nice General Vascovsky and his beautiful wife, now, she could not believe he was on duty twenty-four hours a day.

With a younger vigorous wife like her, Vascovsky would have better things to do, Stentor thought. He did not say it aloud, but his mind drifted away—to the young secretary at the Complex, who was in awe of him; and amazed that he was still able to do it with such strength at his age. She really liked it as well. A man of his age, with a girl young enough to be his granddaughter: he should feel ashamed. Stentor felt no shame, though. He wished, fervently, that she was here in the car fondling him—as she did at the Complex—instead of his wife nagging away like a throbbing boil.

*　　　*　　　*

In London they telephoned Big Herbie straight away. All was well.

256

After an evening of pacing and concern, Herbie Kruger relaxed. He even took a stiff vodka, then telephoned Curry Shepherd.

"I know, cocker, they called me as well. We're on, old son."

"Sooner the better," Herbie smiled his daft, stupid, smile to himself. "I'll see Martha tomorrow. We'll alert our General friend either tomorrow night, or first thing on Monday."

"Leave it as late as you can; I should."

Herbie agreed. He would sleep well after all.

*   *   *

In Moscow, unknown to Big Herbie, his protégé, Michael Gold, was only just starting his drop. For him the night had hardly begun.

They were lovers, in all senses but the physical, before dinner was over. She took his hand, as naturally as a trusting child, when they left the hotel to drive to the Aragvi, on Gorki Street. There, Irina told him, they served the best *shashlik* in all Moscow. Indeed, while strictly a Georgian restaurant, Michael found the specialities covered a wide range, and the portions were very large—a thick *borshch*, which he had always imagined was just the plain beetroot stew, remembered from childhood, but turned out to be a spicy vegetable soup, garnished with chopped kidneys. Irina said that *borshch* came in many varieties. Michael considered that canned soups did the same thing, and began to giggle, which was infectious. In fact it was a night for much laughter.

She was certainly right about the *shashlik*: succulent lamb, marinated in a sauce; delicious to the palate, biting and juicy.

To finish, there was a glorious Charlotte Russe, which Michael silently admitted was far better than those his mother made with such pride.

The vodka was forsaken for a bottle of Georgian *Shampanskoe*—dry, sparkling and inclined to make Irina giggle even more. The bubbles tickled her nose, just like any other young girl.

They joked, held hands, and sat close, while Michael told

257

her about his past, and life at an English University. In turn she spoke of her own childhood, and schooling in Moscow. Between the talk they discovered a similar passion for movies—Irina wanted to know a great deal about the kind of films shown in the West. In and out of the conversation they both wove flirtation, and this deepened, until, at one moment, all conversation stopped and they just sat there, looking at each other.

"You're eating me with your eyes," she said.

He nodded, "And you, with yours. You're devouring me."

She leaned forward, obviously wanting to kiss him, but whispering this was not polite in a public place. "We go back to the hotel, and I come to your room." She gave him a glittering smile. "I want my present."

Michael gave her money for the taxi, and, during the ride back, she initiated him into the ways of handling Floor Ladies. "They all know what goes on, and some are difficult. When you get your key, leave ten rubles."

It was the same the whole world over. Bribes. Still, he went through the charade, finding the room just as he had left it.

Full of food, and a little dizzy, from both Irina and the wine, Michael unlocked the case to remove the neat, beautifully-wrapped, presents. It crossed his mind that, soon, he would have to make some excuse to get away. But, for now, the moment was theirs. Fire, flood or bomb could not have stopped them, let alone the package to be delivered to Stentor.

She smelled of the cold, and a pleasant scent, as she twined her arms around his neck, once inside the room. The kiss, with all its variations—the biting of lips, opening of mouths, and deep penetration of each other's tongues—went on and on, until the need for air pulled them apart. Her fur hat fell off, and the long blonde hair tumbled out around her flushed face. Even fully dressed, through her top coat, she had pressed hard against him. Now, she could not wait to undo the buttons. The coat fell to the floor—"My presents?" she squealed, spotting the gold and silver parcels wrapped with ribbon.

258

"Your presents," he grinned, like a dummy, waving a hand towards them.

Irina was in no mood to take her time, even though she exclaimed at the wonderful wrappings. Then came the cries of delight as she held up the wisps of gossamer. "But these are real silk, Mikhail. Real, true silk. They would cost a fortune."

He moved towards her, knowing he could not stand it much longer; but, suddenly she ducked away. "I give you a show of fashion, Mikhail." Before he could stop her, Irina disappeared into the bathroom, closing the door firmly.

It did not take long. She reappeared dressed only in a pair of the luxurious, heavily lace-trimmed, panties brought from London. Then there was no stopping either of them. As Michael moved, so Irina took the initiative—grabbing at him, undressing him, ripping off his clothes and pulling him down on top of her on the bed.

Perhaps it was the magic of two people attracted to one another; maybe Michael imagined it; or, possibly, it was what he wanted to believe; but Irina made him feel more of a man than any of the dozens of casual girls he had taken in his life.

She groaned, half-delight and half-pain, as he entered her; then their lips were locked, and their bodies docked together, nodding and bowing as though riding great waves.

The first time was over quickly, and they lay—naked and close—quietly muttering endearments until Michael was again ready.

The third time was Irina's own doing, for she reversed roles, thrusting with an athletic vigour which more than matched Michael. When that was done, they again lay panting, Michael's head reeling as she continued to whisper her love, and bite at his ear, leaning over to kiss him, one hand between his loins.

Stentor. The thought came to his head with a rush. Aimlessly he cast around in his mind. How could he free himself? No magic anwer came back, except for the magic of her hand on him, stroking new life to his already throbbing body. He had no desire to leave her. No true motivation for going out

259

into the hostile city—except the consciousness that it was his duty.

By now Michael was tiring, and so found it easier to control the situation. In the far corner of his mind he thought that, if he made it last—made love hard and long and strong—he could tire her: maybe bring sleep.

She told him, time and again, that she loved him; that she had never experienced anything like this. Could she stay for the night? For she wished to wake in his arms. He went on; and, eventually, they both fell apart on the bed, panting and exhausted.

Michael pulled back the blankets and sheets, helping her snuggle into bed, while he excused himself to go to the bathroom. Sleepily she said she should also go. She would later. She loved him so much.

His loins ached as never before. But seldom had he been forced to work so hard at the pleasure; and this pleasure was so different.

When he came back into the room, she was on her side, eyes closed, breathing regularly—the long deep draughts of sleep.

Quietly, he bent over her. She was out to the world; satiated, with a happy smile, her body relaxed and fulfilled. Now, he would have to take the risk. Moving as silently as possible, Michael Gold dressed, changing into heavy grey trousers and boots, pulling a thick rollneck sweater over his head. It was late. Christ, after ten o'clock. In London they would be worrying.

Remember the routine—he kept glancing at the inert form under the blankets and sheets—the jiffy-bag and tapes; then the books: finding the pages, removing the documents and photographs. He checked them over, one at a time, counting them; rehearsing all they had taught him. Everything was there.

Now he packed the good greatcoat in the little plastic holdall. On with the anorak and spectacles; the cap on his head; Piotr Kashvar's passport and documents in the anorak pocket; the jiffy-bag—now containing all the items—sealed with sellotape, tucked into the plastic bag. Money. Check. Double-check. He hoped the Floor Lady would not stop him.

Irina murmured in her sleep; moved, seemed to open her eyes, then closed them again, and moved deeper down into the bed with a contented moan.

Michael reached the door. London still worried him: playing on his mind. After all, the job would be done—the package delivered—in a matter of thirty minutes at the most. If he could put them out of their misery now, without waking Irina.

She did not move. Hesitating for a second, he decided to risk it: crossing to the telephone, and quietly dialling the number they had given him. A nondescript voice answered.

Michael spoke, very low; almost a whisper. "Norman?" he asked. The voice said it was Norman, yes.

"Just to let you know I got back okay. Smooth trip. Everything fine. See you soon."

Irina did not move. Softly Michael Gold replaced the telephone, picked up the plastic holdall, and tiptoed out of the room, closing the door silently behind him.

The moment he left, Irina turned, in half-sleep, and her eyes popped open wide and alert.

21

THE FLOOR LADY nodded at her post, and nobody challenged Michael as he made his way down to the main, marbled hall of the National Hotel.

The nights were still bleak cold, and his breath hung n little clouds, almost solid, dispersing very slowly, as he rudged towards the Sverdlov Square station.

He must remember not to be too late returning. The underground trains only ran until half-past midnight, though—at the moment—there seemed to be plenty of activity on the cold streets. Trams and buses; cars; people, like himself, walking briskly; the occasional wail of a police or ambulance siren.

God, what would it be like in winter, he wondered? This was bad enough: the prelude to the upturn of the year. Near the station he saw a café just closing; an oil lamp in the window. It reminded him of something. A poem? A book? The words came, unbidden, into his head—

> Snow swept over the earth,
> Swept it from end to end.
> The candle on the table burned,
> The candle burned.

He could not remember where the poem came from. Perhaps he would ask Irina when he got back. Lord make her sleep. Please. Just until he got the job done. Then he could return to the soft bed and her pliable body.

Putting his five kopecks into the machine, Michael followed the high-arched tunnel, heading for the platform at Red Square from where the train would take him to the Koutouzovskaya station.

A drunk tried to talk to him on the train; and a young woman got on at Arbatskaya, coming to sit close to him, even though the carriage was not crowded. She smelled of cheap scent, and her cheeks were made up with two bright spots, like a doll.

As they drew into the Kievskaya, where he changed platforms, the woman nudged closer, lifted her skirt, revealing a slip of paper under a frilled garter. The paper had a price written on it. After the clean, scrubbed, loving Irina, the very idea of the whore revolted him. He was glad when he reached the air again, trudging towards Stentor's apartment block.

One of the Militia men, sitting in the discreetly parked

car, saw him first. His comrade was asleep, coming out of a dream, when nudged.

"Looks like our subject." The first Militia man strained forward, his breath fogging the inside of the window. They were both tired, and disgruntled with the assignment—sitting there every night, watching for one missing person: just because he was a relative of some KGB bigshot.

"You think so? How do you tell at this distance?" The second Militia man rubbed sleep from his eyes.

"Just the description. Watch."

"Wind down the window. You can't see a fucking thing inside here. It's like taking a sauna in a sewer."

"Steamy also." The first Militia man wound down the window, letting in a blast of icy air.

Across the road, in the small apartment being used by the KGB team, the man seated at the window slept on duty: his partner was stretched out behind him on the bed—the pair of them surrounded by the paraphernalia of surveillance. But the night glasses, and camera—on their twin tripods—in the window, were unmanned.

In the car, the two men from the MVD examined the description form, and details, by the shaded light of a torch.

"Well, I think it's him." The first man leaned from the car window. "Watch. Look. Yes, he's going to the entrance."

"You think we should report it?"

"See what happens. In a minute."

Gold-Troilus-Piotr Kashvar approached the big glass doors; found them locked, and rapped noisily. One of the night guards left his game of chess: not hurrying himself.

"What you want?"

Gold said he was the General's nephew—Piotr Kashvar. Did not the man remember? He was here the other night. It was important that he see his uncle. He had a present for him. It was the last chance to let his uncle have the present.

"Leave it with me. The Comrade General's out for the evening. Won't be back till late."

The night guard's companion shouted something. The General had asked to be notified. He was expecting someone.

"He would have said if it was his nephew," the man at the door flung back over his shoulder. "Leave your parcel. I'll see he gets it the moment they return."

"That means my aunt's out as well."

"Big party at the Kremlin. Everybody's there."

"Can I come in and wait? My train doesn't leave until the early hours: I'd like to see them, and I'd rather wait here, in the warm, than at the station."

The night guard opened the door, shrugging. "If you wish." He was not going to incur the General's displeasure, by leaving this ragtag nephew out in the cold.

"Well, he's gone in. You think we should report it?" The first Militia man rubbed the stubble on his chin, and pushed his face close to the window. The cold filter of air at least removed the stink of stale vodka, coming from his comrade.

"It can't do any harm." The second man reached for his transmitter and switched on. They had been told to keep radio silence, unless the subject turned up. Now the radio crackled.

The leading MVD man pressed his microphone button, gave his call sign, and was immediately answered. There was a short pause while they consulted the card, and its list of codes. Chief Investigator Fedyanin had passed it on—brief details only, and use the codes. He did not want any Tom, Dick or Harry knowing when the subject was spotted: by which, they presumed in the car, the Chief Investigator did not want the KGB in on the act.

The message went straight into Petrovka Street. Personal and urgent. Immediate for Chief Investigator Fedyanin. Uncle's boy waiting for Uncle now at the Slum.

The man on the radio sighed. Fedyanin would love this—being disturbed at home: though who knew what it meant. There was enough trouble around tonight. All the usual fights, muggings, together with the normal share of drunk and domestic violence.

*   *   *

264

Irina Lobanova had slid into a peaceful, and satisfied sleep. Then, something disturbed her. She drifted upwards, wondered if she was dreaming, before the sleep reclaimed her. The next thing she knew was the sound of the telephone dial, and someone talking softly. Then the door closing.

Suddenly she was fully awake, sniffing the air, trying to clear her head and separate dreams from reality. Of one thing she was certain: Michael Gold was a good lover. Not the best she had ever tasted, but he had brought her on several times, and eventually left her satisfied and tired. Sure, he had not the bull-like power of some Russian men, who treated their women like cattle. She rather liked that; the feeling of being used for the outpouring. That got her going every time. Well, certainly she was sore from the Englishman.

But what else had happened? And where was he now? No, she had half wakened. It was not a dream. Mikhail had been standing by the bed, dressed in a pullover with a roll collar. He was packing something, and there were papers in his hand. Then she had heard him on the telephone. He spoke to someone in English. Then he left.

For a second or so, Irina was outraged. The man who had sworn he loved her; given her presents; taken her body; asked her to stay for the night. This wretched Englishman had upped and left her, alone in the hotel; and where would he go at this time of night?

Fury went through her. Lover? She spat. That was all he wanted. To boast he had fucked a good Russian girl.

Then Irina calmed herself. There was more to it than that. The clothes and papers; the telephone; Michael Gold gone. Something had happened. She lay there for a full two minutes before slipping out of bed, and going to the telephone where she dialled Adviser Pankov's night number.

He answered straight away, and listened quietly as she told her story. There was a long pause once she finished, so that she asked him again—"What shall I do?"

"You do nothing," he said. "I shall look into it. I presume his passport is at reception?"

"Yes."

"Then he has to return. You stay where you are. I shall make enquiries. In the meantime we'll make the Militia do some work for their pay. I'll have a couple of their men sent over to look at his passport, and wait for him to come back. They can take him in for questioning, and we'll follow up, if it turns out to be something really special."

"And me?"

"You? You're a good girl. We won't bring you into it. Just stay where you are for the time being. I'll be in touch. Room number?"

She gave it, and Pankov closed the line.

Ten minutes later there were two plainclothed MVD men in the lobby, questioning the reception staff, and looking at Michael Gold's passport. A little later, a patrol car arrived with some uniformed officers. At least it was warm in the hotel lobby.

*   *   *

The MVD men who watched the apartment block on Kutuzovsky Prospekt, could see the two guards playing chess. Their man, the General's missing nephew, sat to one side watching: clutching a package to his stomach.

Inside the building, the night guards were not on the best of terms. There had been a small argument as to whether the General should be informed. In the end they thought it better not to do anything. It was getting late; though who knew what time they would return? Those receptions at the Kremlin went on for hours; until late into the night; and everybody got pissed out of their heads. But they would be back—sooner or later.

*   *   *

Chief Investigator Fedyanin was watching television. They were rerunning an old series, one of his favourites. Nowadays it always seemed to be repeats and re-runs. *Shield and Sword* was ten years old—more—but still very good: great stories the spies who wormed their way into Nazi Germany—those

266

men and women of darkness, who did so much to win the Great Patriotic War.

Fedyanin's wife did not share her husband's delight in the spy TV series, but sat there, staring into space, her mind a million miles away, as the pictures flashed over the screen.

They both jumped when the telephone rang. Fedyanin cursed, and spoke sharply into the instrument. "Does the General know? Is he with him?"

A pause, for the radio man to repeat the message. "Can you transfer me to the unit on watch? Patch me through to them on the radio?" Fedyanin tapped his foot and waited, craning his neck to see the TV screen. Then the mobile unit came on the air. The General was out: some booze-up at the Kremlin. All right, he would see to it himself.

Fedyanin knew his priorities. Though there was some kind of promise to let a Major Badim, of the KGB, know if the man Kashvar surfaced, Fedyanin had enough sense to consider the General before anyone else. Within minutes he was speaking to the night guards at the apartment block.

Oh, should they have informed the Comrade General? No, it was fine. The Chief Investigator would let him know. Did the General leave a telephone number? Good, well, pass it on. He would see to matters.

Back on Kutuzovsky Prospekt, in the room across the wide street, the KGB surveillance man woke with a start.

"Shit." He looked at his watch, in the gloom, relieved to see he had missed only some fifteen minutes. He struggled to clear his head. Like one of the MVD men, there had been too much vodka during the late afternoon: before he went on duty. He supposed it would be best to take a squint through the night glasses, on their tripod.

Nothing unusual could be seen, as he traversed the area in the line of sight.

Still plenty of traffic, but nothing stopping at the building under observation. The surveillance man adjusted the knurled screw on the glasses, to bring the doors of the apartment block into sharper focus—sweeping on either side. Then, alert: back again. A further adjustment. He could see clearly through the glass doors into the lobby. To the left, the pair of night guards played chess; but another figure sat near them. How had the interloper managed that? Shit on my grave—while I was asleep.

The surveillance man turned, moving to his resting colleague, shaking him awake. He was almost certain the man was their target, but nobody in his position would dare take on the responsibility of reporting it to Badim, unless completely certain.

His story had to be right. Only just now, when the guards invited the man in, had he been able to see the face. The whole thing had to look as though their report followed immediately after recognition. Where this kind of thing was concerned, two voices spoke with more authority than one.

*　　　*　　　*

The party was being held in the huge reception room, reached by escalators, on the topmost storey of the massive Congress Building, which adjoins the old Great Kremlin Palace.

It was an impressive affair, with colour from the dress uniforms and the ladies' gowns; long buffet tables landscaped with food; and an endless supply of drink. The setting is ideal for this kind of gathering, for the walls of the reception room are made almost entirely of glass, giving one of the best views in the whole of Moscow.

An orchestra played throughout the entire evening, and General Glubodkin was trying to enjoy himself. His wife enjoyed herself as a matter of course. Stentor though, having arrived still in a high state of anxiety, found himself now in a very different frame of mind.

The motive force behind this change of heart had appeared within five minutes of their arrival, in the form of the Chairman of the Committee for State Security himself.

The all-powerful man beamed as he approached, and Stentor suddenly realised he was alone in the crowd—his wife having been enticed away by some of her cronies: all wives of senior KGB officers.

"My dear Vladimir." The Chairman put out a hand, and Stentor acknowledged the authority with a stiff bow of salutation.

"I wanted to see you." The Chairman's face betrayed nothing but goodwill. "Time is a luxury. Come, let us talk for a moment." He placed an arm around Stentor's shoulder, pivoting him towards the corner of the long window. There, they stood for a moment or two, looking down at the magnificent view of the Kremlin, and out across the city.

"We've known one another a long time, old friend." The Chairman spoke softly. "But I wanted to make this as informal as possible. It will become official on Monday. Old comrade, you are to be retired on full pay as from the coming week."

Stentor's mouth fell open, and his head turned to examine the Chairman's eyes. "What . . . what have I done?" he blurted.

The Chairman gave a low chuckle. "Served your country, and the Service, with great ability for more years than necessary." He lied, worrying at the lie, and still hoping that Vascovsky was wrong.

"But . . .?"

"You thought, like all of us, to die in harness? Yes, I understand that. My friend, there will be decorations; a fine *dacha*—much better than the one you already have—where is it? On the Baltic coast somewhere? Latvia? You will also have no responsibilities. There will be time to rest and relax. It happens to us all, you know."

So it had come. The news was not unexpected, of course, yet Stentor felt as though a sudden void had opened up. The days, and months, stretched ahead like a weary arid view. Days, months—no, years possibly. Years, with no frame of reference except the past, and the gentle nagging of his wife.

In a fraction, Stentor's life had altered. The Chairman's hand gave his shoulder a squeeze. "Come, comrade. Let's drink together." As they sidled their way through the growing crowd, so General Glubodkin's eyes caught Vascovsky making an entrance with his wife. It would make life easier for Vascovsky, the spy-hunter, Stentor thought. Easy for him to corner a man on full retirement. At least he might have that to come—the inevitable questions; the stone walls and the interrogators—unless Tserkov caught up with Yekaterina, and so dishonoured Vascovsky; or Stentor's London masters managed to do worse. Drink? No, that only made him ill.

The reception was successful—like all official Russian junkets—with a very large number of people quietly leaving at regular intervals to vomit. After a few hours, Stentor judged that over two-thirds of the assembly were well under the influence. He wondered how the meetings with the Eastern Bloc leaders would go tomorrow, as they wrestled with the touchy problems of economy, and political line, among the barbs of deathly sick headaches.

Thank God that he, Stentor, was well-versed in the ways of liquor: spending most of the evening nursing a full glass. So Stentor kept his head, and watched, with wry amusement, as others keeled over.

Even his wife was exceptionally merry. He would leave it until tomorrow before telling her the news; knowing she had waited for so long. For her, his retirement could bring nothing but pleasure.

At one point, he found himself among a group near to General Vascovsky, who conducted himself with superb poise, surrounded by captivated women—and not a few men: telling stories that set them laughing, after the manner of those who take too much alcohol, and so find even the most simple joke hilarious and brilliantly witty.

The eyes of the two men met briefly: Stentor happily noting that Vascovsky broke the gaze first, turning back to the group to make a quip which again set them all off in guffaws of mirth.

There was a tap on his shoulder. Glubodkin turned to see one of the Kremlin Staff officers at attention, a duty armlet around his sleeve. "Comrade General, a telephone message. Personal, and very important, for you, sir."

Stentor raised his eyebrows, following the young officer to the entrance, and small office where a telephone lay

270

unhooked, on a table. With a word of thanks, Stentor took up the receiver. At the far end, Fedyanin spoke rapidly.

A few moments later, Stentor was giving instructions to the young officer of the Kremlin Staff. He would like his car brought around immediately, and would somebody please inform his wife. He had been called away on urgent business, which should not keep him long. Would his wife wait for his return. Fifteen minutes; half-an-hour at the most.

The young officer, slightly overawed, knowing he was dealing with a legend of the KGB, appeared only too anxious to assist. Within five minutes Stentor's car raced, its pennant flying, through the Spasskaya—Saviour's Gate—heading for the apartment block on Kutuzovsky Prospekt.

As the car gathered speed, Stentor was not to know that Major Badim, Vascovsky's aide, was searching desperately for his General—having just received a report that the 'nephew' had been sighted.

The car came to a squealing stop outside the apartment block, and Stentor, giving orders for both driver and body-guard to remain at the ready, leaped out.

The night guards pushed their chairs back, standing, to acknowledge the imposing presence; while Michael Gold, in his role as Piotr Kashvar, made a move towards Stentor, speaking as they drew close. "I was afraid that I would miss you, Uncle. My leave is over . . ."

For the benefit of the night guards, Stentor produced a towering rage. Where did Piotr think he had been? What had he got himself into? Disappearing like that. "Your aunt's been out of her mind with concern. We wait for years to get a glimpse of you, then you disappear like a naughty schoolboy . . ." Stentor kept it up, propelling Michael towards the elevator.

Michael Gold took the hint, trying to get words in between the General's tirade—"My plans changed . . . I . . . I had to . . . There was no time to . . ." and so, and so, until the elevator doors closed, and Stentor gave him a great wink. Holding a finger over his lips, General Glubodkin continued his tongue-lashing—"Well, I have no time. You cannot stay here . . ."

271

"My train leaves at three in the morning, and . . ."

"Then you can wait at the station. I've come from an important reception, at the Kremlin. The Militia's been searching for you since you decided my hospitality was not good enough for you. I've only come back so that I can put your aunt's mind at rest. Now, Piotr, what've you been doing? Drink? Whores? Both?"

Michael Gold spluttered, and the odd conversation continued until they were not merely inside Stentor's apartment, but safe within the General's antiseptic study.

There, Gold handed over the package, which Stentor tore open, examining each item hastily. As he took the photographs and papers, looking at each in turn, the General started to laugh. "Excellent," he whispered. "There's no time to listen to the tapes, and I'm afraid I shall have to act out another little play with you downstairs. This will be the scene where I cut you off without a kopeck, denounce you, and say we never wish to set eyes on you again." As he spoke, Stentor looked closely at the blue flimsy, which contained the coded instructions. He would deal with those later, even though Michael Gold told him that London required Stentor to take special note of the map references, times and fall-backs contained in the cipher. They were particularly important.

Stentor acknowledged this. Then—"You have done well; whoever you are. Can you, perhaps, get one last message back to your people?"

Of course, Michael Gold hoped he could do so with telephone double-talk. It was the only way, except for taking a dive into the Embassy, and he certainly did not want to do that, now he had just found Irina.

"Tell them, first, that I have been retired. As from Monday I shall be a private person—retired honourably on full pay. Next week, I clear out my desk."

"Does this change anything?"

Stentor was silent for a moment. "Yes." Very slowly he swallowed. "I came through my dark night. I faced the fact that Russia is my country, and I could not bear to be

272

anywhere else. But that has altered. One thing I had not really looked squarely in the eyes, was the fact of inactivity. Now I have to do that. I shall carry out whatever instructions they give me here," He tapped the flimsy. "After that—if they have a planned meeting place—they can lift me out. I leave it up to them. If there is a date and time, here, then I shall be there. Waiting. Reluctant, but waiting to leave. You can do that?"

Gold said he *would* do it. "They'll know before morning."

"Good, but you have a further problem. I am in no doubt that this place is being watched. My own Service, naturally, wishes to speak with you. I also had to play along with the Militia. They could pick you up as you leave."

As he packed away the tapes, photographs and documents into a floor safe, Stentor quickly suggested what should be done.

Outside, in the car, the driver and bodyguard were to see the play. First, the General emerged, pushing his nephew in front of him. The nephew tried to argue, almost in tears. They even heard the words—"You understand, Piotr," the General shouted. "Never again. We do not wish to see you. You've abused our hospitality, so you're no nephew of mine. Understand? Now return to the hole out of which you crawled, and don't ever come back." He made for the car, the nephew following at a distance, still pleading.

The General's bodyguard was out, swiftly, as the nephew tried to pull at the General's greatcoat. "Get away. Out. Out. Out of my sight."

The large, young bodyguard came between them, making sure his General was back in the car. "I should do as he says." The bodyguard spoke quietly but with the heavy firmness of his calling. "Really I should. Otherwise I shall have to hit you—and you wouldn't like that." He gave the nephew a small push, sending him backwards, in a series of little steps, ending up against the wall.

They watched the scene from the MVD car; and also from the surveillance room across the street. The curtain came down. End of Act One. The General's car drove away, leaving the lone and pathetic figure in his anorak, peaked cap, and glinting spectacles, standing on the pavement, clutching the little plastic bag. It was then that the radio in the surveillance room came to life. Badim's voice through the speaker, almost hysterical in its pitch—"Pick him up. General Vascovsky says you are to pick him up now. This minute." The two KGB watchers almost collided with each other, as they made for the door.

Major Badim had suffered agonies. It was almost twenty minutes before he got through to the Kremlin extension number General Vascovsky had left for him. Then there was a long wait, while they went to get the General. His reaction had been immediate. "Don't let him go. Not at any price. And don't let the MVD get at him. You hear?"

The two men in the Militia car had no orders; so they just sat and watched, as the downcast figure walked, stoop-shouldered, down the street, turning off into the nearest intersection—a narrow alley leading to the rear of the apartment building.

When the two KGB men reached the street, they were hampered, first by the traffic, and next by the complete disappearance of their quarry. The bird had flown. He could have just walked away, or taken a cab—anything.

One of the men went into the building, to question the night guards. Yes, there had been a tremendous row. The General had disinherited his nephew. The nephew had to get a train back to his post in the Urals. He had gone that way—they pointed to the first turning along the street.

The two KGB officers gave chase—late in the day. The alley was deserted, but for a smartly-dressed foreigner in a heavy overcoat and fur hat.

Michael Gold was pleased with himself. The trappings of Piotr Kashvar had gone into one of the great rubbish bins behind the apartment block. True he now had no papers, as his passport was still at the National. But he was Michael Gold again. It seemed certain to him that the pair of heavily-built men, who bumped into him as he emerged on to

274

Kutuzovsky Prospekt, were after Kashvar. He had beaten them.

At peace with the world; satisfied that the drop had been made, as instructed, Michael Gold hailed a taxi, ordering the driver to take him to the National Hotel. From there he would work out the next step. The message had to get to London. Whatever their plans, Stentor would be waiting. Big Herbie would be pleased with him. Just pray Irina had stayed asleep. No more worries.

The taxi pulled up at the main entrance, and he paid the man—overtipping him: what the hell, it was government money anyway.

As he entered the vaulted marble lobby, so two men detached themselves from the long reception desk, at a word from one of the clerks. Michael took two paces forward, then sensed the danger before even seeing it. He did not consider it might be Irina's doing. Logic said they were on to him. Blown, so run for cover. Take a dive.

The two men bore down on him, one calling in English, "Michael Gold?"

Gold looked to left and right. In a moment, all his confidence drained away. He backed off, then turned, running for the exit. There was a loud shout in English—"Stop. Gold; stop."

In the doorway stood a Militiaman in uniform, pistol drawn; but Michael swerved, made a feint to the left, then shoulder-barged the uniformed man, who was caught off balance, and shoved to one side.

Gold followed through, heading out of the main entrance at speed, the shouts still echoing from behind. Once in the street he could not stop—running, gathering momentum, like some missile projected from a gun.

Before he knew it, Michael Gold was at the edge of the pavement. Another shout; lights, traffic; a few people, some of them recoiling from him. Then his foot hit the rock-hard snow, in the gutter, on a level with the pavement. He felt his legs slide, and his body take off, out of control.

He did not see the truck, only a great light, and a blaring of horns, mixed up with shouts, and a scream. Then a feeling of movement through the air; pain, and a numbness; a great crash; more light. Silence.

He knew who he was; and that he was looking upwards, towards darkness, speckled with a sea of faces; but there was no sensation. He could not move. Christ, he thought, I've got to get the message to London. "Irina," he said, only the words would not come out of his throat. Then he remembered the poem. Of course. He had done the book in the original Russian. It was one of *Zhivago*'s poems. Wasn't he going somewhere, in Moscow, in winter? Didn't he see a candle behind a window, and try to make some sense out of a line which came into his head? The candle in the window—or words like that?

One of the disembodied faces was now close above him. The lips moved, but Gold could not hear a thing. Not a bloody thing, he thought. Cambridge, that was where he should be. It was safe there—the grey stone, and the courts. Books, pubs, good company. He wanted to take Irina there. She would enjoy Cambridge.

The face faded, and he was in the Senior Common Room. People looked at him oddly; and why was he reciting this aloud, in Russian?

> Snow swept over the earth,
> Swept it from end to end.

Christ, it was cold tonight, and getting very dark.

> The candle on the table burned,
> The candle burned.

For Michael Gold; Troilus; Piotr Kashvar, the candle went out for the last time, and the darkness swallowed him up.

22

By six in the morning, General Glubodkin had not got to his bed. When they finally arrived back at the apartment, he felt it was neither timely nor necessary to mention the retirement news to his wife. She was well away, in any case—bouncing off the walls on her short journey to the bedroom. Stentor's wife and hard liquor did not mix.

In his private study, the General went carefully through the material brought to him by Piotr Kashvar. He listened to the tapes, sitting back, still in uniform, smiling to himself as the whole dirty business came into focus. Then he examined the photographs. No expert would dare refute them. Together with the other documents, the pile of evidence was damning. Vascovsky would simply cease.

Last, he deciphered the blue flimsy of instructions. These were not requests, but instructions: orders. They also gave precise details of where Vascovsky would be on one night of the following week—probably in the early hours of Tuesday morning. Stentor's first duty was to be sure that General Vascovsky's phones—private and office—were wired so that the exact date, and time, could be confirmed. All this had to be done quickly. It would be wise—his instructions advised—for Stentor to hand everything over to another officer, and stay well clear.

By six o'clock he knew the way it should be done. It was Sunday, but that made little difference here. They took a day off, but his driver was on a constant twenty-four hour alert. General Andrei Tserkov would be out of town; but, for something as important as this, the Head of Department V would not really worry about being disturbed.

Stentor picked up the telephone, dialling the motor pool at Dzerzhinsky Square; giving orders for his driver, and bodyguard, to be at the apartment for nine o'clock. That would give him time to bath, shave, change and take a little breakfast.

*   *   *

The telephone would not stop ringing, dragging Herbie Kruger out of the very deep and dreamless dark. He caught sight of his digital alarm, with the greenish figures, as he reached for the phone. Five in the morning.

Curry Shepherd, sounding as tired as Herbie, spoke in a low voice, as though he had someone with him, and did not wish to disturb them. "The boss," he whispered. "Wants us up at HQ this minute. There seems to be a flap on."

An hour or so later, in the strange, early-morning, depression of the Director General's office, the magnitude of 'the flap' was made clear. Moscow Embassy had sent a Flash signal to the Foreign Office. Presumably their own resident in the Embassy had put names together; for the signal contained the day's codeword for information to be passed to the Secret Intelligence Service.

A British citizen, on holiday in Moscow, had been accused of raping an Intourist girl at the National Hotel. The DG did not have to spell out the man's name; but, when apprehended, Michael Gold had made a run for it, slipped, and fallen in front of a truck. The report said he was DOA.

"Can we be certain?" Herbie asked, above Curry's loud curse. Curry then expressed concern for the girl. "Sod the girl," Big Herbie's venom seemed to explode into the room. "Mike was young. Inexperienced. Rush-trained. A mystery of mysteries. I warned you; and I doubt if there was any rape. That's a cover-up. A snow job."

A cipher signal had gone off to the Moscow resident. They expected a Flash reply, the DG said. "But that will take time. I simply want the facts. I also need to know how you feel about continuation, now young Gold's been taken out."

"We're sure he's dead?" Herbie realised, with a certain amount of horror, that he would be called upon to break the news to Nataly. There was also the question of being sure that Michael *had* been killed. In situations like this it could be to the Soviet's advantage to have a faked death in the family. Herbie summed it up—"If he's definitely dead; if it's confirmed; then there's no problem. We had his signal. He carried out the drop; so Stentor's primed. I had planned to leave the final telephone call, from Martha to Vascovsky, until Moscow time, Monday morning. Then we go ahead: if he is dead—confirmed, with reliable witnesses—there is no problem."

"Yes." Curry yawned. "If he *is* dead; and if he managed to stash the Kashvar documents, and the clothes—so there's no come-back—we're home and dry; and I see no way of us getting all that cleared up before we start running. If not . . ."

"If not, then we have to abort." The Director General did not even look at them. "So, the decision is up to us. We have to decide, on whatever information comes through, whether the Main Event is on or off."

"We go." Herbie was adamant. "As long as there's certainty about Gold's death, we go. Stentor got the drop. Everything else—the Kashvar documents and all that—must be put to one side. We go. If it's been washed out at the other end, we shall soon know about it."

The DG was equally firm. "At the moment, Herbie, we wait. We wait for whatever information is available." He creased his brow, stood up and looked down from the window on London, beginning its new day.

After a while Curry suggested breakfast. The Director nodded, then seemed to change his mind. "If you'd go ahead, Curry. I'd like a word with Herbie."

Alone with Big Herbie, the Director hummed and hawed; taking his time in getting to the point.

At last—"Look, Herbie, the other day . . . Well, you sort of blew up in our faces. Talked about going private after this. All that kind of thing."

"Yes?" Herbie showed no reaction.

For a little longer, the Director remained embarrassed. Then he plunged. He wanted to know—needed to know—Herbie's true intentions.

Big Herbie spread his hands wide. Until last year's bit of bother; until he did something very stupid, and disobeyed orders, he had served the Firm to the best of his ability.

"You've done that, Herbie. We all know it; and respect you."

"Respect?" Herbie smiled. This time no stupidity showed through. Here was the real Herbie: the strong, professional, craftsman, who knew his trade through and through. "Respect's no good any more, sir. You remember George— George Thomas?"

Who could forget him. George Thomas had played a major part in the history of the Firm, and Herbie had spent many hours with him, during the Nostradamus investigation some years ago.

"George used to quote T. S. Eliot to me. 'We are the hollow men. We are the stuffed men.' I find poets like him difficult. But in this game we do become hollow and stuffed . . ."

To Herbie's surprise, the Director muttered some other lines from the poem. Herbie had never thought of his Director as a man with leanings towards poetry.

> . . . Headpiece filled with straw. Alas!
> Our dried voices, when
> We whisper together
> Are quiet and meaningless
> As wind in dried grass . . .

The Director understood. "You meant what you said, then?"

Herbie nodded. "This is the last one. It is necessary, because . . . well, because it's Vascovsky."

"I don't want you involved emotionally." The Director did not snap, or speak sharply.

Herbie shook his head. Emotion did not enter into it. This was a dirty operation: unpleasant. "It's really a matter of putting the record straight. You understand?"

The Director saw the point. "Not revenge?"

280

"Revenge? Gets you nowhere."

"Good." A long silence. "So, when it's over, you'll go private?"

That was what Herbie intended.

"And you'll do . . .?"

The daft smile this time. "Grow roses; read; listen to music; get married; live. Sorry, but this one's the end."

*   *   *

Some twenty-five miles west of the centre of Moscow, lies the unprepossessing village of Zhukovka. It is a small village. Maybe a collective, people might say, passing through. From the road you see the usual peasant huts, built of logs; and small clapboard outhouses. The place is a roadside clutter, and the rustic surroundings can be glimpsed through thick forests, which straddle the road.

What nobody sees lies past the peasant huts, which are only a front to something very different. Just before entering the hamlet of Zhukovka, a wide metalled track leads off into the forests, on the right hand side.

This track turns into a road, which eventually leads to the real Zhukovka; and the real Zhukovka is, in truth, two elaborate, and luxurious, villages—Zhukovka One and Two.

People who live locally, talk of Zhukovka Two as Academic Zhukovka; Zhukovka One is known as Sovmin—*Soviet Ministrov*. Here live important ministry officials; Cabinet ministers; deputies, and ranking officers of the security forces. In turn, Sovmin is two villages, so finely tuned is it to rank and position. Behind brick and iron fences, the rulers of the Soviet Union live in modern, or old, houses of style and beauty.

It was down this road, to Sovmin, that Stentor's car travelled at around ten o'clock on the Sunday morning. The General wore civilian clothes; as did his driver and bodyguard. No pennant flew from the car; but a telephone call, ahead, made certain that the way was open to them. So the car slid quietly through the thick blockades of trees, broken, at intervals, by iron gates, or sweeping drives.

At last, Stentor's car turned left, through an elaborate archway, up a short, hard, drive and then—pausing for identification—past great wrought-iron gates, which clanged shut in their wake as they purred upwards, tyres crunching on gravel, the shrouding trees giving way to well kept, and watered, lawns.

At the top of a slight incline stood the house—a great rambling wooden structure, rising on three tiers, like a giant wedding cake, and topped with a circular cupolated tower. A veranda encircled the house; enclosed, with its wooden awning held in place by spiral carved pillars, their distances joined, along the top, by fretted decoration.

The whole was painted a gleaming white; immaculate, as if straight out of some fairytale illustration. Stentor picked up the heavy briefcase, brought with him from Moscow, and left the car, to be greeted by General Tserkov who embraced him beaming genially. Even the driver and bodyguard shuddered slightly at the sight of this pleasant old man—the eternal cigarette in one hand—who had power, in secret, over so many.

"Thank you for seeing me with such little notice, Andrei." Glubodkin followed the Head of Department V up the steps, into a wide, panelled, hall.

"It's nothing." Tserkov gave a dry cough. "Though you will not find much activity. Not after last night. To be truthful with you, I do not feel over-well myself. What a party."

"Yes. Quite something. I did not relish the idea of leaving Moscow, but needs must, Andrei."

The elderly man nodded. "This is business then? Important?"

"Very."

"Then we had better climb to my little castle." He gestured, leading the way up a broad staircase, soft underfoot with heavy carpet, the walls hung with priceless paintings, and Daghestan rugs, old, and worth a ransom.

They traversed a banistered first floor galleried landing, then climbed again; turned along yet another gallery, and started the final ascent, up a gently spiralling stairway, which led to a small landing, and a pair of heavy oak doors, which General Tserkov opened to reveal the dome at the top of the house.

It was a plain work room, with windows set at intervals, commanding a sensational view of Andrei Tserkov's estate—woods, lawns, a walled garden, and a great ornate lake. Between the windows, there were rows of books, and electronic equipment. In the centre of the room, a circular modern table-cum-console for television, stereophonic sound, and video. The chairs were steel and leather—soft and comfortable. Stentor dropped into one of them, while Tserkov seated himself behind the console. "I come here to play and to work: the two can be interchangeable, I find."

"Indeed. You have everything for both."

The two men smiled at each other, silent for a matter of seconds. Then, Tserkov broke the silence, asking what he could do for his old friend.

"You may not have heard yet," Stentor began. "Tomorrow morning I am retired; honourably and on full pay. By the end of the week I cease to be on the active list."

Tserkov was unmoved. Yes, he knew. Congratulations; his brother comrade had earned a time of peace for his old age.

"Then, today—and a few other days, I imagine—has to be spent putting the house in order." Stentor paused again, pulling the briefcase towards him. "Andrei, in this strange and secluded world of ours, we do not always share each other's secrets. It may well be that I have quietly trodden on someone else's territory; walked where others are also walking. I have some highly delicate material here, and, after the remarks made at our special meeting, it was in my mind to pass this over to you in any case."

"So?" Tserkov motioned for him to continue.

"General Jacob Vascovsky, our Chairman's representative. He is not all he seems. I was, in fact, more than surprised when the Comrade Chairman appointed him; for I have had people keeping an eye on the General for some years. It was not until yesterday afternoon that I personally went through the entire dossier, and collected certain items. Even I had no idea how serious things were."

Tserkov smiled. "Really? I'm surprised—as I was also surprised at our Chairman's gullibility. I was preparing to speak with him tomorrow. Vascovsky works for the British, of course."

Stentor said that was so.

"Perhaps you realise he is about to defect?"

"As close as that?"

The Head of Department V said that, after the last meeting, he had ordered Vascovsky's telephones to be immediately put on a twenty-four hour monitor. "He has received one message, in clear language, from a woman in England. I should also tell you that his wife—Yekaterina—still works for the French, as was suggested at our last meeting. It's only a matter of time for her. But Vascovsky, himself, has—as I say—received a message since we began listening."

Stentor laughed. He had received more than that. Would the Comrade General like to see the present he had brought for him?

Tserkov became very grave as he glanced through the documents and photographs; and even more silent as he listened, attentively, to the tapes. It was quite a hoard, he announced. "Why have you not made this public within the Service, Vladimir?"

Stentor shrugged. Vascovsky was safely tucked away for some time. One waits often. Perhaps he had waited too long. Now that he was retiring he felt this material should fall into only the right hands.

"It's a bombshell," Tserkov's eyes gleamed. "A major coup. A—what do they call it?—a *coup de main*."

"Quite; and I am retiring. My people have gathered this over a number of years. Yes, I agree, I should have placed it in other hands before this. Already I've said, it amazed me when I found what was here: the sheer volume of it. But I want no glory from this, Andrei. I simply need peace, quiet, and a rest. If I release this information now, they'll keep me on for years. So, my good old friend, I thought of you. It is you who now monitors Vascovsky. Here is the information to bring about a full justice."

"You mean . . .?" The greed showed through that avuncular exterior.

Stentor nodded, "I mean it is yours; all of it. You take the full credit. You can have the sole responsibility, on the understanding that I am kept well out of it all. Are we, as they say, in business?"

*　　　*　　　*

The signal from the Moscow Embassy did not come until late on the Sunday afternoon. There was absolutely no doubt that the Englishman, Michael Gold, was dead—hit by a truck while trying to escape arrest. It was not clear, however, that he was responsible for the rape of a young Russian woman. There was not a hint of other charges; but the so-called rape smelled of a fit-up.

Big Herbie went off to Catford, to break the news to Nataly, and did not get back to the St. John's Wood flat until near midnight. He found Curry Shepherd snoozing peacefully, in one of his easy chairs.

"Thought I might as well stick close from now on, cocker." Curry watched Big Herbie's face, drawn with strain. Never had Curry seen him like this. "You okay, Herbie?"

"Nothing a vodka won't fix. A vodka and a good blubbing—isn't that what your English public schoolboys say? You do a blubbing?"

"You blub, mate; or you *are* blubbing. The verb to blub; to weep; to cry. I blub; you blub; he, she or it blubs. I am blubbing; you are blubbing; he, she or it is blubbing. Cry, Herbie. Yes, have a good blub, right?"

Herbie said yes, he understood. Nataly Gold had taken it very badly, and Big Herbie found the whole thing unnerving.

"Can't be helped, old Herb. One of those things. We erred, and to err is . . ."

"Human."

"Yes. Not losing the old bottle, are we, Herbie?"

"You mean am I frightened?"

285

Curry cocked his head in an affirmative.

"Terrified," admitted Herbie. "Let's not err tomorrow, Curry. Or in the small hours of Tuesday. Okay?"

*   *   *

They woke Martha Adler early. Her friend was coming, they said. Everything was ready for her to make a telephone call.

She wore a towelling robe, when Herbie arrived. He kissed her, cradled her; and she hung on to him. The telephone stood, alone, on the table—like another person in the room, coming between them. She asked when he would return? "You said a day or two, but I know about these things. Really a day or two?"

Herbie's large head nodded. Really a day or two. Then it would be over.

"Will you see me: when you get back, I mean?"

"Straight away. I see you the minute I get into London. Come straight here."

Her eyes were a whole mélange of doubt "Promise, Herbie."

Big Herbie took her gently in his arms again. He spoke quietly, gently, smoothing her hair with his big hand as he spoke—"Martha, my dear. You are a lonely woman. When I return I will also be lonely. We live only with past lives, crowding our real selves from our bodies. We've known each other a long time; we know things that should not be said. Long ago we shared a bed; then, recently—when we both needed comfort. If . . . no, when, I come back, can we try to share more?"

"You mean it? You mean . . .?"

Herbie looked away, feeling clumsy, and too large a physical man for the slim woman, whose bones he could feel through the robe. "Look, I cannot say I love you. Not at the moment. But in some ways I have always cared: you know that—okay, if you wish to play with words, loved you. Can we try?"

"Please."

Herbie nodded, smiling in a way which embraced her more than his arms or body could ever embrace. He disengaged from her, taking out the paper, and placing it next to the telephone. "I'm sorry. You have to do this now; quickly. No hold-ups."

She gave thumbs up; radiant, changed by a few words.

It was eight o'clock in the morning, London time. Eleven, in Moscow. Martha dialled the code for Moscow, then the number for the Yasenevo Complex. In Russian she asked for Vascovsky's private extension, recognising his voice as he came on.

"Lara," she said.

"Yes? It's Yuri. Go ahead."

"Kolya will be there for a pick-up at four o'clock tomorrow morning, your time. Reference number . . ." she went on reading, clipping off the map reference numbers.

There was a slight pause. When Vascovsky spoke, Martha could almost see the engaging smile playing around his mouth. "Good," he said. "Tell Kolya that Yuri will be there on time."

"Fall-back, every twenty-four hours for two days only," she read, parrot fashion.

"I understand. Thank you, Lara." The line closed.

*   *   *

Within ten minutes of the call being made from London, General Andrei Tserkov was listening to the tape. Since the previous morning, he had spent a lot of time going through the documents and photographs; and listening to taped conversations between Jacob Vascovsky and the man called Kruger—the one they spoke of as Big Herbie.

So, he considered, we have him on a meat hook. With luck I might even have both of them on meat hooks. Yuri equals Vascovsky; and Kolya is Big Herbie Kruger, his long-time British control.

General Tserkov rang for his ADC, whom he sent for certain charts and maps. Within the hour Tserkov pinpointed the reference on the Latvian coast: a small inlet, with a bay, almost halfway between Ventspils and Lyserort, in the incorporated Soviet Socialist Republic of Latvia.

With the familiar confidence of a man used to making fast decisions, General Tserkov gave a series of orders. A fast helicopter would be needed, from one of the military bases. He chose four of his best men; then made a long-distance call to one of the bases in Latvia. He would be there that night.

*   *   *

Jacob Vascovsky departed from the Complex within an hour of receiving the call. As usual, his instructions were explicit, and cloaked in secrecy. Major Badim was left to carry the weight of the day's work. It went with the job, so Vitali Badim complied. One of Vascovsky's previous ADCs—it was said—ran a railway station in Siberia.

Vascovsky also made arrangements with speed. By the time he drove from the Complex, there was an aircraft waiting for him; while Badim had telephoned ahead.

On arrival, the General would require an armoured Command Car. He would be working alone, and planned to drive the car himself.

*   *   *

On that same Monday morning, General Vladimir Glubodkin, who was Stentor, still refrained from telling his wife about the retirement. In fact he did exactly the opposite. There had been a message for him while she slept. He would be away for a few days: urgent work of national importance. His wife could not have cared if he was to be away for a whole week. She felt too ill to move from her bed, and had sworn that, never again, would she allow herself to be pressed into drinking so much. A two-day hangover was not natural.

Stentor, dressed in full uniform—his boots, belt and holster gleaming with polish—stood in the bedroom door. It was a moment of ruthlessness. For a fraction of a second he hesitated, then, with dignity, performed his final act of deception.

288

"I shall telephone you if it is to be more than, say, three days."

"Whatever you say," she groaned, turning her face into the pillow.

Stentor went down to the lobby and asked one of the day guards to get a taxi for him. The car would not be coming today.

He carried only a small briefcase, and waited until he was in the taxi, out of earshot of the guards, before ordering the driver to take him to the airport. Yes, he would telephone his wife in a few days. With luck it would be from England. After that, he consciously hardened his heart, refusing to think about the action he was now taking. He was old enough to know his mind; and if things went wrong, the revolver in his holster was loaded.

At the airport nobody questioned the authority of a full General—particularly one wearing the sword and shield badge of the KGB.

Stentor easily got himself a seat on the next flight to Leningrad. From Leningrad he would double back—there were scheduled stopping flights to his final destination: Riga, in the incorporated State of Latvia.

Before the flight to Leningrad, Stentor made another telephone call, organising a car at Riga. It was quite a long drive, but there would be time—just.

*   *   *

Herbie Kruger and Curry Shepherd left Heathrow on the Scandinavian Air Services morning flight—SK526—to Stockholm. They carried only hand baggage, and travelled separately: each watching the other's back. They would be there in plenty of time for the small cocktail party, being given on board the British Island class patrol-craft *Jersey*. The four somewhat burly business men—who had been staying at the Grand Hotel—were also invited.

At about three in the afternoon, the merchant ship, *Artemis*, making her way along the coastal route for Stockholm hove to, and sent out a message that she would be under way again later that night, having stopped to make some engine repairs before heading for harbour.

The small party, on board the British patrol-craft, was due to begin at six in the evening.

23

THE YOUNG LIEUTENANT-COMMANDER RN, Captain of the *Jersey*, sat in the command chair, anchored to the bridge deck. The bridge was small, and very cramped with both Big Herbie and Curry Shepherd standing nearby.

Below decks, the four SAS men found it equally crowded in the tiny wardroom.

Before leaving England, the Captain had been given classified instructions. The sealed orders were to be opened only on a given series of verbal exchanges, made to him personally.

On the previous day, he had received a signal ordering him to invite certain people, for a cocktail party, on board at six in the evening. He was to expect others; and now he sat with this strange pair—the huge, dumb-looking, German; and the jaded, shabby, old-school Englishman—who had just gone through the verbal codes.

He read the sealed orders twice, and considered it all very odd—but this was the first time he had come into contact with men like Herbie Kruger and Curry Shepherd. He did not care for it much. The whole business did not seem to be true to naval form. However, their lordships, who ruled his life, had so ordered matters. He could only obey.

"Going to have to get a shift on, gentlemen." He looked at Herbie and Curry. "You know what's in these orders?"

Curry said they had a rough idea; and Big Herbie gave a

small nod. The patrol-craft was to leave Stockholm, and make a rendezvous with the merchant ship *Artemis*. She would be lying some fifty miles off the coast, at a designated point, north-east of where they were at anchor.

From the *Artemis* they would pick up certain equipment—notably a required number of *Gemini* inflatables with outboard motors; plus arms.

The craft was then expected to head towards the Latvian coast, staying well outside the three mile limit, but making all possible speed. They had to arrive, on station—some four miles offshore—before two in the morning. The whole trip covered around one hundred and seventy-three nautical miles, and the flat-out speed of the patrol-craft was in the region of twenty knots. It did not take immense wisdom to work out that the entire journey would take around their maximum time limit. So the Captain had cause to show irritation and concern.

"Two o'clock, give or take some," Big Herbie grinned. "As long as I can start the run into shore about three—maybe three-fifteen—we'll be on time."

At that point, the Captain did not ask for more details. If he was to make the rendezvous with *Artemis*, and get to the point on the Latvian coast, within an hour of the given time, they had to leave now. With as much courtesy as he could muster, the naval officer requested his two passengers to leave the bridge.

*   *   *

General Tserkov had ordered full surveillance on Jacob Vascovsky from the moment of complete revelation regarding Madame Vascovsky's past. He was pleased to see that the wife remained in Moscow—seemingly unaware of both the teams watching her, and the fact that her husband was about to make a last dash to the West, via the Baltic coast.

As soon as Vascovsky's departure was announced, Tserkov set off in pursuit. Already he had lodged the mass of evidence with his ADC—to be handed to the Chairman without delay if anything went wrong.

291

In the meantime, he sat, with his four chosen men, in the big, relatively fast and comfortable Mi-24 helicopter, that would put them down within a mile or so of the predicted pick-up point on the Latvian coast. They would be there in plenty of time. In position and waiting, long before Vascovsky completed his journey.

Andrei Tserkov was not worried about his old friend, General Glubodkin, who had provided most of the evidence against Vascovsky. His own turn for retirement would come soon enough, he knew. But at least he would be remembered for more than merely the ruthless manner in which he ran his Department. They would speak of Andrei Tserkov as the man who caught Britain's most dangerous, long-term traitor, implanted within the security apparatus itself.

*   *   *

In fact it was Stentor, making his journey in full uniform, and by the most public of means—Aeroflot, and the hiring of a good motor car—who first reached the jumping-off point.

For years, it had been Stentor's maxim that, if you wished to hide your movements, do everything in an open and straightforward manner. It had paid off before, as it did now.

In that part of the Baltic the nights are very long for most of the year; so, when Stentor arrived within a mile of the coastal point, it was already getting dark—the day having stretched itself to around seven hours.

He parked the car, well off a small track running down towards the sea; checked bearings, with map and pocket compass; then set off on foot.

The inlet, or cove, chosen by Herbie Kruger for the operation, could not have been better. The terrain was wooded, with thick pine and fir, the ground sloping slowly towards the sea; then, quite suddenly, descending through a wide gully of rock—a great cleft which rose on either side of the woods, finally petering out to a sandy bay. The trees here grew down to within a couple of hundred metres of the sea;

292

and the bay itself stretched in a crescent, covering just over a kilometre. Yet still the rocks towered over trees, sand and sea.

Against the sky, Stentor caught sight of a small pile of ruins—an old tower, or what was left of some ancient castle: dead stone making a sinister pattern against the darkening sky. Castles, and fortress ruins littered this part of the coast, so this one was not unusual. They were regarded as romantic tourist attractions.

Taking his last look at the rocks—and the silhouetted castle—Stentor chose his vantage point, among the trees to the far right of the bay. He quietly sank out of sight, preparing for the long and silent wait—hoping that Jacob Vascovsky might not also choose this place. He doubted that, for Vascovsky would, in his arrogance, be prepared to show himself. After all, he expected to meet someone on the beach, so had no reason to come with stealth.

*   *   *

Andrei Tserkov, and his men, came with silence and speed. They had the resources and techniques. Yet Stentor was conscious of the helicopter, circling in the distance, just before eleven at night. Then, it seemed to rise again, chopping off into the far distance.

Indeed, the Mi-24 had gone for the time being; dropping its human cargo as near to the inlet as safety permitted, then—remaining in radio contact—moving several miles away: waiting, ready to be called up when the moment came.

Tserkov, and his group, never once broke cover; coming down the steep, sometimes rocky, slope on the far side from where Stentor lay; then fanning out across the central reserve of trees. Tserkov himself stayed as near to the middle of the bay as he thought fit; while his men faced, alternately, outwards and inwards, at regular intervals.

The Head of Department V also imagined that, when he came, General Jacob Vascovsky would walk on to the sand, from the centre of the trees—not concerned with noise or disturbance. This was a dark, secret, and rather beautifully

293

desolate place. It would hold no fears for the excited Vascovsky, waiting—oblivious of other watchers—for his ship to come in, and carry him to some just reward.

*   *   *

They took on two of the Geminis, with their powerful outboard motors, and some small arms—Ingram submachineguns, and Browning automatics: the Ingrams to the disgust of the four SAS men, who said they felt naked without their beloved Heckler & Koch weapons. After all, the SAS had already discarded the Ingram MAC II in favour of the H & K after assisting at the hijack storming at Mogadishu.

It was after leaving *Artemis*, while they settled down for the long, fast, run in to the pinpoint drop, that Curry Shepherd and Big Herbie Kruger went through a last ritual.

The Director had virtually told them he did not want to know who did what. By rights, Herbie should not have been there at all. He had already argued long with Curry. "It will be me, Curry, that he expects to see coming into that inlet. *Me* riding into the bay. So it *should* be me."

Curry agreed in principle. In practice, however, he maintained that, as Herbie was not supposed to be there at all, they would decide, on the toss of a coin, who should be in the leading *Gemini*.

It mattered little, in the end, for Herbie won, and would not listen to Curry's pleas of it really being a 'two out of three' contest. Big Herbie was to have his way, and show himself— like a tethered goat—to his old enemy.

Having made the decision they went, first, to the four SAS men; then to the Captain, explaining what they could about the method, and reason, behind what would happen in a few hours.

The naval officer was appalled; the SAS men resigned to anything. Only Herbie and Curry were happy, in their complete understanding of the ramifications of the strange charade. The two men sat, smoking and occasionally talking; though spending most of their time wrapped in personal thoughts.

For Herbie, it was a time of almost physical climax. At long range, and by devious—almost disastrous—means, he had brought the Firm to a situation which would probably save Stentor's life; certainly allow him several more operating years within the Soviet Union—for there was no way in which he could know of the man's retirement.

Herbie had also gone one better. Whatever had happened to him in the past; however many failures, or successes, lay behind him, the bulky German-born intelligence expert had manoeuvred things so that—in these final hours of a long night—his personal enemy, over the years, would come to grief. In Curry Shepherd's language, Herbie had stitched up Vascovsky, good and proper.

If all worked smoothly, Herbie Kruger had planted the irrefutable lie of all time on Jacob Vascovsky. Though even Big Herbie could not yet believe that the planning, and tactics, would work.

Curry brought him out of his reverie. "The boss man says you're taking a walk after this."

In the dim light, Herbie saw Curry's eyes fixed on him. Curry was like an owl in the dark.

"True."

"After all this time, cocker? Any plans?"

Herbie dipped his head, so that Curry could not see his face, and the smile which lit it. "I get married, Curry. Go private, and go public at the same time. Orange blossom and champagne. Bridal beds, and a steady life."

"Believe it when I see it. Adler?"

Herbie grunted a yes, then added—"You believe it, Curry. It's all going to happen. We all pay some time, you know."

Unaccosted by any Soviet patrol, the British craft arrived at its point—four miles offshore: exactly in line with the inlet—at twenty minutes past three in the black morning.

*   *   *

The sea was smooth as a silk-screen print; the night still as the old ruins, topping the rocks above the bay.

In the silence, with ears attuned, Stentor heard the patrol-craft's engines, coming from over the water; then dying, as the ship hove to. Like a night animal, Stentor could see clearly across the bay. His senses had never been so alert.

General Tserkov also heard the engines, and knew the moment would soon arrive. He lay, smelling the sweet mixture of pine, fir, sand, and sea; stiff with waiting; but ready for the inevitable.

Then—from across the water—all who waited in secret heard the distant rumble of small outboard motors; rising, then dying to an almost friendly throb.

As the motors began to close over the stretch of sea, so the noise grew louder—thrown into the cleft of rock, and reverberating against the rising stone.

At this moment, both Stentor and Tserkov saw Vascovsky rise, as if from the ground, right at the furthest corner of the curve of trees.

They watched, each with his own particular thoughts, as General Jacob Vascovsky walked, unperturbed, to the centre of the beach. He then turned to make his unhurried way down, almost to the water's edge.

His eyes strained out over the sea, hoping to catch an early glimpse of his prize. After years of waiting, endless months of silent battle, Herbie Kruger was almost in the net again. In a matter of moments—Vascovsky thought—Kruger will step on to the beach; trusting as a dog about to be put down.

In three completely different ways, the main protagonists on the beach waited for their personal spotlight of triumph.

Vascovsky, and his capture of Kruger.

General Tserkov, and the unmasking of a Soviet traitor, together with the taking of that traitor's British control.

Stentor, and his own escape from suspicion and Vascovsky's knowledge—together with a chance at making his own leap for freedom, after a lifetime of duplicity.

Then, with an almost shocking suddenness, they all saw the

296

two craft appearing, as though from the bottom of the sea, pluming great white feathers of spray; riding, one in front, the other behind and slightly to port.

*   *   *

Big Herbie Kruger sat for'ard in the first *Gemini*: an SAS coxswain at the back, steering the boat in at speed; while another SAS man held a central position, midships. This second trooper carried an Ingram under one arm, and a cylindrical starshell in his left hand, the right poised over the ring which, when pulled, would shoot the light high and illuminate the entire beach—rocks, ruins, trees, everything.

The second boat was there for cover: in case things turned nasty. Everyone had been warned there was to be no exchange of fire, unless absolutely necessary; but the second *Gemini* was more heavily armed.

Curry crouched for'ard, with the SAS coxswain at the rear, and the remaining SAS man midships. All three were armed. Ingrams, Brownings, and stun grenades.

The ride was exhilarating in itself: a bucketing, bouncing, sliding scream over the placid water—not unlike a ride in a bobsleigh.

Herbie craned almost out of the *Gemini*, his eyes straining to catch the first glimpse of the beach. Then he saw the small flash. Vascovsky had signalled. Herbie turned, moving his hand in sign for the coxswain to cut the power, and prepare for the turn.

As the light flashed from the beach, so both of the *Geminis* lost power—the engines dying, and the sturdy rubber boats lurching, sliding towards the edge of the sand under their own momentum.

This was it. The split second when Herbie's timing had to be as accurate as that of an acrobat.

*   *   *

As Jacob Vascovsky pressed the button on his torch—to signal Herbie on to the beach—he realised what was wrong. In the coolness of his excitement, and moment of triumph, the General had acted automatically. Now, as he sent the little beam of light towards the speeding craft, he saw what was out of tune with everything else. Two boats. There were *two* boats. If Herbie was coming, it would have been one—and without power; without the sound of heavier engines further out to sea.

Vascovsky dropped the torch, glancing about him; instinctively sensing the danger—not only from the boats bearing down into the bay. There was hazard here. Near at hand.

The engines from the boats cut out. They were skimming in towards the sands. Vascovsky's hand reached for his automatic, dragging it from the holster. Then, from the leading boat, a cry—Big Herbie Kruger's voice echoing in the wake of the dead motors—"Jacob. No. Get back. They're on to us. Get out. Get out." Herbie was doing what Curry had called—at the briefing—the Larry Olivier bit.

From behind Herbie, the SAS trooper pulled the ring on his flare, lighting the beach—trees, the walls of rock towering above, and the pile of ruins high over all. The flare gave no shadows; just a clear light, embracing everything—including General Andrei Tserkov, as he stepped from the cover of the trees, shouting to his men as he came forward. Then, to Vascovsky—"Jacob. Stay where you are. It's over for you. Finished."

The words reached Vascovsky as the outboard motors of the two *Gemini* inflatables came to life again: each coxswain leaning on their tillers, and everyone praying they had not come in too far—that no rocks lurked beneath, ready to rip open the rubber bottoms of the boats.

The screws churned lather from the sea, the *Geminis* trembling; then taking up the power, starting to turn.

Vascovsky looked back—the boats so near, and Herbie Kruger clear, smiling, in the first craft. He turned to see Tserkov advancing on him, a pistol in his hand. Other men following.

In an instinctive gesture, Vascovsky's hand came up. He was ready to turn back; to vent all his feeling, and frustrations, on the boats: but the action was mistaken. Andrei Tserkov shouted again, telling him to drop the weapon.

For too long, Vascovsky stood, uncertain: turning to Tserkov, then to the boats, in the middle of their sliding turn, still well inshore.

Tserkov dropped to one knee, his arms up, in the classic double grip. Well, he thought, maybe it's better like this, squeezing the trigger twice; then twice more.

Vascovsky felt nothing: only the first thump, and the odd sensation of his heels dragging backwards, making twin furrows in the sand; then the dark, as his body hit the sea.

As though their General's shots were a signal, the other men began firing—raking the water around the boats.

In the halved second, as General Tserkov fired, Stentor made his move. The turning boats had not picked up speed, and seemed to him, close enough, slow enough, for a gamble.

Launching himself from the trees, the elderly General ran to the water's edge, splashing in, his legs fighting the strength of the sea, then his whole body immersed so that he could swim.

His head went under; then, within yards of the skidding first boat, he called out—"Kruger. Kruger, it's me. It's Stentor."

Then the hail of bullets hit the water around him.

*   *   *

Herbie took it all in, in that camera-flash moment—the men on the beach; Vascovsky's indecision; then the shots, and his enemy dragged back into the sea.

In the second *Gemini*, Curry Shepherd began to shout, "Hold your fire. For God's sake don't shoot."

The boats had begun their turns, close to each other, the screws biting, and the craft lifting, picking up speed. Herbie's *Gemini* was side on to the shore when General Tserkov's men opened fire. Clearly, he heard the rip and thwack, as the metal tore and ripped at the rubber.

Herbie's *Gemini* continued to skid, its outboard motor

screaming, as the screws came out of the water. Then the nose went down. The coxswain and the other SAS trooper were thrown over the side. Herbie, at the front, felt a sudden agony, as a bullet ploughed into his calf. He coughed—dizzy with the shock, and pain—then fell forward, gulping water as he went.

Curry's *Gemini* had already begun its run back, the speed starting to increase nicely; but the coxswain leaned on the tiller, bringing the rubber boat around in a sickening skid, before Curry could even shout the order.

The SAS man sitting midships, lifted his Ingram—and pointing high—fired two quick bursts, yelling that it would keep their heads down, on the beach. Like Curry, he was intent on saving the three men in Herbie's *Gemini*.

They circled, the SAS coxswain and trooper, both conscious, reaching from the water to grab at the fast-moving boat. Another two bursts from the Ingram as Curry sighted Big Herbie, rolling, like a sick porpoise, in the foam.

Hands stretched out, heaving and hauling the dead weight into the *Gemini*. The other men from Herbie's boat were in now, balancing the craft, trying to help by clinging on to Curry, and their comrade.

With one final immense pull, they hauled the massive man over the curved sides. The moment they had him in the boat, Curry yelled—"Out. Get out of here." The coxswain piled on the power, the nose lifted, and the *Gemini*, swaying and off trim, spewed out its white feather and, slamming up and down over the sea, shot away from the beach.

Curry bent to examine his friend—now conscious, and throwing up the water swallowed when he went overboard.

"You're okay, cocker. Nasty gash in the leg; but you're okay."

"Got him." Big Herbie smiled up at Curry. "They got the bastard." He winced with pain. "Leg hurts a bit."

The bullet had chewed out a long runnel in the flesh, and there was a lot of blood. One of the SAS troopers passed over a field dressing, and Curry staunched the wound, as best he could in the swaying *Gemini*.

300

Herbie would be fine once they got him aboard the patrol-craft. "You'll take that trip down the aisle yet, old Herb. Lucky Martha."

"There'll be people doing a blubbing that day." Herbie smiled up at him. A hard smile, but one of triumph.

"I shouldn't be surprised, old cocker. Shouldn't be surprised at all." Curry could see the patrol-craft, engines running, waiting to accept them aboard.

*　　　*　　　*

Stentor could not really understand it. They had not waited for him. They did not even seem to have seen him. He knew he was in the water, floating on his back. He also knew about the numbness. It had nothing to do with the cold. Somewhere—probably in his back—a bullet had ground its way through flesh and bone.

Yet he felt remarkably tranquil; just floating, and at peace with the world. He could even see the shape of the trees and cliffs. Then the ruin of the castle, like a cut-out in the theatre—at the Bolshoi. Was it the house, he wondered? The house in the Lear Song?

He was not conscious of his body at all now; everything appeared to be drifting away. The quiet dogs, Stentor thought, and tried to laugh, but could not. From a long way off—he thought it was in his head—he heard the Lear Ballad, and the ruin on the cliff came into focus for a moment—

> Beyond the dark on a rock
> Stands a tall house.
> Birds are nesting on the rock,
> But the house is empty.
> But the house is empty . . .

His very last sensation was that of a breeze, fanning over the sea, touching his cheek. The wind was getting up. Then the song again—

No voices are heard,
And only the wind, a wild guest,
Alarms the quiet dogs;
He has brought news from afar,
That the master . . . has . . . disappeared . . .

* * *

On the beach they were dragging the late General Jacob Vascovsky's body from the surf. Tserkov felt saddened: but all the evidence was there. He had witnesses; and the documents, and tapes. As he had thought at the moment he fired, perhaps it was better this way. Less of a mess. But a pity they had missed Kruger. He wondered about the two boats. One for cover, the General presumed. Giving a dry laugh, Tserkov lit a cigarette. They had certainly needed cover.

A shout came from the water's edge. "General, sir. There's something in the sea. I think we got one of them."

Tserkov threw down his cigarette, grinding it under his heel, into the sand. By the time he reached the edge of the water, two of his men, waist deep in the sea, were floating the body in.

The other two held torches, to guide their comrades; and, as they brought the corpse ashore, Tserkov could see it was not one of those from the boats. The immaculate uniform was soaked, but the face looked at peace as they laid him on the sand.

Tserkov went down on one knee, his hand brushing the forehead of the old man. What was he doing here? Tserkov's face contorted with pain. After all these years; and the retirement. Life played strange tricks. He presumed—could only presume—that Volodya could not bear to miss the last act. He had to be there—unannounced—to see his brave work come to its full fruition.

One of the men spoke. "Comrade General? It's the Head of Special Service I, isn't it? It's General Glubodkin?"

Tserkov nodded. "Yes. People used to think he was a dandy."

302

"And a man for the ladies, they said, Comrade General."

"He was a man with great authority, and responsibility. General Vladimir Glubodkin was also my friend. A veteran in the Service. A good, courageous, man to whom Russia owes much." Nobody, he thought, would ever know how much. But if he, General Andrei Tserkov, had anything to do with it, General Vladimir Glubodkin would have a hero's burial.

He rose, and saluted the body of his dead comrade with great pride.